Praise for Rachel Neumeier

"The characters are vivid, the action scenes are intense, and the mythology of the shape-shifting 'black dogs' is fascinating. It's the kind of book that made me resent the obligations of ordinary life because I just wanted to keep reading."

Sharon Shinn, author of Archangel

"A self-contained novel, *House of Shadows* is an imaginative fantasy complete with a strong trio of main characters – including two wonderful heroines – and some truly awesome worldbuilding."

The Book Smugglers

"When I need a book to just *get me,* I know where to look: Rachel Neumeier."

Ivy Book Bindings

"*House of Shadows* is enchanting with lovely writing and a character-driven story. It reads like an original fairy tale, full of magic, wonder, and beauty."

Fantasy Café

"Neumeier excels at complex, neatly tied up endings, and I really enjoy seeing how she resolves her plots. If you're in the mood for a heavy, richly written tale, *The City in the Lake* is right up your alley."

Starlight Book Reviews

"I was delighted when *The Floating Islands* was exactly what I wanted: a captivating and gorgeously written fantasy world."

Steph Su Reads

RACHEL NEUMEIER

Black Dog

STRANGE CHEMISTRY

An Angry Robot imprint
and a member of the Osprey Group

Lace Market House,   Angry Robot/Osprey Publishing,
54-56 High Pavement,   PO Box 3985,
Nottingham   New York,
NG1 1HW   NY 10185-3985,
UK   USA

www.strangechemistrybooks.com
Strange Chemistry #25

A Strange Chemistry paperback original 2014

Cover art by Paul Young

Distributed in the United States by Random House, Inc., New York.

ISBN: 978 1 90884 483 5
Ebook ISBN: 978 1 90884 484 2

Set in Sabon by Argh! Oxford

Printed in the United States of America
9 8 7 6 5 4 3 2 1

1

With one fingertip, Natividad drew a pentagram on the window of the bus. It glimmered faintly, nearly invisible, light against light: protection against danger and the dark and all shadowed things.

Well, almost all. Some, anyway.

The glass of the window was cold enough to numb the tip of her finger. The cold was always a shock; she somehow never expected it, even after all these days of travel. It was cold inside the bus, but she knew it was much colder outside. Of course winter temperatures here fell way below zero, but she hadn't guessed what that would be *like*. She hadn't known that air could be so cold it actually hurt to breathe. She knew it now.

The countryside framed by her pentagram's pale glimmer was as foreign and comfortless as the cold. The mountains themselves were almost familiar, but Natividad recognized nothing else in this high northern country to which she and her brothers had come. Driven by enemies behind and hope ahead... though now that they were here, this didn't look much like a country of hope. But they had

had nowhere else to go. No other choices.

Natividad glanced surreptitiously sideways, reassuring herself that, even in this cold and unfamiliar country, her brothers hadn't changed.

Her twin, Miguel, in the seat next to her, was reading a newspaper he'd scrounged somewhere. *That* was certainly ordinary. He turned the pages carefully in a vain attempt to avoid irritating Alejandro. Across the aisle, Alejandro was staring out the opposite window, pretending not to be annoyed by the rustling pages. Natividad saw the tension in his shoulders and back and knew how hard his dark shadow pressed him. Despite everything she could do to help her older brother, his temper, always close to the surface, had been strained hard – not only by the terror and rage and grief so recently past, but by the unavoidable awareness that they were running into danger almost greater than they'd escaped.

All the strangers on the bus didn't help, either. All along, wanting no one behind them, Alejandro had insisted that they sit together in the rear of the bus. Though it was nice to sit in the front so you could get off faster when the bus stopped, sitting in the back was alright if it helped Alejandro keep his shadow under tight control. Even if it was harder to get a good view of the road. Natividad looked out her window again. She could still see the pentagram she'd drawn, though by now it would be completely invisible to ordinary human sight.

Out there in the cold, mountains rose against the sky, white and gray and black: snow and naked trees and granite and the sky above all... The sky itself was different here, crystalline and transparent, seeming farther away than any Mexican sky. The sun seemed smaller here, too, than the one that burned across the dry mountains of Nuevo León: *this* sun poured out not heat, but a cold brilliant luminescence that the endless snow reflected back into the sky, until the whole world seemed made of light.

Beside Natividad, Miguel leaned sideways to look past her, curious to see what had caught her attention.

"Nothing," Natividad said in English. She had insisted on speaking nothing but English since they had crossed the Rio Bravo. Miguel and even Alejandro had looked back across the river, toward the home they were leaving behind. She had not. She wanted to leave everything behind: all the grief and the terrible memories – let the dead past *drown* in that river; she would walk into another country and another life and *never* look back.

"It's not *nothing*," her twin answered. "It's the Northeast Kingdom. It's Dimilioc." His wave took in all the land east and north of the highway.

"Just like all the other mountains," said Natividad, deliberately flippant. But Miguel was right, and she knew it mattered. Since St Johnsbury, all the land to the east was Dimilioc territory. She said, "I bet the road out of Newport is paved with yellow bricks."

Miguel grinned. "Except the road is lined with wolves instead of lions and tigers and bears, Dorothy."

Natividad gave him a raised-eyebrow look. "'Dorothy?' Are you kidding? *I'm* the witch."

"The good witch or–" Miguel stopped, though, as Alejandro gave them both a look. Alejandro did not like jokes about Dimilioc or about the part of Vermont that Americans called the Northeast Kingdom – almost a quarter of the state. Natividad knew why. Americans might be joking when they called this part of Vermont a "kingdom", but she knew that there was too much truth to that joke for it to be funny. Dimilioc really was a kind of independent kingdom, with Grayson Lanning its king – and everyone knew he did not like stray black dogs. They were all nervous, but Alejandro had more reason to be afraid than Miguel and far more reason than Natividad. Fear always strained his control. Natividad ducked her head apologetically.

"Newport," Alejandro said, his tone curt.

It was. Natividad had not even noticed the exit signs, but the bus was slowing for the turn off the highway. Newport: the town where all the bus routes finally ran out. Just visible past Alejandro's shoulder, Lake Memphremagog glittered in late afternoon light. Natividad liked the lake – at least, she liked its name. It had *pizzazz*. She stretched to catch another glimpse of it, but then the bus turned away from the lake and rolled into the station and she lost sight of the bright water.

Newport was the town closest to Dimilioc that did not actually fall within the borders of the Northeast Kingdom. It was smaller than Natividad had expected. Clean, neat, pretty – all the towns this far north seemed to be clean and neat and pretty. Maybe that was the snow lying over everything, hiding all evidence of clutter and untidiness until the spring thaw should uncover it. If there was a thaw. Or a spring. It was hard to believe any spring could thaw this frozen country. As she got off the bus, Natividad pulled the hood of her coat up around her face and tried to pretend she was warm.

"You must get out of the cold," Alejandro said abruptly. He closed one long hand around Natividad's arm, collected Miguel with a glance, and led them across the street toward the hotel on the opposite corner. He scanned the streets warily as they moved, scenting the cold air for possible enemies.

Natividad made no effort to calm her brother. She hoped and believed they'd left all their enemies behind them – even Vonhausel would not dare intrude on Dimilioc territory – but *they* were intruding here, so how could Alejandro be calm? She didn't argue about the hotel, either. It looked alright. It looked like it might be expensive. But everything in Newport was probably expensive, and her brother needed to feel like he was in control, and they would only be there one night, after all.

Miguel heaved their pack up over his shoulder and hurried to catch up. "We need to find a car–" he began.

"Not today," snapped Alejandro. "It gets dark too early here. You can't go alone to look at cars, and Natividad is tired and cold and needs to rest."

Miguel, catching Alejandro's tone and not needing Natividad's warning glance, said meekly, "Maybe tonight I can find a newspaper with ads. Then I can figure out which cars we should look at tomorrow." Alejandro nodded curtly, not much interested.

The hotel *was* expensive, but they only needed one room. They got a room with two beds, but Alejandro wouldn't sleep, of course – certainly not after dark. He stretched out on his stomach on the bed nearer the door, on top of the bedspread, his chin propped up on his hands, his eyes open and watchful.

"One night," Natividad said, counting the money they had left. "I think we can afford one night – if we don't have to pay too much for a car. We won't need–" she stopped herself, barely, from saying that after tomorrow, one way or another, they probably wouldn't have to worry about money. She said instead, "Try to find a car for less than two thousand dollars, Miguel, but we can pay more if we really need to."

Miguel muttered a wordless acknowledgement, not looking up. There had been newspapers in the hotel's lobby, and he had collected them all. Natividad read the stories while her twin looked at the ads for cars. Big headlines shouted about recent werewolf violence. The part about the weather included warnings about the dates of the approaching full moon as well as about expected snow. All the way north, in one hotel and bus station after another, the headlines had been like that.

Certainly the newspaper people were right about the great increase in "werewolf" violence, though the writers did not yet know enough to distinguish between true black dogs and mere *cambiadors*, the little moon-bound shifters. What ordinary people thought they knew about "werewolves" was still mostly wrong, even now, when the vampire magic that had fogged human perception for so long had thinned almost to nothing. The vampires had not been gone long enough, yet, for people to figure out the real shape of the world. Miguel said that human ignorance about the *sobrenatural* could not last very much longer.

Natividad wasn't sure. She thought people wouldn't want to think about or believe in scary monsters that hunted in the dark.

"Your *maraña mágica*," Alejandro said abruptly.

Natividad looked up in surprise. "You think it's important? Here?" Even if Vonhausel had managed to track them all the way north – which was impossible – but anyway, even *Vonhausel* would hardly attack them here in this nice hotel so close to Dimilioc.

"It's always important," Alejandro snapped. "All the time."

Natividad said, "Alright," in her very meekest tone and slid off the bed. Before she got out her *maraña*, she drew a pentagram on the glass of the window, for safety and peace, to help calm her brother. But she drew a mandala on the floor, too: a simple crossed circle, just in case Alejandro was right and somebody *was* looking for them. Unwanted attention just sort of slid off a circle. Mamá had taught her–

Natividad stopped for a second, breathing deliberately. For just a heartbeat, she could almost have believed she really was back with Mamá, out behind the main house, where the great oak reached its heavy branches out over the ring of young limber pines, twenty-seven of them, each with its trunk only a little thicker than her own wrist. She could almost believe she stood amid rich light slanting through the oak leaves, dust motes sparkling in the sunlight pouring down around her.

Mamá had planted those pines when she and Papá had first built their house in Potosi, because there was strength in bending as well as in standing firm. She said Papá and

Alejandro could have the rest of the mountain, but the circle was *her* workshop and she wanted no shadows to fall uninvited beneath the oak or between the pines–

Natividad flinched from that memory. She would not remember the other shadows that had come there, at the end – she *refused* to remember that. She wanted to remember Mamá the way she had been before, long before, when the pines had been hardly taller than a little girl of five or six or seven. Mamá smiling and happy, teaching Natividad to draw circles in the gritty soil. Circles, and spirals, and mandalas strengthened with their interior crosses. She had said, "Spirals draw attention in, but circles close it out, Natividad. Attention slides off a circle. Remember that, if you ever have to hide. But then, of course you will remember, my beautiful child. You remember everything." And she had reached out and touched Natividad's cheek gently with the tips of her fingers. She had been smiling, but she had been sad.

"Hide from what?" Natividad had asked. The sadness worried her. She had not understood it. She remembered that now: the naivety of the child she had been, who understood already that the Pure always had to hide but thought that was just the way the world was and did not understand why that truth should make Mamá sad. Who did not understand yet how carefully Mamá had worked to hide them, their whole family. Or from what.

Or what would happen when they were found.

She *would not* allow herself to remember. She breathed deeply. Only after she had again locked the past in the past did she go on to borrow Alejandro's knife, prick her finger, and anchor the mandala with a drop of her blood at each compass point. She did not remember Mamá showing her how to do that – she *would* not remember, and did not, focusing fiercely on the immediate present. As she closed the circle with the last drop of blood, she murmured aloud, "May this cross guard this room and all within, against the dark and the dead and any who come with ill intent." And then she added, "And this night let it guard us, too, against ill memory and dark dreams." Her brothers both looked at her sharply, but Natividad pretended not to notice. The mandala closed with a sharp little shock of magic. She nodded firmly to show them that everything was fine.

"The *maraña*," Alejandro reminded her, not commenting on her addition. He watched her, worried. He thought she couldn't tell when he worried about her, but she always could.

"I know," said Natividad. She slipped her *maraña mágica* out of her back pocket and held it up. Folded, it was about the size of a credit card. She snapped it open and spun it across the door from top to bottom. It clung there, a tangled net of light and shadows, trembling like a dew-spangled spider web, insubstantial as a handful of light but ready to confuse the steps of any enemy who tried to cross it. Natividad didn't dare remind Alejandro about anything in case he thought she was nagging, but she remarked to the air, "If we call out for pizza, we'd better remember to take that down again, or we'll be waiting a long time."

Miguel looked up, suddenly alert. "Pizza?"

Natividad made a scornful sound, pretending to be offended. "You and pizza! Anybody would think you'd grown up Gringo."

"It's probably genetic," Miguel said, pretending his dignity had been injured. "It's not my fault I got the pizza gene and you got the tamale gene. Can we order pizza if we put jalapenos on it? Jalapenos and onions and ham and extra cheese."

"It's not very good cheese on those pizzas–"

"It wouldn't be very good on anything else, but it's perfect on *those pizzas*."

"Order whatever you want," Alejandro said from the other bed. He spoke in Spanish, visibly beginning to relax at last as this casual, ordinary bickering persuaded him that his sister felt safe and cheerful again. "Better than going out." He rolled over, reached out to snag a pillow, and shut his eyes at last.

Natividad gave her twin a quick grin and an OK sign. Miguel raised a conspiratorial eyebrow and went back to his ads, careful not to rustle the papers.

"I like this one," Miguel announced in the morning, waving a slice of cold pizza illustratively in the air over the newspaper. "See? It's old, but those Korean cars last a long time, and the ad says it's got good tires for snow. It's a little more than you said, but maybe we can bargain the price down. The phone number is the same as the hotel; I mean the first three numbers, so I think the address is maybe not too far away. I bet we could get a map at the desk."

Natividad had figured out how to use the coffee pot in the room and now she sat on her bed, drinking coffee and watching Miguel finish the pizza. The pizza looked disgusting, but the coffee was good. She would have liked to add cinnamon, but it was alright the way it was. The shower was running. Either Alejandro was feeling safe enough to leave off guarding the room for two minutes, or else he'd realized it was important to look as civilized as possible when they met the Dimilioc black dogs. Natividad was betting on the latter: she didn't think Alejandro *ever* felt safe anymore. She said, "Newport isn't very big, is it? You think we can walk?"

"I'll have to call, find out where this is." Miguel looked at the phone but didn't reach for it. Natividad understood perfectly. Black dogs, especially when they were nervous, liked to feel like they made all the important decisions. Her twin would wait until he could ask Alejandro for permission to make that call. He finished the slice of pizza instead. Then he looked wistfully at the last piece in the box, but he didn't touch it in case Alejandro might want it.

"Maybe we can stop somewhere for cinnamon rolls or something," Natividad suggested.

Miguel made a face. "Those cinnamon rolls! Too much sugary goo."

"I got the cinnamon roll gene," Natividad said smugly. "All *you* got was the gene for pizza. *Cold* pizza." She pretended to shudder. Then, since Alejandro had opened the bathroom door in a puff of steam, she went to see what things she might have clean. Things that would make her look civilized and grown up.

To her, the steam seemed very faintly scented with charcoal and ash. She touched Alejandro's arm in passing, taking the edge off his tension and anger. Pausing, her brother looked down at her and smiled suddenly, the way he could: a swift hard-edged protective smile that said more clearly than words, *I won't let anything bad happen to you.* "I know," Natividad said. She patted his arm again and went on into the bathroom, closing the door behind her.

The water was hot and came down hard, stinging. The shampoo smelled of lemons and pine needles. Natividad used the hotel's blow-dryer – really, American hotels were so thoughtful – and put her hair up, pinning it carefully so it would stay. She chose pink crystal earrings to match her pink blouse. Then she stood and looked at herself in the mirror for a long time, tilting her head one way and another, trying different expressions, trying to see if she looked grown up and confident. She thought she did. She was thinner, now. That made her face look different, more like Mamá's. Only not really.

Turning abruptly, she went out into the main hotel room, and said, just a little too sharply, "Are we ready? Can we go now?"

They bought Miguel's second-choice car. It was a little more expensive, but the woman who owned it was telling the truth when she said it was in good shape and would handle snow well. The owner of the first car had lied about those things. It was hard to lie to a black dog, and not so easy to lie to Natividad, either. That man hadn't understood how he'd given himself away, but he'd been too scared of Alejandro to protest when Natividad told him he should be ashamed of himself.

This woman was much nicer. Alejandro stood back, arms crossed over his chest, his attention on the peaceful streets, not looking at the woman because he was trying not to scare her while Miguel and Natividad handled the purchase. Buying the car took almost all the rest of their money, but it was worth it because the woman had delivered mail for twenty years and turned out to know all the roads. She was happy to go over the directions Miguel showed her.

"I'm retiring, but this was my work car. It's old, but it's a good one. It can handle the roads as long as the snow doesn't get too deep. It'll get you to Lewis, right enough. Got family there, do you?" The woman's eyebrows went up on that last. She didn't sound exactly *doubtful*, but Natividad thought that was just because she was polite.

"Papá was from there," Natividad assured her. "He met Mamá in Mexico."

"Of course." The woman's gaze lingered on Natividad's face. "Your mama was a beautiful woman, I can see." Then, possibly noticing Natividad suddenly blink hard, she turned briskly back to Miguel. "You'll get to Lewis alright, I expect. Good thing you didn't wait to come in right at Christmas, there'll be a lot more snow by then. But it's easy enough. You take state highway 105 east just like it says here, but then you jog south a mile or so on Derby Line Road. You're going to skirt along the western edge of Derby Lake, then take highway 111 east and a bit south. Let me draw you a map." She fished in her purse for a pad and pencil. "See, you'll go right through Island Pond and Brighton, that's all one town these days so don't let yourselves be confused by the signs."

"Yes, ma'am. I mean, no, ma'am," Miguel promised. "I won't."

"You sure you're old enough to drive, young man? Well, never mind. Look here, the highway goes off this way, but you'll take McConnell Pond Road north and then keep on it. It'll turn into Eagle Nest Road and then into Upper Tin Shack Road, but you just keep on and you'll get to Lewis alright." The woman hesitated, glancing at Natividad. "You know – you *do* know, that's all the Kingdom Forest, really? Lewis is right on the edge of the Forest. It's no place for..." she stopped again and finished, "Well, if you've family there, you'll be alright."

Natividad tried to guess what the woman had intended to say. No place for foreigners? Mexicans? Kids? Ordinary humans? She wondered how much a mail driver might have learned about Dimilioc in twenty years of delivering letters and packages to Lewis and Brighton and Island Pond and all those little towns and villages in Dimilioc's territory.

"Thanks for the directions," Miguel said, his tone bland. He opened the back door of the car and threw in their pack, then shut the door again and looked at Natividad. She began to count out the bills. Everyone was distracted by the sight of all that money. At least, Natividad thought afterward that that was why none of them, not even Alejandro, realized the black dogs were there until they attacked.

There were two of them, though in the first instant of the attack Natividad thought there were more because they took up so much space and moved so fast. They were huge, more like mastiffs than wolves, with broad heads and heavy shoulders, and blunt muzzles set with jet black fangs. To experienced eyes, they didn't look like any natural animal at all – they were much too big, their eyes blazed fiery gold and red, and the snow exploded into steam with each bounding footfall as they rushed forward.

Black dogs usually didn't work together very well, but these separated as they rushed forward, the larger attacking Alejandro and the smaller lunging up and over a parked car to get to Natividad. She saw, in that one frozen moment, how his long black claws, almost bearlike, left gouges and slashes not just in the paintwork, but even in the metal itself.

Without thinking, she ducked backward into the car they had just bought, slammed the door, and locked it – she knew in her mind how little protection the fragile metal and glass could provide, but it might slow the black dog down a *little*. She drew a pentagram on the car window with a shaking hand, whispering words of warding – that was better protection than the car itself, and the black dog veered away, screaming with frustration and hatred, his voice rising to an inhuman keen that ended in a hiss. Rearing up on his hind legs, he swayed back and forth, torn between bloodlust and the dread of Pure magic.

Miguel knew better than to stay close to Natividad during a black dog attack. He looked horrified, but he also jerked the woman who had sold them the car almost off her feet in his rush to get them both away from Natividad's attacker and back to the dubious safety of her house. Natividad was as horrified as her twin looked: *Miguel* couldn't ward the house, and that wooden door would be no protection at all. The black dog dropped back to all fours and rushed after them, and she could see he would catch them before they reached the house. He would kill Miguel and the woman, and then come back to deal with Natividad at his leisure.

The other one would kill Alejandro and together they would get her out of the car somehow–

Alejandro caught the black dog before he had gone three strides. Alejandro, Natividad realized instantly, was *glad* to fight – fiercely glad of the chance to let go of all his hard control, all the tight-held fury and frustration of the journey, all the grief and rage he had carried from Nuevo León. His shadow had come up fast and hard, bringing with it the *cambio de cuerpo*, the change of body, in plenty of time to meet the attack. Alejandro was lost in the battle-lust of his black dog shadow – but he had not for an instant forgotten about his sister or brother.

He had not stayed to meet his own attacker. He must have ducked and gotten away, because now he leaped onto the hood of Natividad's car, and then the roof – the thin metal boomed and deformed under the impact – and then flung himself from that height down upon the black dog pursuing Miguel. Alejandro did not flinch from Natividad's magic, but their other attacker, coming after him, was forced to take precious seconds to go around the car rather than over, and in that time Alejandro tore into the smaller one, who had plainly not looked for attack from the rear. Alejandro's claws tore across his spine, and his massive jaws crushed and tore the black dog's neck. The creature cried out, collapsing, dying, his body contorting and twisting back into human shape, horribly piecemeal so that half his body and the lower part of his face were still black dog when the rest was human. Black ichor and red blood spattered the snow, and the black dog's shadow, torn free from his body, shredded into the cold air, dispersing, gone.

Alejandro did not pause to roar his triumph, but whirled to meet their remaining attacker. Alejandro's jaws dripped with ichor, fire flickered behind his black fangs, the powerful muscles of his shoulders bunched and rippled as he lowered his massive head. His snarl was a terrible, ripping sound of threat and bloodlust.

His opponent hurled himself forward, shrieking his rage and hatred.

Alejandro leaped away sideways, then pivoted and met him after all. Natividad thought she could almost feel the shock of their collision, even from inside the car. Then there was a *real* impact, as Alejandro flung his enemy into the side of the vehicle. The car's back door *crumped* inward. Natividad screamed, a small, embarrassing sound, and pressed her hands over her mouth, shrinking back. But her magic flared as the black dog hit the warded car and the black dog shrieked again, this time in pain as well as fury. In that instant, while he struggled to get clear, Alejandro tore into him in deadly earnest. There was a fast series of blows Natividad couldn't follow, and then black ichor sprayed, smoking, against the windows of the car. Both black dogs vanished below the level of her sight, and only one rose again.

Natividad opened the door on the opposite side of the car, very carefully and slowly. She wanted to hide in the car forever and never get out again, but of course she couldn't. Alejandro needed her. She knew it. That was why she had the courage to get out. He snarled at her as she came around the front of the vehicle, a long ugly sound with a wicked hiss in it.

"Hush," said Natividad. She put a hand on her brother's massive shoulder, feeling the muscles rock-hard under his shaggy pelt. "Hush. We're alright. *Somos bien.* There aren't any more, isn't that right? Only the two and you killed them both. Isn't that right? We're safe. It's alright now." She thought he understood her. He lost language when his black dog came up, but she thought he understood her anyway. She looked past him, checking on Miguel. Her twin was halfway back to the car, bringing the woman with him. She didn't try to get away from him. She looked stunned. Natividad knew how she felt.

"We're alright," Natividad said to Miguel, then suddenly found herself almost in tears, which was ridiculous because *now* everything was *fine*. She leaned shakily against the car, rubbing a hand hard across her mouth. The bodies crumpled in the snow looked completely human now. The black ichor had all burned away, leaving only red spatters across the snow and the car and everything.

Alejandro's massive head turned from side to side, his nostrils flaring as he scented the air for more enemies. But at last he shifted, slowly, and with some unpleasant fits and starts, back toward his human form. It took several minutes, during which Miguel, with cool practicality, dragged both bodies away behind a hedge and began kicking snow over the worst of the blood. It was already bitterly cold. Natividad had almost forgotten, until she saw the blood freezing into crystals in the snow, how cold it was. Shivering, glad of her mittens, she got a handful of snow and began to scrub the blood off the car. She glanced at Miguel and then at the woman who had sold them the car, wondering what they could do about her. She would obviously call the police as soon as they were gone...

"*Now* I believe your father was from Lewis," the woman said, her voice shaky but emphatic. She stared at the blood, cast a horrified glance at the half-concealed bodies, and *didn't* look at Alejandro at all, which must have taken quite an effort. "I sure *do*. Oh, my God. I never... My *God*, in broad daylight... Jesus *Christ*."

Alejandro straightened at last, looking almost entirely human. He stared at the woman. She met his gaze for a moment with horrified wonder, but looked away again before Miguel, once more at her side, needed to warn her about that. She said rapidly, "I don't know anything, I don't *want* to know anything, I don't *care* what you people do, anyway *they* attacked *you*, not that it's any of my business, alright? Take the car, just take it, that's fine, I don't care, somebody else can find the bodies, it won't be the first time lately, alright?"

"Alejandro..." Natividad began.

"You won't call the police," said Miguel. Though he spoke to the woman, his raised-eyebrow look was for Natividad.

"No. No! I swear I won't! I swear!"

The woman was starting to cry, which was kind of awful. Natividad said quickly, "She's telling the truth, you know. She really is. You must be able to tell that as well as I can, 'Jandro." That was why her twin had made the woman deny it, of course: so Natividad and Alejandro could hear the truth in her voice. She patted her brother anxiously on the arm. The human shape of his arm was reassuring, but his muscles were still hard with tension.

"We can leave right now, get out of town immediately," Miguel put in smoothly. "Anyway, I bet the police here don't *want* to interfere with Dimilioc. Whatever they know or don't know or have figured out since the war, you know there's got to be a long, long tradition in this town of staying way out of Dimilioc business."

Alejandro rubbed his hands across his face. The anger was ebbing at last, or at least he was getting it under control. He dropped his hands, stared at Natividad for a moment, and then said, his voice gritty with the remnants of black dog rage, *"Me de igual. Está bien."*

"Right," said Natividad, relieved. "Right. *Bien.*" She patted his shoulder.

Natividad thought the woman might change her mind and call the police after all as soon as they were gone, but she didn't say so. Anyway, Miguel was right, of course. The people of Newport, including the police, undoubtedly did have a long tradition of staying out of Dimilioc business, so probably there would be no trouble. Or not from the *police.* Natividad wished she knew whether those black dogs could possibly have belonged to Vonhausel. But Vonhausel shouldn't have dared trespass on Dimilioc territory. She looked at Miguel.

"They can't be Vonhausel's," her twin said, answering her exact fear. "Right on the edge of the Kingdom Forest? I don't believe it. They were strays." But despite his firm tone, Miguel was frowning. He said abruptly, "Dimilioc should have tighter control than this. Strays, here? I wonder how strong Dimilioc actually *is,* now…" But then, as Alejandro shifted his weight, Miguel fell abruptly silent.

Natividad said nothing. She didn't want Alejandro to know how scared she still was. Then he would be angry again, and his shadow would press at him, and she didn't dare cost him even a shred of his control. They had this good car now, and soon they would be at Dimilioc, and then her brother would need every bit of his control. So, Natividad tried to think of cheerful things – hot chocolate, say. Except then she thought of Mamá's kitchen, and Mamá, and that was worse. So, then she tried to think of nothing at all.

2

The car finally got irretrievably stuck a few miles north of Lewis, on a nameless road that twisted up the sides of steep rocky hills and then chopped its way back down again.

Miguel was much better with cars and driving than either Alejandro or Natividad, and someone had to drive, but the road got worse and worse, and Natividad was not surprised when her twin finally lost control on one particularly steep curvy bit. When the car skidded, Alejandro put out an arm to brace her, and Miguel took his foot off the gas, and the car slid gently sideways off the road and tucked itself into a snowdrift at the base of a granite ridge. The gentle impact was little worse than when the bus had hit potholes in parking lots on their way north. Natividad uttered a small scream, mostly to tease her twin. Miguel winced, embarrassed. "Sorry," he said to both of them. "Sorry. It's not like normal driving. I thought I slowed down enough."

"*Está bien,*" Alejandro reassured his brother. "It doesn't matter."

He didn't sound angry at all. Natividad guessed her older brother might even be glad that the car had run off the road. He might not mind if there was one delay and then another, so that the moment they came to the heart of Dimilioc remained a moment in the future and not yet *this* moment. She would understand that. *She* was Pure, so she was safe – pretty safe – and Miguel was only human. But Alejandro – black dogs were so *territorial*. Miguel thought it would be OK, but Natividad thought her twin might be too sure of his logical analysis of what Grayson Lanning *ought* to do to really believe he might do something else.

"So, I guess we'll walk the rest of the way," Miguel said, once they were all sure the car was stuck. He patted the steering wheel wistfully. "Maybe we can get the car back later." He reached into the back seat for their pack, glancing over his shoulder at Natividad. "It can't be so far now. Three or four miles, maybe. And it's not that cold."

This was optimistic. It was very cold. No part of Nuevo León ever got so cold, not even the mountains. Here, their breath trailed white and frozen through the brilliant air, puffs of living steam against the stark black branches of the trees. And there was a great deal of snow here. Natividad could not remember snow ever falling at home in Potosi, far less at Hualahuises where Mamá's family had lived.

They pushed their way through knee-deep snow all afternoon. The whole world was white and black: the occasional green of needled pine and the flash of red as a bird flew by only served to accent the bleakness of the winter forest. Natividad could not imagine how the bird could live in this frozen world, where there seemed neither fruit nor seed nor insect nor anything else that might sustain living creatures. She thought this must be a hard country for bird or beast. A hard country for people, too. Even for black dogs.

Yet this cold northern world was not perfectly silent. Pine needles rattled in the occasional breeze; now and then a clump of snow fell softly from a branch. Somewhere not far away a bird called sharply, unmusically. Perhaps the red one, perhaps another; Natividad did not know the birds of this country. They had occasionally seen others through the afternoon: little ones of gray and buff and white; once a small flock of large black ones, like crows but bigger, which might have been ravens.

She stumbled over a snow-covered rock, and Alejandro touched her arm, stopping her. "You are alright?" he asked her. "Not too tired?"

"I'm fine," Natividad said, waving away any concern, but she could tell from the way that Alejandro looked at her that he didn't believe her. She smiled at him reassuringly, but the smile took a deliberate effort. She *was* tired. And the cold was awful. But she didn't want to make her brothers stop for her sake. Miguel, hovering protectively at her elbow, looked alright, but Miguel had spent his whole life trying to keep up with their older brother. He was not tall, but he was sturdy and strong for an ordinary human, and the cold did not seem to bother him as much as it bothered her.

Alejandro himself, of course, did not really feel the cold. Black dogs didn't. It wasn't fair. Natividad gave Alejandro a look in which she tried to combine scornful amusement and impatience. She said, again, "I'm fine." Her breath, like Alejandro's, hung in the air, a visible echo of her words.

"She's fine," Miguel said, putting an arm around her shoulders.

Natividad leaned against her twin, her smile suddenly genuine. "See?"

Alejandro was not convinced. "We could stop, rest. We have not come very far. I think we still have a long way to walk. You should rest. We could make a fire. You have those *cerillos*? Matches?" He looked at Miguel. "We could boil water, have coffee. Eat something. Then you would have not so much to carry."

Miguel grinned, a flash of white teeth in his dark face. His smile was their father's. Just recently, as Miguel had shot up in height and lost the plump softness of childhood, Natividad had begun to see echoes of their American father's bony features emerging in her twin's face. "I'm fine, too," Miguel said "But I wouldn't mind carrying some of this weight on the inside instead of the outside."

Miguel, though much less strong than Alejandro, was the only one of them carrying a real burden. Natividad carried a shoulder bag with matches and a thermal blanket and some food, and her brothers had insisted on her carrying their small remaining cache of American money. Her twin carried everything else: the little pot to boil water; mugs and powdered cocoa; jerky and nuts. Extra clothes, too – especially for Natividad, of course, which was a little embarrassing, but only a little. It wasn't *her* fault her brothers didn't care about clothes.

Since they had known their car might not be able to get all the way to Dimilioc, they had brought the things she and Miguel might need if the cold got too bad. More than that, they had not wanted to abandon every last trace of their past. Buried in the middle of Miguel's pack, Natividad knew, was Mamá's special wooden flute, wrapped up in Natividad's favorite dress, the one with all the ruffles.

They hadn't had to argue who would carry the pack. Last year, when she and Miguel had been only fourteen, he might have argued. Even Natividad herself might have argued. She might have thought Alejandro should carry the pack because he was the biggest and had the black dog strength. But this year, they all understood that Alejandro could not carry any burden because he needed his hands free.

Alejandro carried only a knife: the silver one she had blooded for him. If worse came to worst, he would fight. If he fought well enough, if Natividad had time to use her *maraña*, then maybe she and Miguel would be able to get away. Lewis was not so far behind them, and if they could get another car, maybe they would be able to get all the way off Dimilioc territory.

The truth was, if worse came to worst, probably they would all die. But that had been so since the day Mamá and Papá had been killed. Even before that, in fact, though they had not known that when they were younger. So short a time ago, when they had all been children, before the war between black dogs and the blood kin had weakened Dimilioc, and Vonhausel had renewed his own war with Papá… Natividad shut those memories away with a sharp effort.

"I'm not too tired," she said. "I can go on." She looked at her watch, a cheap one with a black plastic strap and a pink face, and a white kitten to point out the hours and minutes. She put back the hood of her coat and looked at the sky, where the sun lay already low above the horizon. So comfortless and distant, that sun. She could almost believe cold radiated from it, and not warmth at all.

Alejandro said, "No. You two should eat something. Is that not what you said, Natividad? People need to eat more in the cold. *You* told us that."

"You did say that," said Miguel, so placidly that Natividad could not argue. Her twin was very hard to argue with. "Of course you should eat something. Some jerky, maybe. I'll take one of those nut bars with the chocolate, if you've got any more. And we should drink some water."

Natividad shrugged. "*Matón*," she said, but without heat. Then, remembering her rule about English, she corrected herself: "Bully." Tucking back several wisps of hair that had worked out of her careful pins, she began to search through her light pack for something to eat. Miguel walked a little aside from the trail they'd been following, kicking knee-high snow out of his way, and swept more snow off a fallen tree so she could sit down. "I really don't need to rest," Natividad protested, but then shrugged. "But I suppose I wouldn't *mind* coffee." She followed him, peeling the wrapping away from one of her nut bars and handing her twin another.

"Well, look at this," said a new voice, sharp and quick and nasally American. "Black pups trespassing. Do you know, when we got the call, I walked out in the middle of breakfast? If I'd realized it was a pack of *puppies*, I'd not have troubled myself."

Natividad jumped and spun around fast. Miguel caught her arm to steady her and Alejandro took several quick steps to put himself between them and the newcomer. Natividad touched her pocket, but didn't grab her *maraña mágica*, not yet: she didn't want the newcomer to guess she had it. If they *did* have to run, she wanted it to take him by surprise.

Alejandro moved a step forward, toward the threat. He stared directly into the newcomer's face for a breath, which between black dogs was a challenge. Then, with an effort Natividad could see, that she thought she could almost feel in her own body, he lowered his eyes.

The American was taller than Alejandro, but seemed hardly older at all. Surely he couldn't be as young as he appeared, but the way he stood and moved and looked, no one would have dismissed him as a boy anyway. He stood with his weight forward, relaxed, but holding himself with the kind of balance that meant he could move fast in any direction.

His was a very American face: bony and narrow, with a thin, unsmiling mouth crooked now with disdain, as though nothing he looked at pleased him and he didn't expect it to. His hard stare implied arrogance; the set of his mouth suggested impatience and an inflexible temper. Despite his youth, it was the face of someone already long experienced with killing and death, someone who would not be easily touched by anger or fear or grief. It was the face of the Dimilioc executioner, who killed without mercy or regret.

She knew his name. Everyone did – everyone who knew anything about black dogs. This was Ezekiel Korte, old Thos Korte's nephew: the youngest man ever to be made Dimilioc's executioner. Stray black dogs always feared the Dimilioc executioner. Even in Mexico, a thousand miles south, black dogs whispered his name and looked over their shoulders when they broke Dimilioc law, afraid that someday they would find the executioner behind them – and for the past six years, when they did, it was this face they had seen before they died.

The young Dimilioc executioner was dressed with a black dog's indifference to cold: narrow black pants that tucked into boots, a blue shirt, a black leather jacket clearly chosen more for its looks than its warmth. Other than his shirt, there was no color to him. His hair was the color of bleached straw. His pale blue eyes, many shades lighter than the shirt, seemed to Natividad to be the color of the winter itself. She was immediately afraid of him, but she also found that she was sorry for him, which she hadn't expected at all. He had drawn danger and disdain around himself as closely as that leather jacket, but what she thought was that she had never in her life seen anyone who seemed more *alone*.

Alejandro took another step forward and then dropped to one knee in the snow, but he did not reach for the knife he carried. Natividad was very glad of his restraint. She could see her brother was trying to strike a balance between respectful acknowledgement of the executioner's superior strength and his own pride – *black pup*, the young executioner had said, and him only a few years older than Alejandro himself. She knew it would be harder for Alejandro to defer to Ezekiel Korte than to one of the older Dimilioc black dogs. Black *wolves*. Papá had said the Dimilioc black dogs called themselves wolves. She wished desperately that Papá was here now. Or Mamá, even more. Though if their parents had lived, none of them would have come here.

"Well," said the Dimilioc executioner, looking them over with leisurely derision, "It's a little late for courtesy, isn't it? What is this? One black pup and a human boy and a girl Pure as the white snow? One doesn't expect to find such a mixed pack of strays in the winter woods. Still less walking on foot straight into Dimilioc territory. There are quicker ways to find death, if that's what you seek."

"We ask to speak to Grayson Lanning. We ask for a proper audience. Is it your place to refuse?" Alejandro said. Natividad could hear the edge of strain in his voice, but she hoped a stranger would not.

Ezekiel tilted his head to one side, smiling. "Oh, it is."

Alejandro hesitated. Behind him, Miguel said, "Of course it is, but, Ezekiel Korte, would the Master of Dimilioc thank you for exercising your prerogative?"

The young man's wintery eyes went to Miguel. "You know me, do you?"

"Everyone knows you."

"Black dogs. Not humans, generally." Ezekiel's pale gaze shifted back to Alejandro. "Your brother, is he? And the girl's your sister, I expect. She's pretty."

Alejandro stiffened at this provocation, delivered so indifferently it was almost an insult. Natividad shook off Miguel's restraining hand and went forward to touch Alejandro's shoulder, trying to calm him. She knew – they all knew – that no Dimilioc wolf would attack *her*. If Ezekiel Korte attacked anyone, it would certainly be Alejandro.

Ezekiel's pale eyes remained steady on Alejandro's face. He said softly, "You think you can fight me? Give your brother and sister time to run?"

"She's Pure," Alejandro said sharply. Too sharply, despite Natividad's touch. He obviously knew it, because he took a breath, then, and lowered his head. "I don't want to fight you, but why should she have to run? She is Pure."

"I see she is. But she's with you. And you're trespassing. Aren't you?" The young executioner's gaze shifted to Natividad, then to Miguel and finally back to Alejandro. "You think she can run in this cold? The Pure are just as susceptible to cold as ordinary humans. You got your car stuck at the bottom of some hill, I suppose. It's a long way back to Lewis from here. Too far for children on foot – especially children who don't cast real shadows."

"I'm fast," Natividad said sharply. It was dangerous to show a black dog fear. She was sharp instead, so she might seem less like prey. "We're *not* children, and I'm fast, and strong. You might be surprised."

Ezekiel's pale eyebrows rose. He laughed, briefly, but with real humor.

Alejandro's muscles tightened under Natividad's hand, but he kept a tight leash on his rising anger. "Fighting you is not my first choice. *Usted eliges* – it is your choice. What we want is to speak to Grayson Lanning. Not a challenge – *not* a challenge, or would we have walked openly into Dimilioc territory?"

"Perhaps not," murmured Ezekiel. "No, perhaps not. And you're not up to my weight – though perhaps you're just old enough to think you are. You're what – sixteen?"

"*Eighteen*," Alejandro snapped, then visibly caught himself. Natividad tried not to wince. She could see Ezekiel had been deliberately insulting, and her brother had let his temper slip. Just a little, but enough to show that no, he was not up to Ezekiel's weight. Which, of course, they had all already known.

Ezekiel's cold gaze rested on Alejandro for a moment longer. Then he looked at Natividad. "You're younger than he is, aren't you? You *are* pretty. But can you run?" He shifted his weight, stepped forward, focused on her with clearly predatory intent.

Just that fast, Alejandro was on his feet, flinging Natividad back, his knife in his hand, his shadow rising behind him and around him in response to his sudden blaze of fear and anger. The cold air smelled of ash and burning.

Her brother couldn't win a fight with the Dimilioc executioner. Natividad knew that. But if he could injure him with silver, there was a better chance she and Miguel could get away. They had all agreed to that, but she hadn't thought they would have to actually fight – Miguel had been so sure they would not have to fight. Though her heart raced with sudden fear, she still thought Ezekiel didn't mean it. But Alejandro was *ready* to fight, even if he knew he couldn't win. The silver in the blade sparked against his fingers, but it did not burn him. If he cut Ezekiel, though, that cut would burn, and resist ordinary black dog healing.

"You *would* fight," Ezekiel said, easing back. He was smiling again: a thin, dangerous smile. "I thought you would. But with a knife?"

"It is your choice," Alejandro repeated. "If I must fight you, I will use a knife, yes. Because I would need the advantage. But I do not want to fight you."

"Don't you? Down, then. *Down* – and drop that knife."

Alejandro did not move.

"Do it," muttered Miguel, his voice low. The executioner had frightened him, too, Natividad could hear it in his voice. But he whispered to their brother, urgently, "It's a test, I'm sure it's a test. Do what he says."

Alejandro's mouth tightened. But after a moment, he turned and threw the knife, a sharp motion that left the slender blade buried in the smooth bark of a tree twenty feet away, chest high. Natividad understood: if he had to fight the Dimilioc executioner now, maybe he could recover it, use it. Ezekiel couldn't: it wasn't blooded for *him*.

Then Alejandro turned back to face Ezekiel and dropped again to one knee.

Ezekiel smiled, a mocking expression. His own shadow had gathered around him, heavy and dense, clinging to his pale skin, almost as obvious to her as it would be to another black dog. It smelled of ozone and bitter ash and burnt clay. But he did not go into the *cambio de cuerpo*, and after a lingering moment, his shadow ebbed back down to lie again on the white snow.

Ezekiel took a step forward. Another step, wary. That was a compliment, sort of: that Dimilioc's executioner approached Alejandro with caution. The American eased forward a third step. Alejandro shuddered. Natividad knew her brother was on the edge of leaping up, backing away, letting his shadow bring the *cambio de cuerpo*. Miguel caught Natividad's arm, pulling her back, leaving Alejandro alone. She yielded, reluctantly, and only because she knew that their presence would only make Ezekiel's close approach harder for Alejandro to bear.

He did not move. Natividad was so proud of him. Her brother stayed still, even when Ezekiel reached out slowly and set one hand on his shoulder, close to his throat. Black-shadow claws tipped the young man's fingers. It was naked aggression, that touch. It was a threat, and an arrogant show of control over his own shadow.

"I could tear out your throat right now," Ezekiel said softly. "Could you stop me?"

Alejandro said, harshly, "No."

"You're in a bad position. Why did you let me put you in such a bad position?"

"Because the only choice I saw was fighting you, now. We didn't come here to fight."

"No. Of course not. You want to talk to Grayson." Ezekiel stood for a moment, staring down at him, and then lifted his hand and eased back a step. "You have something resembling control, it seems. Maybe he'll want to talk to you." He backed another step, glanced past Alejandro toward Natividad, and added, "It's another few miles to the house. Can your sister walk so far?"

"Of course I can!" snapped Natividad, insulted. She strode forward again, laying her own hand on Alejandro's shoulder, exactly where Ezekiel had touched him. His black dog shadow did not take *her* touch as a threat. Their mother had worked the *Aplacando* on her black dog son as soon as he was born. To him, the touch of the Pure, especially Natividad's touch, was strengthening, reassuring... calming.

Alejandro took a long breath, glanced up warily, and got to his feet.

There was no sign that Ezekiel took that movement as

a challenge. The young American only raked his wintery gaze across them all. Then he turned his back and walked away, leaving the road to walk directly into the stark forest. He did not turn his head to see Natividad detour briefly to recover the knife, but she thought he must know she had. Probably he didn't mind if *she* had it. She kept it – that was probably best, because Ezekiel would no doubt care a lot more if Alejandro took it again.

The countryside was rugged. The snow, mostly knee high, was in places up to Natividad's hips. It was hard to wade through. Natividad had discovered long since that snow was not as light and fluffy as she had always imagined: it was brittle and hard on the top, so one broke through with every step; and it was heavy to push aside. A black dog like Alejandro or Ezekiel could wrap himself in his shadow and walk, weightless, along the top of the snow. But they didn't. Alejandro walked in front, and then Miguel, breaking a trail for Natividad. They had done that all along, but she was surprised to find that Ezekiel Korte also, without comment, walked heavily through the snow, helping make a trail.

Another red bird clung to a branch overhead, scolding them in sharp little chirps. Its mate, brown touched only lightly with red, joined it. Farther away, a trio of deer stood motionless and watched them pass. There was far less clamor of life than in the oak forest near Potosi, or even the dry scrub around Hualahuises where the coyotes and javalinas lived. But at least the frozen forest no longer seemed completely barren. This seemed, in an odd way, a sort of reassurance. An omen – as though life might be possible here also for black dogs out of the south and their human kin. She wanted to point the deer out to Miguel, but none of them could say anything that Ezekiel would not overhear, and she was afraid he might think her silly. So they walked in silence.

The Dimilioc house was a great sprawling mansion of white stone and red brick, nothing that invited burning, which was a sensible precaution for a black dog's house. Natividad thought that three of their mother's house could have tucked themselves into just the first floor of one wing of this house, and there were two wings and three stories. There was no landscaped garden, only a sweep of clear snow-covered ground that ran out to the edge of the forest. Near the house, low stone walls edged the road. There were no tracks through the snow, but here and there were light scuff marks that might have been made by the weightless steps of black dogs.

Four men waited on the wide porch of the house, framed by red brick pillars and the leafless stems of some tough vine that clung to the brickwork. Natividad clung tightly to Alejandro, not for her own reassurance, but to help him keep his temper. She held Miguel's hand, too, but that *was* for herself.

Ezekiel Korte lengthened his stride and went up the stairs onto the porch, with a short, ironic nod for one of the men there, unmistakably disclaiming any continuing responsibility. He might as well have said aloud, "*That's my part done; now this is your problem.*"

Natividad knew the man to whom Ezekiel nodded must be the Master of Dimilioc. Grayson Lanning. She would have known him anyway by the density and strength of his shadow, by the way it had eyes that flickered with fire. She had thought Papá strong, but even Papá's shadow had not had eyes like that, through which one could glimpse smoke and burning.

Grayson Lanning was not as tall as Ezekiel, but broader. Not as old as Natividad had expected: probably not yet even forty. But authoritative, even so. To a merely human eye, he would have looked like... a banker, maybe, or the director of a wealthy company, or maybe – and this was a little more accurate – the head of a ruthless drug cartel. Natividad knew exactly what he was: an extremely dominant black dog with a dangerous temper and a murderously strong shadow.

The Dimilioc Master's eyes were deep-set and dark, his brows heavy, his mouth straight and humorless as an axe cut. Where Ezekiel Korte was lithe and light as a dancer, Grayson Lanning was rugged, broad, strong-boned, and powerful. Natividad didn't have to remind herself to drop her eyes when he stared at her. The scent of charred wood and smoldering coal that surrounded him was, to her senses, very strong. It enshrouded the entire house. If any ordinary humans were in that house, she could not tell. She was almost sure no one else Pure was in there. She already knew that all the men on the porch were black dogs. No. Not black *dogs* at all. Dimilioc black wolves.

Alejandro glanced sideways at her. She pressed his hand hard, trying to steady him. Then she let go, because her brother would have to face the Dimilioc wolves without her help. She was sure he could. She could feel her own heart beating quickly and lightly, like the heart of a bird. Her brother would be able to hear it, probably. She smiled at him anyway, a bright, brave smile that denied fear. On her other side, Miguel did not smile. He looked very solemn.

Alejandro took one step forward, putting himself out in front of Natividad and Miguel, and went to his knees. To both knees. Natividad knew why: he was acknowledging that now it was impossible either to run or to fight. She dropped to her knees as well, knowing the Dimilioc wolves would expect that from all of them. Beside her, Miguel swung the pack down to the ground and also knelt. Alejandro did not glance back at them, but lifted his eyes and looked into Grayson Lanning's face. Then he deliberately lowered his gaze to the ground.

"Well," said the Dimilioc Master, speaking to Ezekiel Korte, "When I sent you out after our trespassers, I did not expect you to bring them to back to our very doorstep. Certainly not alive. I gather you believed I would benefit from meeting them personally?" His voice was heavy, a deep gritty bass that was almost a growl.

"They thought so," Ezekiel answered, his tone faintly amused. "They'd left their car stuck someplace and were walking in on foot. Along the road, obvious as you please. Asked for you by name." He leaned his hip on the porch rail and crossed his arms over his chest, looking cool and not very much concerned, for all the world like any posturing teenager. But he was not just any teenager, and he was not posturing.

"The boy's human, but that girl's Pure," one of the older men said. Dark and heavyset. Old, at least fifty, but still strong. That would be Harrison Lanning, Grayson's older brother. He was frowning, but did not look actually hostile.

The other dark one, about Ezekiel's age, that one must be Harrison's son, Ethan Lanning. He had the look of the Lannings and he was the right age. *He* looked hostile – the only Dimilioc wolf to seem truly antagonistic rather than merely scornful. Natividad wasn't sure she blamed him, though. It must be hard to be just ordinary when you lived in the same house as Ezekiel Korte.

"Yes, Harrison, we all know she is Pure," said the oldest of the men, fair and light boned. That would be Zachariah Korte, Ezekiel's uncle. He certainly had the same supercilious tilt to his head.

Grayson studied Natividad. "She may be Pure, but she's a child."

Natividad looked the leader of the Dimilioc in the face. As he had addressed her, she could answer. She said, as meekly as she knew how, "Fifteen, sir, though I have cousins my age who are married, so I don't think I'm a child."

Heavy brows lifted. "No? Well, perhaps you are right. And you believe your Purity will protect you. What do you think will protect your brothers? Especially that one?" He nodded toward Alejandro. "A black dog openly trespassing on our very doorstep."

Natividad's brows drew together. She opened her mouth to say, "*We came in right along your road, didn't we? You didn't exactly plaster "No Trespassing" signs along the way, did you?*" But Alejandro put in quickly, before she could say anything, "We all thought at least Natividad would be safe, and probably Miguel, and if we were wrong, sir, it's my fault. I argued them into coming to you, so it's my fault and not theirs."

Grayson lifted a skeptical eyebrow.

Alejandro said as sharply as he dared, "It is! Because of what our father said about Dimilioc and about you. He said Dimilioc was lucky you were Master, he said Thos Korte might have started the war, but you could finish it; he said you would fight the war *cueste lo que cueste*. He said, when the vampire miasma failed, Thos Korte would have failed too; he would have let the vampires regain their strength, he would have been afraid to lose the miasma, afraid of what ordinary human people would do when they became able to see us all. But you would pursue the war to the end, no matter what it cost…" He faltered and stopped.

Natividad knew her brother had been silenced by the stark memory of exactly what the true cost of Dimilioc's war had been: emboldened strays hunting as they pleased; and worse, far worse, Papá's own bitterest enemy tracking him down at last. She wanted to touch Alejandro's hand, say something to help him, but she could think of nothing to say.

Then Alejandro drew a hard breath and said, "Papá said you were a good Master and an honorable man. So, I said we should come. So, our offense is my fault, sir, and if you punish our insolence, you should punish me and not my brother and sister. No matter how many of our cousins married young, Natividad *is* only fifteen and that's a child. And Miguel – he's not a black dog and he's no older than she is, and anyway, what would she do without a brother to protect her? You must not punish them."

"Your father?"

Alejandro had, of course, deliberately provoked Grayson

to ask that question, but now he wasn't quick to answer. A whole lifetime of silence was hard to overcome.

"Edward Toland, sir," Miguel said. Very respectfully.

Grayson's heavy brows rose. "Edward. Well. I wouldn't have guessed that at all." He paused, studying Miguel, and then went on, "Though perhaps I see a similarity. A subtle likeness, but now I look for it, I might believe that you come from the Toland bloodline."

"Yes, sir. We do," Miguel assured him.

Grayson examined them all, one after another. "You all have the same mother? A Pure woman? Do I understand that correctly?"

"Yes. Yes, sir."

"How very imprudent of Edward. Thos would not have liked that at all. No wonder he hid himself and his family so carefully. Well... Well, he is now dead, I imagine? During the war?"

Natividad looked down, swallowing. Her dark grief was nothing she wanted to show strangers; it was too ready to tear open, a chasm that could swallow her whole. She was grateful when Miguel answered because that meant she didn't have to. "After the war, when the black dogs began hunting so boldly," her twin explained. "Papá hid from Dimilioc well enough before, but not... after the war..." Miguel stopped, taking a hard breath, not as unaffected as he tried to seem.

"Yes, I understand. There are many more stray black dogs in Mexico than here, of course." Grayson's hard gaze moved to Natividad, then to Alejandro. He said to Alejandro, "Thus, your decision to cross the border."

"Yes, sir," said Alejandro. He didn't look at Miguel. He said, "We needed to get Natividad somewhere safe. We couldn't protect her – I could not. Our father's enemies, they would not stop."

"Your father's enemies," Grayson Lanning repeated, his voice expressionless.

Alejandro had argued that they shouldn't explain the real reason they'd had to leave Mexico, in case the Dimilioc Master wondered whether he really needed another enemy. But Miguel had said they had better not start at Dimilioc with a lie and Natividad had sided with her twin. So now Alejandro said, still not looking at Miguel, pretending everything had always been his idea, "Vonhausel."

"That old enmity," said Zachariah. His tone was dry and unamused. "Yes, I recall that quarrel vividly. So, it did not die even after both Edward and Malvern Vonhausel were cast out."

"No, sir," said Alejandro. He started to say something else, but Miguel, interrupting, said quickly and earnestly, "At first I think Papá thought he might track Vonhausel down and kill him, but then I guess Vonhausel got too strong, and Papá met Mamá, and after that Mamá kept us hidden, but I guess maybe there was a lot of magic loose during the war, and somehow Vonhausel learned where we were–"

Alejandro said, overriding Miguel's lighter voice, "I cannot protect my sister from Malvern Vonhausel. But Dimilioc can surely protect her. If you will. Master."

Grayson regarded him thoughtfully. "Well, that is likely true. But am I seriously meant to believe that at some point before he died, Edward Toland actually advised you to appeal to Dimilioc for protection?" A slight incredulity had come into the Master's voice.

Alejandro answered, "Yes, sir. He told... He told us about Dimilioc. He said that the only black dogs who do not live in fear belong to Dimilioc and call themselves wolves. He told us that Dimilioc black wolves live together with humans and with the Pure. That Dimilioc wolves use the *Aplacando*, the Calming, and cherish the Pure. We know... Everyone knows Dimilioc has always killed any black dog who dares hunt the Pure." Alejandro paused, then went on, "And then we heard that Thos Korte was dead and you were Master. Papá said if we had to... to leave Mexico, we should come to you."

What Papá had actually said was, "*Don't stand and fight, hear me?*"

He had been speaking to Alejandro; it would not have occurred to Natividad or even Miguel to stand and fight. And he had not exactly been speaking. He had been snarling, the change half on him. They had known by then that Vonhausel had come, that he was close. That they would not be able to fight. The dry forest around Potosi was already burning, the oaks smoldering into slow flames and the pines going up like torches. Black smoke had veiled the whole sky.

Mamá had been trying to show Natividad a special way to hide, always hard for the Pure. Natividad had been trying to learn it, crying with fear and trying not to beg to stay with Miguel. She had known if she stayed too close to her brother, she might draw black dogs to them both. She had had to hide by herself, at the base of the live oak, concealed by its living shadow, and Mamá… Natividad wouldn't think about that.

But she couldn't help but remember how desperate and furious Papá had sounded when he'd ordered Alejandro: *"Get clear of this, don't fight, lead those bastards off of us, as many as you can get to follow you. Come back if you can, find your brother and sister, take them north. Dimilioc's the only chance you'll have, understand me? You'll have to throw the dice. Grayson Lanning has got to be better than old Thos, he could hardly be worse, and Toland is a name he'll recognize."*

Alejandro said only, "He told me Dimilioc would remember his name. He said you might take us in."

"Is that what your father told you?" Grayson was silent for a moment. He did not seem to expect a response, but at length went on, quietly, his deep voice dropping into a still lower register, "It's been, what? Twenty years, since your father quarreled with Vonhausel and then, like a lunatic, with Thos Korte. At least twenty years. I find it interesting that your father, though exiled from Dimilioc, nevertheless found himself a Pure woman. That he even married her. I find it incredible that he lived long enough to have children your age and yet never once brought himself to our attention."

Alejandro apparently could think of no response to make to this. Natividad certainly couldn't. Not even Miguel seemed to have anything to say.

"And now you are here. Possibly with Malvern Vonhausel snapping at your heels. Well. And you think Dimilioc should lay claim to your father's old quarrel?"

Here it was, this moment, which held either life or death,

which held their futures and all their lives. Natividad wished she could answer. Or Miguel, who could always find words that were smooth and polite and persuasive. But the Dimilioc Master would expect Alejandro to answer before his younger human brother or Pure sister.

So it was Alejandro who took a breath, met Grayson's eyes, and answered, "Dimilioc hunts down *descontrolados* black dogs and sends them into the fell dark; Dimilioc clears moon-bound shifters out of the sunlit world and protects the Pure. Twenty years ago, Vonhausel did not dare challenge Dimilioc. Now the war is done, if there still exists any civilized House of black wolves he will not dare challenge, it is this one. So, I brought my sister here. Will you not take her in?"

The Dimilioc Master did not answer. He regarded Alejandro with narrow-eyed intensity.

Alejandro lowered his gaze, but from the angle of his head, Natividad knew he continued to watch Grayson covertly. He said suddenly, "Was the cost of the war with the vampires so high?" Alejandro looked from man to man on the porch: Grayson and Harrison and Ethan Lanning; Zachariah and Ezekiel Korte. "Is *this* all your strength?"

Grayson said nothing.

"You are weak," Alejandro said harshly. "Dimilioc is *weak*. All the *callejeros* were hiding before, they were quiet, but now why should they hide their shadows? Never mind Vonhausel: if even ordinary stray black dogs look north now, who is here to stop them?"

"I expect we'd manage somehow," murmured Ezekiel, cool and mocking and totally unimpressed.

"Oh, yes, will you? Should black dogs fear the Dimilioc *verdugo*?" Alejandro asked him. "The Dimilioc executioner, who can find you anywhere and will step silently out of the night to tear out your heart – every black dog fears the *verdugo*! But even the executioner himself cannot fight ten black dogs at once... or twenty... or fifty."

"You might be surprised," said Ezekiel, smiling a little.

Alejandro shook his head. "It's fear that defended Dimilioc. It was fear of you that kept the *callejeros* quiet in the world. But now Gehorsam is gone from Germany, and nearly all the Lumondiere wolves dead in France, so we hear, and who knows about the Dacha? Or the cartels in Syria and Saudi Arabia; not that *they* are a loss, but they were strong and now they are gone. If not even Dimilioc remains strong enough to make all the *norteamericano* black dogs afraid, then the *callejeros* will hunt the Pure, and never mind what Malvern Vonhausel will do! Any black dog with strength enough to force another to follow him will come to pull you down. If you have only five wolves to meet them, they will do it–"

Grayson gave Alejandro a burning look, and Alejandro stopped. The Dimilioc Master said, his tone harsh, "I assure you, pup, black dogs everywhere are still wise to fear Dimilioc."

Alejandro lowered his eyes, but Miguel, less impressed by black dog aggression, said, "If Dimilioc can't hold against stray black dogs, that would be... Look, you *have* to hold. If Dimilioc was gone, even the weakest of the black dogs would hunt as they please. There would be another war, this one between black dogs and humans, and no one would win that one either, but black dogs would lose it."

Grayson transferred his burning look to Miguel.

Miguel didn't seem to notice. He said earnestly, "Dimilioc needs to be stronger, whether Vonhausel comes or does not come. You don't have *time* to breed more black wolves of Dimilioc bloodlines. You need us as much as we need you! Toland used to be Dimilioc. We could be again. Alejandro is strong right now – Papá trained him all his life–"

"Enough!" snapped Alejandro. But he said to Grayson, "But that is true. That is all true. We came to ask Dimilioc to take us in. If you *can* protect my sister and brother, then we will strengthen Dimilioc."

Grayson Lanning tilted his head, amusement and something else in his hard face. "You amaze me."

"I will be loyal to Dimilioc," Alejandro insisted. "We all will be. Six wolves would be stronger than five. Enough, maybe. Miguel will make himself useful to you – and, after all, our sister is Pure."

Ethan Lanning said with contempt, "Pimping your sister, are you, pup?"

Only Natividad's grab at his arm kept Alejandro in his place. She was furious and didn't mind letting it show, because meekness was all very well, but there were *limits*. She said sharply to Grayson, ignoring Ethan, "I *told* Alejandro he should say that. It's obvious anyway. Did you think it was an *accident* I said that about my married cousins? I'm not a *puta*; I won't lie down with them all. But if you take us into Dimilioc, I'll take any one of your wolves you say." She jerked her head scornfully at Ethan. "Even him."

Ethan Lanning flushed and snarled, his shadow rising fast through him so that his jaw distorted and his claws slid out of his hands, which Natividad affected not to notice. But, with impressive control, he stopped the change there, his shadow subsiding, at no more than a look from his father.

"If we kill your brothers and keep you?" Harrison said to Natividad. He glowered at her, though she couldn't tell whether that was because he was angry with her, or irritated with his son, or whether that was only his normal manner.

She tossed her head, glaring back at him. "Then I'll hate you all. You don't want that."

"We don't," Grayson agreed, his rough voice cutting across Harrison's response. The Dimilioc Master walked down the steps and put one thick finger under Natividad's chin, tipping her face up. She met his eyes, though she knew perfectly well how dangerous that was. She could see Alejandro staring at her, willing her to be meek and submissive. But *she* wasn't a black dog. *She* didn't have to drop her gaze. Nor did the Master of the Dimilioc wolves seem offended. After a moment, he let her go.

He looked carefully at Alejandro, and then at Miguel. To Miguel, Grayson said, "You also want to come into Dimilioc? Human as you are?"

Miguel gave Alejandro a wary glance. "It was the only thing any of us could think of to do, after Vonhausel killed our parents. We... We hid. Papá wouldn't let us fight..." he cut that thought off.

"If you had fought, you would be dead, too," Grayson said, his deep voice quiet. "Especially you, boy. Our human kin don't belong in black dog battles." He paused. Then he said to Ezekiel, much more curtly, "Take them downstairs. When they have been secured, come up, and we will talk about this. Ethan, go get their car. If you can't get it up the road, at least get it out of sight." The Master himself went back into the house without a backward look. Zachariah Korte and Harrison Lanning followed him, and Ethan shot them a contemptuous look and strode away toward the forest. Then only Ezekiel remained, watching them where they still knelt. He was smiling, but his pale eyes were cool and watchful.

"That was not precisely what I expected, when I brought you here," he commented.

Miguel looked Ezekiel in the face as he got to his feet. "Why not?" he asked. "I'd have thought it was obvious."

Even if Miguel had been careful not to meet the young executioner's eyes, he might have put that better. There was no challenge in his tone: as always, he was simply curious. Nevertheless, Natividad wasn't surprised when Alejandro stood up quickly, in case the Dimilioc executioner took offense at Miguel's familiarity.

But Ezekiel showed no sign of affront. He said merely, his tone dry, "Perhaps it should have been." Then he offered Natividad a hand to help her rise. Alejandro moved to stop her taking it, then caught himself. She smiled tiredly at her brother, but she took Ezekiel's hand without hesitation. His thin smile as he offered it told her that he expected her to be afraid of him and she wanted to show him she wasn't. And she wasn't, really. Not *really*.

Ezekiel's hand was warm and firm, his grip strong. He met her gaze as he lifted her to her feet. He was not smiling now. She could not read the expression in his eyes.

Alejandro put a hand under her elbow, easing her back, away from the Dimilioc executioner. "You're tired…"

Natividad let go of Ezekiel's hand, allowing her brother to draw her back. She knew Alejandro had been pushed far enough already, so she agreed cheerfully, "Tired and stiff! I think *every* muscle I own is going to be stiff." But then she looked straight up into Ezekiel's eyes, not smiling, and asked, because she thought he might answer, "What's downstairs?"

"Nothing too alarming," Ezekiel said, still dry. "You can relax." She could tell he was telling the truth, though there was a slight emphasis on the *you* that she wasn't sure she liked. But when he stepped back, waving them all up the porch stairs so they had to go past him and let him come at their backs, she went. Especially because, under the circumstances, she didn't think they had much choice.

3

Alejandro found "downstairs" more than a little alarming. The term turned out to refer to a big, half-finished basement, with brick walls, tiles on the floor, exposed pipes reaching across the unpainted ceiling, and – this was the part he didn't like – a huge, heavily barred cage taking up fully two-thirds of the available room. The cage bars were wrapped top to bottom with silver wire. The lock itself didn't have silver on it, but Alejandro could see it would be out of reach from inside the cage. There were plumbing attachments in the cage, as well as a single cheap plastic chair and a narrow cot. Outside the cage was a small table.

Ezekiel tipped his head toward the cage. "It's plain, I know, but amenities tend to get destroyed." He looked thoughtfully at Natividad. "You'll leave your little knife on that table."

Alejandro didn't like that either, and his black dog liked it less. Losing that silver knife, stepping into that silver cage... His black dog pressed at him, wanting to fight now, while fighting was still possible. He closed his eyes, breathing carefully. Natividad's attention was on him, not Ezekiel. She had the knife in her hand, waiting for his nod. He couldn't make himself give it, but he took the knife out of her hand himself and, without looking at the *verdugo* set it carefully on the table outside the cage.

The young *verdugo*, evidently satisfied, gestured toward the cage door. Alejandro lowered his gaze, put one hand on Miguel's shoulder and the other on Natividad's, and guided the twins into the cage, because whatever his black dog thought, there *were* no other options.

"Good," said Ezekiel. But he made no move to shove the door closed. He said instead, "Of course, the cage is for black dogs. A nice little Pure girl could have a room upstairs."

Alejandro stiffened. He set his hands protectively on Natividad's shoulders, glaring a warning at the young Dimilioc *verdugo*. The cage door was still open. He wanted to explode out of the cage, fight the *verdugo*, kill him. He longed to tear that mocking expression off his face, rip through his spine, send his shadow screaming into the fell dark, leave his body bleeding on the concrete floor. Impossible, stupid urges. Papá would have said, "*Is that what you want to do, or is that your black dog?*" He would have said, "*You call up your shadow and you put it down, don't let it start going the other way.*" Alejandro took one slow breath after another and did not move. Natividad *would* be safe here. Alejandro clung to that conviction, blocking his shadow's longing for blood and violence with the solid refusal of a lifetime's practice.

But he would not let anyone take his sister away from his protection, either. They would have to kill him first. He stared at the young *verdugo*, letting him see that.

Ezekiel Korte met his eyes, smiling.

"No, thank you," Natividad said, in her meekest tone, the one she used on Alejandro when he was angry. It was all show, that tone, but it helped calm his black dog.

Ezekiel shifted his gaze to her, and his smile changed, the mockery in it giving way to genuine appreciation. "A *private* room," he told her.

"Thank you," Natividad repeated. "But no. I'll stay with my brothers." She patted one of Alejandro's hands, where he gripped her shoulder. But she also smiled at the *verdugo* and added, "Some extra blankets would be nice, though. And a cord. So we can hang blankets across the middle," she added, when the young man lifted an eyebrow.

"Of course," Ezekiel murmured. He shoved the door closed behind them with his foot. It swung against its iron frame with an echoing crash, a disturbingly final sort of sound. When he walked away up the stairs and closed the door on the landing as well, the silence that folded down around them was even more disturbing.

Natividad sat on the cot and sighed, then groaned dismally as she looked at her boots. "I don't think I can bend down that far!"

Without a word, Alejandro knelt and began to unlace the boots for her.

"I think that went well," Miguel said tentatively. "Didn't you think that went well?"

"Compared to what?" Alejandro asked, managing to keep most of the growl out of his tone. He pulled Natividad's first boot off, then the second, set them aside and helped his sister swing her legs up on the cot.

Natividad lay down slowly, groaning, and closed her eyes. "Oh, I'm going to be stiff tomorrow."

"Your coat," Alejandro reminded her.

"Cold down here," she said, not opening her eyes.

Of course. He should have realized. Alejandro took off his jacket and draped it across his sister's feet. She wiggled her toes in weary gratitude. Alejandro dropped down to the floor beside the cot, leaning back against its edge. He looked at his brother with lifted eyebrows, then shook his head. "*How* did you talk us into this?"

"You did well," Miguel told him, ignoring this question. "It *did* go well. Grayson listened to you. No wonder, with so few black wolves left here. Maybe some we haven't seen yet, though." Since Alejandro was sitting on the floor next to the cot, Miguel sat gingerly in the single chair. It didn't collapse, so he leaned back and sighed.

"Or maybe not. You think six black dogs are enough to face Vonhausel, if he comes?" Natividad asked. "You think so, really?"

"Better than one," growled Alejandro. But he hated to think how slender a protection Dimilioc might prove, weakened as it clearly was.

"Lots better! Remember what Papá said about the Dimilioc executioner," added Miguel. "And I bet Grayson is one tough *hombre*." He pretended to shudder, then added more seriously, "No, Natividad, I still think this was the best place to come. I really do."

Alejandro said absolutely nothing.

Natividad, no doubt aware of his temper, said quickly, "Lots of silver on those bars. How long do you think we'll

be left alone? Do you think it'd be long enough for me to–"
She stopped as the door at the head of the stairs opened.

Alejandro immediately got to his feet, taking an aggressive stance between his siblings and the door – then caught himself. Stupid, stupid, he knew better – stupid to challenge when you could not fight. He could not bring himself to sit down or even step back, but he forced himself to look at the floor.

Ezekiel came down the stairs with a stack of blankets. He surveyed them all for a moment, then unlocked the door and toed it open. He tossed the blankets to Miguel, said, "Someone will bring food," to Natividad, and added, "You come with me," to Alejandro.

Alejandro's stomach clenched. Natividad had come up to one elbow. Her eyes were wide, but she was trying to smile. "That was fast. We'll leave you the crumbs, if there are any."

"*Bueno*," Alejandro said, and in English, "Right, you do that." He stepped out of the cage, not looking at the *verdugo's* face. He knew Ezekiel Korte must be aware of his anger and fear and he hated that, but there was nothing he could do about it, either – along with so many other things he could do nothing about. But the *verdugo* offered no insult, only stepped aside and gestured Alejandro up the stairs before him.

The room to which Ezekiel brought him was much larger, much warmer, and much more richly furnished than the basement. A massive granite fireplace occupied most of one wall, huge logs burning within it. A wide window took up most of another wall. The sunset was already streaking the sky over the mountains with carmine; below the mountains, the forest was shadowed with lavender and indigo.

Before the window, on a thick wool rug, stood a grouping of chairs with heavy carved frames and thick cushions. Grayson Lanning occupied one of the chairs, Zachariah Korte another. Their shadows stretched across the floor, flickering around the edges in the uncertain light, but palpably dark.

Harrison Lanning, his shadow not quite so dense, was leaning on the back of another chair on the other side of his brother. Ethan Lanning stood behind Harrison, his arms crossed, frowning, nakedly hostile. But at least his shadow was no darker than that of any ordinary black dog. Alejandro was not afraid of *him*. It was nice to have one Dimilioc black dog he did not have to be afraid of.

Ezekiel Korte drifted across the room, trailing, despite his youth, a shadow almost as heavy as Grayson's. He perched with negligent grace on the broad arm of a chair. Even that was a threat, in a way, because he was so ostentatiously poised to move fast from that position.

Since no one had told him what he should do, Alejandro walked the little distance necessary to stand before Grayson's chair. He glanced up briefly into the Master's face, then dropped his gaze and stood still.

"Your father raised you," Grayson said without any preliminary. "Edward Toland. He trained you. Taught you control. You lived as a family – you and your brother and your sister and your mother. And your father. All in the same house. Is that right? Don't lie to me."

"Yes, sir," Alejandro answered. "No, sir. That is the truth."

"Edward showed you how to deal with stray black dogs and those damned blood kin... Did he teach you to kill them or avoid them?"

"Both, sir. Either. Whatever would be safest for our family."

"So, he taught you to keep quiet," Grayson Lanning said thoughtfully. It was not a question. "To live quietly and hunt quietly." He paused, then said at last, without any change in his deep, calm voice, "I remember your father. We were not precisely contemporaries; I was a boy when he left Dimilioc. But I remember him quite clearly. Edward was a strong man. A decent man. I'll tell you a truth: I much preferred him to Vonhausel. Thos did not agree, of course."

Ezekiel said lightly, "Thos was always partial to black wolves of Gehorsam descent. No accounting for taste."

Alejandro said nothing. He had no idea what response either of them expected.

"Your father had a great deal of control," the Master continued after a moment. He had paid no attention to Ezekiel's interruption at all.

Alejandro said, "Papá had to keep tight control over his shadow," but then stopped abruptly. His grief made it impossible to keep his tone steady.

"Not merely because he feared enemies. Because you and he would have killed everyone in your neighborhood. Is that what you mean?"

Alejandro nodded.

Zachariah Korte said quietly, "Your mother helped with that, I suppose."

"Yes, sir."

"Of course," said Grayson. "Only a Pure woman could have given your father both a black dog son and a Pure daughter. How fortunate for your family she should have produced a Pure daughter. I imagine that by the time you had grown into a dangerous little puppy, your sister was already old enough to help your control. Is that so?"

Alejandro controlled a strong impulse to ask Grayson what he would do with Natividad. He longed to beg for reassurance. He knew it was a stupid impulse, which made very little difference. He said, "Yes, sir," and waited again.

"And your control when you do not have your sister by your side? I wonder about that." Grayson glanced at Ezekiel, who straightened.

Alejandro turned to face the *verdugo*. He knew very well what was coming. His father had trained him for this. He had expected it. But he found his stomach clenching with fear anyway. He had trusted his father. It was not the same, to face Ezekiel Korte. He did not know how far Ezekiel would go. How far Grayson Lanning would let him go.

Ezekiel came around the chair and walked forward. He was not smiling now. His shadow did not rise, but it gathered around him, dense and heavy. As soon as Ezekiel was close enough, without any apparent emotion, he hit Alejandro across the face. It was an open-handed blow, but hard enough that Alejandro staggered. And it was *fast*.

Alejandro found himself struggling, to his shame, with a sudden visceral fear of the Dimilioc executioner. The shame was worse because of the *verdugo*'s youth. He knew he did not have Papá's strength, he knew he might never be so strong, but he had never expected to be afraid of a black dog his own age. But he was afraid of Ezekiel Korte, with a primitive instinct-driven terror that made everything hard – holding to any shred of control was abruptly ten times more difficult than it should have been. He knew Ezekiel could see that fear in him and he hated that, but even so it was all he could do, when the *verdugo* hit him a second time, to take the blow without attempting to attack in turn.

He could feel his shadow rise through him, trying to take on shape and substance, trying to force him into the *cambio de cuerpo*. He knew his face was distorting, his hands, his feet; his shoulders hunched as his body tried to twist itself into the shape that *ought* to cast its shadow. A thin snarl crept from his throat. It was not a human sound. Alejandro set his teeth against that sound, forcing his shadow down, holding grimly onto human form. He took a third blow, this one to the stomach – if Ezekiel had been using claws, that blow would have had his guts out, and for an instant he was not sure the Dimilioc *verdugo* had not done it. His terror gave the executioner's shadow sharp teeth, not only metaphorically.

When Ezekiel Korte tried once more to hit him across the face, he blocked the blow – then found the Dimilioc executioner gripping his arm instead, shoving him back, pinning him against one of the heavy chairs. Ezekiel was strong, stronger than Alejandro, and there was a terrifying ruthlessness in his cold eyes, something harder and more deliberate than ordinary black-dog savagery. Alejandro wanted to change… He *needed* to change… He *would not*. He fought his shadow instead, struggling to hold to human shape. His shadow began to yield, began to sink down once more.

Then Ezekiel said, with deadly, unemotional contempt. "This is what you call control?" His grip tightened, close to crushing Alejandro's arm. "If you had been there when black dogs attacked your mother, would you have fought them? I don't think you would. I think you would have yielded to the scent of death and joined them instead. I think you would have fought the rest, but only for the chance to spill her blood yourself–"

Alejandro's shadow flooded abruptly upward as rage jolted his control and the change took him. He snapped at Ezekiel's wrist with savage fangs, slashed at his belly with ebony claws. But Ezekiel was not there to meet his attack. He had melted back, away from Alejandro, but he did not seem alarmed. He had not allowed his own shadow to rise, but watched Alejandro coolly from his human form, unmoved by visible fear or anger. Alejandro understood with the rational part of his mind that he was right to be afraid of Ezekiel, but his black dog, thoroughly ascendant, wanted to stalk the Dimilioc *verdugo* and tear his human body into bloody pieces.

"Stop," Grayson said calmly. The Master's power rolled out through the room, smothering all the shadows, pressing Alejandro's shadow down flat, forcing it back into an insubstantial darkness.

This was not a thing that Alejandro recognized. It was not something Papá could have done, nothing Papá had ever described. But Grayson Lanning forced him back into human shape as though it was nothing, as though it took neither thought nor effort. Alejandro found himself on his hands and knees on the thick rug, hardly able to tell what shape he wore. He was trembling with reaction, which shamed him, but he could not stop.

He did not want to look up. The flat contempt in Ezekiel's

voice still echoed in his memory, and he knew when he looked up he would find that contempt staring back at him from the eyes of all the Dimilioc wolves. Worse, he knew that if Papá were here, he would look at his son in the same way. He would say with Ezekiel, "*This is what you call control?*" Alcjandro wanted to slink out of this room, into the gathering dark of these strange cold mountains, and run south, a shadow hardly more substantial than the natural darkness.

Above him, having never stirred from his place, Grayson's heavy voice asked, "Well?"

Alejandro fixed his gaze on the gray and red pattern of the rug. His shadow's claws had scored heavy lines through the wool. He stared at his own hands. Human again. They looked like anyone's hands. He said nothing.

"Alejandro," said Grayson, and waited.

Alejandro did not want to look at the Dimilioc Master. But at last, having no choice, he straightened his back and forced himself to meet Grayson Lanning's eyes. To his surprise, he did not find contempt there. There was even a kind of sympathy in that dark stare.

"Ezekiel can break anyone's control," Grayson told him quietly. "I would have been amazed if he had not broken yours. Did you think otherwise?"

Alejandro stared at him. He felt young and stupid, and violently resented being made to feel that way. His shadow snarled in the back of his mind. He set himself to hold his human form and mind against it.

But Grayson said, "I am not holding you now. Let your shadow rise. Let it up, boy, and let us have a look at your black dog. Ezekiel – loose your shadow as well, if you please. I would not like to have to replace the furniture in this room."

Ezekiel tilted an amused eyebrow at the Master of Dimilioc and melted into his shadow, so swiftly and cleanly that Alejandro could not keep from staring.

Ezekiel's black dog form was shaggy, huge, with massive bones and powerful shoulders. Its skull was broad, its muzzle blunt, its wide-set yellow eyes gleaming with fire as well as with vicious intelligence. Alejandro would have said that there was nothing of Ezekiel Korte in that malevolent stare, and yet he would never have mistaken this black dog for any other man's shadow.

Alejandro had seen his father's shadow form. He had worn his own like a mask that had seemed at times more real than his own body. He had wrapped himself in his shadow to run or hunt or to fight stray black dogs and the moon-bound curs they had made. But Ezekiel's black dog was more frightening than any other he had ever seen. It was not larger than his father's shadow body. But it seemed somehow more solid, more *auténtico*. More real. When Ezekiel dropped his jaw in a terrible black-dog laugh, the contained heat of his fiery eyes seemed to burn out across the entire room, until Alejandro was amazed the rug and the chairs did not catch fire.

"Now," said Grayson Lanning said to him, "let your own shadow rise."

Alejandro had almost forgotten the Dimilioc Master. His gaze jerked that way, startled, when the Master spoke. He felt the blood rise into his face, and told himself the heat there was anger and not shame. His shadow was ready to be angry. It rose, hot and fast, and the shame fell away. The uncertainty burned like dry grass in a fire as his body molded itself to his shadow. He stretched and yawned, enjoying the deadly, confident strength of the black dog. He stared around the room looking for someone to kill... Grayson Lanning met his eyes with a complete absence of fear that made him pause despite his confidence.

But he thought he could kill Ethan Lanning, perhaps. He was eager to try. He stared at the youngest of the Dimilioc wolves, looking for any sign of fear, of uncertainty. When Ethan met his gaze without showing either, he whined, disappointed – then snarled, a long singing snarl, trying to make the other flinch. He eased forward a pace, flexing a broad foot, thinking about the brutal rake of claws, the spilling blood, the scents of burning and ash and death.

Ezekiel stood up and looked at him, only that, and he stopped, recognizing that the other was stronger. Where Alejandro in his human form might have been angry or frightened or ashamed, his black dog only acknowledged the other's strength, accepted it, found no urgent reason to challenge it, and turned away from the fight.

He found himself looking again at Grayson Lanning. Grayson looked fearlessly into his fiery eyes and said, "Now put down your shadow, Alejandro, do you hear? Come back up."

For a long, long moment these words did not make any sense. Alejandro heard the Dimilioc Master, but Grayson might as well have snarled like an animal rather than spoken in any human language. Then the Master patiently repeated, "Come back up," and suddenly the sounds reordered themselves into understandable speech – into a command.

The black-dog shadow did not want to yield to any *command*. It recognized Grayson's strength, but not his authority. Besides, it did not want to subside back into shadow, to give way to the human form – not so soon after rising, not while the night waited outside this house. It stared out the wide window, at the darkness that filled the world. Even if it could not kill any Dimilioc wolf, maybe it could crash through the glass and fall into the night. It could run across the snow, find some living creature with sweet blood to hunt... Run all the way back to that town... A house crowded with ordinary humans would provide an exciting hunt...

This, at least, was a familiar urge. Alejandro blocked it with the forceful skill of long practice. He locked his gaze on Grayson's, caught at the dim memory of his human body, knocked his black dog off balance while it was momentarily checked by its awareness of the Dimilioc Master's strength, and struck out of the shadow that enfolded him, back toward his human form, as a swimmer might strike for the surface of a lake far above.

It felt like that, coming out of the shadow, sliding from the black dog back into his human body. Like coming into air when he might have drowned. Like pulling free of gripping hands.

In another way, reclaiming his human body felt like accepting a prison, or like drowning.

It had made him sick, that change, when he was a child – the difference between the shadow and his own body. Eventually he had learned to step from one shape to the other, from one mind to the other, from black dog to human and back again, with reasonable ease. But it was always harder to come back through his shadow than it was to let the shadow rise. He held very still for a long moment, his eyes closed, one hand gripping the back of a chair for balance, waiting for his body and his soul to accept human shape once more.

Then he opened his eyes and looked at Grayson Lanning.

The Master of Dimilioc turned his head to meet the fiery gaze of Ezekiel's black wolf. "And would you call that control?"

Ezekiel laughed silently, black fangs gleaming, and straightened easily, with flawless control, back into his human form. His smile held no less malice in human form. He said smoothly, looking at Alejandro and not at Grayson, "Who could fail to be impressed?"

Alejandro could not quite keep from flinching, could not quite force himself to meet Ezekiel's mocking stare. He told himself that was only sensible, that he must be careful, that the moment after the *cambio de cuerpo* was a dangerous time to meet any black dog's gaze. That was all true. But he knew that was not why he lowered his gaze.

"Take him down," ordered Grayson. "Bring the human boy."

Alejandro wanted to protest, which was stupid. He wanted to ask for reassurance, which was childish. He lowered his eyes and obeyed Ezekiel's gesture. It was hard to walk past the American, hard to leave the Dimilioc executioner at his back – he did not like to do that even though the rational part of his mind knew it made no difference. His black dog liked it even less. It trembled as the shadow of a leaf might tremble. A dying leaf, as the leaves must come down in the autumn, *cuando se caen las hojas,* in this land of winter. He told himself that Ezekiel would not see his shadow tremble. But he knew the *verdugo* would in fact see it. He did not look into the young American's face. It might have been dangerous to look at him, but that was not why Alejandro avoided his gaze, and he knew Ezekiel would know that also.

Miguel got to his feet as they came down the stairs. He had been sitting, not in the chair, but on the floor next to the cot, his head tilted back against its frame – listening, probably, in case he might hear anything of what passed upstairs. Or maybe just listening to Natividad's breathing as she slept. To the reassuring steadiness of her heartbeat. Alejandro could hear both her easy breaths and her heartbeat from the stairs, and found the proof of his sister's peace easing past the edge of his own longing for violence.

He met Miguel's eyes. He did not know what to say – anyway Ezekiel was listening. In the end, after the *verdugo* unlocked and opened the cage door, he stepped into the cage without saying anything at all. Neither he nor his shadow liked being forced to pass so close to Ezekiel, and the silver on the bars made the feeling of being cornered worse still. He tried not to flinch.

Miguel's too-perceptive gaze flicked from the Dimilioc *verdugo* to Alejandro's face. "*Te hizo daño?*" he asked in Spanish. *Did he hurt you?* He did not whisper, but he spoke quietly, and the soft, even rhythm of Natividad's breathing did not change.

Alejandro shrugged. He wanted to say, "*Be careful.*" He
wanted to remind Miguel that lots of Americans understood
Spanish – not so many this far into the frozen north, but
still, one should be careful. But after all, what did it matter?
After that first hesitation, he said, "*Estoy bien. Lo sé–*"

Ezekiel said briskly, "That's enough! You, out you come.
Let's go."

Alejandro moved aside so that his brother could pass by.
He wanted to say to his brother, "*You'll do well, you'll be
alright; watch out for anger, he will use your anger as a
weapon against you.*" But he did not know what test or
interrogation Grayson Lanning might have in mind for
his human brother, and anyway, he did not dare offer any
advice or reassurance after Ezekiel had ordered him silent.

And Miguel saw that he did not dare. A wary anger came
into his eyes. His mouth tightened, and he glanced sidelong
at Ezekiel's face.

Ezekiel, of course, saw both the wariness and the anger.
"Save it till it might do you some good," he told Miguel,
clearly amused, and shut the cage door behind the boy. He
did not slam the door, but even so, metal rang against metal
as the door swung to. Even then, however, Natividad did
not wake.

Alejandro looked down at his sister, at the hollows of her
face – last year she had not had those hollows; last year her
wrists had not been so thin nor her bones so prominent.
She had lost too much of her strength in the grief and terror
of their flight from Mexico. And she was thinner now than
even those few days ago.

Looking up, he said abruptly to Ezekiel, who had just

turned to follow Miguel up the stairs, "She's tired. She ought to be left alone tonight."

Ezekiel turned back, one eyebrow rising. Alejandro looked aside. But he also said stubbornly, "You should leave her alone until morning."

The Dimilioc executioner glanced past him at the slight figure on the cot. Then he shrugged. It was a wry shrug with more than a touch of mockery to it, but it was not unfriendly. "I agree with you. But it's not my decision."

Alejandro said nothing. He watched Ezekiel turn and follow Miguel up the stairs and through the door at the top. That door shut, quietly. Then there was only silence, and the dark, and the quiet sound of his sister's breath. He knelt down on the floor by her cot, drawing comfort from that sound.

Alejandro was sure that the Dimilioc wolves would not kill Miguel. Not now, not tonight – not at all, if they wanted to keep Natividad. He was sure of it.

He had told Grayson that he had persuaded his brother and sister to trespass into the very heart of Dimilioc territory. But who knew what Miguel would say if Grayson asked him about that? Alejandro should have claimed responsibility again, should have made the Dimilioc wolves all believe that the offense was his fault. He had been frightened, like a child. He had forgotten he needed to protect Miguel. How could he have forgotten?

He rested his forehead against the wool of the blankets that covered Natividad, listening. He heard nothing but his sister's even breaths, her heartbeat. His own, muffled by his shadow. Which, cowed by this silent cell with its silver-bound bars, was tenuous and very quiet. He was not even sure he could get his black dog to rise if he called it... He remembered Papá teaching him to call his black dog up. At first it came up whether he called it or not, whenever he was angry or frightened or upset... When he had been very little, his shadow rose when it chose and went down when it chose. He had had no control over it at all. Or he had not understood he might win control over it.

One of his earliest memories: he must have been about three, he knew that, because he had just begun to talk; like many black dogs he had been late to talk. The black dog did not understand language, and it had pulled at him all the time then, so that a lot of the time he had not really been separate from it. And the twins had been born that year.

At first Alejandro had not been allowed to come near the new babies. But one day – Alejandro remembered this vividly – one day when Mamá had gone out to the garden, Papá had taken him to see the two infants, tucked together in the little crib they shared. They had been sleeping, but woke when Alejandro leaned over the crib. Little Miguel had screwed up his face and cried, which had given Alejandro a pleasant little thrill of power and excitement as though he was hunting. His shadow had pushed at him, tipping his chubby baby fingers with claws and filling his mouth with the tastes of ash and blood. But Natividad had stretched out her hands to him and cooed and laughed, and he had liked that in a different way.

"Cut her," Papá had suggested to him. He had lifted Miguel out of the crib and tucked him against his shoulder, but he left Natividad lying where she was. "Go ahead," he said. "It's alright. Rip her up. Spill her blood. Look how little she is! You could kill her so easily. Don't you want to?"

Alejandro sort of did. He leaned forward eagerly, his mouth distorting toward the muzzle of the black dog, the bones of his shoulders and arms shifting. But his baby sister smiled and cooed, not at all afraid, and another part of him wanted her happy just like that, wanted to protect her and was horrified at the idea he might hurt her, that anybody might ever hurt her.

"Part of you wants to hurt her," said Papá. "But a different part of you would destroy anybody who tried to hurt her. That part stops the other. Isn't that so?"

Alejandro hadn't been astonished that Papá understood so well. Papá understood everything; he knew that already. He had nodded and waited for Papá to explain things.

"The part of you that wants to hurt your sister, that isn't you, Alejandro. That's the black dog. That's your shadow. The part of you that stops it, *that* is you. You always need to know which one wants something: your shadow or you. And sometimes you can let your shadow have what it wants, like when we go hunting in the forest, but mostly you have to stop it. You will always be able to stop it, though, if you want to. Understand?"

Alejandro couldn't remember now how well he'd understood his father, then. How well could any little black dog pup really understand where his shadow stopped and he started? But he reached out now as he had reached out then and touched his sister's cheek gently with fingers that were human right to the tips of the blunt nails. He had protected her from that moment, protected her all her life.

Until he had brought her here, where he could not protect her from anything.

He couldn't fight the *verdugo,* anyway. He told himself firmly that it didn't matter: Dimilioc would not kill a Pure girl. He told himself that, and tried to believe it.

They had all thought themselves very brave, when they had decided to come to Grayson Lanning and ask Dimilioc to take them in. Papá might have said that Grayson was an honorable man and a good Master for Dimilioc, but he had also said, all their lives, *Dimilioc does not tolerate strays, remember that. You never want to catch Dimilioc's attention.* They all knew it was a desperate thing to do.

Alejandro had wanted the twins to run east instead, to Japan maybe, or China. To some country where Natividad would not need to fear Vonhausel's pursuit or the violence of *perros negros.* But she had refused. Because she did not want to go to so foreign a country, she had said. Really, he knew, she had refused for his sake. The Chinese dragons loathed black dogs almost as much as they had loathed vampires. Black dogs could not go into the Far East, and so Natividad would not go.

For himself, he was glad she had refused. He would have gone with them, guarded them along the way despite the danger. In the Far East, his brother and sister would have been safe from every demonic threat, certainly safe from Vonhausel. But Miguel had said no, who knew if the Chinese dragons would hate the Pure as they hated black dogs, the magic was all tied together after all, they should come to Dimilioc instead. Now Alejandro wondered how his human brother had made this sound like such a good idea. He thought of Ezekiel's dispassionate contempt, of Grayson's massive strength, and running north no longer seemed so clever. He wished very much for Papá, for his strength and his confidence – but even Papá's strength had not been enough, and his confidence had been misplaced, and he was dead. No one but Alejandro was left to protect Natividad and Miguel, and how could he do that here?

He wanted to get up, to pace. That might disturb Natividad. He did not want to wake her. They had pushed her too hard today, too hard for many days before this one. She was tired – she was exhausted still with grief, though she would never admit it, and then Alejandro had pushed her to keep up with the killing pace a black dog did not even feel. *Miguel* could keep up, more or less, for a while. But Natividad?

He wanted to break the chairs, tear the blankets, hurl himself at the bars of the cell. He did not move, except to stare restlessly up the stairs.

How long could it *take*, for Grayson Lanning to question Miguel? It seemed a very long time, but was probably not even an hour, before the stairway door clicked open. Alejandro was on his feet at once, all his muscles tight. He saw Ezekiel first, and for a moment no one else. His breath caught.

But then Miguel came down the stairs after Ezekiel, and Harrison Lanning behind him. Harrison was carrying a platter. There was the smell of fresh bread and grilled venison.

There were two platters, in fact: one for the meat, and the other for the bread and a wedge of soft cheese and a crock of fruit preserves that smelled of sugar and lingering summer. Harrison carried one of the platters, but Miguel himself carried the other. As before, Ezekiel unlocked the cage door and gestured for Miguel to enter. Miguel moved easily – he did not seem to have been harmed at all. But as he stepped past Ezekiel to enter the cell, as Ezekiel shifted his weight, he flinched, just perceptively.

Someone else might have missed that little *encojo*. But to Alejandro, his brother might as well have cowered like a beaten child. Miguel never cringed from anyone. He had never been beaten or abused – he had always had his father and brother to protect him. Until tonight. Alejandro set himself against a sudden savage desire to challenge Ezekiel right there, an effort of will that might have failed except that he was himself afraid of the Dimilioc *verdugo*. Besides, Harrison was there also. Alejandro set his teeth hard and stayed where he was, by the cot. But he could not stop himself glowering at Ezekiel.

Ezekiel, smiling, met his furious stare with a look of cool mockery. "Well?"

Miguel, perfectly well aware of Alejandro's rising fury, said quickly, "I'm alright. I'm fine." And then, more forcefully, "*De verdad, estoy bien!*"

Alejandro made himself lower his gaze. "Yes," he said grimly, in English.

But the anger and danger in the room was so palpable that Natividad opened her eyes and sat up, flinging off her blankets with a sharp, terrified movement that recalled the dangerous life they had all led for the past year.

Alejandro shuddered with the effort to put his shadow down. He took a step backward, put an arm around his sister, and tucked her against his side. "*Estas bien,*" he said, then, wary of Ezekiel and even of Harrison, switched to English. "You see: we are all well."

Ezekiel tilted his head to one side, but did not contradict this piece of optimism. Harrison grinned outright. "That's right, boy," he said. His voice was deep and harsh, but not actually unkind. He stepped forward to bring them the platter he held, brushing past Ezekiel with a careless lack of concern that Alejandro could not help but read as *riesgoso* – risky. But the young *verdugo* only stepped aside, not seeming to resent the familiarity.

Natividad shivered, caught her breath, stared from one of the Dimilioc wolves to the other – then sighed in exasperation and straightened. Although she did not move away from Alejandro, her heartbeat steadied and her breathing slowed. As she calmed, the level of aggression and anger in the room settled as well.

Harrison Lanning rolled his shoulders, stretched, and grimaced – not a smile, but not an unfriendly expression. He said to Natividad, "You, we need." Then he said to Alejandro, "You and your brother, we'll talk about that. But you're safe tonight."

Alejandro made himself bow his head. "Sir."

"So respectful," murmured Ezekiel, but there was less of an edge to even his mockery. He gestured Harrison out of the cell with a minimal jerk of his head – it might have been a command, or not, and Alejandro realized that part of his black dog's uneasiness was due to uncertainty about the relative ranking of the Dimilioc wolves. Black dogs wanted – needed – to know who was stronger and who must give way; it created a constant uneasiness to have matters of rank unresolved or unclear. Harrison was so much older – but Ezekiel was the Dimilioc executioner, and unquestionably more dangerous one-on-one. Alejandro's black dog could not tell which of them was more dominant and did not like the uncertainty.

Harrison moved back a step so that Ezekiel could swing the cell door shut, but even then Alejandro could not tell whether he was watching a weaker black wolf respond to the command of a stronger, or whether he was simply seeing one man disregard matters of rank and age to cooperate with the suggestion of another.

"Have a nice night," Ezekiel said to them all. "Pleasant dreams." He glanced casually at Miguel, but held Alejandro's gaze until Alejandro dropped his eyes – no question whether *that* was a matter of rank. But then Ezekiel grinned and clapped Harrison on the shoulder – rare, for one black dog to touch another, but he did it – and the two Dimilioc wolves went up the stairs together. The door at the top of the stairs closed behind them.

Miguel let out a deep sigh and came to take Natividad's hand in both of his, clearly needing that contact more than he needed rest or food. Alejandro knew how he felt.

So did Natividad, *por supuesto*, but though she put an arm around her younger brother's waist, she also said wistfully, "Is any of that meat actually cooked?"

After a moment, Miguel laughed, a little unwillingly, and pulled away from his sister's embrace. "Sit down again and you can have supper in bed."

"*Comida*? Is it still supper and not breakfast?" Natividad rubbed her face. "I feel a hundred years old. How long was I asleep?"

"Not long," Alejandro assured her. He moved to inspect the contents of the platters. "Supper, and then you can sleep again. Some of the meat is only a little rare. It's fine – it's venison," he added, putting some of the most well-done slices aside for Natividad, along with some of the bread and all the berry preserves. He added to Miguel, as though casually, "Grayson wanted to see my shadow rise. Ezekiel did it. I think it took that *cabrón* less than a minute to break my control."

"*En serio?*" said Miguel, disbelievingly. "*Your* control, 'Jandro?"

Alejandro didn't look at him. "It's more than his strength. Though he's very strong. He sees too much about what will rouse anger and fear. And it's not like when Papá made me practice control. The *verdugo* is much scarier than Papá."

"But less than a minute?"

"Truly."

The boy looked a little happier. He rolled a slice of meat up with focused concentration and ate it in two bites. Another. Then he said, not looking at Alejandro, "I guess it took him maybe four or five minutes to make me lose my temper. I didn't think *anybody* could do that to me."

Alejandro nodded. "Grayson told me Ezekiel could break anyone's control."

"I think he could," Miguel agreed. He shivered, exaggerating it, but it was real, too. "I think so. I think Ezekiel's the strongest black dog here."

"But Grayson's the Master." Natividad had made sandwiches with some of the meat and cheese and bread, then eaten her first sandwich with concentrated intensity.

But now she put her second sandwich down and frowned at Miguel. "Are you sure Ezekiel's really the strongest?"

The boy shrugged. "No. But I think so."

"I think he's right," said Alejandro. "I think that's exactly why Zachariah and Harrison backed Grayson when he took the Mastery. Because they knew none of them could beat Ezekiel one on one. I think maybe they all draw a lot of their strength from one another, even now."

"But…" said Miguel, frowning. "I don't think Ezekiel *wants* to challenge Grayson anyway."

"Of course he wants to challenge him–"

"His black dog might want to fight him, but I don't think *Ezekiel* wants that."

Alejandro thought about this. "Maybe."

"I think they're all very strong," Miguel said. "Even Ethan. But their control–"

"Yes," said Alejandro. "Their control is more important than their strength. No wonder Dimilioc could keep all the other black dogs down so long. Dimilioc *lobos* really *are* ruled by human will, not black dog bloodlust." He had not really believed that until this moment. Not really. He had never known any black dogs like that – except Papá. He said slowly, "You see how they are with one another – you see how they are a family." Ordinary black dogs, even blood relatives, seldom tolerated one another well enough to share a single territory. A very strong black dog could force others to submit to his control and hold them as a pack, but that was not the same. Alejandro had known Dimilioc was different. Papá, *por supuesto*, had been different himself, and tried to teach Alejandro to be different the same way.

He said bitterly, "And then I showed them tonight how little control I really have." He had not understood what *real* control was until Ezekiel Korte had demonstrated to him that he didn't have it.

"We're still alive," Miguel pointed out, having effortlessly followed this thought out to its obvious conclusion. "You think that's just because of Natividad? I don't. You said yourself Ezekiel could break anybody's control."

"Yes," said Alejandro, trying to believe it.

"What about the bars, though?" Natividad asked, seeing his distress and wanting to help. "If they leave us alone for a while, I could blood them for you. That would make you feel better, wouldn't it, even if you don't think we should really try to get out?"

"Do you think for one second they haven't thought of that?" said Miguel

"They wouldn't be able to tell," protested Natividad.

Miguel looked at her. "Are you willing to bet 'Jandro's life on that? Remember Dimilioc's always been associated with the Pure. Maybe they know more than you think about things like that." Miguel turned to Alejandro. "I know you really, really hate being locked up, but if she bloods the silver for you and they find out, they might not take it out on her, but you?" He shrugged. "*Estás chingado.*"

"Language!" said Natividad, rolling her eyes. But she didn't argue with her twin's assessment. She swung her feet to the floor, holding up a hand to stop him when Miguel started to object. "I'm just going to look at it. I think maybe you're right about Dimilioc thinking about that already – I think otherwise I'd have a private room right now, whatever I said."

"Looking" at the silver meant running her fingertips along the wire, frowning, her eyes actually closed. She followed the silver wire up and down the bars of the door, reaching through them to touch the lock. Finally she said, still frowning, "We don't need to worry whether they'd notice if I blooded this silver. They've done something to it."

"Something?" Miguel, curious about anything new, wanted details.

Natividad shrugged. "Something to stop it being blooded." She looked at Alejandro, lifting her shoulders in an apologetic shrug. "I think Mamá said something about this, but I don't remember. I'll have to think about it, 'Jandro."

"Yes," said Alejandro. "It's fine. It doesn't matter. I think Miguel was right – we wouldn't have wanted to mess with their silver anyway." He waited for her to sink back down on the cot and then tucked her in, ending by draping his jacket over her feet again in case she was still cold.

"Well, what *I* say," Natividad declared in a very different tone as she settled back again, "is tomorrow can take care of itself. I don't even *care*, as long as we don't have to hike miles and miles through the snow. It's just really *disappointing* to find out how hard it is to walk through. Why would anybody live here?" She waved a hand in theatrical disgust before either of her brothers could answer. "I know, I know, because Dimilioc's always been here and black dogs like space and territory. Even so. No wonder Papá came to Mexico. He ought to have been glad to come south." She made a face and tucked one of the extra blankets around herself. "Cold, huh. *Who* thought coming here was a good idea?"

Alejandro grinned despite himself.

"I'm going to sleep," Natividad announced. "You can talk if you want, you won't keep me awake. Wake me at... Wait! On second thought, *don't* wake me." She stretched out ostentatiously and shut her eyes. She was showing off how calm she was, Alejandro knew that, but she was also still worn to the bone. Her breathing smoothed out again almost at once.

"And you – you're really alright?" Alejandro said to Miguel once he was certain their sister was truly asleep once more. "*De verdad?*" He held out a hand, inviting his brother to sit next to him.

Miguel nodded. He came over and sat down on the floor beside Alejandro. After a moment, he said, "And you... the silver..."

"*No importa.*"

"Right," said Miguel. He added eventually, in a different tone, "It was not as bad as I feared – and also, in a different way, worse than I feared. You understand?"

"Oh, yes." Alejandro touched his brother on the shoulder. It was hard for a black dog to touch anyone gently, but he made the effort, and Miguel leaned against him for a moment, a closeness they rarely shared. Then, aware that this kind of contact strained Alejandro's control, Miguel straightened and rested against the cot instead.

"*No está bien tartar así a la gente–*" Alejandro began.

"Of course it's not right to treat people so roughly, but if you wanted to find out about someone, human or black dog or whatever, about his control and strength, how else would you do it? You're angry because your black dog is angry and also because you're..." Miguel hesitated, then shrugged. "Because you're embarrassed. So am I. It's harder because Ezekiel is our age, nearly, isn't it? But what else should they do but what they did? It was nothing personal, what Ezekiel did."

"Hah," said Alejandro, and grinned at last, leaning back against the edge of the cot in a deliberate echo of his brother. "I don't have to like it. You're far too sensible, Miguel." Sometimes he wondered what that would be like, to be that way – to be calm and rational, the way an ordinary human could be. Not to be pulled always toward violence and anger by the black dog shadow. Miguel had so much more choice over what he did, or at least over what he felt; a kind of control a black dog achieved only through constant struggle.

Miguel's mouth crooked. "No such thing as *too* sensible. Which we can hope Grayson thinks as well."

Alejandro nodded. "You understand people. What will they do? Miguel, you did not tell them *you* argued us into coming here?"

"*Estas bromeando*? You'd kill me yourself if I told them."

"I might." Alejandro gave his younger brother a long look, trying to decide whether he was lying. But Miguel met his hard stare with evident sincerity.

"So," Alejandro said at last. "What I think is, maybe they will send me away and keep you. I don't think they will kill me. They want Natividad, and if they are wise they will want you. It must be useful for Dimilioc to have some ordinary humans and I don't think they do right now. I think they will say to one another, 'That young one, he is only a boy, he shows promise and he can be brought up to be Dimilioc in his heart, and anyway he is not a black dog so he is no threat.' I think they will say, 'That black pup, though, he does not have such good control of his shadow, and at his age he will challenge everyone and never rest from violence.' If they say things like that, Miguel, then it is important that you let them blame me for our trespass. It will not matter to me, and maybe it will help you."

Miguel nodded, but this was not exactly agreement.

Alejandro said, a little more forcefully, *"Harás lo que yo te diga.* If they keep Natividad, and they will, it is important she have a brother near her. You understand?"

"Yes. Yes! I understand. You don't need to keep on about it!" Miguel got to his feet, taking an impatient step away.

"If you understand and agree, then I don't," Alejandro said grimly. "If you tell them and then they don't kill us both, I really *will* kill you myself."

"Papá suggested we come here," Miguel said. "And you decided we would. Natividad and me, we never make decisions, we're just along for the ride."

"Good."

"But if they send you away, they're fools, and if they kill you, I won't forgive it."

Alejandro nodded. "So, what will they do? Do *you* think I worry for nothing?"

Miguel shrugged, glancing up to meet his brother's eyes and then down again, uncomfortably. "Nothing about this is obvious. I don't know the Dimilioc wolves well enough to guess. I don't know." He looked at Alejandro earnestly. "I *really* don't. But Grayson's smart and he doesn't care a lot about tradition. I mean, once so many vampires got killed that there weren't enough to keep their miasma going and people began to see vampires and blood kin and then black dogs? No one expected that, right? But Grayson figured out he could use that by just sending the right information to the right people so the humans themselves would attack the blood kin where Dimilioc couldn't reach them. That was really clever, and usually a black dog wouldn't think of things like that. So, I get that Dimilioc didn't used to let anybody just walk up and join, but Grayson's different – and Papá *was* a Toland."

Alejandro thought that Miguel might be partly right, but that unpredictability was not the most reassuring quality the Dimilioc Master might possess. But he said only, "Maybe you are right. So. Rest, then. You rest, and I will also, and as Natividad said, we will let the morning take care of itself."

But the morning came, and nothing happened.

The windowless basement room offered no sign of the brightening dawn and the soundproofing was too good to allow any sound from the house above to filter down to the cell, but Alejandro felt the sun anyway, a pressure against his shadow. No one brought more food. There was still some bread left, and some of the berry preserves. Alejandro left the food for the twins, who woke stiff and bleary. Miguel did not complain. Natividad complained about the lack of a toothbrush, and the lack of a hot shower, and the lack of clean clothing: their belongings, *escaso* – scant – as they were, had not come down to the cell with them. But she did not complain about the silence from the house above, or admit that she was afraid of what this silence might portend.

Alejandro could not touch the silver-wrapped bars of the cage, but Miguel stood on a chair to string cord across the width of the cell and then hung blankets across the cord. There were even clothespins to make the job easier – Alejandro would not have expected Ezekiel to think of such a detail, or to bother finding a handful of pins even if he did. He almost thought well of the *verdugo* for a moment, until he caught himself.

After the blankets were hung, Natividad managed something of a bath in the sink – "*Cold* water!" she declared, splashing. "I thought water this cold was ice!" But she looked refreshed and even cheerful when she pulled the blankets aside and rejoined them. "No television, no books, not even a deck of cards," she said, looking around at the blank cell. "Not very good service! I don't know if this is a hotel I'd care to patronize next time we're wandering through the wilds of Northern Gringolandia."

"Half-civilized barbarians," Miguel said solemnly. "Be glad they have running water." Natividad grinned. Papá had had a great deal to say about the lack of running water at home in Potosi, and, when the twins were six, had at last put in a pipe from the spring. "I think–" Miguel went on, but stopped as the door at the head of the stairs opened at last. For one moment, he looked as frightened as any ordinary fifteen year-old boy. Then he hid the fear behind the calm mask he had learned through living with a black dog father and brother.

Alejandro found his own anger and fear almost impossible to hide. If the Dimilioc *lobos* decided to kill him, kill Miguel, keep Natividad as their prisoner – if they decided to do that, he would not be able to stop them. The vivid awareness of his own helplessness was almost unendurable. How had *this* seemed the best among all possible risks?

It was Ezekiel who came down the stairs. Ezekiel alone. Should they find this reassuring? Or was the presence of the Dimilioc executioner alone a bad sign?

Ezekiel gave Alejandro a cool stare, forcing him to lower his eyes; he did not trouble to make any such show of authority with Miguel. Was that a good sign? He gave Natividad an unsmiling little nod as he unlocked the cell door – she met his gaze, and he didn't seem to mind. That was surely good? Then the *verdugo* gave them all an economical little jerk of his head: *Come on out.*

Alejandro kept himself between Ezekiel and his brother and sister as they went up the stairs. He knew this could not possibly make any difference; he even knew that he might better put Natividad nearest Ezekiel, forcing the *verdugo* to get around her before he could attack either Miguel or himself. The extra seconds this might buy them could be invaluable if Ezekiel *did* attack. But he could not help himself. He could not possibly put his sister so close to the Dimilioc *verdugo*. And Ezekiel knew it, and laughed. Not out loud. But Alejandro knew he was laughing inside.

He took them to the same big room Alejandro had seen the previous night. The view was even more spectacular in the clear morning light. The forest looked… wild. Dangerous. It might have stretched on forever. The naked trees ought to have looked dead, ugly. Instead, the black branches drew lines across the white snow and the brilliant sky in a stark, unexpected beauty. Alejandro longed, suddenly and fiercely, to be outside this house, free in that winter forest, far away from any other black dog who might threaten or challenge him. From Miguel's wistful glance at the window, he likely felt some human version of the same longing. But Natividad's attention, hopeful and hesitant, was all for Grayson Lanning.

The Dimilioc Master occupied his customary chair. This time all the other black wolves were seated, their chairs drawn into a semicircle. Only Ezekiel stayed on his feet, leaning his hip on the arm of a chair as he had done the previous evening. Alejandro and his brother and sister stood before the Dimilioc wolves like prisoners brought into a court, only a court where everyone besides themselves was a judge.

Grayson Lanning let his glance pass over Miguel and Natividad, but met Alejandro's eyes. Alejandro immediately dropped his gaze to the floor. He could still make out the marks of his claws in the wool of the rug. He did not know what to say, and so said nothing. Even Natividad was silent, amazingly enough.

Grayson said without preliminary, "Dimilioc has seven wolves, not five. Two are away just now on an errand for me."

Alejandro understood what Grayson was saying: *we are not as weak as you supposed*. He said nothing.

"I will tell you," Grayson continued after a moment, "I am astonished at what Edward Toland accomplished. I am astonished that Edward found a Pure woman, that he lived with her for something like two decades, that he raised a human son without killing him and a black dog son without losing him to bloodlust. I do not expect black dogs outside one of the civilized Houses to do such things – or to wish to do them. Even a Toland raised in Dimilioc. Those who are cast out do not find it an easy matter to retain such civilized behavior. Even with the *Beschwichtigend* to help them." He paused.

Alejandro thought the Dimilioc Master was going to say, *But...* – and then go on to order his death, and maybe Miguel's. He tried to steady himself against fear and anger, tried to think what he might do or say to persuade Grayson to spare at least Miguel.

Then the Master went on, instead, "You might say, seven wolves is still weak. This is true. You assure me that you and your human brother and Pure sister are capable of loyalty, that you are worthy of some degree of trust, that you will all, in the long term, be an asset. I am inclined to take you at your word – at least so far as to try you."

Alejandro, braced for a different decision, looked up at him in surprise and mistrust.

"Well?" said Grayson. "Even if Vonhausel's grudge against your father drove him to follow Edward south, I doubt he will trouble overmuch, now, to seek Edward's children here in the north. But if he should follow you, well, after all that we have faced and fought and overcome, I hardly think we need to fear Malvern Vonhausel."

"If he dares come against us at all, him and whatever shadow pack of strays he might have compelled to follow him," added Zachariah, his lip curling. "Which I doubt. I never cared for him, myself; give Edward credit for choosing his enemies."

"Not wisely," Harrison rumbled.

"If not wisely, at least well," Zachariah said smoothly.

"Sir…" Alejandro said, in some confusion, glancing from one of them to the other. He stopped, made himself take a breath, and said to Grayson, "Sir, you won't regret it–"

"Of course not," muttered Ethan.

Harrison snorted. "Why should you complain?" he growled to his son. "You'll have a black wolf younger than you in the pack. How is that bad?"

Ezekiel was a few years younger than Ethan, Alejandro was fairly sure, but of course the *verdugo* did not count. Ethan grunted, giving Alejandro an assessing stare. Alejandro looked away, but a long beat too late to appease the young Dimilioc wolf, who glowered. Ezekiel grinned, clearly amused by this byplay.

"You'll find your own level in Dimilioc," Grayson said to Alejandro. Then he said to Miguel, "But humans don't fight wolves. Remember that."

"No, sir, I know," Miguel assured him earnestly. "I mean, yes, sir."

"Now, you," Grayson said to Natividad. "Dimilioc needs the strong black dog sons and Pure daughters you can give us. You're not a whore, but you *are* a valuable commodity. You understand that?"

"Yes," Natividad said, in her most submissive manner. "I mean, yes, sir. We knew I would be." She did not *look* frightened, but her heartbeat had picked up. Alejandro prepared to intervene, if Grayson tried to do anything with her that she couldn't tolerate. Though he did not know what he could do–

Grayson gave Natividad a long, assessing stare. "You are also a child, and never mind telling me about your married cousins. Fifteen, are you? When is your birthday?"

Natividad said cautiously, "April seventh, sir."

"April. Nearly four months. So. When you turn sixteen, you may choose any Dimilioc wolf you wish. Until April seventh, I'll not have any black dog touch you." He looked deliberately across the half circle of chairs, at Ezekiel. "That includes you."

That did not seem to amuse Ezekiel. His mouth set hard. He straightened, shoving himself away from the chair on which he'd been leaning.

"Well?" growled the Master.

Ezekiel did not even glance at Natividad. He said, "April is alright. I can wait. I don't care about that. But if she doesn't choose me, I'll kill any other black dog who touches her." Holding Grayson's eyes, he added deliberately, "That includes you."

There was a long pause, heavy with tension. No one moved or spoke; all the black dogs looked down or away, except for Grayson and Ezekiel, whose gazes had locked.

Then Grayson, though he did not look away, grunted and moved a hand dismissively. "In April, maybe. And today?"

Ezekiel dropped gracefully to one knee and bowed his head. "Master," he said formally.

"Then that will do," said Grayson, with no sign of concern.

Natividad, frightened or perhaps only shocked, leaned against Alejandro. He put an arm around her shoulders and wished she had thought to claim a November birthday instead. Four months did not seem long. It did not seem like any time at all.

4

It was strange that such a cold world could be so beautiful.

The light was the key to the beauty of winter, Alejandro decided. Natividad had been joking when she'd said it was a different sun here, but she had been right, too. The light here *was* different. Pale, fragile... purer, somehow, than the southern sun.

He stood with his hands on the sill of a window in his sister's room. It was a large, airy, cluttered, pink, frilly room that Natividad clearly loved, although she pretended to scorn pink as girlish. The room boasted pretty tables and chairs and a nice couch, and a bed with pink muslin curtains onto which Natividad's whole room from home would almost have fitted. Alejandro wondered whose room it had been last year, and how that unknown girl had died.

Miguel had immediately claimed the larger of the adjoining rooms. It was much plainer than Natividad's, with a narrow bed tucked into one corner next to an equally narrow window – no curtains around that bed – and, in the opposite corner, a big sturdy desk with one chair. The computer on the desk was the thing that had caught

Miguel's eye. He had gone to it immediately and was now scrolling through the news, calling out the most interesting headlines. "'*Vampires in retreat*'?" he quoted, and laughed, looking over his shoulder into Natividad's room through the adjoining door. "Well, more or less! If being all dead and burned counts as 'in retreat'. But, here, here's somebody who's figured out the war's over. It's Fernandez, you know, that *tipo* from New Zealand. He says he thinks the fighting now is all infighting between 'werewolf' rivals. That's pretty good, for a human."

"You think he's really *un perro negro*?" Alejandro asked.

"No, no." Miguel's eyes were back on the screen. He pulled the chair around and dropped into it, clicking rapidly as he followed one link after another. He said absently, "Fernandez is no black dog. He writes all from his head, you know? I think he's just a sharp guy who puts things together. He was one of the first to figure out about the vampires, I mean about what their magic had been doing to ordinary humans all along, and then last August he worked out some good tactics for clearing vampires out of inner city slums without firebombs. You remember what happened in Russia."

Natividad groaned. "How can you stand to read about things like that?" She lay flat on her bed and put a pillow over her head.

"Oh, now he's just writing this great series of articles about possible vampire influence in the Ottoman Empire and France during the fifteenth and sixteenth centuries. Anyway," Miguel added, a little apologetically, "he's human, alright, and I'm not surprised he's also one of the first to figure out the war's over."

"The first war," Alejandro said.

"What we have now, this isn't a war. Except it's kind of a war of all against all, I guess. And Vonhausel against us – but I guess we've left him behind now, alright."

Miguel sounded very satisfied about that. Alejandro wasn't so confident they'd traded the greater danger for a lesser. Though... Natividad had. Miguel, too, probably. That, at least, they had achieved with their flight.

But it had been a flight. A defeat. When they had been attacked, Alejandro had abandoned the battle and run. He closed his eyes, hearing Papá shout in memory, *Run, 'Jandro! Lead those bastards off us!* He had obeyed, the raw desperation in Papá's voice overwhelming his shadow's bloodlust. Maybe that had done some good. Some of Vonhausel's black dogs had pursued him. He had run and dodged all night and all the next day, fighting when he was brought to bay amid the broken country at the base of the mountains; he had killed one and another of Vonhausel's black dogs and broken away and run again and never known whether Mamá had succeeded in hiding his younger brother and sister, whether Papá had managed to win time for Mamá herself to run.

When he had at last made his way back to the burned village, he had believed at first that everyone was dead. Everyone. That everything was lost. He had longed to scream out his rage and grief, to let his shadow rise and never try again to chain it. Only then he had found Miguel, pale with shock and fear, hiding in the hole beneath the root cellar, his scent masked by the stench of charred coffee and chilies. And then Natividad had crept out of the ring of burned pine-stubs which were all that remained of Mamá's circle, covered with ash and blistered where burning pitch had rained down on her. She had been shaking, unable to speak at all for days, but she had hidden there somehow, by some trick of Pure magic, and was not hurt.

But Mamá was dead. And Papá. Both dead. They had found pieces... Alejandro flinched from the memory. If he had stayed... If he had disobeyed Papá and stayed to fight... He knew there was no logic to those doubts. Vonhausel had brought too many black dogs against them. If he had stayed, he would be dead, too. But... if he *had* fought, maybe he and Papá together could have won enough breathing room for them *all* to run. If Edward Toland had brought them here himself... if he had brought his Pure wife... obviously Grayson would have welcomed them all.

No way to know. He had obeyed Papá's desperate command; Papá and Mamá had died, and he and Miguel and Natividad had lived. No way to know what else might have happened...

"Could we *please* talk about something else?" Natividad asked plaintively, probably aware of his rising rage and grief. She put the pillow aside and propped herself up on one elbow to look at him. "'Jandro, is your room alright? It's awfully small."

"It's fine," Alejandro said. Natividad was exaggerating the plaintiveness of her tone, but behind her teasing he could tell she was worried. She thought he couldn't tell when she was worried about him, but he could. Deliberately shaking off memory and grief, he said, "I like it small. I like the windows." This was true. His room, on the other side of

Natividad's, *was* tiny. But the windows were huge, taking up
almost all of two walls, so that the room seemed suspended
in the air. From the scars on the window sills, this room
had belonged to black dogs before him. He wondered who
had lived in this set of connecting rooms last year: siblings,
friends, lovers? It was horrifying, how much space had been
abandoned in this house, how many rooms waited for new
tenants to move in.

The sense of dead ghosts whispering around the edges
of perception was very strong in the whole suite. But these
were the rooms Grayson Lanning had told them they could
have. In a strange way, Alejandro was even glad of the
sorrow that clung to these rooms, this house: he could not
help but feel that the whole world should share his own
grief. He wondered whether Natividad also felt that, and
thought she did. He thanked God and the Virgin every
hour, every minute, for Natividad. He was sure that only
her presence had persuaded the Dimilioc *lobos* to accept
her human brother, far less a stray black dog pup.

Alejandro only wished he thought it a good bargain for
Natividad herself. But the back of his neck and his spine
pricked when he thought of Ezekiel Korte's cool, uninflected
voice: *If she doesn't choose me...* He wondered whether he
should begin planning now for some kind of ambush, some
ataque sorprendió, a surprise attack that might let him kill
Ezekiel and free Natividad from his threat.

Papá had taught him about that when he was still a
pequeño, a kid. "You won't always be the strongest,"
Papá had said. "Right now, if you had to fight a stray, he'd
probably tear you up, right? So, you'd need to be tricky

about it. For example, you could use Natividad or your mother as bait, right? Because we know *callejeros* haven't got much sense, especially not when they're chasing down a Pure woman, right? Only you don't want to risk Mamá really, but you could bait a trap with her blanket or blouse and maybe a little of her blood."

Alejandro had grinned. He could envision perfectly a stray black dog rushing down a game trail toward the scent of a Pure woman, completely missing a black dog hidden and waiting in ambush.

"Only you have to keep your shadow *all* the way down until the right time to let it up," Papá had added. "Or ninety-nine *callejeros* in a hundred will scent *you* hiding! So, let's play it out, right? I'll be the stray, and you've baited a trap right outside the village; that's all good, but how are you going to make sure I come along this trail and not a different one? Or right through the forest and not on a trail at all?"

Traps and ambushes and tricks, and hunting, and straight-up battle, and always, always control, because a black dog who couldn't control his shadow was just a *callejero*, a stray, to be put down like a rabid dog. Alejandro had been so proud the day a trap of his own making had made it possible for him and Papá to ambush and kill a pack of five black dogs. One *had* got past them, but Alejandro had set up the trail to lead the *callejero* right in between a pentagram and the cliff face, and Miguel had shot him with one of the special silver bullets that Tío Fernando had shown him how to make. Alejandro had been even prouder of the forceful control that had let him walk out of the forest in human form to congratulate his young brother.

And now Ezekiel Korte had shown him how little control he really had.

Probably Ezekiel guessed he was thinking about ambushes. Ezekiel was hardly a *callejero*. Probably the Dimilioc executioner would prove, in practice, impossible to surprise.

Since he did not want to say any of his thoughts aloud, Alejandro stood by Natividad's window, staring out at the endless sweep of sky and black forest and snow that stretched out below. People said snow was frozen water. It seemed to Alejandro that snow was really frozen light. He wondered if, when it melted in the spring, it did so with bursts of luminous brilliance as well as rivulets of water.

"*Desolado*," Miguel said. He had, surprisingly, left the computer and now leaned in the doorway of his room, watching Alejandro's face rather than looking out the window. His comment might well have been meant to apply to Alejandro and not the brittle winter forest.

Natividad, lying now on her back on the pink bed, one leg crooked casually over the other upraised knee, shook her head. "*Espléndido*," she said. "But it's not a friendly splendor, is it? This is a country that doesn't care if you die. I mean, neither does the desert, but this isn't the same." She tilted her head, peering sideways and almost upside down at Alejandro. "Do you feel that also, even though you don't feel the cold and can run on top of the snow?" Her tone dropped. "You'll go for a run later, I guess."

She meant, with Ethan Lanning and maybe one or another of the other Dimilioc *lobos*; she meant more than a run. And she was right. There would be a run, and a fight.

Alejandro shrugged, meaning "*Sí*". Knowing that Natividad couldn't help but worry, he said, "The country out there may not care if anyone dies, but Grayson Lanning would be furious. Nobody wants that. I don't, either." Although he wouldn't mind killing Ethan – well, that was his black dog shadow snarling. But he would not lower his gaze for Ethan Lanning. He would *win*.

"You'll beat him," Miguel said. "I don't know him, but I know *you*. You'll beat him."

"I wish you didn't have to fight, even if you do win!" Natividad rolled abruptly to her feet and came to stand beside Alejandro, looking out the window. Leaning forward, she breathed on the cold glass and then drew a circle on the misted surface with the tip of her finger. She fitted a five-pointed star into the circle and then watched it fade. But if she breathed on the glass again, it would reappear. Her pentagram was still there on the glass, even though it was invisible. Like light, in a way.

Alejandro shrugged again.

"Oh, yes, I know. Shut up. You black dogs…" Natividad made a face. "I don't want to think about black dogs. Or Dimilioc wolves. What*ever*." She sighed, and the window misted from her breath, her pentagram glimmering briefly back into visibility.

Alejandro wanted to ask her which of the wolves she would choose, but how could she know yet? He wanted to ask what she thought about Ezekiel's threat. But she probably did not know yet what she thought about that, either. Maybe she didn't find Ezekiel as frightening and offensive as Alejandro did. She probably wouldn't tell him if she did. She would talk to her twin about her fears, maybe. But then Miguel wouldn't tell Alejandro what she said, either. Too good with secrets, both of them. Especially for fifteen.

"Well, children," someone said behind them, and Alejandro only just stopped himself from whirling violently around. Instead, he made himself slowly unclench his hands from the windowsill and turn with something like control.

Natividad did spin about, but that was alright: girls never looked stupid even when they were surprised.

One ought never to flinch from a black dog. You never backed away, because if you ran, a black dog would chase you. Not so much someone Pure, like Natividad, but it would be worse for Alejandro to look surprised or wary. Worse still if Miguel flinched. Alejandro tipped his chin up and looked deliberately into Zachariah Korte's face for a long moment, to focus the black wolf's attention on himself before he lowered his gaze.

From the voice, he'd thought it was Ezekiel. The two were alike in more than voice. Like his nephew, Zachariah looked very *American*, all bony gringo height and pale coloring. His voice, too, was much the same. His eyes were the same cold blue, the color of the winter sky outside. They had even less expression, Alejandro thought, than that sky.

"Pup," Zachariah said to Alejandro, with a scant nod of acknowledgement. He ignored Miguel entirely, but he offered Natividad a cool smile. "Natividad. That's an unusual name: Natividad. Do they call you Nattie?"

In reply, Natividad picked up a pink frilly wastebasket from beside the nearest table and pretended to throw up in it. "Anyway," she added, to Zachariah's surprised laugh, "it is not unusual. It's a good Catholic name, and besides it was Grandmamá's name. *Nattie* would be silly. It wouldn't *mean* anything. It just sounds strange to you because gringo names have no pizzazz." She gave the Dimilioc wolf a sly, sidelong glance. "I guess they call you Zack?"

Zachariah Korte smiled, barely, as though expressions were meant to be horded, as though if he might use up his share and never be able to smile again. "Very seldom."

He thought Natividad was funny, Alejandro could tell. The Dimilioc wolf thought she was *cute*. Zachariah looked at her the way he might look at a precocious four year-old baby, not the way a man looked at a pretty girl. Alejandro exchanged a glance with Miguel as a tension he hadn't exactly known he'd felt suddenly eased. Zachariah thought Natividad was too young for him. Or maybe he just didn't mean to set himself up to oppose his nephew. Either way, Alejandro thought that was fine. He could tell by Miguel's crooked smile that they agreed Zachariah was definitely *much* too old for Natividad.

"I don't suppose they call you Alex?" Zachariah said to Alejandro, with another of those faint smiles.

"No," said Alejandro shortly.

"'Jandro, sometimes," Natividad said cheerfully. She put the wastebasket back where she'd got it and bounced over to sit cross-legged on the bed, coquettish as a kitten. She did not seem, this morning, to be afraid at all of the Dimilioc wolf. She gave him another sly look. "*I* could call you Zack. I bet everybody really calls you Zack when you're not trying to be scary. And everybody probably calls Ezekiel Zeke, too,

and Harrison, Harry. What is it for Ethan? Eth? Than?"
She did not suggest that anybody called Grayson by any
nickname, Alejandro noticed.

Zachariah laughed. "No, indeed – though I'd enjoy
watching you call my nephew 'Zeke'. But, in the interests
of a convivial breakfast, it might be best if we all agree
to refrain from any nicknames whatsoever." He turned to
Alejandro. "After breakfast, I think you'll find Ethan invites
you for a run. Among other things."

Meaning he, too, expected Ethan and Alejandro to fight.
Alejandro didn't allow himself to smile, but the thought of
violence and blood prickled pleasurably down his spine.
His shadow flexed, wanting to rise. *Later*, Alejandro told
it silently. *Later*. Patience was not a black dog quality, but
after a momentary struggle his shadow subsided.

"You like the idea, do you?" Zachariah had missed
nothing. "Good. But breakfast first." He turned to lead the
way, gesturing them to go in front of him.

The kitchen was big. Actually, it seemed a little overdone to
Alejandro. Nothing like their mother's kitchen, where they
had all used to gather. Natividad had helped Mamá make
tortillas every day, and at Christmas everyone had helped
her make tamales. Mamá's kitchen had always smelled of
chilies and cumin and cinnamon and hot oil and, to a black
dog, vividly of blood from cleaned chickens and meat.

This room was not like a real kitchen. It was too big
and too shiny and artificial. It smelled more of soap than of
food or cooking. The sink and refrigerator and oven were all
steel, and the counters were lined with gray granite almost

as shiny as the steel. And the kitchen was cluttered with tools he did not recognize; all those things looked big and shiny and artificial as well. Pans hung suspended from the ceiling, but there were no strings of garlic or dried chilies. Mamá's kitchen had been the heart of their home. It was hard to think of this kitchen as the heart of anything.

To Alejandro's silent astonishment, Zachariah made breakfast as though he was accustomed to the task. Maybe he cooked all the time. In Monterrey, where people were rich, a house like this one would employ twenty servants. Here there didn't seem to be *any*, but after all somebody had to cook. Natividad perched on the edge of a tall stool drawn up to one of the stone-topped counters, uncomfortable until Zachariah gave her two dozen eggs to beat with cream and salt.

Miguel touched Alejandro's shoulder, tipping his head toward the door, and the two of them wandered out into an immense, ornate dining room. The room held a polished table with space to seat at least twenty people – black dogs, who needed plenty of space – and two matching sideboards, and glass-fronted cabinets in which were displayed crystal glasses and silver platters and fragile-looking dishes painted with intricate designs in blue and red and black.

Harrison and Ethan Lanning were already seated at the table. Ethan gave Alejandro a direct stare, curling his lip. Alejandro deliberately glanced away, as though he merely happened to be interested in the display cabinets.

"Quit your nonsense," Harrison growled at both of them. He said to Miguel, "A few ordinary humans around the place are exactly what we need. Black-pup posturing makes me tired." He waved a broad hand. "Sit, sit. Anywhere."

Anywhere not at the head of the table; Alejandro and Miguel both understood that. Alejandro wanted to put Miguel at the end, with himself between his brother and the next nearest black dog, but Miguel slid around him and instead took the seat directly next to Harrison.

"How many humans did you used to have here?" he asked. "Were they all somebody's relatives? Because that's pretty bad, losing them, if they were brothers and sisters, cousins and wives. That's tough."

"Too many were, as you say, kin," said Harrison. "Far too many." His tone lowered, so that Alejandro wondered what kin he might have lost. He added, almost more to himself than to Miguel, "They... Humans are so vulnerable to vampires."

"Were," said Miguel. "*Were* vulnerable to vampires."

Harrison's dark eyes focused on Miguel. After a moment, he smiled, though grimly. "*Were* vulnerable. Yes. That's done."

Alejandro found the Dimilioc wolf's obvious grief profoundly reassuring. They had carried one or another of the Dimilioc names, he guessed, those dead human brothers and sisters and cousins and wives. They had counted as part of the Dimilioc pack. Maybe a subordinate part, but they'd had an accepted place, a place that Miguel could move into and make his own.

"We'll bring in a few human servants in the spring," Ethan said, his tone tight and annoyed.

Alejandro looked at Ethan in surprise. They would? How? Would the Dimilioc wolves just hire ordinary people as servants? That was hard to picture. Maybe Dimilioc actually made a practice of kidnapping people when they ran short of servants? Could that possibly be what Ethan meant: that in the spring maybe a few early hikers might disappear?

"Oh, servants," Harrison said, with a dismissive little tilt of his head.

"Useful creatures, servants. Or do you enjoy dusting?" said Zachariah, coming into the dining room with a platter balanced on each hand and Natividad, similarly laden, behind him. He slid his platters onto the table with the neat grace of experience and turned to help Natividad with hers.

"You don't seem to mind the cooking," Ethan said, not quite snapping.

"But do I dust?" Zachariah was clearly amused, but the glint of humor in his pale eyes faded as he looked around the table. "Where's Ezekiel? Grayson?"

"Busy, one supposes," Harrison said. "We won't wait."

Breakfast was ham and eggs and biscuits with honey and fig jam. The eggs were fine. Plain. Not very interesting, was Alejandro's reluctant judgment, and he didn't even care about food. Natividad, if she had been cooking, would have fried strips of day-old tortillas to scramble with the eggs, and added chilies and onions. The biscuits were alright, though. Much better than the squishy bread you could get at the roadside places where buses stopped. Alejandro watched Natividad tuck ham and fig jam into a biscuit. She was avoiding the eggs. He suspected she was planning a takeover of the kitchen. He wondered whether Zachariah would mind if she made some good Mexican food. Did he think of that kitchen as his? He might be territorial about it, hard though that was to imagine when the room was so free of personality.

"Do you make bread, too?" Natividad asked, and Zachariah said, "I do," and passed her the platter of ham. Alejandro found it was actually not hard to imagine Zachariah's long clever hands kneading bread dough on one of these fancy stone-topped counters.

"In the spring—" Harrison began, and was interrupted by Zachariah suddenly putting down his fork and lifting his head. "Yes?" said Harrison.

"I don't quite know." Zachariah stood up, not urgently but not wasting time either, and said briefly to Harrison – not so much to the rest of them – "I'll let you know." Abandoning his plate, he walked out, heading for the front of the house.

Harrison ate two more bites of eggs, then put his fork down and glowered at Ethan. "Anything?"

Ethan shrugged. "Not so I can tell." He shoved his chair back, preparing to get up. He said to his father, pointedly not looking at Alejandro or Miguel, nor even at Natividad, "I'll go find out, shall I?"

Harrison began to nod, but was interrupted by a deep-throated cry – a sound midway between a howl and a roar, violently aggressive. There was the sound of shattering glass and the long ripping sound of splintering wood. Harrison was instantly on his feet, striding toward the door, his back bowing and twisting as his shadow rose: it had been a man who'd got to his feet, but it was a massive-shouldered black dog who slammed the door open and lunged through it, moving in long bounds that seemed almost more suited to a lion than a wolf. Ethan was a step or two behind his father, still mostly in human form, his dense shadow gathered close around him.

Alejandro spared one fast, alarmed look for the twins. Miguel had already turned and bolted – the right way, away from the trouble – but Natividad had frozen, staring at him. "*Vamos*!" Alejandro snarled at her, meaning: "*Go after Miguel.*" He himself whirled to follow the Dimilioc wolves. His shadow rose around him as he ran; his claws sank into the hardwood floor as he flung himself through the doorway and forward.

Perhaps thirty black dogs were scattered across the open ground that lay between the edge of the forest and the Dimilioc mansion, some of them leaping forward toward the house like great cats, some of them stalking low to the ground, some even creeping on their bellies. They panted, coal-black fangs gleaming in hot red mouths, smoke wreathing into the air from their breath, the snow melting where they passed.

They were Vonhausel's black dogs. Vonhausel's shadow pack. They were here. They had come all the way north after all, right into the heart of Dimilioc territory. Alejandro could not believe they had done such a thing. He *did* not believe it. He told himself they must be merely a clutter of American strays, bold and stupid with the waxing moon, temporarily gathered together by some black dog stronger and more ambitious than they. But then he saw Vonhausel himself, unmistakable, huge and flame-eyed, behind the rest, and after that he could not tell himself comforting lies.

He saw Vonhausel's black dogs through a fiery haze of bloodlust and anger, so that they seemed to cast bloody shadows and the snow itself was tinted crimson. The enemy black dogs approached in a ragged half circle. A dark miasma of smoke and evil followed them and clung to them and reached out before them. It was hard to see how many they were or exactly pinpoint their locations, but Alejandro thought that those at the edges were racing ahead while those at the center approached more cautiously. That was reasonable because, thirty feet from the front door, Ezekiel Korte anchored the center of the defense, with Grayson Lanning supporting him on one side and Ethan on the other.

Harrison was beyond Ethan, well out to the left, facing half a dozen black dogs. To the right, Zachariah had been the first to actually close with enemies, and now one of his opponents was rolling on the ground, screaming, half his face torn away. Blood and black ichor splashed madly across the snow as Zachariah used his weight to bear down another of the intruders and tore at his throat and chest, but in the next moment another of the invaders hit the oldest of the Dimilioc wolves and knocked him away from his writhing enemy. The wounded black dog, neither dead nor dying, twisted into his human form, letting his shadow carry away his terrible injuries. In far too little time, his shadow would rise around him once more and then he would attack again.

Five Dimilioc wolves were far too few; Alejandro had said so, and he had been right. Six was not much better, and for an instant he hesitated. He might find the twins and run, let the Dimilioc wolves cover their flight. But if Vonhausel won here, he would win everything, and then he would come after them again and kill them all, and he knew they would never get away.

His black dog, if it was not free to abandon the Dimilioc wolves, was perfectly happy to attack the invaders. Desire and counter desire fused, and with almost no perceptible hesitation, Alejandro hurled himself against the cluster of black dogs that surrounded Zachariah. There were four of them now, heavy and massively muscled. One faced Zachariah directly, fangs snapping, while two others closed in from his flanks, claws sharpening to needle points as they reared up to grapple, while the fourth swung wide to come around from the rear. Zachariah whirled in a tight circle, threatening them all.

Concentrating on their enemy, the strangers did not realize they faced another attacker until Alejandro slammed into one of them as he reared upright. Unprepared for the brutal impact, the stranger went down, but he twisted as he fell, striking at Alejandro's face with savage claws that lengthened as they slashed up at him. Alejandro jerked his head to the side, neatly evading the blow, and darted his head forward, closed his jaws on the invader's foreleg. *Yes!* howled his black dog, and Alejandro shook his head violently, knocked his opponent's attempted return strike aside with one forefoot, extended the shadow claws on the other, and ripped him across the belly, and then upward across the chest to tear through ribs and crush his heart.

More blood and ichor sprayed across the snow; his enemy's shadow writhed and howled and his body began to twist back into human form as he died. Alejandro also howled, but with savage pleasure, as he whirled around to look for another enemy; Zachariah was still battling furiously with two of the invaders. The third, his forelimb wrenched nearly off and his intestines spread in gory loops across the trampled snow, stared in glaze-eyed shock; the great, smoky cloud of his shadow struggled and failed to retain purchase in his dying body as he shifted piecemeal toward death and his human form.

But ichor and red-tinged smoke also poured from Zachariah's side where one of his opponents had torn him open. The two that were left harried him hard, and two more black dogs had cut away from the main force to come against him and Alejandro. Beyond them, in the midst of the wild twisting knot of battle, Alejandro could see Ezekiel Korte tearing into a cluster of enemies. He belatedly realized that the heave and surge of black dogs there marked Grayson's position – the enemy black dogs had pulled the Master down and now worked to finish him. But even while Alejandro watched, Ezekiel shifted fluidly from black dog to human and back, twice, impossibly fast, hardly a flicker between forms. The *verdugo* was using his shadow to clear away any injury even while eviscerating his enemies, and now Alejandro half believed Ezekiel alone truly might destroy a dozen enemies, or more.

He could not see Ethan or Harrison at all, but even in the midst of wild rage and bloodlust, even while he lunged to attack one of the Zachariah's opponents, Alejandro found himself astonished at the number of intruders who had been torn apart and lost their shadows and now, in death, dwindled back into their human bodies.

But there were still too many enemies and too few, far too few, Dimilioc wolves. Grayson had not made it back to his feet. Maybe the Master was dead – there was no choice but to fight;

he knew that and his black dog knew it, and he closed with one of the strangers. They crashed against each other with a shock that shook the world, claws lengthening as they both reared to slash, each of them using his weight to try to bear the other down, jaws snapping. Alejandro's claws scored across his enemy's chest, missing the belly stroke he'd aimed for. His enemy twisted and closed a crushing grip around Alejandro's shoulder, forcing him off balance and down, and though Alejandro tried to tear himself free he could not get loose–

The flat crack of a pistol shot snapped out like a whip stroke, loud even across the ugly clamor of battle, cutting alike across the roars of enraged black dogs and the screams of those whose wounds were too terrible to be absorbed by their shadows. Another shot. Then a third. Alejandro's enemy reared up and tried to shake him as a dog would shake a rat, but the strength of his grip was already failing, his body already writhing back toward his human form as Alejandro tore out his throat and flung him away.

The pistol cracked again, and after a careful, stretched-out pause, again. And again. Alejandro took longer than he should have to realize the shooter was now targeting Ezekiel's opponents. The pistol cracked once more, and then again, and, as the attackers hesitated, Alejandro found himself actually at leisure to watch Ezekiel fight. The black dogs attacking Ezekiel had found him a terrible enemy even without the support of the gunfire, and now, freed from the hard press of crowding enemies, Ezekiel lunged forward with astonishing speed and tore one of them almost in half.

The Dimilioc executioner fought almost casually. He showed no sign of the bloodlust and rage that engulfed

Alejandro, which Alejandro had assumed always consumed any battling black dog. That deadly calm was not the only advantage Ezekiel's formidable control gave him. As Alejandro watched, Ezekiel flickered from black dog to human form and back again between one stride and the next, using the change to slide between baffled opponents, then tear into one enemy after another. With a toss of his head, Ezekiel flung part of a recent opponent's torso thirty feet through the confused shadows and smoky light, contemptuously dropping the rest of the body, then leaping, with an air of lazy ease that almost disguised his speed, to tear once more into the pile of attackers that hid Grayson Lanning from sight. One black dog spun away to the left and another to the right, a third flung his head back, screaming, and Grayson surged at last out of the horde of his enemies.

Dark blood and black ichor clotted the Master's shaggy pelt; smoke streamed from his gaping jaws, and actual flames flickered, dark crimson edged with blue, in his mouth and along the edges of his terrible wounds. He twisted his head down and to the side, drew breath, and roared at his attackers, and two of them contorted helplessly back into human shape, though plainly they tried to hold onto their black dog forms. Grayson instantly tore those two apart, and the rest fled backward, a wavering retreat that yielded a lingering pause in the midst of the violent battle.

For a long moment, Alejandro thought that the Dimilioc wolves had, against all possibility, actually won. Just like that: so fast. Fully half of the intruders were down, some with wounds that were closing, but many more dead or near death. He even believed the Dimilioc wolves might destroy Vonhausel himself, and they would all be rid of him – so fast.

Then Vonhausel, well back from the fighting, lifted his head and howled, a long terrible cry that echoed and re-echoed around the icy forest. All across the cleared land before the house, snow exploded into steam. Fire, the crimson-edged hellfire that burned black at its heart, licked out across limp winter-brown grasses. Three pines at the edge of the forest burst into flames, burning with incandescent violence, and the momentum of the battle shifted again. There were still a lot of black dog intruders to rally to that burning cry – fifteen, maybe twenty, and every Dimilioc wolf except Ezekiel staggered under wounds there had been no time to shed. Alejandro did not see Harrison Lanning, maybe he was among the dead or hidden by the smoke; Ethan, one forelimb crippled, stalking back and forth on three legs, the frozen earth charring where he stepped.

There were no more gunshots.

Vonhausel howled again, powerful haunches bunching as he sank down, preparing to spring forward. The rest of the black dogs rallied to him with a cacophony of howling and snarling, gathering into a tight pack. They meant to rush Ezekiel, Alejandro understood suddenly: they would take Ezekiel and Grayson, and after that they would find it no great task to bring down the rest of the ragged Dimilioc wolves. And after that they could do anything they wished to the children of Edward Toland and Concepcíon Ramerez.

Zachariah suddenly left Alejandro, running toward the Dimilioc Master. Alejandro saw Ethan pressing in from the other side, still on three legs, blood dripping from slashes across his head and neck but following the same instinct: the Dimilioc pack gathering to face down its enemies. Alejandro leaped forward, following Zachariah, because there was nothing else to do and anyway he was angry, angry, angry. How dare these black dog *callejeros* attack Dimilioc *now*, when they would cost Alejandro so much, cost him everything? Visions of the destroyed village came to him, Mamá and her kin tumbled bloody and abandoned, Papá torn and dead and looking so small in human form, so small in death, when he had always been so powerful. Vonhausel had done that. It was all Vonhausel's fault. Alejandro dropped into a crouch, flanking Zachariah, snarling, a low savage note that vibrated in his chest; he longed for blood and hellfire and destruction.

Four more black dogs emerged from the forest, surely a superfluity of enemies. Two were big, heavy, broad-headed; the other two small and slight, but they looked like they would be fast – if the four fought as a team, they would be very dangerous – but Grayson tipped his torn head toward the sky and howled, and Ezekiel joined him with a long high-pitched ripping shriek of aggression and scorn, and Zachariah gave voice to a deep, grating sound that was more roar than howl. All four newcomers answered savagely and loped forward to cover the left flank of the little group of the Dimilioc wolves. The crowd of intruders hesitated, Vonhausel rearing high up, staring at the newcomers.

A pistol shot rang out, sharp and crisp against the voices of the Dimilioc wolves and the black dogs, and Vonhausel spun about, snapping at his own side. Grayson Lanning howled and leaped forward, pulling his Dimilioc wolves along in his wake, the four newcomers with them. The pistol cracked again, and Vonhausel must have wondered whether the shooter would find more silver bullets, because he whirled around, racing for the shelter of the forest, and all his followers scattered and fled after him.

The Dimilioc wolves let them go, though the shooter fired once more, so that one tardy enemy tumbled over, yelping, before scrambling to his feet and bounding away. Miguel –for it could only be his brother firing in their defense – really had run out of silver bullets, Alejandro guessed, or that black dog wouldn't have gotten up again. He regretted, savagely, that Vonhausel himself had not come in range while Miguel still had silver bullets in his gun.

Por otra parte... on the other hand, Miguel had rashly brought a gun – had hidden and brought a *gun* along, a gun and *silver ammunition*, right into Dimilioc territory. Their mother's gun, by the sharp sound of its retorts. Alejandro had not known. Miguel had not told him – well, of course he hadn't, Miguel would have known how furious his black dog brother would be.

Thank God and the Virgin for the little fool's *audacia*. That audacity had very likely saved all their lives. But, *Madre de Dios*, if the Dimilioc Master had guessed, if Ezekiel had found that gun before this fight... Alejandro found himself snarling under his breath, racing toward the house. If Grayson did not kill Miguel, he was going to do it *himself*.

5

Once the shooting was done, Natividad got Miguel to put the gun down as quickly as she could. Then there was nothing to do but wait for trouble to arrive. Natividad only hoped she could help keep the trouble from getting too big and serious.

She'd had no idea her twin had brought a gun with them into Dimilioc, no idea how he'd gotten it past Ezekiel Korte – loaded with silver ammunition, even! But she had a *very good* idea how the Dimilioc black wolves were going to respond to that particular bit of smuggling. She didn't know whether Miguel had been totally stupid to smuggle a silver-loaded gun into Dimilioc, or totally brilliant. Although if he hadn't, they might all be dead now, so she guessed he'd been brilliant.

Which didn't mean he wasn't going to be in big, serious trouble.

They waited in a big room on the second floor, right above the front door; a formal room with heavy furniture and gloomy landscape paintings and, which was the important thing, a sliding glass door that let onto a wide balcony. From the balcony, Miguel had been able to direct his fire straight into a crowd of enemies only forty or fifty feet away. But he'd come inside again now. He stood in the middle of the room, his arms at his sides, his gaze fixed on the floor. Natividad hovered anxiously to one side. The gun lay on a table, spent casings piled neatly beside it. It was their mother's light little .22 pistol. Miguel was a good shot, but Natividad had to admit, hitting anything at all with that gun at forty feet was amazing.

Alejandro arrived first, which was good, or should have been good, but he was really angry – scarily angry. He was still mostly in his black dog form when he strode through the doorway, which wasn't a good sign, though he was gathering himself into human form as he moved. He was dripping with ichor and blood from horrible deep slashes Natividad couldn't bring herself to look at, but his shadow carried away his injuries as he shifted. Usually he'd clean himself up when he shifted, but this time he had been too badly wounded or else he was too angry, because even after the change blood still spattered his clothing. Black ichor smoked against his skin as it burned away, but he didn't seem to notice. His black dog's anger still surrounded him like choking ash. He strode forward, not even seeming to notice Natividad, and grabbed Miguel. It was a human hand that closed hard on Miguel's arm, but when Alejandro lifted his other hand to hit him, black claws extended from the tips of broad, blunt fingers.

Natividad jumped forward to catch his hand. "Alejandro!"

Miguel flinched, but didn't try to get away or defend himself. He bowed his head, a meek attitude both he and

Natividad used to defuse black dog aggression. It was all
show, and even Alejandro knew it, really, but sometimes
you had to put on a show with black dogs, and they had to
let you get away with it.

Alejandro, jaw clenched, shaking with rage, nevertheless
lowered his hand. Natividad let him go, cautiously. Their
older brother had never hit Miguel, never since they had all
been children, but for a second she had really thought he
might. But Alejandro only shook him once instead, hard,
and let him go. Even then, though, and even with Natividad
right there, it took him a moment to get rid of his claws
and force his hand back into a fully human shape. When
he spoke, the growl of the black dog was still in the back of
his throat. "Fool! *Estupide!* You brought Mamá's gun *here*?
With *silver bullets*? What if the Dimilioc *lobos* had found
it? What would they think?"

Miguel started to answer, but Grayson Lanning spoke
first. "We might have thought," the Dimilioc Master's deep
voice said from the doorway, gravelly with the echoes of his
change, "that whatever pretty speeches you made, you had
come here hunting black wolves."

Grayson was in human form, but his eyes still burned
a dark and fiery crimson, utterly inhuman. All his injuries
were gone – well, nearly gone. One must have nearly
exceeded his shadow's ability to absorb it, for it showed
even on his human body: a wide red weal that ran across his
throat and disappeared beneath the collar of his shirt. His
shadow clung close to him, smelling of ash and blood, but
he was obviously in perfect control of himself.

Alejandro spun about at Grayson's first words, putting

himself between the Dimilioc Master and Miguel, so fast Natividad hardly saw him move. His own shadow was surging upward again in response to this new threat. His jaw began to distort into a muzzle, his bones to shorten and thicken, his back to bow with the change.

"No!" cried Natividad, darting forward to catch his wrist again, now really frightened. She tried to get between Alejandro and the Master, knowing neither of them would hurt *her*, but Alejandro shook her away, snarling. Natividad clung to his arm, refusing to be protected, and her brother snarled again, his rage terrifying–

"No," said Grayson, without emphasis. The Master did not physically move, but his power slammed through the room like a soundless sledgehammer coming down. Even Natividad felt it, and Alejandro actually staggered. The Master's power smothered her brother's shadow, forcing it down, forcing Alejandro back into his human form.

Alejandro straightened, panting, clearly sick with the stress of too many changes coming too quickly one on another – and maybe, Natividad thought, with the knowledge of his own powerlessness. He tried to speak, but the change had made human language foreign to his tongue –and now, though he tried, he could not shape coherent words. Natividad still held his arm. She shook her head when Alejandro tried to shove her back. "No," she went on quickly, praying it was true, "No, *está bien*, 'Jandro. The Master won't harm us."

"You sound very confident of that," Grayson said, his tone harsh with anger, or maybe just with the echo of his black dog. "What *is* this you brought us? Is *this* Malvern

Vonhausel, with upwards of *thirty* black dogs under his shadow? This is a detail I do not recall you mentioning! Now he has come here and seen that we are weak, do you think he will go away again?"

When he put it like that, it did sound bad. Natividad stared at him, trying not to look frightened because it was always dangerous to be afraid of black dogs, even if they were your friends. Even if they were your family. And the Dimilioc Master was neither.

"We didn't know how many wolves Dimilioc had lost," Miguel protested. "How could we know?" He walked forward, touched Alejandro on the arm in passing, and faced Grayson. He dropped to his knees before the Master, turning his head to expose his throat in formal submission.

Grayson stared down at him, but did not, at least, seem inclined to hit him. "Well, boy," he rumbled at last. "You feared your father's enemy enough to bring a weapon, I see. *Silver* bullets. Shall I understand that Edward actually encouraged you to involve yourself in black dog battles?"

"Not exactly, sir, but Papá thought we should be able to defend ourselves, especially when the war–"

"Do not parse law with me, boy! Did your father never teach you that our human kin *stay out of the fighting?* Which is for your own safety, boy; humans take their *own* wounds!"

"Staying back from the fighting didn't protect *your* human kin," Miguel pointed out, his calm voice sliding like an unexpected knife through the Master's anger.

Grayson, taken aback, stared down at Miguel in a silence that might, Natividad was afraid, become far more dangerous than his previous anger. She shuddered, shifting closer to Alejandro, grateful for the arm he put around her shoulders.

Miguel said quickly, "Forgive me, sir, but it's the truth! It *is* the truth, and anyway, if I broke black dog laws, they're Dimilioc laws, made in a different time, when Dimilioc owned the world. They're your laws, you can change them – you *have* to change them." His voice rose with the urgency of his need to persuade the Master. "It's different now! Those laws only made sense when there were lots of Dimilioc wolves! Everything's different now!" Forgetting himself, he looked up into the Master's face and met his hard, dangerous stare.

Natividad tensed, and beside her Alejandro went stone-still, but Grayson still did not hit Miguel, who, remembering caution, looked down again. He said stubbornly, "If you will trust your human kin to use guns loaded with silver, then we can be an asset to you, not a vulnerability. Sir, please, respectfully, you're right about Vonhausel not just going away again – I don't think he will, sir, no. Wouldn't this be a good time to change outdated laws to match the world as it is now?"

Ezekiel came in, quietly, in time to hear Miguel's plea. He stood with his arms crossed over his chest, his head tilted at a sardonic angle. He completely lacked the echoes of anger and blood that clung to Alejandro and even to Grayson and ought to trail after any black dog who had been fighting. It was a level of control Natividad had not even imagined. He looked poised, cool, unapproachable, and very dangerous – it was more than just physical presence, Natividad thought, though Ezekiel had plenty of that. This was an intense psychic presence, sort of. He just seemed to take up more space than anyone else in the room, even Grayson.

He said into the fraught pause that followed Miguel's words, "The boy has a point."

Grayson turned his head to stare at Ezekiel. He asked in his hard, gravelly voice, "How did you miss that gun?"

Ezekiel angled his head to the side, showing Grayson his throat. "I have no idea." He lifted an eyebrow at Miguel. "How did you hide it?"

Miguel hesitated. He said after a moment, "It's a light gun, a LadySmith .22. It was Mamá's gun. I took that one because it would be easy to hide." He hesitated again, flushing, and then added, "I wrapped it up in Natividad's extra, um, underthings, with a strong rose sachet to hide the scent of the silver."

Natividad straightened in indignation. "You did what?"

"Well, you like rose scent," Miguel said to her. He added to Ezekiel, "Then I wrapped all of that in two layers of plastic. I thought even if you looked in the pack, even if you searched it, you'd probably not go through Natividad's, uh, personal things. The gun's so light I thought you might not notice the weight."

Ezekiel was smiling: a thin, cold sort of smile, but a smile. "Clever. I didn't." He looked at Grayson. "My mistake. I beg your pardon, Master."

"Arrogance is your besetting sin, Ezekiel," the Master said, not angrily. Simply stating a fact. "Next time, you'll remember this."

"Yes," said Ezekiel.

"And you," Grayson growled, once more focusing on Miguel. "You brought that gun and that ammo because you *knew* your father's enemy, having killed him, would stalk you. Is that how it was?"

"Not exactly," Miguel said in a subdued tone. Alejandro tensed, his weight coming forward on his toes.

"Settle down, pup." Grayson growled, rather testily, but, to Natividad's relief, without real anger. "I hardly intend to beat answers out of your human brother."

Natividad almost laughed in nervousness and surprise, but bit her tongue and choked it back to a strangled-sounded cough. Ezekiel tilted a sardonic eyebrow at her, but she couldn't guess what he was thinking. She looked away from him.

"We didn't *know* Vonhausel would come after us," Miguel protested, but without any great conviction. "Anyway, we *really* didn't know you would have so few wolves here to meet him."

Alejandro fixed the Master with a brief, hard stare and put a supportive hand on Miguel's shoulder. Natividad said quickly, trying not to sound too anxious, knowing she wasn't able to pull that off, "If anybody can stop Vonhausel, it's Dimilioc. That's still true. Isn't it?"

"I'm not quite confident *he* thinks so," Ezekiel said, light and sardonic and amused. He glanced sidelong at the Master. "I must admit, I've become quite curious about this Vonhausel."

"Long before your time," growled the Dimilioc Master. "Somewhat before mine. The man I remember did not have the strength we saw this morning. One gathers he has become more than a typical vicious hot-blooded stray black dog." He sounded disgusted, but no longer angry. He gave Alejandro a hard look, but added a curt nod when Alejandro looked down. "Got your shadow under control, pup, do you?"

Natividad gave her brother an anxious look, wondering if he had recovered language enough to answer, but Ezekiel said smoothly before Alejandro could try to answer, "Master, I agree we may wish to discuss many things, including our interesting new enemy and the possibility of revising Dimilioc law to match this brave new world of ours. But possibly of more immediate importance, you may want to, ah, welcome, our newest guests. I believe they are in the dining room. Zachariah is making a second breakfast."

"How industrious of Zachariah," growled Grayson. "I presume this is his subtle method of reassuring our... guests."

"Exactly," Ezekiel agreed. "Which they may need, after the welcome they've already had. No doubt it's hard to believe Dimilioc's facing an existential threat when it's stuffing you with biscuits and eggs. Nevertheless..."

"Indeed," said Grayson. He turned his shoulder to Alejandro and gave Miguel an impatient wave. "Oh, get up, boy. Got any more silver ammunition?"

Miguel jumped to his feet. "No, sir. I only had a little–"

"You used it to excellent effect," said Ezekiel. "Which I'll also remember."

Grayson gave Ezekiel a sour look, but only asked Miguel, "Got any more surprises tucked away? Bazooka in your back pocket? Grenades tucked inside a stuffed animal? Rocket launcher wrapped up in frilly petticoats, right along with its rockets? Well?"

"No, sir," Miguel repeated, very meek.

"Then come to breakfast," Grayson said. "We'll hear your story, boy, and no equivocations." He turned toward the door, jerking his head for Ezekiel to go with him.

The young Dimilioc executioner turned to follow, but over his shoulder, he said, "You, kid. Miguel. That was good shooting." He added to Alejandro, with casual authority, "We've all seen now you can keep your head when you're fighting, which is admirable. Keep it now, hear me? Don't be rough on your brother." He walked out without waiting for an answer.

Once they were gone, Natividad lifted a theatrical hand to her brow and pretended to collapse into the nearest chair. Alejandro ignored her. He glared at Miguel.

His younger brother dropped his gaze, but he also said stubbornly, "I'm sorry, Alejandro, but I did save your lives, you know. Grayson Lanning knows it, too. So, I was right to bring the gun – and you wouldn't have let me, so I was right not to tell you."

Alejandro was not prepared to admit this, though Natividad knew they all knew it was true. He glared harder. "Lucky fool," he said in Spanish. "What if he'd killed you?" He'd gotten language back, obviously. Natividad was almost sorry, although he was going to yell at Miguel eventually and she supposed they might as well get it over with.

"He wouldn't have," Miguel said, unfortunately using that patient tone of his that drove Alejandro wild. "For saving all your lives?"

Alejandro bared his teeth in an expression that was not a smile. "He's the Dimilioc Master! *Estúpido!* You don't know what he'll do! We've led an enemy to his doorstep, haven't we? And now you defy him to his face, and you may say, '*Oh, it's all fine*,' but what if it hadn't been? If he'd tried to hurt you, if he had, I'd have fought him, Miguel, but I couldn't have won, and then Natividad would have been alone here! Did you think of that?"

Miguel started to answer, but Natividad protested first. "Leave me out of it! And don't you fight Grayson, Alejandro, you hear me? No matter what! Promise me!" She knew already that he wouldn't promise, and couldn't, but she glared at him anyway.

"I didn't shoot until it was obvious I had to," Miguel put in. He took a step toward Alejandro. "Don't be angry, 'Jandro. I tried not to shoot at all. But there were so many against you. If I hadn't had the gun–"

"I know!" Alejandro snarled, and stalked away, out the door. He stopped in the hallway, facing the wall, obviously wanting to slam his fist right through the fine wood paneling. Then, with a hard, jerky movement, he swung away and strode down the hall. Natividad thought he showed amazing control not to let his shadow rise in the *cambio de cuerpo* when he was clearly longing for violence.

"He knows I'm right," Miguel said in a very low voice, meaning for only Natividad to hear him.

"Of course!" she said, looking after Alejandro. "Do you think that helps? Come on! He can't manage Grayson Lanning by himself."

Though neither Harrison Lanning nor his son was in the dining room, Grayson and Ezekiel and Zachariah were already there, devouring cold ham and hot biscuits and eggs fried in butter. It seemed incredible that after everything that had happened, the Dimilioc wolves meant to just sit down and go on with their breakfast... but Natividad had to admit, if you wanted to reassure somebody that everything was fine, eggs and biscuits and bacon were one way to do it. The smell was seductive. She hadn't realized her appetite had returned until presented with the promised biscuits.

But she couldn't just go in and take a seat. Those guests Ezekiel had mentioned were already there: black dogs they didn't know, so there was reason to be cautious. Two men, but also, to Natividad's dismay, two *girls*, one maybe Alejandro's age and one younger, just a baby, maybe twelve or thirteen. There weren't a lot of female black dogs, which was good – Natividad vividly remembered Mamá telling her, *A woman shouldn't ever be born a black dog.* Then she had explained why.

Natividad flinched away from thinking about what happened to nearly all of the sons and too many of the daughters of black dog women. Not that either of those girls would welcome pity – especially not from a girl who was Pure. They were probably going to hate her.

They weren't Mexican, those girls; they looked maybe Egyptian or something. The older one was extraordinarily beautiful and obviously knew it. She wore tight black jeans, low black boots, and a silky white blouse. Her earrings were moonstone and crystal, dangling on fine chains that looked like silver but had to be steel. She had settled into her chair in an explicitly sensual pose, one long leg extended and the other drawn up, her hands linked around her knee. Her head was tilted back, her eyes half closed in an expression of amused contempt, her black hair falling sheer and straight almost to the floor. She had wide-set slanted eyes and broad cheekbones, a small mouth and a pointed chin. She made Natividad think of a praying mantis, not only because of her delicately triangular face, but also because of the violence hidden, barely, behind the stillness she showed on the surface.

The other girl, obviously her sister, was small and delicate and looked like she might also grow into a beauty, except for a long curved scar that started at the corner of her mouth and cut across her cheek toward her ear, pulling her mouth awry. Someone must have cut her with silver, to leave a scar like that. *She* wasn't striking sexy poses – and it wasn't just how young she was: her hair was cropped short with a total lack of attention to how it looked, and she was wearing faded jeans and an equally faded T-shirt that had probably once been black, and no jewelry at all. She was staring down at the table, not in ordinary black-dog submissiveness, but like she was trying to make herself invisible. Natividad felt sorry for her, a scarred young girl black dog with a showy sister like that.

"*That's* unexpected," whispered Miguel, coming up beside Natividad and looking over her shoulder. "They *are* black dogs, aren't they? Too bad," he added, even more quietly, too quietly for anyone farther away than Natividad and Alejandro to hear him, but with considerable fervor. "Look at that girl!"

He meant the older one, of course. Both her brothers were staring at her. Natividad couldn't even blame them, but they were stupid if they thought a girl like that would want anything to do with either of them. But boys *were* stupid. Natividad nudged Miguel, frowning hard at him. He raised his eyebrows at her, pretending not to know what she meant. Then he stared at the girl again.

Natividad muttered, "They're going to hate me."

"You can handle them," Miguel said, with infuriating assurance. He looked at Alejandro. "Can we go in? I'm starving."

"And you want to meet that girl. *Pendejo!*" Natividad whispered back, but her twin just grinned at her.

"*Allí*, at the end of the table, by Ezekiel," Alejandro murmured. "You see there are places on the left side of the table." He led the way forward, allowing his black dog shadow to rise just a little – Natividad felt it. It wasn't lack of control, but a warning to those strangers.

Everyone looked up as they entered the room. The beautiful girl curled her lip and looked away again; her little sister stared at Natividad for a long moment and then realized she was staring, flinched, and looked away. That was strange, a black dog showing submission to a Pure girl; Natividad frowned. Then she was distracted as the older male black dog, red-haired and good looking, probably about Grayson's age, looked her up and down with a close and insulting attention. "Pretty as well as Pure," he said approvingly.

Natividad glared at him. He laughed and indulgently glanced down, as a powerful black dog might in humoring a pup. Natividad took a breath, but Alejandro closed his hand hard on her wrist under the pretext of guiding her to a chair. She pretended not to notice, but she also didn't say anything. Yet.

Alejandro also stared steadily into the red-haired stranger's face, letting his shadow come up a little more: *Back off.*

"Meaning no offense," said the black dog easily. He glanced casually aside: a concession because he knew he'd been insulting.

The other male, a round-faced young man, blond-haired and freckled, said casually to Alejandro, "Don't raise your hackles at us, hey? Grayson's already said it's hands-off till she's sixteen. But, hey, pretty bird," he added to Natividad, "We're not *blind*, you know. Can't blame a guy for looking. When you're sixteen, how about you and me…"

"Watch it, *amigo*," Natividad warned him, ignoring the hard pressure of Alejandro's hand on her arm, "or your irresistible charm will sweep me off my feet and I'll swoon in your arms on my sixteenth birthday – and you might ask Ezekiel how he'd like that before you say that's fine with you."

Ezekiel glanced up and grinned. He leaned back in his chair, stretching out his long legs and resting one elbow on the table, the very personification of arrogant self-satisfaction. Natividad almost laughed, but that would have ruined it. The rude black dog, who had already started a smart rejoinder, closed his mouth, looking unsettled. Satisfied, Natividad let Alejandro seat her between himself and Miguel.

"James Mallory," the Dimilioc Master said to Alejandro, pointing a blunt finger at the red-haired man. He indicated the younger man. "And the irresistibly charming Benedict Mallory. James, Benedict, this is our newest Dimilioc wolf,

Alejandro Toland, who approached us on his own initiative."

"A Toland pup?" James said. "Well, well."

"So, we have recovered all of the traditional Dimilioc bloodlines except Hammond," said Grayson. "Yes. And that is Alejandro's brother Miguel, who shot a number of our attackers with silver bullets before your timely arrival, or you might have found half the black dogs in creation waiting for you in the ashes of our house when you arrived." The very flatness of the Master's tone acted as a kind of emphasis. All four newcomers looked at Miguel with respect but Natividad stared at the Master. She was sure he had done that on purpose, deliberately raising Miguel's status with all the Dimilioc wolves. She decided suddenly that she might actually *like* Grayson Lanning, even though liking the Dimilioc Master seemed as if it might be against the rules or something.

Miguel, with the black wolves all staring at him, said apologetically, "When you don't have a shadow, you have to improvise."

Benedict Mallory laughed. "Improvise, is it? Shot three of 'em, did you?" He looked at Grayson. "Don't we have a law about that?"

"I believe we may possibly find this an appropriate time to reassess several Dimilioc laws," Grayson said, his tone very bland.

Miguel coughed. Ezekiel laughed openly. Natividad grinned, now certain she really *did* like the Dimilioc Master, which she had not expected at all.

"And this," said the Master to Alejandro, "is Keziah, who descends from one of the Saudi cabals, but has declined to claim a specific line or name. She has been living rather quietly on the west coast with her sister, Amira. James and Benedict took Keziah my invitation, which, as you see, she accepted. So, Dimilioc increases." He lifted an ironic eyebrow. What he meant, Natividad was sure, was, *So, you see you are not the only one who thought of your plan.* Alejandro glanced aside, color rising in his face. Miguel looked suddenly thoughtful.

"And barely in time, we find," said Zachariah Korte. He looked at Grayson. "I admit I would never have expected that sort of concerted attack from mere strays – even with a Dimilioc exile to lead them."

Natividad looked quickly at Grayson, but the Dimilioc Master merely ate a bite of ham, not seeming immediately inclined to begin with the hard questions.

Zachariah lifted his shoulders in a minimal shrug. He held the plate of eggs out to Natividad and added, smiling at her, "Your enemies seem disconcertingly determined. Even so, I trust you will not swoon in my arms in revenge if I say that acquiring *you* is a piece of luck for us all, whatever nuisance has tracked you to our doorstep."

"Luck, indeed," said Keziah scornfully. "Of course, we must be pleased to have a Pure bitch to protect from her special enemies."

"Keziah," Grayson said, his voice dropping into a register even lower than his usual deep rumble.

The girl lifted elegant eyebrows at the Dimilioc Master. But then, as he did not look away, her eyes dropped.

"It's not the girl's fault she's Pure," Grayson said. He looked deliberately from Keziah to Amira and back again.

"Dimilioc does indeed protect the Pure. We have protected them since St Walburga coaxed the first Pure birth from a black dog mother."

That was not exactly what Walburga, daughter of St Richard of Wessex and niece of St Boniface of Germany, had been trying to do, nor why she had later been canonized, Natividad thought, but it did explain why she had later been recognized as the patron saint of those attacked by mad dogs and werewolves.

What St Walburga had been trying to do was cleanse the black dog taint from the unborn daughter of a black dog woman. She had succeeded, sort of. And sort of failed. That had not been a miracle, or that was the decision of the Church, though Mamá had always said maybe the magic had been divinely inspired. But everyone agreed the saint had made a powerful spell that no one else exactly understood. On Walpurgisnacht, the Pure as well as German peasants still laid out gifts of honey and wheat for the saint, and with similar prayers.

Later, when she was an abbess at Heidenheim in Germany, St Walburga, with the first of the Pure girls who had become nuns at the abbey there, had also developed the *Beschwichtigend*. The *Aplacando,* Mamá called it, the Calming: the magic that protected a black dog from his most savage urges, especially the bloodlust that drove black dogs to hunt and kill the Pure. Very soon after that, some black dogs had realized the advantage the Pure could bring them: not merely better control over their own shadows, but also black dog sons born with superior control and, if they were lucky, Pure daughters who could bind families together and let a civilized black dog patrimony carry on from one generation to the next. Gehorsam had been founded in Heidenheim, first of the black wolf Houses; and Dimilioc in Britain; and Lumondiere in France; and much later, and not the same, the Dacha in Russia.

But despite the *Aplacando*, it was no wonder that many black dog women, whose sons were always destroyed by their shadows and half of whose daughters were stillborn, hated any Pure girl they might meet. Natividad looked at the table, though she guessed it was hopeless to try to appease Keziah.

"You knew, when James made you my offer, that Dimilioc values the Pure," Grayson told the girl. "You knew it when you came here. I do not want to lose you. You and your sister are both valuable. But you are not more valuable to Dimilioc than Natividad Toland. You need not like one another. But you must be civil. And, preferably, not homicidal. I expect you both to permit Natividad to work the *Beschwichtigend* for you. I'm perfectly certain James explained that this would be a necessary condition for anyone wishing to belong to Dimilioc."

Amira looked away. But Keziah said, her voice smooth, beautiful, and chillingly indifferent, "Of course. We knew it anyway. Everyone knows that you Dimilioc wolves breed for Purity. You want your sons to rule their shadows and your daughters born with light in their hands. That's well enough, for those who care about such things. Whatever Dimilioc wishes is well enough."

"Indeed," Grayson said, with a slight, ironic lift of his eyebrows. He glanced around the table. "Dimilioc now numbers ten wolves. This is an improvement, but, as has recently become clear, far from adequate if we are to be challenged by a determined enemy." He looked grimly at Alejandro. "Perhaps now is an appropriate time to hear a less condensed version of your father's relationship with Malvern Vonhausel. And your own."

Natividad saw her black dog brother stop himself from glancing at Miguel. He met Grayson Lanning's hard stare and said, carefully, "This Vonhausel, he was our father's enemy forever, and our mother's. Of course he has forced other black dogs into a shadow pack, or he would not have been able to kill Papá. But I did not think he would bring them and follow us here. I did not think Dimilioc would have so few black wolves to face him."

"And volunteered nothing, even when you saw how few Dimilioc wolves remain," Grayson said, his tone still grim.

Zachariah leaned back in his chair, ostentatiously relaxed, deliberately breaking the gathering tension. "Malvern Vonhausel," he said thoughtfully. "He was a strong black wolf. Not so personally strong as to be a threat, as I recall. He couldn't have forced so many strays to follow him. Not then. But he was ambitious. I remember that. Ambitious to find a way to harness black dog magic, codify it... make it *useful*, as Pure magic is useful. He wanted to work out a far more aggressive kind of magic. He quarreled with Edward about that, because he wanted to use the Pure in his studies. Just one or two, he said: a reasonable sacrifice if we could gain a better understanding of demonic magic. Edward was vehemently opposed, but Thos was interested, James, do you remember?"

"That whole thing was before my time, a bit," James Mallory said. "You and Harrison were Vonhausel's contemporaries, not me. I remember the quarrel, but the reason for it, that's something else, isn't it?"

Zachariah smiled, without much humor. "Well, that's it in a nutshell: Malvern wanted to work out a useful kind of demonic magic. *Thos* hoped he might find a way for black dogs to gain permanent ascendance over vampires and those damned blood kin of theirs. Thos didn't mind breaking eggs, but Edward was dead against anything that would require sacrificing the Pure, and was damned vocal about it."

"Indeed," said Grayson. He tapped his fingers thoughtfully on the table. "Yes. I had forgotten the subject of that dispute, but I remember the quarrel."

"Oh, yes," Zachariah agreed. "Edward could match Vonhausel, but not Thos, of course. That's the part you remember, I'm sure. There was a huge argument, but a very short fight. After that Edward had no choice but to lower his eyes and hold his tongue."

"Edward Toland defied Thos, and lived?" Benedict asked, clearly incredulous. "Thos didn't kill him?"

"He couldn't. Remember, this was right after Thos first took the Mastery. He hadn't yet gained the strength he had later." Zachariah glanced briefly at Ezekiel. His nephew gazed back at him without expression. Zachariah went on, "Edward was popular in the house, especially with the Pure. He had strong support from plenty of black dogs, too. Thos didn't dare kill him."

"So, he exiled him," James surmised. "But then, why exile Vonhausel too?"

"You're getting ahead of the story. No, what happened next… The way Harrison and I put it together afterward, what happened was this: Malvern murdered Linda Hammond. You remember that, of course, Grayson, though probably not the story behind it. He murdered her and used her blood somehow to capture her magic… or something. Made something, or worked out something, I don't know. I don't think anyone ever knew exactly what he'd done. Except Thos, perhaps. *He* was apparently happy enough with whatever it was that he was willing to accept Linda's murder. Edward wasn't."

"But Edward still couldn't fight Thos," said Benedict. "Right?"

"Exactly. He couldn't. As had been so recently and vividly demonstrated for us all. But immediately afterward, Edward was gone."

"Yes," Grayson said slowly. "I remember that. Thos said he'd exiled Edward, and then he exiled Vonhausel as well, with some explanation or other no one believed – I don't remember what. I thought most likely Vonhausel had killed Edward in defiance of Thos's order, and Thos exiled him for that."

"That's right, that's what everybody thought," agreed James. "But even at the time, you know, it didn't make sense. *I* always thought Thos himself murdered Edward, then put the blame on Vonhausel and exiled him to hide what he'd done. I was damned sorry about it."

"But you didn't dare challenge Thos over it," said Zachariah, then quickly lifted a hand to forestall a hot response. "No, neither did I, and I thought the same, at first. But after Malvern left – left of his own will, mind you; he was gone *before* Thos gave the order of exile, and by all accounts he went in a rage and in a hurry – after that, Harrison and I came to believe that Edward had stolen something of his, and fled with it." He glanced at Miguel, then at Alejandro. "We decided Malvern had gone after him, and Thos covered everything up after the fact with orders of exile so he'd look like he'd been in control all the time."

Ezekiel lifted an ironic eyebrow. He had leaned back in his chair, his legs stretched out and ankles crossed, his hands in his pockets. He said nothing, as he had said nothing to any of this account, but Natividad thought he might be trying to make it all make sense in terms of the Thos Korte he'd known. She somehow thought he might be having trouble with that, though she wasn't exactly sure why she thought so. *She* was having trouble imagining what in the world Vonhausel had done with that poor Pure woman's magic when he murdered her. Or thought he'd done, or meant to do. It ought to be impossible for a black dog to make or do anything useful with his shadow magic – but if he hadn't, then what had Papá stolen? However, if Papá had stolen something from Vonhausel, then Mamá must have known, too, and then why hadn't Mamá ever told *her* about it?

She remembered when Mamá had explained about the blood of the Pure, about what the blood kin did with Pure women when they caught them. "Pure blood to break Pure working," Mamá had said. She had been showing Natividad the pentagrams on the village church: on the windows of blue and pink glass, on the carved wooden door, and on every individual stone at a woman's shoulder height, inside and out. Those stones were head-high for Natividad, who had been about eight. She had reached up to lay her hand on the stone nearest the door. The stone was warm under her hand, only it wasn't really warmth, but a good feeling *like* warmth.

"Grandmamá and Tía Maria drew all those stars," Mamá explained. "And I and Tía Maria did the mandala around the church yard. This church is the safest place in Potosi. But always remember, a vampire can shatter even our protections if they pour our lifeblood out over our mandala or across the threshold of the church. You must never let the blood kin catch you alive, Natividad, because they will use your death against the innocent if they can."

Natividad had shivered.

"Do not be afraid. I will show you a better place to hide if they come," Mamá told her, and took her to the live oak standing inside the circle of young pines. "Twenty-one pines and one oak," Mamá said. "You may not wish to hide in the church, Natividad: that is for innocent people and children, but there are some things you may do better if you are here and not in the church." Mamá looked down at Natividad and sighed. "Someday soon I must show you…"

Natividad didn't understand. She was puzzled by that sigh and by something else in her mother's tone, something she did not understand. "Mamá, are you sad?"

"No, no, *mia hija*. No, I am not sad. Only… No, never mind. Put your hands on the tree. Do you feel the pentagrams I carved into the wood when you were born? Also there is a saint's finger-bone buried among the roots.

Saint Louisa's bone, they say it was. My Great-grandmamá
buried it there when she planted the oak. If you must hide
quickly, come here for safety. *With* Alejandro. Come here
with your brother if you can. A tangle of shadows can hide
you from any who would do harm to you, whether your
enemies are blood kin or black dogs."

Natividad had not understood how shadows could
tangle up, or which shadows were supposed to. And when
Vonhausel had come with his shadow pack to kill them all,
Alejandro had not been at home: he had been miles away,
hunting in the desert near Hualahuises, hunting under the
moon. She had run to the oak all by herself, through the
smoke rolling down the mountain from the burning village.
She had tucked herself down in among the oak's heavy
roots where they heaved out of the gritty soil, and no one…
no one had found her, all that night.

She swallowed, pulling herself, with brutal effort, out
of unbearable memory. She rubbing her eyes hard with
the back of her hand and looked quickly around the table,
trying to be subtle, hoping no one had noticed her sudden
struggle with tears.

James was looking grim, and his younger brother
Benedict a little bit scared, or maybe confused, or maybe
both. Ezekiel was sardonically unreadable, an expression
Natividad was sure he practiced in front of a mirror. Keziah
looked contemptuous and bored and sexy – she probably
practiced that in front of *her* mirror. Every day, probably.
When Natividad accidentally met her eyes, her lip curled,
and she looked away again with ostentatious indifference,
but at least she didn't seem to think anything odd about

Natividad's own expression. Her little sister Amira had drawn her legs up and tucked herself back in her chair, trying to be unnoticeable. Grayson tapped one finger gently on the table, frowning with a heavy grimness he probably didn't have to practice.

Zachariah, oldest of them all, looked calm and a little abstracted, with a faintly self-derisive edge to his mouth – he was thinking, probably, of those difficult days: murder and secrecy and a Master he hated, or at least didn't trust; the sort of Master who would let an ambitious Dimilioc black dog get away with killing a Pure woman. He said, "Harrison and I might have taken Thos down right then, if we'd worked together. We did think of it. It would have saved us all a good deal of grief if we'd done it. But everything calmed back down after Edward and Malvern both disappeared, and Thos consolidated his hold, and we lost the moment."

"If you had tried to fight him then, Thos would have killed you both," Grayson said, dismissing this putative failure with a curt gesture.

Ezekiel leaned back in his chair, a casual movement that nevertheless gathered all eyes. He said, "So, I'm sure this is all very interesting, but now we must wonder what light Edward's sons might be able to shine on all this ancient history." He lifted an eyebrow at Alejandro.

Alejandro hesitated.

Miguel said, calmly, "Malvern Vonhausel allied with a blood kin clique. He allied with the blood kin to get access to vampire magic. Papá tried to stop him and then tried to kill him, only he couldn't, and Papá tried to tell Thos Korte, but Thos wouldn't listen, and finally Papá ran south, and met Mamá, and Mamá hid us all. But Vonhausel's making common cause with the blood kin, that was the first move in the war, twenty years before anybody realized it had even started, Papá said."

Everyone, including Alejandro, stared at Miguel. He shrugged apologetically, ducking his head. "Papá used to talk to me about it. But if he stole something from Vonhausel first, I don't know about that."

"And then the war came," said Grayson. "And Vonhausel came after your father. I think we may surmise that was more than a casual or personal enmity."

"Oh, well... Actually, he came after Mamá, not Papá," Miguel said. He could not keep his tone level, though Natividad knew how hard he tried. "He took her sister, first, our Tía Maria..." He stopped.

"He did not come alone," Alejandro said. His voice was harsh with anger and grief. "Without Dimilioc to stop him, Vonhausel found a lot of black dogs to follow him. They came. I wasn't... I wasn't there. Natividad and Miguel hid. I found them there... later. Afterward."

"They killed everybody," Natividad said. Her voice sounded small and shaky, even to her. She fixed her eyes on the smooth grain of the table between her hands and tried not to see or think about anything else. "Even the goats and the... the chickens. So, we had to go... we had to go somewhere."

"I said we should come here," Alejandro said, with considerable force, not looking at Miguel. "Vonhausel had already killed our father and mother. I did not think he would follow us. There seemed no reason for him to follow us."

"He wants Natividad," Miguel said apologetically. "Because she's Mamá's daughter, and I think there's something about Mamá's magic. Something she passed on to Natividad."

Natividad stared at him.

"I kind of think so," Miguel said to her, even more apologetically.

"Well," said Zachariah when Natividad did not say anything further, "And how excited he must be, now that he has not only found Natividad but also discovered Dimilioc's weakness. The vampire blood kin lost the war, but I imagine *Vonhausel* still hopes to win it." He looked at Grayson. "You were *very* right about our need to recruit. Unfortunately, this trouble is worse than I think even you expected."

"It seems we've joined Dimilioc precisely in time to watch it destroyed utterly," Keziah said smoothly. "How delightful."

Grayson gave her a look. He said to the other Dimilioc wolves, "I think we must indeed recruit in greater numbers than I had anticipated. And with a little more alacrity. James, you had better go to Boston this afternoon. Ezekiel, you will fly to Chicago tomorrow morning."

James looked disconcerted, but Ezekiel nodded casually, as though he'd expected this order. Miguel asked, "Sir? Who are we recruiting?"

Grayson deliberately spread fig preserves on a biscuit. Then he leaned an elbow on the table and looked at Miguel, his expression unreadable. "There is a pair of black dogs in Boston that may do well for Dimilioc. Brothers. They have never caused difficulty enough there to provoke us into killing them; now we may be glad of it. They also have two human sisters who might prove useful. I believe they will be glad to receive my invitation, which is why James will deliver it, using," he glanced at Natividad, "the famous Mallory charm."

Miguel nodded. "And in Chicago, sir?"

"Yes. There we have a black dog named Thaddeus Williams. I knew his father slightly: a very strong black dog with more sense and less temper than one would expect of a stray. I believe Thaddeus takes after his father. For example, he has taken a Pure wife. That's against Dimilioc law, of course, but now it only increases his value to us. I want both Thaddeus and his wife, but I suspect they will not be inclined to cooperate. Ezekiel will bring them here for me."

Yes, Natividad understood that. If Grayson sent the Dimilioc executioner, it was not to deliver a suggestion, but a command. She wasn't sure she liked the idea of... *forcible* recruitment.

Miguel didn't seem worried at all. He asked, just as though it was a matter of academic curiosity, "How many other black dogs will you ask to join Dimilioc, sir?"

Grayson cut a slice of ham into small, neat pieces and began to eat them, one at a time. Natividad thought he was not going to answer. But after a moment he paused, his fork in the air, and said, "I had initially thought to stop with the Meade brothers and Williams. Now... I think we had better recruit to something like full strength. I think Dimilioc will need... shall we say, a minimum of thirty wolves."

Neither Zachariah nor Ezekiel looked surprised, and

Keziah leaned back in her chair, looking suddenly both thoughtful and pleased. But Benedict and James both stared at Grayson. "Thirty?" said Benedict.

"They'd outnumber us three to one!" James protested.

Grayson looked thoughtfully at the Mallory brothers. "I think it would be better if there were no 'them.' No 'us.' Only Dimilioc. Thirty black wolves and a reasonable number of humans with proper blood ties, and as many of the Pure as we can find."

Benedict seemed subdued by the Master's flat tone, but James smacked his hand down on the table in open anger. "You'll turn Dimilioc into a mockery of itself! A wild pack filled with internal division and murder, black dogs with no history, with no ties to each other or to us! They may call themselves by our name, but whatever exists by that name, it will not be Dimilioc! How can you consider this?"

"I think the proper phrase," Keziah said to him, with cutting sarcasm, "is, 'a mockery of what Dimilioc *once was*'. You are much reduced, aren't you? A fact I don't think you emphasized much during your invitation. *That* is why the Master considers this. When this enemy of yours brings his pack of black dogs and shadow shifters against Dimilioc again, what do you want to do? Face him with seven true Dimilioc wolves, pure of heart and bloodline? That would certainly end your difficulties."

James Mallory stared at her.

"So, we do thank you for your invitation, which has brought us into your danger," Keziah added mockingly. "And you had better thank us for accepting, Irishman, and for fighting alongside Dimilioc, and for remaining now, when we might go to your enemy instead."

James opened his mouth, but then closed it again without saying anything.

Before the silence could become too fraught, Grayson said smoothly, "We are pleased you and your sister accepted Dimilioc's invitation, to be sure, Keziah. When we win, you will be well placed within Dimilioc."

"Yes," murmured Keziah, smiling with slow, deliberately seductive aggression. "That's why we're still here." But Natividad saw how she glanced at her sister, a swift fleeting glance, and was suddenly sure that Keziah had come to Dimilioc for exactly the reason Alejandro had – to protect her sister. It almost made her want to like the beautiful black dog girl, which was uncomfortable because she was scared of her.

"Fine. Fine. Wonderful." James glared at Grayson. "But we need wolves who are truly Dimilioc! Not ragged strays with less control than a moon-bound shifter! Not stray black dogs who can't walk down a city street without dealing out wholesale slaughter…"

One corner of Grayson's mouth twitched upward. "James, please. No, certainly not."

"The ones we bring in will be Dimilioc," Zachariah said quietly. "Given time. They or their sons."

"Dimilioc will be burned to ash and dust before they have sons!" James said furiously. "The ones who can *have* sons!"

Amira's face tightened and she looked down, though Natividad thought James had not deliberately aimed that barb at the black dog girls. Keziah's lips curved in a faint, amused smile. She ate a bite of ham, appearing untouched by any of this argument.

"We can control them until they learn to control themselves," said Ezekiel.

"*Control* them! They will be a worse enemy to us than that Vonhausel, because they'll be on the inside rather than the outside! How can you not see that?" James looked from Grayson to Zachariah to Ezekiel and back to Grayson. Meeting only a bland, blank look from the stronger Dimilioc wolves, he shoved his chair back, got to his feet, and turned to walk out.

"James," said Grayson, and despite his fury the other man stopped, though he did not turn.

"Go to Boston," Grayson told him. "Bring me Andrew and Russell Meade and their sisters. They already believe that belonging to Dimilioc is a privilege. Bring them to me burning with a desire to earn that privilege."

James still did not turn around. But before he stalked out, he gave a short nod.

"He'll do well for us," Zachariah said after he had gone.

"Of course he will," said Grayson, and ate a biscuit.

Benedict, who had been sitting very still while his brother argued with the Master, now risked a glance up. "I could go with him, Master."

Grayson gave the young man a brief smile. "Thank you, Benedict, but no. I want you here." He transferred his attention to Ezekiel. "And I want you to return from Chicago as quickly as possible."

"If Vonhausel–" Natividad began.

"Our enemy lost many of his black dogs today," Grayson said calmly. "I imagine that those who remain will be wondering whether attacking Dimilioc was such a clever idea. Some will certainly slip away into the forest to look for easier hunting elsewhere. Vonhausel himself may want to attack again today or tomorrow, but I believe he'll discover he must find black dogs to replace his losses, or else he will have to make a good many moon-bound shifters and then wait for the full moon before he can attack."

"That's all true," agreed Miguel.

Grayson's eyebrows rose at this impudence, but he said nothing. Natividad hoped Miguel was right and Grayson's analysis was correct. It had better be. If Alejandro was gone, if he and Ezekiel and James Mallory were gone and all those black dogs came again… Her brother had already come home once to find burned rubble and the bones of his kin. Natividad didn't think he could bear that again. She and Miguel wouldn't like it very much, either.

"You are finished with your breakfast?" Grayson said to Benedict Mallory. "Good. Go see how the cleanup is coming. Tell Harrison I want to see him. Then you may help Ethan with any little chores that may remain. Zachariah, if you would be so kind as to take Miguel into town and buy him a real gun. Whatever he wants."

"Half a dozen rifles," said Miguel, adding hurriedly when Grayson turned his head and lifted one heavy eyebrow, "Please, sir. Maybe a dozen, if that's alright?"

The Master surveyed him. "You plan to break them? Lose them? Designate each for a particular day of the week?"

"Well," Miguel said cautiously, "Any human can handle a gun loaded with silver. Those two human women James is supposed to bring? And there's Natividad, sir. She isn't as good as I am, but she does know how to shoot."

Grayson said, "How reassuring."

The Master's dry tone evidently reminded Miguel of the obvious fact that not every Dimilioc black wolf would wish to put silver-loaded guns into human hands. He said quickly, "You should make use of us; you know you should, especially right now when you're so hard-pressed. Human allies are something Vonhausel won't have, isn't that right? Not if his black dogs are so violent and shadow-driven, they won't tolerate humans, will they? Or if they do they'll kill them too quickly to use them properly–"

Grayson held up a hand, stopping this urgent flood of persuasion. He said to Zachariah, "A dozen rifles. Let the boy choose them."

Zachariah nodded. "If you're certain."

"Certain of the necessity," said Grayson.

Benedict started to speak, stopped. Grayson looked at him. "Nothing, sir," muttered the younger black wolf, dropping his gaze.

"Good. You may help Ethan, but first I want you to get on the Internet and order a lot of silver or silver alloy – Miguel, make a list of what you need. Include the proper equipment for casting your own ammunition. You do know how to make ammunition? Good. Go make up that list now."

The Master shifted his gaze back to Benedict as Miguel pushed back his chair and went out. "Be certain to ask for same-day shipping," he said to the young black wolf. "I don't imagine they'll manage that, but it would be good if they made the attempt. Remember to call the post office in town and tell them to notify us when the parcels arrive."

"Sir," Benedict acknowledged.

"I will show you appropriate rooms," Grayson said to the girls. "Natividad, you may come with me. You are, I trust, capable of working the *Beschwichtigend*?"

Natividad nodded, trying not to look nervous. The Calming would counter their natural bloodlust to kill the Pure, but it would not actually make the black dog girls like her, she knew. Amira just looked scared, Natividad wasn't afraid of *her*, she felt sorry for her – but she was afraid of Keziah. Alejandro laid a supportive hand on Natividad's shoulder, glaring warningly at Keziah. Amira cringed, but Keziah met Alejandro's eyes, arched an elegant eyebrow, and smiled faintly.

Ezekiel stood, a smooth movement that somehow implied menace. He said to Grayson, "You intend to give them the brown suite? I'll show them where it is." It was not *exactly* a challenge, Natividad thought – but it was not far off. It certainly was not a request.

Grayson met the younger black wolf's eyes for a long moment. Neither looked aside, but Ezekiel said easily, "If that's alright with you, Master."

Grayson lifted heavy shoulders in a minimal shrug. "That might be best. Yes, very well. I'll have instructions for you before you leave, however. See me tonight. Benedict, since Ezekiel will be otherwise occupied, book an early flight for him." He looked at Alejandro. "You'll go to Chicago with Ezekiel."

"We'll be leaving early," Ezekiel said. "Be ready to go an hour before dawn." His voice, light and mocking, made it clear that he knew perfectly well that Alejandro wanted to protest Grayson's order but did not dare argue with the Master.

Natividad gave her brother a quick look. Of course this was a test of his obedience, and maybe of Ezekiel's, and probably of the black dog girls as well. She didn't like that at all. She trusted Grayson – well, mostly – but not Keziah. And what if Vonhausel brought his shadow pack back against Dimilioc while Alejandro was gone to Chicago with Ezekiel? What then?

She could see the same questions had occurred to Alejandro. He wouldn't like to go anywhere and leave her or Miguel behind in Dimilioc – he didn't even want to let her go anywhere alone with Ezekiel and Keziah right now, whatever Grayson said. At least she could help with that. She said quickly, "You can come with me, you can help me, 'Jandro, alright?"

"With the *Beschwichtigend?*" Ezekiel said, amused.

Natividad tried to look astonished, as though every Pure woman needed her black dog brother to help her work magic. "Of course!"

Ezekiel lifted his eyebrows, but merely stood aside, looking expectantly at Keziah. The girl rose with graceful poise. Amira stood up reluctantly, keeping her sister between herself and the Dimilioc executioner. Ezekiel appeared not to notice. Natividad wondered if he was actually trying to be kind to the little girl, or if he just didn't care about her at all.

Ezekiel led the way into the hallway and lifted a hand, directing them all toward the stairs. "You'll find the brown suite comfortable," he said easily, speaking to Keziah. "Or if you don't, simply tell Grayson so. I'm sure we have rooms that would please you." He added without a pause and in exactly the same pleasant tone, "If you touch Natividad while I'm gone, I'll make you into an example for the ages."

Alejandro's jaw tightened – he was offended, Natividad knew, because he thought it was his place to make threats like that on her behalf. But he said nothing. *She* wasn't a bit offended. She was relieved and even flattered, because if Ezekiel would defend her even after looking at *Keziah*, well, wow.

Amira flinched, but Keziah just smiled and tossed her hair back over her shoulders, the crystals in her earrings ringing against one another like tiny bells. She looked very beautiful and elaborately sexy. "Will you?"

Ezekiel turned and strode up the stairs. As he walked, he shifted to his black dog form and instantly back to human, then the black dog, then human again – shifting completely with each step, a sharp blinking strobe of alternating forms, impossibly smooth and fast. The steps creaked every time he shifted to the massive black dog shape. His claws scored the wood, smoke and ash swirled with his movements; then the next step would be a light human tread. He turned at the first landing and leaned negligently on the banister, a slim human youth. But his shadow pooled at his feet, so dense even Natividad could see it clearly. He said softly, straight to Keziah, "Do you think Thos Korte made me his executioner as a *joke*? You can challenge me, if you like. I wouldn't mind at all."

Keziah smiled and said, her tone amused, "Well, perhaps not today." But she also looked aside.

"As long as you're sure," said Ezekiel. "The brown suite?" He turned and walked up the stairs, not at all concerned to have the black dog girls at his back.

The brown suite consisted of five interconnecting rooms, all in taupe and gold, brown and warm ivory. The largest room, with a beautiful fireplace, soft chairs and lovely wrought iron lamps, had plenty of space to do the *Aplacando*. Alejandro helped Natividad roll the thick rugs out of the way, then, at her gesture, opened a window to let in unfiltered daylight and air – the air was *freezing*, but that was alright. She gestured for the girls to stand several feet apart in the middle of the bare floor and drew a separate pentagram around each with a handful of sunlight and the whispered words her mother had taught her. Amira cowered when her sister gave her a little push away, but Keziah gave her a stern look and said something in Arabic or whatever language it was they spoke, and the little girl obediently crouched down inside her own pentagram. Natividad wished she could say something to reassure Amira, but of course there was nothing she could say that would help. She hurried a little so Amira would feel better as soon as possible.

But working the *Aplacando* itself actually felt kind of… strange. Natividad hadn't actually *done* it before – of course she knew how, of course Mamá had shown her, the *Aplacando* was the most important magic of all and every Pure girl learned it early. But actually *working* it felt strange. Almost, Natividad thought, like lifting a stone that was actually made out of paper, or stepping off a step that wasn't there. She *might* be doing it wrong… but she didn't *think* she could have made a mistake doing it now, when it really mattered.

She did the *Aplacando* for Amira first – maybe it just felt strange because the little girl was so young or because

Amira didn't resist. But then it was exactly the same for Keziah, and Natividad just didn't believe *Keziah* should be especially easy to work magic on. Stepping back, she frowned at Keziah. "I think… I think maybe that wasn't the first time anybody ever did the Calming for you. Was it?"

Keziah smiled, though without much humor. She shrugged. "All the Pure know how to do the *Beschwichtigend,* so why not? Anything to make Dimilioc happy. We found a Pure woman as soon as we could, as soon as we came to this country." Her voice was smooth and mocking, but she also put out a hand to gather her little sister close to her side.

Amira bowed her head and rubbed a thumb along the scar on her face, glancing covertly at Natividad through her lashes. Natividad smiled at her, and though the little girl didn't exactly smile back, she almost seemed to want to.

Alejandro said unexpectedly to Keziah, "No one will touch your sister, you know. You think you don't like the Pure, but Natividad would be very upset if anyone harmed your sister – so no one will harm her. That is what the Pure do for black dogs. If you become part of Dimilioc, you will learn that."

Keziah opened her mouth, but shut it again without making the cutting response she probably thought of first. Her uncertainty made her seem suddenly younger and less… sophisticated, or something. She looked at Natividad as though it had occurred to her for the first time that she might be a real person even though she was not a black dog.

"And you won't harm Natividad," Alejandro added. "Because everyone else would be very upset if you did." His gaze met Keziah's, and neither of them looked away. After a moment, Keziah said, still not breaking that stare, "Yes, that part was clear enough."

"Well, then, how nice we have everything settled," Ezekiel said briskly. "I'm sure Grayson will be ecstatic. And even more so if we are all still alive in the morning, so please keep that in mind if you choose to fight. Also, please, not indoors. Grayson is liable to be quite annoyed if the furniture gets broken." He glanced at Natividad and tipped his head toward the door, an invitation she accepted with alacrity, though not without a quick backward glance at her brother, who, surprising her, showed no inclination to follow.

"They *are* going to fight," she said uneasily, as soon as the door closed behind herself and Ezekiel. "I should–"

"I suspect not today or tonight," Ezekiel interrupted her smoothly. "No, Natividad, trust me for this. After your *Beschwichtigend?* She may posture, and so may your brother, but neither will actually want to fight for some time. I only warned them because the furniture can suffer merely from posturing and Grayson really would be annoyed."

Ezekiel sounded uncharacteristically relaxed himself. Natividad gave him a sharp look, but didn't say the first thing that came to her tongue, which was, "*You don't want to fight now, either, do you?*" She wondered if a really big clue to why Ezekiel was so determined to have her had just hit her between the eyes.

"Now, where shall I escort you? Plenty of time left for packing the paltry few tools of my trade…" Natividad didn't even want to know what those might be, "and with Benedict haranguing the airport into a convenient flight time on my behalf, I'm entirely at leisure. Shall I show you the rest of the house? Alas, the gardens are not very scenic at the moment..."

"The kitchen?" Natividad suggested diffidently. "Do you think Zachariah would be offended if I made bread or something? Cinnamon rolls? If you have cinnamon?" She added, at Ezekiel's raised eyebrow, "I would like to. I would like to... to do something with my hands."

Ezekiel nodded soberly. "I think I can safely promise you that no one will be offended if you make cinnamon rolls."

He helped her find mixing bowls, and then the flour and sugar – the canisters were hidden in a cabinet. The cinnamon was in the spice rack, but the *levadura* was in the freezer, which Natividad would never have guessed. It took her some time to remember the English word – yeast – but then she was pleasantly surprised to find that Ezekiel knew where it was kept. Waving away the offer of measuring cups and spoons, she began to scoop things together in the largest bowl. She asked, tentatively, not looking at him, "So, how long ago *did* Thos Korte make you his executioner?"

"Ah!" said Ezekiel. "Your ulterior motive appears! An interrogation over the eggs and butter! Nearly seven years ago. I was almost fourteen."

"Fourteen!" Natividad looked at him quickly. Ezekiel was leaning against the refrigerator, looking relaxed and amused and not at all offended. He was watching her steadily. Though his tone was light, there was no mockery in his eyes. She was sure he was telling the truth. It was hard to believe. "You were younger than I am!" she protested.

"There wasn't a black wolf in Dimilioc who could take

me, one on one." Ezekiel's voice was cool, completely matter-of-fact. "I knew that. I enjoyed it. I believe it amused Thos to have a child for his executioner, but I certainly didn't object. I liked having the older black wolves look aside from me."

Black dogs did like people to be afraid of them. Natividad stirred the dough together into a shaggy mass and scraped it out onto the floured counter. She didn't say anything.

"I expect Thos also liked the idea of training a black wolf pup to be exactly the executioner he wished. He'd been Dimilioc's executioner himself, once. He had strong ideas about the role, which he naturally passed on to me."

"Oh," said Natividad. She kneaded the bread dough, forcefully.

"He also undoubtedly wanted to instill the habit of obedience in a pup he thought might otherwise eventually be a rival. I imagine he also thought it desirable to separate me from other potential rivals. The Dimilioc executioner is everyone's worst nightmare, and certainly no one's friend." Ezekiel paused and then added, "I didn't understand any of this at the time, of course."

"Oh," said Natividad again.

"It didn't work out very well for him in the end," Ezekiel said, his tone bland. "Working out your frustrations, are you?"

Natividad blinked down at the bread dough, which had become nicely silky and elastic. "It's very therapeutic," she said austerely. "You should try it sometime. Much better than killing people."

Ezekiel grinned, that flashing grin that was so unlike the smile he wore when he was threatening people. "Speak for yourself." Then the grin disappeared. He pushed himself away from the refrigerator, took a step toward her. Natividad stared at him, taken by surprise. He seemed suddenly both taller and older. He said, the mockery gone from his voice, "I won't hurt you. You know that. I won't hurt your brother, either, if I can help it. I won't kill him. Even if he pushes me. Which I think he will, eventually."

"He thinks he has to… to protect me," Natividad explained, feeling awkward and suddenly breathless. She wanted to take a step back, but she couldn't because that would be retreating and you never retreated from black dogs. If you did, they might chase you. Of course, she sort of had the idea Ezekiel would chase her no matter what she did. She held her hands up, powdery with flour, to warn him back.

"Someone needs to protect you. Little kitten, little Pure girl, surrounded by all the big bad Dimilioc wolves." Ezekiel reached out with slow deliberation to touch her cheek, ignoring the floury palm she put on his chest to keep him at a distance. His chest was hard with muscle under Natividad's hand. She swallowed.

He said softly, his tone deliberately, mockingly, husky, "You had better depend on me to protect you, little kitten. Otherwise you'll be shooting people with your mama's gun and your brother's silver ammunition, and we can't have that."

Natividad laughed. She couldn't help it.

There was a stifled sound from the doorway, and they both turned.

Alejandro stood there, staring at them both. Natividad twitched guiltily and stepped hastily backward, though she wasn't guilty of *anything*, so it wasn't *fair*. Ezekiel gave a little mocking tilt of his head and smiled his slight, dangerous smile. He didn't step back at all.

Alejandro stared at Ezekiel. After that first searing look, he didn't glance again at Natividad.

"Well?" Ezekiel asked him softly. "There's still plenty of time left in the day, if you want to fight me."

Alejandro glared at him.

"I won't hurt you too badly. Nothing your shadow can't carry away for you."

Alejandro took a long, slow breath. He let it out. Then he turned his head aside and lowered his gaze. Natividad felt the effort of that submissive gesture in her own body. She swallowed, wanting to apologize, although she had nothing to apologize for and anyway she didn't dare say a word.

"It's not your job to protect her anymore," Ezekiel said, still very softly. There was no mockery in his tone at all, now. "When you put her into Grayson's hands, you gave that up. It's not your job, it's not your right, and you can't protect her from me anyway. Nor does she need your protection." He paused, then said with sudden exasperation, "You're not a child and I don't think you're a fool. What did you think would happen when you brought her to Dimilioc?"

Alejandro said nothing.

"It's not the same when it's for real," Natividad said, not very coherently.

"It's always for real," Ezekiel said. "All the time." He paused, then jerked his head sharply toward the door. "You can apologize to your sister later. Get out." When Alejandro did not move, he smiled and added, his light voice flicking like a whip, "I really don't advise that. I really don't. *Get out.*"

Alejandro took a stiff step back toward the door. Another. He darted one swift unreadable look at Natividad and was gone.

Ezekiel looked away, the tension running out of him like water. Natividad hadn't even been aware he was tense, until she saw that. He slanted a quick, sideways look at her face. "I'll apologize now," he said. "I don't, often, so I hope you appreciate it. I'm sorry. I should have known your brother was there."

Natividad wondered if she should feel flattered because she'd distracted him. She actually sort of did. She also felt embarrassed. She said, "It wasn't your fault. Or his."

"Certainly not *yours*," Ezekiel said. His voice was once more light, unconcerned, amused. Now that he'd recovered his balance, he looked at her directly. "I should leave you alone. You'll be alright?"

Natividad realized he was actually worried that Alejandro might be angry enough to hit her or something. She said emphatically, "You don't have to worry about *that*. But... you don't have to leave. I mean, if you want a cinnamon roll."

There was a short pause. Then Ezekiel said, "I love cinnamon rolls," and pulled a kitchen stool around so he could watch her put the dough in a bowl to rise and start getting out the things to make the icing.

6

Embarrassment and anger and shame were not good companions for the journey from Dimilioc to Chicago. Alejandro knew it. He met Ezekiel at dawn, just as ordered, and pretended hard to a cool indifference, as though that awkward encounter in the kitchen had never happened. Avoiding the subject felt like cowardice. But he was sure that bringing it up would be worse.

They drove through Lewis and then past Brighton while it was still dark, and boarded Dimilioc's little plane at Newport while the clouds above were still pink and gold with the dawn. Alejandro was embarrassed again because he had not guessed that Dimilioc owned its own planes. They were small planes, but even so Alejandro revised his estimate of Dimilioc's wealth upward.

Ezekiel flew the plane. Of course.

Despite his youth, the Dimilioc *verdugo* flew exactly the way Alejandro would have expected: with disdainful competence. He barely seemed to pay any attention to the instruments on the flight deck, but somehow he always seemed to correct for any errant gust of wind almost before it ever touched the plane.

Despite everything, Alejandro discovered that he loved flying. He loved the speed of it, the edge of danger, the roar of the motor and behind that the half-heard sound of the rushing wind. He loved the long rolling view of the world below and the towering clouds that turned into fog when they flew into them. He thought this was something *he* loved, something clean that his black dog did not care about at all, something his shadow did not touch. He wished Miguel and Natividad could be here. Someday they must certainly fly. Except that Natividad would probably love it so much she would insist on flying lessons and her own plane. Alejandro smiled at the thought. That was exactly what she would want.

"Like it, do you? Want to learn to fly?" There was an edge of mockery to the question, but Ezekiel's tone was not actually hostile.

This seemed a peace offering, or at least an offer of civility. Alejandro kept his own tone polite. "I was thinking that it may be a good thing Natividad never realized how much fun she could have if she badgered a crop duster into giving her lessons."

Ezekiel tilted his head. "She'd like flying, would she? I'll have to teach her."

That thought made Alejandro flinch. Natividad *would* want Ezekiel to teach her to fly. Alejandro had not intended to throw his sister back into Ezekiel's company. He said, "Natividad–"

"Stop," said Ezekiel. "Say the wrong thing now, and I promise you, we'll take this up again later, when I've leisure for it."

Alejandro closed his mouth. Ezekiel's hands, resting on the controls of the plane, had not tensed. His tone, still light and cool and amused, had not changed. Nevertheless, Alejandro knew that the Dimilioc *verdugo* meant that threat seriously.

After a while, as though there had been no pause, Ezekiel said, without apparent rancor, "I've no intention of hurting her, you know. Now..." and his voice took on a razor edge of threat "whether you believe that or not, shut up about it."

The dangerous edge in those last words made bright fear run down Alejandro's spine and set the hairs on the back of his neck prickling. His silence felt like cowardice; it felt like he was abandoning Natividad. But he did not dare defy Ezekiel Korte.

Alejandro was not afraid of Ezekiel because he thought the *verdugo* would kill him here and now. He was simply afraid of him. He'd thought he'd begun to get over that simple physical fear and now found he had not, and was ashamed that he had not, but the shame made no difference. And he knew that Ezekiel must be aware of all of this.

Ezekiel turned back to the plane's instruments. "I'll show you the controls," he said, his voice rough, but no longer holding that razor sharp threat. "It would be useful if you could fly this thing."

Alejandro made no attempt to answer, but he paid attention. Even if he hadn't been interested, he wouldn't have dared do otherwise.

The plane landed in Chicago almost on time. There was no snow in this city, but everything – the vast lake they had seen from the plane, and the ground, and all the buildings, and the sky above – was gray and unpleasant. The air felt heavier despite the wind, and everything smelled thickly of car exhaust. It was nearly 5 o'clock in the afternoon. In Vermont, it would have been dark. Even here, it would soon be dusk, and the heavy moon would rise for the first night of its full strength. Alejandro thought he could already feel the moon's tidal pull, for all that the moon itself still lay hidden in the light above.

"Get a map," Ezekiel said, waving Alejandro toward a kiosk as they made their way out of the airport. "Chicago's pretty easy to get around in, but get a map anyway. We should have a car waiting for us. They'll have lost their record of it, I expect, but try not to kill anyone at the rental place no matter how much they deserve it."

Chicago had tremendously crowded highways looping around in all directions, but Ezekiel only glanced at the map. Though Alejandro held it folded to what he thought was the right page, Ezekiel left him in no doubt about his superfluity.

"Williams lives outside Chicago proper. In fact, he lives, if our information is correct, west and north of a town called Joliet." Ezekiel took an exit without seeming to pay any attention to it, as though he drove this way all the time and knew exactly where he was going. "This time of day, it'll take us quite a while just to get out of the city, never mind all the way to the Williams' place. I want to get back to the airport no later than midnight, so we'll have to move things along once we get there."

Alejandro nodded.

"You know what your role is?"

"To do what you tell me, I guess," Alejandro answered, then flinched, expecting an amused, scornful, "*Is that what you guess?*"

But Ezekiel said, his tone merely *eficiente*, "Yes, but not only that. I'll deal with Williams, but if I have to take him the hard way, you'll keep his wife safe – keep her from running, stop her from shooting me if she's had the same bright idea as your brother. You're used to handling your temper around your sister, your brother. Grayson assumed you can do this. Tell me now if there's a problem with this assumption."

A role he could actually play. A *useful* role. That was both unexpected and welcome. Alejandro said, "No. No problem."

"Then this should go perfectly smoothly," said Ezekiel, his tone once more slightly mocking.

Thaddeus Williams and his wife turned out to live way, way out of the city, where the air smelled of turned earth and cows and growing things. Alejandro liked this much better than the bewildering crowded city, though it was a poor area. They found the place eventually: a trailer, not a house. Other trailers and ramshackle houses were scattered back along the road, though none were actually in sight.

The car already parked in front of the trailer was a battered Chevy. Clotheslines stretched between rusty poles, though nothing hung on the lines in the chill damp. Beyond the clotheslines, pieces of broken bricks outlined neat beds within a small garden, bare in this season. Alejandro was surprised by a surge of homesickness. This place only lacked half a dozen *gallinas* pecking around in the garden to give it very much the feeling of his mother's village.

He had wondered what they would do if Thaddeus Williams and his wife were not at home. He had not asked only because he was afraid of Ezekiel's temper if the *verdugo* did not have a plan for that. But both Thaddeus and his wife were in the trailer: he could smell the ash-and-burnt-clay scent of a black dog, and behind that, the clean, bright scent of a Pure woman.

Ezekiel did not trouble with subtlety. He turned off the SUV's engine, opened his door, got out, and slammed the door behind him. The sound echoed aggressive as a gunshot in the evening quiet.

Then Ezekiel just leaned against the hood, waiting, his arms crossed over his chest and his head tilted in cool disdain. "Go around the back," he said to Alejandro, and, when Alejandro did not move quickly enough, snapped, "Go!"

The door of the trailer slammed open and a tall man came out in a rush. Alejandro hadn't known he'd had an image of Thaddeus Williams in his mind until the real man completely failed to match it. Thaddeus turned out to be black, bald, enormous, and gripping a bright silver-alloy knife almost as big as a sword in one hand. His other hand was a massive paw with needle-sharp black claws; his heavy jaw and shoulders also showed signs of the *cambio de cuerpo*. That he could change just so far and then hold those changes amazed Alejandro; no wonder Grayson Lanning wanted him for Dimilioc–

"Move!" snapped Ezekiel at Alejandro, straightening, and ordered Thaddeus Williams, *"Stop right there."*

Alejandro did not stay to see what Thaddeus would do. He sprinted around the trailer just in time to stop the woman there from getting into a truck. He caught her arm, trying not to grip too hard. She did not scream. She whirled and struck at him with a silver knife, a much shorter and slimmer weapon than her husband's, but more than sufficient to disable a black dog.

It was exactly what Natividad would have done, so Alejandro had half expected it. But this woman was neither as fast nor as agile as Natividad, and besides that she carried some dark, heavy bundle in the curve of her other arm. He evaded her blow, caught and twisted her wrist to make her drop the knife, and dragged her back away from the truck.

Then the bundle tucked under her other arm squirmed around and slashed at him with a second knife, and Alejandro was forced to let go of the woman and leap backward. The little boy – five? six? – fought free of his mother's frantic grip and landed on the dirt in front of Alejandro, snarling. He was already partly into the *cambio,* his back hunching, his jaw distorting to accommodate fangs, the scent of ash and burning thick around him.

Alejandro's shadow tried to rise in response. If it did, Alejandro knew, he would *kill* this little black pup. His black dog longed to tear the boy away from his shadow, rip him apart into bloody, smoking pieces, then turn on his mother – that was *just* what it wanted. Alejandro shook with the brutal longing.

"*You're used to handling your temper,*" Ezekiel had said. "*Tell me now if there's a problem.*" And Alejandro had promised him there was no problem. But he had not expected to have a black dog puppy lunging for him, slashing with a little silver knife and snarling. He snarled back at the boy, fighting his shadow and its vicious longing for blood and death.

He backed up, then backed up again, his shadow crowding him, rising, rising. He could feel his hands twisting, claws stretching out of his fingers; he could feel the burning rise through him, trying to pull him into the *cambio de cuerpo*. He had lost track of the Pure woman – no, there she was, and she had her own knife back in her hand – she was screaming, running toward him, but he could not make out her words. He had lost the precious trick of human language – he was losing himself. Fury and horror mingled, blurring the boundaries between himself and his shadow. He caught the little boy's wrist to make him drop his knife. His claws scored the boy's skin, blood beading along the thin wrist. The scent of blood pulled at his shadow, hard.

And, because he could not stop it, he let his black dog rise. But he did not let it come up through him – he *would* not. He set a determinedly human jaw and *refused*. He was *not* his shadow. He *would not be*. And instead of letting his black dog come out, he cast it forward across the boy's shadow, smothering the black pup with his greater strength, crushing the boy's shadow back and down, forcing him into human shape. It was exactly what Grayson Lanning had done to him, twice. He hadn't thought he understood what the Dimilioc Master had done until he needed to do it himself and found he actually could.

The boy was screaming in rage and twisting to get away, but he was fully back in his human form, and when he hit

Alejandro, it was only with a human hand, clawless and ineffectual. Alejandro picked him up, leaned his head away from the boy's furious blows, and glared at his mother.

She stopped dead, holding her hands out in front of her body. After a second, realizing she still held the knife, she threw it down. "Don't..." she said to Alejandro. Her voice was husky with terror. She was a tall woman, big, with a strong-boned plain face, black eyes, short-cropped black hair, and skin the color of caramel. She said again, "Don't..."

"No," Alejandro told her. His own voice was unfamiliar in his ears, harsher and deeper than it should have been, a sign of how hard his shadow pressed him. He was furious with reasonless black dog anger, hardly able to bring human words to his tongue. He was so close to the change. He knew it. But he did not change, he *would* not. He growled, "Come. Come," and, still carrying the boy, caught the woman by the arm and dragged her with him back around the house.

In front of the trailer, the battle was less comic. Alejandro might have been injured by those silver knives, and never heard the last of it – a Pure woman and a little black dog pup, oh, such enemies! But Thaddeus was huge, powerful, and desperate. And he was *using* his black dog fury – his shadow was gathered around him, under tight control. He now did not look at all human, but he had still not fully changed, so he was able to grip his silver blade. He attacked Ezekiel, slashing.

Thaddeus was trying to kill Ezekiel, but, Alejandro realized, Ezekiel was still trying not to kill Thaddeus. He was fully changed, but he, no less than the other man, was still in full control of his shadow: even as they watched, he drew Thaddeus into a reckless attack that left him seriously overextended, but then pulled his return blow so that rather than ripping right through Thaddeus's belly and tearing out his spine, he only left a set of incisions that, though bloody, barely sliced through the skin.

And he made it look easy. Surrounded by the dense anger and pounding heat of battle, Ezekiel still somehow looked lazy, disdainful, barely involved even when he spun away from a backhanded sweep of the silver knife that might have taken off half his face. Black ichor dripped from his shoulder, so an earlier stroke of that blade must have cut him, but he was still unbelievably fast–

"Oh, God," whispered the woman, seeing as well as Alejandro how the fight was going.

"Scream," Alejandro growled at her urgently. When she only stared at him, terrified and defiant, he let claws slide out of his fingertips and held his hand up threateningly near her son's face. The boy squirmed and fought, tried to bite with blunt human teeth. Alejandro shook him hard, snarling, his shadow pressing at him as it tried to rise, and the child, at last frightened into submission, whimpered and shut his eyes.

"Con!" said the woman, half reaching toward her son, hesitating, afraid of Alejandro, terrified for her husband.

Alejandro thought his face was no longer exactly human. When he snarled, "Scream!" at the woman, he couldn't tell whether he spoke in English or Spanish or in any human language at all. If he frightened her enough, it wouldn't matter–

The woman threw her head back and screamed, a shriek they could probably hear both in Mexico and Vermont.

Thaddeus whirled around and saw his wife, his son, and Alejandro, with his black dog shadow thick around him and his claws threatening the boy. He made a guttural noise, half scream and half roar, gathered himself for a lunge–

"Thad, no!" cried the woman. "Oh, God, no!"

Thaddeus tried so urgently to stop that he slid sideways and nearly fell, a cloud of dust and ash pluming up around him. Ezekiel, in exactly the right position to tear out his throat and crush his spine, instead hit his arm to make him drop the silver knife and then backed away, folding himself upright, back into human shape, with his amazing smooth speed.

There was that sudden cessation of all action that sometimes happens in a fight, a frozen moment in which no one moved or spoke or sobbed, in which the whole world seemed to pause. Ezekiel stood poised and balanced despite the ugly cut across his shoulder from Thaddeus' silver knife. Thaddeus made no move to reclaim the knife, though it had fallen only a few feet away. He was panting heavily, head lowered, blood and ichor clotting his black pelt. He should change, let his shadow carry away his injuries, but it was clear to Alejandro that he couldn't, that he was too distraught. He tried, his black dog shadow shivered, but the moon's hard pull supported the shadow; it would not subside willingly, and Thaddeus clearly could not, at this moment, force it down.

Ezekiel moved forward a step, young and slim and arrogant, totally in control of the situation. "Enough!" he said, without a hint of the black dog growl. "Williams, that is enough! Get your shadow down, and keep it down! Where's your control? Well? Will you force me to kill you even now?"

Alejandro tried to imagine explaining to Grayson that they'd come this far, fought this powerful black dog to a standstill, and then had to kill him after all because he could not be controlled. It was all too easy to imagine what Grayson might say in return. Closing his eyes, he shoved his own shadow out and forward as he had done to stop the boy's attack. He used the weight of his own shadow to press Thaddeus Williams's shadow down and back, supporting Thaddeus's own efforts to force it down.

At last, Thaddeus shuddered and straightened as his black dog retreated. Then it was finally a man who crouched there in the dirt, on his hands and knees, in torn jeans and a plain black T-shirt. His gaze locked for one helpless moment with his wife's before he moved to stare at Alejandro and, still in his grip, the boy.

Ezekiel gave Alejandro an odd look, not quite pleased. "Picked up Grayson's little trick, have you?"

Alejandro had no idea how to answer that.

But Thaddeus turned at once toward Ezekiel. For an instant he looked into the Dimilioc *verdugo's* face. Then, dropping his gaze, he said, his deep voice rough with terror and fury and the remnants of battle, "Please. Please. Whatever you do to me – damn you, you son of a bitch! Do anything you want to me, but don't hurt my wife or son!"

Ezekiel relaxed. He straightened his shoulders and smiled. Despite the blood oozing from the cut across his shoulder, he looked for all the world as though he'd just concluded a civilized conversation with the man, not fought a roaring battle with him that might well draw the more foolhardy neighbors and maybe the *policia*. He did not seem worried about either possibility. He said, "How kind of you to offer. Another time, you might try that first, do you think? However, this time I'm not hunting. I'm merely a messenger. Grayson wants to see you himself."

"Oh, God," said Thaddeus. He rubbed his big hands over his face and was silent for a moment. Then he looked up again, met Ezekiel's eyes for an instant, and bowed his head again, bowed his whole body down. It took an obvious effort. "I'll come. I'll come with you – I won't fight you. Just don't... Please. I don't know why Grayson Lanning gives a shit about me, all these years, all he's got to have on his plate right now, you'd think... but if it's me he wants, let them go. Please."

"You know that's not the way it's going to be," Ezekiel said, still smiling.

Sádico son of a bitch, Alejandro did not say. All black dogs were more or less cruel, but a *man* tried to be decent despite the pressure from his shadow. He said sharply to Thaddeus, "Do you think the Dimilioc Master would hurt a Pure woman?"   •

The man laughed harshly, a sound almost like a snarl and almost like a sob. He did not try to get up, but the muscles of his back and shoulders bunched and his big hands closed into fists. "Fuck, kid. Oh, God. Do you think I don't know what *Grayson Lanning* will do with a Pure woman? He'll tell his little bastard of an executioner to pin me up as an example, and then he'll pass my DeAnn to one of his black

wolves. He'll murder my son to clear the way for her to
bear a pup from one of the Dimilioc bloodlines–"

"He will not!" snapped Alejandro – then stopped,
surprised at the anger in his own voice.

Ezekiel, from the ironic lift of his eyebrows, had caught
Alejandro's sudden uncertainty. But he only said, "Well,
we'll all find out, won't we? Because we are all going to
get in this SUV and drive back to the airport and get in my
plane and fly back to Vermont. No one is going to fuss or
cry…" He glanced at the silent boy in Alejandro's grip, who
was now standing on his own feet. The child was shivering,
but no longer struggling. He mostly kept his gaze on the
ground, but flicked quick little glances at his father – black
dog instinct kept him from looking at Alejandro, far less
Ezekiel.

"Or try to run away, or cause a scene," Ezekiel continued,
lifting an eyebrow at the woman, and then finished, straight
to Thaddeus. "Or let his shadow up so we can enjoy another
little tussle like this one. You've lost the fight, Thaddeus.
Don't start another. Hear me?" Staring hard at the black
man, he added in a much quieter tone, "Because Grayson
told me to bring you and your wife, but he didn't say a
word about your black pup here. Do you understand me?"

Everyone understood him. Only Alejandro doubted he
would carry out that threat, and then only because he realized
Ezekiel knew that Grayson would want the boy alive.

"Good, then," Ezekiel said briskly. "We'll be moving
quickly, but let's tie up a few loose ends first. You, woman.
DeAnn. Get that silver knife and put it in the car. Alejandro,
bring that pup here to me and then get my kit out of the

car. The black bag," he added impatiently when Alejandro hesitated.

That wasn't why Alejandro had hesitated, but he nodded and said quickly, "There are two more knives. They each had one, even the *niño*."

Ezekiel clicked his tongue. "Of course they did," he said, sounding annoyed. He looked Alejandro over quickly. "You cut?"

"No."

"Good. Let me have the kid. You go get a blanket or something from the house, wrap up all the knives, stow them in the car. Then get me the black bag."

Alejandro shoved the boy toward Ezekiel – the *verdugo* wouldn't hurt him, surely, not if he wanted to use the child as a *rehén*, a hostage. But even so, Alejandro hurried.

The interior of the trailer was surprisingly cheerful, very much a home made by a Pure woman, with none of the grim atmosphere of a black dog lair. The furniture was cheap, but covered with bright throws; there were equally bright rag rugs on the floor. The walls were lined with brick-and-board shelves, which were stuffed with paperbacks and the occasional hardcover – all kinds of books: mysteries and thrillers shoved in alongside romances and a battered copy of *Don Quixote*. Again, Alejandro felt an unexpected surge of homesickness: Mamá had loved books. He thrust it down, grabbed a red throw off a chair, and ran outside again to gather up the silver knives.

Ezekiel's black bag proved to contain, among other things, first aid supplies and half a dozen broad silver bracelets lined with black leather. Someone Pure must have blooded the bracelets for Ezekiel, because he handled them without hesitation, although Alejandro and the little boy both winced away from their bright, clear fire.

"You planning to fight me over this?" Ezekiel asked Thaddeus, holding up the bracelets. "Because if you fight, you'd better win, or I'll beat the hell out of you and then I'll gut your pup like a fish. And you won't win."

Thaddeus looked at his wife. She shook her head, a swift, urgent gesture. He slumped, a subtle change, more of attitude than posture. "No," he said to Ezekiel, not looking at him. "No, you bastard. I won't fight you."

"Good." Ezekiel dropped all but two of the silver bracelets back into his bag, and said over his shoulder to Alejandro, "If he starts to change, stop him."

"Yes," Alejandro agreed. He did not know whether he could do it again if he needed to. But he did not need to try, because Thaddeus, true to his word, did not fight. He held out one arm and then the other, allowing Ezekiel to bend a silver band tight around each of his thick wrists. The wide bracelets looked like the proper sort of jewelry for such a big man, showing bright against his dark skin. But, of course, they were not meant as jewelry.

Thaddeus did not even wince from the silver, which had to be pride – the silver was vivid enough in the evening to make Alejandro flinch, and no one was forcing him to *wear* it. At least the leather backing ought to keep the bracelets from burning Thaddeus. Probably. If he did not wear them for too long.

Ezekiel stepped back, not precisely relaxing, but seeming less edgy. "Alright," he said to Alejandro, tossed him the first aid kit, and shrugged out of his shirt. The long cut from the silver knife gaped wide, deeper than Alejandro had guessed; blood ran sluggishly down Ezekiel's arm. The *verdugo* craned his neck to survey the damage, which, inflicted by a silver weapon, would heal almost human slowly. Then he gave Thaddeus a cold look. The black dog turned his head away.

"It could use stitches," Ezekiel told Alejandro. "You ever stitched somebody up? Hell, just tape it up for now and we'll get moving. I'll drive. The pup will ride shotgun–" that was a threat, because it would keep the boy within Ezekiel's reach "–the woman behind me, Williams beside her, you behind him. Move."

They all moved. Alejandro more than half expected to find *policia* on the road as they drove toward the highway, but there was nothing. And there had never been any outcry from the neighbors. Maybe they were too far away to have heard anything, or maybe this was one of those neighborhoods where no one wanted to run toward trouble. He guessed that the neighbors might specifically not want to run toward any trouble Thaddeus Williams got into. Even if they knew nothing about black dogs, they probably knew he was dangerous and *escalofriante* – uncanny, was that the word? Eerie, unnatural.

It seemed a long way back to the airport. No one spoke. Traffic was not as maddening on this return drive, but with the sun down, the streets became even more confusing. Alejandro could feel the pull of the moon even through the brilliance of the city lights – it dragged at his shadow, tinted his vision with the crimson of bloodlust, made him want to surrender to his shadow and leap out of the car into the wild hunting ground this immense city would provide.

Alejandro kept a wary eye on Thaddeus, but maybe the silver bracelets countered the moon's influence, for he seemed indifferent to its tidal pull. Alejandro set his teeth against the forceful, dangerous drag of the moon until the long drive at last returned them to the airport. Alejandro was almost as glad to see the planes raking their paths of light through the sky as he would have been to come home after a dangerous, difficult hunt.

Alejandro had worried that Thaddeus or DeAnn might make a scene at the airport, their last chance to make trouble where there was a crowd for confusion and protection. But Ezekiel had Alejandro carry the boy and he then tucked DeAnn's arm through his as though he was her escort. Although their little group got the occasional odd look, they were not, after all, passing through the commercial terminal. Then they climbed into the Dimilioc plane, and that risk, at least, was past.

Alejandro sat in the back of the plane with Thaddeus and his wife. Ezekiel took the boy – Con, his parents called him, but Alejandro did not know whether that stood for Conner or Conrad or what – up to the cockpit with him.

Young Con did not cry or, which was more likely for a black dog pup, try to fight. Alejandro wondered what kind of bedtime stories his father had told him about Dimilioc wolves, but the boy's rigid quiet came from more than scary stories. Any black dog puppy must feel directly, personally, the dense burning strength of the Dimilioc executioner. Where a human child might have screamed himself hoarse and fought like a fool, a black dog pup naturally flattened down before a strong black dog, hoping to buy tolerance with submission.

There were half a dozen comfortable seats in the back of the plane. Ezekiel left the door between the passenger area and the cockpit open, so Thaddeus and his wife could look forward and see their son in the seat next to Ezekiel, a constant reminder to cooperate.

Thaddeus deliberately placed himself between his wife and Alejandro, exactly as Alejandro would have done if their positions had been reversed and he had needed to protect Natividad. Thaddeus must know that this protective gesture was pointless. Even if he were not bound to his human form by those silver bracelets, the man would realize that with his son in Ezekiel's hands, he could do nothing but stay quiet. Of course, he must also know that if he did nothing, then later when they landed and put themselves into Dimilioc power, Grayson Lanning could do anything he chose to any of them. The back of Alejandro's neck prickled with his awareness of the man's anger and fear and unvoiced despair. It pleased his black dog, but Alejandro did not like it – and DeAnn was also frightened, which he liked even less. But he couldn't say anything to reassure either of them, partly because he didn't know what to say but mostly because Ezekiel had made it clear he wasn't to say anything at all.

"These people are Grayson's to deal with," he'd told Alejandro before they boarded the plane. His tone had been flat and uncompromising. "Don't muddy the water. You can't make any promises. I don't want you offering reassurance or threats or so much as a word of advice. Understand?"

Alejandro understood. But it made for an extremely uncomfortable plane flight, and all the more uncomfortable because before they took off, Ezekiel also said, leaning back in his seat to look back into the passenger compartment, "The last word from Dimilioc is to make all possible speed on our return. We will therefore not stop before we arrive at Newport. I believe we have enough fuel to manage. We should reach Dimilioc at roughly seven in the morning. Get some rest if you can, but don't relax too far. Call me if Williams gives you any trouble. It's for moments like that they invented the autopilot."

Alejandro nodded. "At Dimilioc... What...?"

"I don't know," Ezekiel snapped. "Everyone is fine right now, the message says. Trust Grayson. He won't let anything happen to your sister."

Alejandro heard just the faintest growl vibrating under that assurance. For the first time he realized that it might be a good thing to have Ezekiel Korte interested in Natividad: it had not occurred to him until this moment that Grayson might work hard to keep Natividad alive just to avoid trouble with Ezekiel.

But he said merely, "Yes."

"Keep an eye on things back here," Ezekiel added, and stared hard at Thaddeus, who stared back for a heartbeat before he looked down. "Don't give me any trouble," he said at last. "Or him, either." By which he meant Alejandro. "I'm sure I don't need to point out that trying to kill the pilot of your plane while thousands of feet in the air lacks a certain *je ne se quoi*. But I will also add that I'm tired and I'm going to get more tired, that the moon's call will be stronger once we're in the sky, that this damned cut from your damned knife hurts like a son of a bitch, and that I'm not long on temper at the moment. Is that clear?"

Thaddeus bowed his head low. And, after Ezekiel turned back to the plane's controls, Thaddeus did nothing more threatening than sit between his wife and Alejandro, his head still down. None of them spoke, Alejandro because of Ezekiel's warning and Thaddeus probably because he was afraid Alejandro would take offense at something he said and complain to Ezekiel. Or maybe because he was afraid that if he said anything, he wouldn't be able to stop himself from making threats, then from trying to carry them out – he was so angry, and they both knew that he was stronger than Alejandro.

DeAnn did not speak, either. She sat close to her husband, leaning her head on his shoulder, her eyes closed and her fingers laced with his, *dulce de leche* against dark chocolate. The close presence of two hostile black dogs was surely enough to explain her silence, though Alejandro would have liked her to talk, would have welcomed the sound of her voice. If not for Ezekiel's order, he would have talked to her as though she was Natividad: anything, nonsense, just to hear her answer.

Was Natividad safe? What trouble had led to that order to hurry back? Alejandro did not want to think about that, but of course he could think about nothing else. *Everyone is fine right now*. Well, good, even that assurance made it clear there had been trouble.

If Thaddeus did anything to slow them down, Alejandro decided, he would help Ezekiel beat the hell out of him.

7

Natividad hated the way she felt after Alejandro left with Ezekiel – frightened and timid, like a little mouse trapped among wolves. She was afraid to leave her room. It was ridiculous to feel this way. She *never* felt this way. But when she stood at her window and watched Ezekiel drive away with her brother, the big car crushing the snow of the driveway, its headlights plunging into the pre-dawn darkness of the winter forest, even though it was totally ridiculous, she *did* feel that way.

"He'll be fine," Miguel said. "Ezekiel won't hurt 'Jandro." He was sitting cross-legged on her bed, watching her rather than looking after Alejandro.

"*Eso es, lo sé*," said Natividad. Her twin *was* right. Alejandro would be perfectly safe with Ezekiel, because Ezekiel wanted her.

Who would have thought the one Dimilioc wolf most determined to have her would be her own age? Well, almost, anyway. Although he didn't exactly want *her*. It would be so easy to fool herself about that, but Ezekiel would probably keep *any* Pure girl company while she made cinnamon rolls.

There was nothing flattering about it. He probably didn't actually *like* her at all. Which was *fine*. Nothing about the deal with Dimilioc depended on anybody actually *liking* anybody else. It certainly didn't matter whether *she* liked the Dimilioc executioner or thought he was *muy atractivo*.

"You'll be fine, too," Miguel said, too perceptive for comfort. Natividad tried to smile. When her brother held a hand out to her, she crossed the room and tucked herself on the bed next to him, curling up small among the pillows. Miguel moved over to give her room. "The famous Mallory charm's got nothing on you," he promised her. "They'll all be wriggling like puppies for you in a week."

"Oh, right..." Natividad said.

Miguel laughed at her. "Oh, yes, they will. Benedict's already making eyes at you, and Ethan's going to come around, you wait and see, and of course you've already got Ezekiel. All the boys looove you. Puppy love, all cute and wriggly, you wait and see."

"You're an idiot," Natividad said, but she gave up and laughed, as he had intended. "Wriggling I don't need! Anyway, Ezekiel..." She stopped, not knowing how to finish that sentence. Thinking about Ezekiel didn't make her want to laugh at all. He was courting her, obviously. That was better than him not bothering, right? At least he cared what she thought. She was pretty sure.

Executioner at fourteen. *Almost* fourteen, he'd said. That was hard to imagine. What would that *do* to somebody? Nothing good, she was sure. She sighed. If Mamá was here... Mamá could have handled Ezekiel and Grayson and Keziah and *everybody*...

"Yeah, about that thing with Ezekiel…"

Natividad didn't want to talk about that with her twin. That she couldn't talk to *Mamá* about Ezekiel hurt so much she couldn't think about it more than an instant. She didn't want to let Miguel guess about that because it would only bring back his own vivid grief and anger. She jumped up, went back across to the window, and drew a pentagram with her fingertip on the window glass, just below the one she had drawn there the previous morning. The pentagrams might be invisible to ordinary sight, but when she turned her head so that the light fell on the window at just the right angle, she could see them. They glowed on the glass, milk pale, as though they reflected moonlight even though no visible moon rode in the overcast sky.

She drew a third pentagram above the other two, then traced a finger across each one. "*Que la paz este en esta casa*," she said, and then repeated it in English: "Let there be peace in this house."

"In *this* house?" Miguel said.

Natividad nodded, acknowledging his tone. "Everyone here is unhappy or afraid." She thought about this and sighed. "Mostly both."

"Well, you know, black dogs. I'll see if I can work with Ethan. Grayson wants him to help me make silver bullets, so that'll give him a chance to get used to me. He's not really so bad, I think."

"It's hard for him," Natividad agreed. "I bet it always has been hard for him. Imagine growing up in the same house as Ezekiel. I bet he couldn't ever match Ezekiel in anything even when they were both little."

"Exactly. And he probably knows Alejandro is stronger – which I think he is – and *now* there's *Keziah*. Oooh." Miguel clutched his chest, pretending he'd been struck by an arrow, but Natividad was pretty sure he wasn't really kidding. "Ethan's afraid he's going to wind up right down on the bottom of the whole younger set," Miguel added. "He'll like having me around."

Natividad laughed. "Oh, yes, of course he will, until he finds out what a bully you are! No, you're right, I thought he was kind of a *bastardo* at first, but I think you're right. He's just scared and worried."

"So, I'll see what I can do with him. What do you think about his father?"

"Oh, well…" Natividad had barely exchanged two words with Harrison Lanning. She said slowly, "He's worried about his son, I expect, but that isn't all. There's something else there. He doesn't like me – or something. I'm not sure."

"We'll figure him out. If he doesn't like you now, he will – everybody does." Miguel sounded perfectly confident. "What about Zachariah?"

Natividad grinned. "Oh, I like him! I do. I think Grayson really depends on Zachariah – I didn't think black dogs could really be *friends*, you know, but you can see they are. And maybe Harrison, too. I think Dimilioc is lucky all three of them came through the war."

"Yeah."

"James, I can't tell yet. He seems like kind of a jerk, but at least he really cares about Dimilioc. That Keziah, though – wow."

Miguel nodded. "Oooh," he said again, appreciatively.

"Poor little Amira, though, you can see somebody cut her on purpose. I hope the vampires got *all* the black dogs in the whole Mideast." Natividad mimed spitting on the floor. "I bet they had a black dog father and black dog brothers. Everyone betrayed them, nobody protected them – except Keziah protected Amira. That's what I think."

"She's something," Miguel agreed. He lay back on her bed, crossing his arms under his head. "You think she'll want to be friends?"

Natividad rolled her eyes. "With you? She's too sexy for you. She'll eat your heart."

"You're talking about the love of my life, here."

Natividad ignored this plaintive protest. "You know she got somebody to do the *Aplacando* for her before? And for her sister? She's smart and she knows what she wants – and what she wants is to be inside Dimilioc's power. Grayson wants her to be Dimilioc–" she touched her own chest "–in her heart. But I think she hates Grayson. I think she hates all black dog men. She hasn't even noticed you – and you'd better hope she doesn't, *gemelo*. She'll chew you up and spit you out. That's what I think."

"Um." Miguel looked unhappy.

"Black dog or human, in some ways, guys are all the same." Natividad gave her brother a knowing lift of her eyebrows. "When I say she'll eat your heart, I mean *literalmente*. She's dangerous. Anyway, she's too old for you. I bet she's eighteen, or seventeen anyway. Why would she notice you?"

"I like you better when you're not so serious," Miguel complained.

Natividad ignored this. "Now, Grayson..." Grayson kind of had that extra-sexy older guy *muy masculino* thing going, but she didn't say that. Anyway, it wasn't important, as long as Ezekiel... She didn't want to think about that. She said instead, "Grayson lost almost all his wolves in the war, didn't he? And now there's Vonhausel. He's grieving and he's scared. And he's angry, of course. With us, too. But..."

"But?"

"I think I like him. He cares about his people." Natividad turned back to her pentagrams, and traced them again with her finger. If peace was too much to hope for... "Let there be happiness in this house," she said. She drew light into the pentagrams, a soft moonlight that would hold them in place and keep her wish alive.

But she already knew that no one, Pure or not, could bring either happiness or peace to Dimilioc. Not while so many of the people within the house were afraid of one another or angry with one another. Not while they were surrounded by enemies who wanted to kill them all.

A rap on the door made Natividad turn quickly. Ethan shoved the door open and put his head through, scowling. "Bullets," he said shortly to Miguel.

Miguel jumped to his feet. "Right! Coming."

"What should I do?" asked Natividad, since even though it was still dark outside, the day was apparently officially starting.

"What do I care?" Ethan said, and withdrew again.

"*Bastardo,*" Natividad said under her breath.

Miguel grinned. "I can handle Ethan. But the Master's the key. *You* need to work your magic on Grayson. Or if you see Keziah, you might put in a good word for me, huh?" He waved, jaunty and irrepressible, and dashed out.

Boys were idiots. Miguel was right about one thing, though, Natividad knew: the Master really was the key to Dimilioc.

Natividad found Grayson Lanning in the room with the fireplace and the great view, seated in one of the chairs closest to the window. There was no fire in the massive fireplace now, only ashes and a few dully smoldering coals. The room was cold for a human, though of course a black dog would not care.

The Dimilioc Master's hands were steepled in front of him, his elbows resting on the arms of the chair. He was staring out into the dark, frowning, mouth set in a grim line, heavy brows pulled down in thought.

There was nothing Natividad could do about the grief and loss Dimilioc had suffered or the danger it now faced. But the Pure could do other things, sometimes. She slipped quietly into the room and crossed to the big window.

Grayson turned his head, awareness coming into his eyes. In a moment he would ask her what she wanted.

Natividad didn't wait for him to speak. She walked across the room to the window and drew a pentagram on the glass, a big one, flanking it with two smaller ones. Then, tracing the lines of the pentagrams, she called light into them and said softly, "Let there be peace in this room. Let this room be a refuge for the weary heart."

Grayson lowered his hands to the arms of his chair and shut his eyes. "Thank you," he said after a moment, and opened his eyes again.

"*Por nada*," Natividad said. "It's not much. I know somebody else already put her wish on this house. I found her stars. A Jewish woman? Because they're the other kind of star – Stars of David."

Dark grief had come into the Master's eyes. He stared at Natividad, a hard direct stare, until she belatedly remembered her manners and turned her face away. Then he asked, his voice deep but not angry, "Can you add to what has already been done?"

"I can reinforce it, but I can't do better." Natividad wanted to look Grayson in the face, but was pretty sure she shouldn't. She stared out the window instead, at the rose-and-pearl light gleaming through the trees. She said gently, "No one could have put any better protection on the Dimilioc house than she did. She was strong and loving, that woman." She glanced toward the Master and then away again. She knew that the unknown Pure woman who had woven her protection around the Dimilioc house had been someone important to the Dimilioc Master: sister, lover, cousin... Trying to break the moment, Natividad perched casually on the broad arm of one of the other chairs, not too close to Grayson. It was a sturdy chair and gave no quivering warning that her weight might tip it over. She said, "We've added to Dimilioc's trouble, bringing our enemies here. I'm sorry."

Grayson Lanning lifted an eyebrow and tilted his head. "You have, in one way. In another, you..." He stopped, his attention directed past Natividad, out the window.

A car was approaching. It was a heavy blunt-nosed vehicle, neither truck nor car but like a cross between the two, with tires that looked about twice as big as normal. No wonder Miguel hadn't been able to get their car all the way along the road, if you needed a car like that one. But it slowed as it came into the cleared area before the house, where its headlights picked out streaks and spatters of frozen blood and ichor from the battle, visible against the white of the trampled snow.

"Pearson," said the Master. "We'll go down and meet him." He didn't sound exactly angry, but there was a dangerous growl in his voice.

Sheriff Pearson was a slight, slim man, probably in his forties. He was nothing like Natividad had expected from a small-town American sheriff. She suppressed a smile, thinking about sheriffs in American movies – at least, the good-guy sheriffs: tall and rugged, with tanned faces and wide-brimmed cowboy hats. Sheriff Pearson wasn't like that. He wasn't much taller than she was and actually kind of... *elegant*, Natividad decided, was the only accurate word. But there was a tension in him that prevented him from looking delicate. His eyes were almost the color of the pearl-gray sky. The tracery of fine lines at the corners of those pale eyes had been made by smiling, but he wasn't smiling now, nor did he look like he planned to smile any time soon.

He knew something about black dogs. Enough to lower his eyes when Grayson Lanning stared at him. Enough to wait, despite the tension in his slim hands and the set of his shoulders, for Grayson to speak first. He carried a gun, but he kept his hands away from it, though she could tell from Grayson's manner that his gun couldn't be loaded with silver.

She thought of the black dogs that had attacked Dimilioc. The sheriff *should* have silver bullets. She wondered whether Grayson would think so, or think to warn him, or allow Miguel to make some for him; whether she should suggest it. Not now, though; not with the Master glowering like that.

"Well?" growled Grayson, his posture stiff and aggressive.

Sheriff Pearson took this rough query for permission to look up, which it wasn't. He also leaned forward slightly, which Natividad could tell was from tension and urgency, but which a black dog might take as challenge. She edged forward, not exactly between the two men, but finding a place to lean against the wall of the entryway about an equal distance from each.

"We had someone bitten last night," the sheriff said without preamble. His voice was sharp and precise; he spoke as though each word was an edged weapon. Natividad wanted to put a hand on his arm, urge him to calm down as though he was a black dog, but she was afraid that if she tried he would only get angrier. "I don't suppose that was one of your wolves, Grayson," the sheriff continued icily, "but your warning was neither timely nor adequately specific. We trusted you to keep *us* clear of your black dog violence, at least–"

Grayson said, grimly, "I regret this. It was unexpected. I doubt that Dimilioc's new enemy is interested in you or yours, but stray black dogs are rabble, difficult to control. We are taking steps to deal with the problem. This man who was bitten. I gather you have brought him to me?"

"It was a girl. Yes, I brought her to you." The sheriff leaned forward, speaking rapidly and with gathering intensity, either unaware of the challenge he seemed to be making or else indifferent to the danger. Natividad pushed away from the wall in alarm, but Grayson didn't move, and the sheriff continued, his voice rising, "You kill people who've been bitten. Of course you do. But I don't want this girl killed. You have other ways of controlling–"

"Caging is merely a temporary measure," said Grayson. "We seldom find moon-bound shifters worth the trouble." His shadow, dense and misshapen, had gathered up around him in defiance of the light in the hallway. But the black dog anger barely showed in his voice. Even now, he did not threaten the man. Natividad didn't think this was due to her presence. The Master just had that much control.

"My *daughter*," said Sheriff Pearson tightly. "It's my daughter, and I assure you, I didn't bring her here for you to kill her. You *have* other ways of controlling bitten people, and you will use those other methods, Grayson–"

Grayson said, his deep voice coming down heavily across Pearson's fury, "This moon will come upon her too swiftly for her to learn even a vestige of control before the change takes her. It is almost upon her now. Later, after the nights and days of the full moon, there are methods she may be able to use. Ways you can help her. We will teach these to her and to you." He paused. The two men stared at one another. Then Grayson added, his gravelly voice almost gentle, "I am sorry for the harm that has come to your daughter, Sheriff Pearson. Dimilioc will not add to that harm."

"Alright," said the sheriff, more calmly. "Alright." He

took a breath. "Thank you. I'll bring her..." He began to turn back toward the door.

"No," said Grayson, stopping him. "Clearly she has not yet changed. But tonight the moon will rise full. Possibly you would still be safe to approach her today, but we will not take that chance. I will send Harrison for her."

Sheriff Pearson looked at him.

"We will not harm her," Grayson promised him.

The sheriff shook his head, then nodded wordlessly, opening and closing his hands. "She'll be alright," he said at last. He stared at Grayson. "You'll be kind to her. You'll tell me if she... if I..." he stopped, not seeming to know how to finish this plea.

"We will do all we can for her," Grayson promised him.

"Yes," the sheriff whispered. "Alright. Thank you." He looked down at last, letting out his breath. Then he suddenly turned his head to stare at Natividad. "You're Pure, aren't you?" He turned back to the Master. "Grayson, I need to borrow this young lady. We can't have anyone else bitten. These are enemies of yours, you said; you owe us some help, here. A Pure girl might help Father McClanahan set up something better than–"

"I will not put the girl at risk," Grayson said flatly. "She stays here, under Dimilioc's eye and hand, where we can protect her."

"Grayson, dammit–"

Natividad, stepping away from the wall, said at the same time, "But–"

The Dimilioc Master cut them both off without a word, with nothing but a hard look. His eyes had gone burning crimson, and Natividad, if not the sheriff, could see how tightly his shadow clung to him. He growled, his voice gone harsh and low, "You are the only Pure woman Dimilioc possesses. We will not put you at risk." Turning back to the sheriff, he added, "I regret the damage your daughter has suffered. I will see to it she is safe through the rising of her dark shadow. That is all I can do for you. The measures your priest can take must suffice you in other matters. He should act as against vampires."

"Nothing a priest can do works as well against black dogs as against vampires," Natividad protested. "I could–"

Grayson flashed a snarl at her. "Natividad. Stay in the house. That is an order. Sheriff Pearson. Dimilioc is fully engaged against its enemies. If we lose, it will be soon. Winning may take a little longer. As long as the outcome is in doubt, there is danger – as I believe I did inform you. Instruct your people to stay watchful, together, and close to town–"

"I'm sure that'll help," the sheriff said, with understandable sarcasm and not nearly enough caution. But still Grayson did not threaten him. His shadow shifted and twisted, distorting the fall of light around him, but the Master showed no sign of the *cambio de cuerpo* except for the change in his eyes and the dangerous snarl in his voice. Natividad was starting to *really* admire his control.

"Harrison will bring your daughter into the house," Grayson rumbled. "Wait for that. Then go back to town, Pearson. Drive swiftly. Do not stop. When next you have any urgent need to speak with me, I hope the telephone will suffice."

"The damned phone makes it too easy for you to hang up on me." Sheriff Pearson was almost as angry as the Dimilioc Master.

"I can do nothing for you. It does not make me happy to refuse you, Pearson. *I can do nothing for you.* Dimilioc cannot spare the strength to protect you. *We do not have the resources.* When that changes, I will inform you. For the present, I advise you stay as far as possible out of black dog battles–"

"And when *as far as possible* leaves us with blood in the snow–"

"Go," Grayson ordered him, voice low and gritty.

After a fraught pause, the sheriff lowered his gaze, disengaging. He said formally, "I am grateful for Dimilioc's protection of my daughter." Then he backed away, one step and another, toward the door and safety. So, he did know when to concede, after all. Natividad had been prepared to leap forward, catch Grayson's arm, hope he would let her help settle his hot fury. Instead, she leaned against the wall again, letting out her breath.

Grayson gave her a fierce, fiery stare. "Go to your room," he ordered, and stalked away.

Natividad didn't go to her room. She couldn't. It was all her fault, that man's daughter being bitten. Nobody needed to point that out to her. Well, not *just* her fault, but if she and her brothers hadn't led Vonhausel north, it never would have happened.

The Pure were supposed to protect ordinary people. Natividad knew that. Mamá had taught her that. Mamá, and Grandmamá and Tía Louisa and Tía Maria in Hualahuises. Only sometimes they weren't strong enough, and sometimes they weren't brave enough...

Mi hija valianta, Mamá had called her. *My brave daughter*. Mamá had shown Natividad how to draw the kind of circles and mandalas that could protect a whole village. Natividad had been about ten when Mamá had shown her the mandala at Hualahuises. Mamá had knelt on the dry earth beneath the shade of the buckthorn and the blackbush acacia and the twisted narrow branches of Devil's claw shrubs, and laid her hands on the ground. Then she had lifted them up, drawing light into the air out of the ground. Natividad had looked, awed, to the left and the right, and seen how the light went on and on in a gentle curving arc of light that cut across the arroyos and the steep foothills of the dry mountains to enclose nearly all of Hualahuises.

"I and my sisters and your Grandmamá drew this circle long ago, before you were even born," Mamá had told her. She had smiled at Natividad, the smile that seemed to illuminate not only her face, but the world around her. "You are not yet strong enough to draw such a large circle, *mi hija valianta*, but you have my blood in you. You will work hard and learn everything, and in not so long you will have such strength."

Natividad had been so proud that day, because she was Pure and would be able to protect everyone. She had believed every word. She didn't want to remember that, now; only she sort of *did* want to, except remembering made her feel ashamed and small and young. So, she *didn't* want to remember. She wouldn't remember.

"There wasn't any time," she whispered. "I didn't have *time* to do anything."

That was true. When Vonhausel had come to Potosi, she had really, truly, not had time to find out if she had the strength of her Mamá's blood in her own veins. She had not had time to find out if she had learned enough. But now there was this other town that needed the kind of protection a Pure woman could set into the earth and the air, and Natividad knew there would be time to protect *this* town. There *would* be time. There had to be, so there would be. If she was strong enough. And brave enough.

And Grayson ought to see it was her responsibility to help the townspeople, but he wanted to keep her safe. She thought maybe she liked the Dimilioc Master. She knew she admired him – he was trying so hard to protect Dimilioc, and yet he was almost kind, when he could be. He hadn't even hesitated to take responsibility for the sheriff's daughter. There were so many other demands on his attention, and a moon-bound shifter was not easy to handle, at least not if you wanted to *help* her. But he thought protecting his own family was the only important thing there was. He was like Papá that way. *Mamá* had known there were more important things than being *safe*.

Natividad, blinked hard, rubbed her hand across her eyes, took a deep breath, and ran up the main stairway so it would look like she meant to obey Grayson. But then she ran back down the kitchen stairs and poked her head cautiously out the side door into the cold morning. It was hardly light even now: clouds had thickened overhead and fat flakes of snow were beginning to wander down from the heavy sky.

Pearson was leaning against his big vehicle, watching, his body rigid and his hands clenched hard, as Harrison led a thin girl into the house. He took a step after them, but stopped himself, his face tight, his thin mouth a hard line.

Natividad thought the girl couldn't be more than thirteen or fourteen years old. Her father's elegant features were, in her, a fragile delicacy. She didn't look like a girl who could survive disasters. She looked stunned and blank, like she had not yet figured out whether she ought to feel grief or rage or despair or terror. All those emotions would crash in on her at once, Natividad knew. Soon. Probably as soon as Harrison locked her in the cage downstairs to wait, alone, for her corrupted shadow to rise. It might not come up until nightfall, but really it could happen any time, with the moon so near full. Natividad wanted to go sit with the girl, talk to her, try to get her to believe that her life might still go on despite being moon-bound.

But the girl probably wouldn't be able to believe anybody's reassurances. Not right away. Not till after the moon began to wane and her shadow subsided again. Besides, if Natividad went to help her, she would have to leave Sheriff Pearson to drive back to Lewis alone, without anything to stop Vonhausel's black dogs biting more of his people to make more moon-bound shifters. Whatever Grayson said, somebody needed to help Pearson or all the townspeople would be terribly vulnerable.

The sheriff was not cursing, but he looked as though he might have liked to. He stared at the blank facade of the Dimilioc house as though he was considering storming it like a castle and prying the help Grayson had denied him out of the Master's hands like a prize of war.

Natividad liked him. She liked the way he hit the side of

his car with the palm of his hand: she liked the clean, human anger in him. She should ask Miguel what he thought before she did anything really risky, but there was no time; in just a moment the sheriff would get in his car and drive away.

So, she walked boldly across the snowy drive, opened the passenger side door, and leaped up to the seat. It was warm in the car – a measure of how brief the sheriff's visit had been. "Quick," she said, while Sheriff Pearson was still staring at her. "Unless you want somebody to peek out and think you're kidnapping me. Quick, let's go!"

That got the man moving: no questions, just swift, economical movements. He, too, had to jump to get into the vehicle. Then he started the car, swung it around without pausing, and drove toward the forest. He glanced once and then again into the rearview mirror. So did Natividad. She more than half expected a sudden uproar, Grayson or Harrison or somebody to race out of the house and after them.

But there was no sign anybody had seen her get in the sheriff's car. She faced forward again, but then found that the trampled, torn-up snow, spattered with the remnants of battle, looked even worse up close. Natividad was glad of the drifting snow in the air: let clean snow cover up all the ugly reminders of blood and fire and death...

"I gather you had a fight here?" said Sheriff Pearson. He glanced sidelong at Natividad. "Miss…?"

She shrugged. "Natividad. Natividad Toland."

"Ah," said the sheriff, obviously recognizing the name of one of Dimilioc's bloodlines.

"My mother was Mexican," Natividad volunteered, although this was no doubt obvious.

"Ah," the sheriff said again. He gave her a sharp look, but didn't ask any other questions. Not about her family, anyway. He gestured out at the blood-spattered snow. "What happened?"

"Oh. It could've been way worse. Nobody got killed. None of us, I mean." Natividad wondered whether she would still be able to say the same in twenty-four hours, in a week. She didn't want to think about that. Surely in a week it would be all over? She said unhappily, "I guess maybe it'll get worse before it gets better."

"Um." The sheriff gave a nod of grim agreement. "We thought... In town, we thought we were *done* with these damned vampire wars."

"Oh, yes," Natividad agreed. "Yes." She remembered those days. "We thought how much safer we would be after the vampires were all gone, how much better everything would be. Maybe soon everything will really be over." She hoped that would be true. She put all that hope into words: "Dimilioc will kill Vonhausel and his black dogs, and build back its own strength, and everything will be better. Your daughter will be alright, you know; I'm sure Grayson wouldn't lie about that. What's her name? Your daughter?"

"Cassandra. Cassie." The sheriff was silent for a while. Natividad did not press him to speak, but tried to make her silence as supportive as possible. At last he went on, "She's no one you'd think... no one who ought to be a... a..." He didn't seem able to complete this sentence.

"We don't say *werewolf*," Natividad told him. "Maybe you know that? That's Hollywood and the TV *noticieros informativos*, what do you say in English? The talking heads?"

It was a good term. She said, not hiding her scorn: "They pretend they've figured everything out, but they don't know anything. Not even now, when it's been months and months since the vampire magic stopped clouding their minds."

"Yes," said the sheriff. "We..." He stopped.

"They don't know about black dogs except bits and pieces. And lots of the pieces are wrong, anyway. Them, they only know about the bitten ones. They say *werewolf* when they mean moon-bound, and then they think that's all there is." She glanced sidelong at the sheriff. "It's different for you, I guess, since you're right here, almost part of Dimilioc. Isn't that right?"

"Yes. More or less. But I don't..." the sheriff's voice shook a little. He looked at her, a quick glance, and away again. "I don't know, I don't think I ever... No one I knew was ever bitten, Dimilioc wolves don't *do* that..."

"Oh, well..." Natividad tried to think what she could say that would be both true and reassuring. "It's not like in the movies, you know?" It was both better and worse than movies made it seem. There was a lot she didn't want to say. "You can have a good life after you've been bitten, if you have a black dog to help you." It wasn't really that simple, and hardly any moon-bound shifter could trust a black dog to actually *help* her, but what good would it be to say that? Besides, she was sure Sheriff Pearson and his daughter really could trust Grayson Lanning.

The sheriff glanced at her, then back at the snowy road. After a moment of silence, he said, his tone once again controlled, "Grayson had to search hard to find you, I suppose. I expect he'll be angry when he discovers you came with me."

He would be. Natividad knew *she* was safe, but she looked at the sheriff in sudden concern. "Will you be alright? It's all my fault," she added, thinking aloud. "*I'm* the one who disobeyed him..." Even to her, this argument seemed disturbingly weak. If Grayson lost his temper with the sheriff... She frowned, worried.

"It's you I'm thinking of, Miss Toland."

"Oh, me? You don't have to worry about me." Natividad put her hands together in a pose of angelic innocence, then pretended to remove and polish an invisible halo. "You said it yourself: I'm Pure." Dropping the pose, she leaned an elbow on the armrest and studied the sheriff. He didn't look afraid. He ought to. She said, "But *you're* not. If Grayson is very angry with you – if he loses control of his black dog..."

"Grayson Lanning? Lose control?"

Natividad bounced around in her seat to face Sheriff Pearson more directly. "No?"

"No," said the sheriff with finality. "He won't lose his temper and kill me, and he won't hurt my daughter to punish me. Grayson doesn't scare me: I dealt with Thos Korte for years, and Grayson's no Thos Korte. Thank God." He negotiated a sharp curve; the vehicle lurched and swayed, thumped over an unseen obstacle, and eased onto a part of the road that was thankfully both straight and nearly level. There was more light now, but the snow whirling through the air made it hard to see. That didn't seem to bother the sheriff. He said, "He *will* help Cass–"

"Nothing can keep her from the change, if her shadow's been corrupted," Natividad said. She said it apologetically, because she knew it wasn't what the sheriff wanted to hear.

He must already know that, but he probably didn't want to believe it. "But Grayson or any Dimilioc wolf can control her even when she's in her other form, and when the moon wanes she'll change back."

"She'll still be herself…"

This was kind of a question. Natividad wished she could just say, "*Oh, yes, just like she used to be.*" She said, "Pretty much. Way more than if she had to deal with shadow memories of, well. Of hunting." She didn't want to say *killing*, or think about what kind of prey the girl might have hunted if the sheriff hadn't brought her to Dimilioc. The bitten ones almost always went after their own kin first.

"I see," said the sheriff. "Yes, I see."

Natividad had an idea he understood a lot of what she hadn't said. He was shrewd, and he obviously knew at least *something* about black dogs and moon-bound shifters and the Pure. His voice was nice when he wasn't so upset. His accent was interesting. Stronger, or at least different, than the accent of the black wolves.

She said, "Grayson Lanning didn't find us. We came here on purpose." She didn't explain why, or what they had brought with them, but added instead, "My brothers and me."

"Black dog brothers," the sheriff guessed.

"One," Natividad corrected. "The other is human." She looked out at the whirling snowflakes. They were coming down even more densely now, and the clouds had thickened so that they still needed their headlights even though it should have been full daylight.

"I'll get you back safe," Sheriff Pearson promised her. He patted the steering wheel. "This girl can go up and over anything that doesn't need a plow – and we can mount a plow on her, if the snow gets that deep."

One *plowed* snow, like a field in the spring? Natividad tried to visualize this. It was a strange image. It didn't make sense to cut furrows in the snow, so she supposed he meant something else. Shoving it out of the way, maybe. How deep would snow have to get, before one had to plow it? Natividad had thought that the knee-high snow they'd hiked through on their way to Dimilioc was deep enough. She wondered how deep it could get. Hip high, chest high, head high? Higher? That was hard to imagine, but what if it kept snowing and didn't stop? Would Ezekiel and Alejandro be able to get back?

She said impulsively, "Stop, stop for a moment?" And, to Pearson's startled, wary glance, "It's nothing, there's nothing, only stop just for a moment, will you?"

The sheriff eased off on the gas pedal, letting his big vehicle coast to a halt at the top of a hill. He killed the engine. Silence immediately pressed in around them. It was not a welcoming silence. Natividad peered into the dim light under the trees, barely able to see through the falling snow. She wished the sheriff had silver bullets. She wished she'd thought to stop in her room and get her *maraña mágica*. A way to confuse the steps of her enemies would be better than nothing – if there *were* enemies. She was sure there weren't. She told herself that, very firmly. She said, "Watch the woods, OK? If you see anything, yell, right?"

"You–"

"I'll only be a minute," Natividad said. She opened her door and slid down into the snow before she could change her mind. It was shockingly cold. She had a hard time remembering between one venture outside and the next how cold it really *was* here. The air felt like ice in her throat. She ought to have remembered her coat – a lot of good it did her, back in her room – well, the cold was another reason to hurry, if she needed one.

Stooping, she ran her hand through the snow on the surface of the road. Then, shivering, she knelt, scooped as much snow as possible out of the way, and drew a line on the packed ice below. Another line, parallel to the first. Straight, clean lines of light, showing the way the road ran, reinforcing its road-ness. Roads were for people to come and go. She said, "*Que esta carretera escoga a los viajeros.*" She drew a pentagram between her two lines, stood up straight, and lifted her hands, palm up, toward the sky. She repeated, only this time in English, "May this road welcome travelers who come with good will in their hearts. May they find their way safely to their journey's end." Light, pale and cold, filled her hands. The snow still fell all around, but somehow seemed to blow sideways and away from the road.

Smiling, Natividad said "*Bueno.*" She walked back around to the open passenger's door.

Sheriff Pearson started the car again. He said softly, fervently, "I swear I'll do everything I can to get you back to Dimilioc safely, but God, I'm glad you came with me."

Natividad was surprised. "You've had Pure women work with you before – you've had somebody put protection around your homes and along your roads, surely? I mean... you have, haven't you?"

"I've never seen anyone do what you just did," Pearson

said. He drove on in silence for a few minutes while the snow came down harder and harder, and yet didn't accumulate on the road before them. At last he added, "It's why we support Dimilioc – even when a bastard like Thos Korte is Master. We support Dimilioc because it protects people like you." The sheriff paused, then added more briskly, "Alright: tell me what you can do for Lewis. What do you need from me, from us?" He took out a cell phone and waited expectantly.

Natividad thought about what she could do. About what she could do even if she didn't have a lot of time. About really big circles. How would Mamá have done this? She closed her eyes and tried to let the memories come.

"Pure magic is for defense," Mamá's voice said, out of memory. Mamá looked up at her and smiled, patting the ground. Natividad had nodded – she knew that. She had knelt down in the dusty sunlight of the afternoon. The sun-warmed carpet of needles beneath the pines smelled sharp. It was a good smell that mingled with the dusty scent of the hot earth and the tang of wood smoke and the fragrance of the chilies one of the neighbors was smoking over a slow fire: it smelled like home, and peace, and childhood.

"Pure magic is for defense," Mamá repeated. "But sometimes it can be an *aggressive* defense." She had smiled at Natividad, a warm, amused smile that invited Natividad to share the joke. Natividad had grinned in return, because no one could resist Mamá's smiles.

But it hadn't been a joke after all, and not even an aggressive defense had been enough, in the end. The pines had burned like slender torches, twenty-one columns of flame in a circle around the great oak – demonic fire, that burned black at its heart.

The air had smelled of burning and bitter ash – in the distance, someone had been screaming...

Natividad caught her breath, her heart racing. She had been wrong to try to remember; she realized that now. She was trembling. She couldn't work good strong magic if she was scared. You had to be brave to work Pure magic – she almost remembered Mamá saying *Mi hija valianta,* and something about courage and strength, something about Pure magic and light and darkness.

Only right at the end, everything had failed after all.

She flinched from the memory and said, very quickly, "I can do defensive things. That's what Pure magic is for, you know? I can't make you weapons or anything, but I'll make you a big mandala, a crossed circle." She was *almost* sure she could do it. It would have to be a *very* big circle. But she *thought* she could do it. She said, firmly, to keep her voice from shaking, "It's protection, but kind of an *aggressive* protection, you know? It shoves bad things out, if you do it right. And stops them coming in, of course. Is that OK?"

"If it works at all, it's better than OK."

Natividad nodded. Mamá had said – she tried to remember without really *remembering* – something about anchoring really big mandalas, something about the cross... Oh, yes, of course, the *cross.* "You have a church in your town, don't you?" she asked. "A Catholic church?" And, at the sheriff's surprised nod, "Alright, good. That's what I'm used to – that'll help. I think I'll draw a mandala with your church at the center of the cross, you know? I'll do the biggest mandala I can, but then anybody who lives outside the edge should maybe come in. But a circle to keep out the fell dark, that would help, don't you think?"

"If it would keep out black dogs, it will be a great help," the sheriff assured her fervently. "I'm sure everyone will be very glad to have you draw your circle anywhere you like. You can draw one big enough to enclose the *whole* town?"

"Well, nearly. I think so." Natividad tried not to doubt it. Doubt wouldn't help. She said quickly, "I can do it, but it won't work as well against black dogs as it would against vampires. Nothing will. You know that, right? But it'll work way better than nothing. Mamá said…" She stopped, took a breath, and said, "I want crosses, too."

"Crosses?"

"Yes, to make into, you know…" She didn't know the words for what she wanted to say. "Aggressive protection" was about as close as she could come. She wasn't sure there were English words for what she meant. "Mamá taught me to make, well, these things. *Aparatos*. Tools, I guess. Things to call light, to catch and trap shadows, you know? So they can anchor the mandala. You know about that?"

"No," said the sheriff. "But that sounds fine."

Natividad was surprised. What in the world had Dimilioc's own Pure women done to protect people, if not made the same kinds of *aparatos* Mamá had shown her? She said, "Well, what I want is big wooden crosses to anchor the mandala. Wrapped with silver. You probably have crosses like that left over from the war?"

"Oh, yes."

"OK," said Natividad. "Good. Four crosses. The biggest you have. As tall as I am, if you have any that big. We'll put them at the compass directions. As exactly as possible, so somebody should figure out where on the circle they should go. The crosses can be plain, but Mamá... Mamá always said it's better if they have writing on them. 'Though I walk through the valley of the shadow of death, I will fear no evil' – things like that, you know? And your priest should renew the blessings on them, that'll help almost as much as the silver."

"Crosses, we've got," repeated the sheriff. He nodded. "A plan for where to put your circle and four big crosses." He smiled at her. "What else?"

"...I think that's all." Natividad rubbed her face. Had she missed anything obvious? If Mamá was here... She wasn't. She never would be, never again, never... Natividad was on her own. She turned her face away, squeezed her eyes shut, and thought fiercely about mandalas.

8

Lewis was very small. It seemed even smaller than Natividad remembered from their brief pause on the way to Dimilioc, but then they had been too tired and anxious to explore. She looked around as they drove through it now. This town was much more prosperous-looking than Hualahuises, but not very much larger than Potosi. If there were even a hundred families here, that would surprise Natividad.

There was a tiny brick post office, and an even smaller police station, which looked like somebody's house and not like a government building at all. She and her brothers had eaten sandwiches at that little place adjacent to the post office. It was a small, shabby diner, only half a dozen tables covered with cheap faded cloths that might once have been yellow, centered with narrow vases holding plastic flowers. But the sandwiches had been good. Also on the main street were a few shops, one with farm equipment and one with coats and sweaters and shoes, old books and children's toys and little statues in its window, really *toda clase de cosas*. There was a little grocery store, and a bar that Natividad thought might also be a restaurant. Everything else in sight was a private home, those big American houses, with a lot of space around each as though Americans wanted to pretend they didn't have neighbors.

Nearly all the buildings were made of wood, but at the far end of the street, in the center of an open town square, reared a great stone church, far bigger than was reasonable for a town this size. Except, of course, that Lewis was right in Dimilioc's backyard. No wonder the people who had founded the town here had wanted a big church. A proper Catholic church, too, which was good. Its bell tower was easily the tallest thing in the whole town, and the glass of its windows sparkled blue and red and gold even in the dull light that filtered past the clouds.

Natividad immediately felt happier, more at home, especially because when she experimentally turned her head to glance at it sideways, she saw that the whole church was immersed in soft light as though illuminated by the glow of the full moon, even though it was daylight and *nublado*. Overcast. She smiled – then lost the smile, thinking about the Pure woman who must have wrapped those layers of protection around the church. She would be dead now, whoever she had been. The war between black dogs and the blood kin had been terrible for the Pure.

Sheriff Pearson drove straight past the police station and tucked his big vehicle by the curb in front of the church. It took up enough space for two ordinary cars. He turned off the engine. Immediately the silence of the town seemed to fold itself around them. Natividad realized that she had seen only a few other cars moving on the road, and no one on foot. Was that the snow? Or was everyone so afraid?

Then someone opened the church door and people flooded out into the town square, young men with shotguns and in their midst a priest, the white collar at his throat a reassurance in any time of trouble. At first it seemed like a crowd, though when Natividad sorted them out, she saw that besides the priest, there were really only three men.

"Father McClanahan," Sheriff Pearson said briskly. "He's worked with the Pure now and then. And my deputies – I only have one, ordinarily, but I thought it just as well to do a little recruiting yesterday. Now I'm glad of it. Shotguns may not be magic, but they slow most things down." He opened his door and jumped to the street before Natividad could ask him what kind of ammunition those guns were loaded with.

The priest was a big man with a round, soft face and a rounder, softer body. His thinning hair was reddish, his eyes blue, his nose crooked, his mouth made for smiling. But he wasn't smiling now. He took Natividad's hands in his, looked at her with concentrated attention, and said, "Pure, are you, then? Good. That's good. God knows I spent the night praying Grayson Lanning would send us real help." Before she could answer, he added to Sheriff Pearson, "How is Cassie?"

"Fine," the sheriff said, clearly meaning he didn't want to talk about it. "Natividad, these men are my deputies – Belliveau, Harris, and Denoux. Well, Denoux? How have things been here? Quiet?"

The deputy addressed, a stocky man with fair hair and a round face and blue eyes set at a slight slant in his face, shook his head and opened his hands. "Not as quiet as we'd wish, Sheriff. The Stewarts found all their cows slaughtered. Torn up in big chunks, partly eaten, blood everywhere. Not an hour past. They turned around and drove right back here, seeing nothing worse than ravens on the way."

"They're in the rectory now," Father McClanahan put in. "Thanking God the kids weren't out making snowmen when the killers came by."

Pearson nodded, his mouth tightening.

"That was never vampire work," Father McClanahan said to Natividad, a faint question in his tone. "Black dogs, I guess. But we've never had trouble with black dogs before…"

"With Dimilioc right there on your doorstep, I guess not! But you're going to have trouble now. Until Dimilioc builds back its strength." Natividad didn't want to be so blunt, but it was true. She didn't want to think about what would happen to Lewis if Dimilioc couldn't build back, if instead it got overrun by Vonhausel's black dogs.

"You trust that damned Lanning bastard?" one of the deputies, Belliveau, asked her. His tone was more than a little hostile. He was clearly the oldest of the three, a man with grizzled hair and a hard mouth.

Natividad tried not to wince visibly. She said quickly, "Some black dogs, you *can* trust. My Papá, he was a black dog, you know? And my brother, he is, too." She looked from one deputy to the next and then the next. Their expressions ranged from intent to suspicious, though Denoux did not look actually hostile and Harris, youngest of the three, gave her a swift grin when she met his eyes. She smiled back and said to all three of the men, as firmly as possible, "If you don't want to run for Newport, you'd better trust Grayson

Lanning, and Dimilioc, and me, because if you don't have us you don't have *anything*. Shotguns and prayers are both good, but they're not going to be enough."

"That's true, by God," Father McClanahan said. "That's true, and we know it." He looked anxiously around at the three deputies, then back at Natividad. "We don't know you, young lady, but we know what you are. Don't worry about us."

Natividad nodded, grateful for his support. She said, speaking quickly because she hated what she had to say, "Dimilioc beat them once, you know, those other black dogs, but I don't think they're giving up, I really don't. I think they're going to stay right here and try again, and as long as black dog strays are gathering in the woods around Lewis, you're all in a whole lot of trouble. You really *ought* to leave. Newport…" The men were all shaking their heads.

"This is our home!" Harris said right out, almost as fierce as a territorial black dog. "We didn't let those damned vampires drive us out, and we won't run from black dogs!"

Belliveau nodded with grim conviction, and Denoux said, "That's right, miss. That's how it is."

Natividad supposed after the vampire war, these people probably knew their own minds pretty well. She shrugged. "Then at least you've got a good church to anchor my circle. I guess you had some trouble with vampires during the war?" This was met by a grim laugh from the oldest man. She nodded. "Then you'll want to remember, black dogs aren't vampires. A church, a good solid church with Pure magic all through it, like this one you've got…" She nodded to the ornate building with its clean stone and tall bell tower and finished, "No vampire or vampire magic could get into a church like this one. But black dogs aren't vampires, you know? A church is pretty safe against black dogs, but not all the way safe. So, a protective circle will give you another line of defense. It won't keep out everything, but it'll help, and it'll give you time so you can figure out other things to do."

Sheriff Pearson nodded, and when different people started to ask questions or argue or whatever, the sheriff lifted a hand to stop them. Then he nodded again to Natividad. "You'll draw your circle. We'll start in fifteen minutes." Belliveau began to interrupt, but the sheriff stared him down effortlessly. "We'll move as fast as we can," he said flatly. "Grayson Lanning didn't want Miss Toland to leave Dimilioc House. He's going to come after her soon enough, I figure. We don't want half a circle."

"Damn black dog son of a bitch," Belliveau muttered.

"Don't say that!" Natividad told him instantly. "Really, don't. Black dogs walk so close to the edge of Hell anyway. Never damn a black dog, it could happen, do you see? And Grayson's not your enemy."

Belliveau looked first taken aback, and then embarrassed. Father McClanahan said, "Good advice for us all, isn't it?"

Denoux added to the older deputy, "Don't be an ass, Frank. You know nobody would be left alive in this town – hell, this *county* – if it weren't for Grayson Lanning and Dimilioc." He gave Natividad a firm nod and added, "We do know who the enemy is, miss – and who it isn't."

Sheriff Pearson lifted a hand to reclaim all their attention, then turned to take a map from one of the young men. He flattened this out to show Natividad. The deputy had drawn a neat circle across the map in red ink, centered on the church and cutting ruthlessly through all other property. Natividad wished she'd thought to say not to use red. But the map was good. And red ink could stand for cheerful things just as easily as it could stand for blood, if she was careful how she thought about it. The map would do. She nodded.

Lewis was tiny. But when you had to go from one house or shop to another and draw pentagrams on all the windows; when you had to brush snow out of the way on all the streets between and draw lines along them; when you had to climb over fences and pick your way across a stubbled, snowy field and then across a frozen creek, it all made the town seem much larger. She already knew she wouldn't have time to make little *aparatos* for people to wear. Just laying the mandala and setting up the big crosses would take all the time there was.

Especially with the snow coming down so hard you could hardly see one building from the next. Natividad hadn't ever imagined snow could fall like this, in whirling curtains, so thick you could hardly see through it, driven by an icy wind that cut like a silver knife. Anything could be hidden behind that blowing snow. The three deputies might have shotguns, but they only had regular ammunition. Silver was expensive, Denoux said, and they'd used a lot during the vampire war, and if they wanted more, they had to buy it themselves. She bet now they wished they had.

But there was only a little way to go to find the place they would set up the first cross. This proved to be a nice warm home with a woman and a lot of children. Natividad liked them all immediately. She accepted a wedge of ginger cake the woman pressed on her – it had a wonderful cinnamon cream with it, dolloped on with a generous hand.

She let the children watch as she set up the first cross, off-center in a fancy, formal room right at the front of the house. It was a good cross, almost as tall as Natividad herself, made of some soft gray wood. It might have been plain except for the care with which it had been made. Its maker had wound a thin silver chain in a spiral around the horizontal crosspiece and painted, in silver paint, "I will fear no evil, for God is with me," in elegant calligraphy down the front. A stand for the cross had also been supplied, but of course Natividad did not need to use the stand – she set the cross where it needed to go and drew the beginnings of her protective circle out to either side of it, and it stood firmly when she took her hands away.

"Leave somebody to watch to make sure nobody moves it before I've finished," Natividad told Sheriff Pearson, while the magic she'd begun buzzed in her ears and sparkled along her nerves. "It'll stand forever then. Nobody will be able to knock it down while the circle holds."

"And a fine conversation piece it'll be," commented the woman who owned the house. "But don't be telling the brats it can't be knocked down; they'll take it as a challenge, won't they?" She wasn't exactly smiling, but Natividad thought she liked the cross. "Don't you fret, young lady: no one will overset your cross. Is that done, now?"

"Almost," Natividad murmured. She drew pentagrams on all the windows of the house, filling the signs with moonlight as she went, and then for fun demonstrated to the children how they could now throw a ball or toy against a window and it would only bounce off, the glass ringing like a bell.

"Hah!" one of the boys said triumphantly. "We can *so* play baseball in the house! Can you do Mrs Wilson's windows, too?"

"Edith Wilson's next on our list," Denoux said, amused and indulgent, while the children's mother pretended to be horrified.

"Use your back door now, not your front door," Natividad told the woman before they left. "Every place behind you is safer now – not all the way safe, but better – but don't go out the front, OK?"

The woman promised that everyone would remember, scowled fiercely at her children until they promised, too, and made a show of locking her front door after Natividad when she and her deputies left.

After Mrs Wilson's house there was another house, and another after that, and then a shop, and a long curving driveway, and then more houses, and finally another cross to set, directly in front of somebody's kitchen sink, which might be inconvenient for them but that's where it needed to go. Then there were more houses and shops; and annoying fences; and a brush-tangled gulley to climb down into, which was hard, and then up out of, which was even harder; and then *more* houses and shops. And more after that.

"How much farther?" she asked, foggy with weariness and magic. She felt like she must have laid signs of protection and goodwill on every house in Lewis, not just the ones set in the planned mandala. Only after she'd spoken, with the sound of her words echoing in the air and Sheriff Pearson looking at her blankly, did she realize her words had been in Spanish. This must be like Alejandro, when his shadow closed around him: this struggle with language and memory and thought... The sheriff pointed, saying something she didn't understand, and she walked that way, blindly, trusting it was the right way to go.

But alarm broke into her weariness when she saw one of the deputies – Harris – pick up the last of the crosses as though it weighed nothing. The young man started ahead, and she realized the cross needed to go right out in the middle of a field.

The cross was a good one, Natividad's favorite of the four that the townspeople had provided. Taller than she was, this one had been made of some smooth polished wood riveted together with silver fittings. She'd thought at first they must really be steel, but no: they had the clean, bright feel of silver. Across the crossbar, letters spelled out "Christ Our Light," and down the front, "Thanks Be To God." The letters had not merely been painted on the cross, but carved into the wood before being highlighted with silver paint that had real silver in it.

So, the cross was fine. It wasn't the *cross* that was the problem; it was the field: a measureless blind white space with snow underfoot and snow blowing in whirling curtains through the air.

The cold was horrible, much worse than when she and her brothers had walked those last miles through the forest toward Dimilioc. There had been no wind that day. Today the wind bit like a vampire: ferocious and draining. Worse, it was impossible to see through all that white, impossible to see a man who walked ten steps away. Anything could hide in the blinding snow just as easily as in the dark of night, and Natividad found herself certain that something *was* hiding out there in that field, something – someone – that knew where they were, where *she* was, by a strange kind of vision that used malice instead of light to find her.

She stopped, trying to look in every direction at once, as frightened of the blind field as she was pressed by the need to finish the magic. Behind her, a line of soft light arced out, visible despite the blowing snow. This should have made her feel better. Safer. But if she could see the light of her protective circle by using senses that didn't exactly involve sight, didn't that mean Vonhausel might see her the same way?

Sheriff Pearson touched her arm. His hood was back; snow caught and melted in his hair, on his face. He said something... Natividad stared at him, shook her head, took a step out into the open field. The sheriff said something else, more loudly, not to her, and the deputies all got serious expressions and checked their guns.

Nothing came at them except the wind. Natividad drew her circle across the field with every step, feeling it sink down into the frozen ground beneath the snow. She felt the shape of the mandala humming in the earth, slightly discordant, waiting to be completed with this last little arc and its anchoring cross. There was so little left to do, and still the only enemy they had to face was the savage wind...

They came to the right place. Natividad knew it was right. She was surprised she had to catch Sheriff Pearson's arm to make him stop: it seemed to her that anybody ought to know that they had come to the exact eastern limit of the protective circle.

Deputy Harris brought her the cross. Natividad showed him where it needed to go, and he knelt earnestly to fit it exactly where she showed him. She touched his shoulder in thanks and he looked up and smiled at her, then got to his feet and steadied the cross as she stroked her fingers across the carved letters and smooth wood. She drew a breath and touched the top of it, reaching for the clean gift of magic to seal the cross into her mandala, and Harris suddenly staggered and fell into her. His gun spun away, into the air, lost instantly in the blowing white, which was suddenly spattered with red. Blood was on her hands, on the cross – Natividad could *smell* it, like meat and hot metal. A dark, hot magic swirled by her, so strong it shoved at her with almost physical weight. Natividad staggered, and the cross toppled over, threads of light from her shredding magic trailing after it.

Natividad tried to catch the cross as it fell, tried to catch the shreds of her light and magic before they could dissolve into the air, but the cross was too heavy or the light too delicate, and she fell instead, floundering in the snow. She was, she found, more outraged than terrified. *Her* cross, thrown down in the snow! And poor Deputy Harris was *dead*, there was death and violence all around her – someone was screaming, one of the other deputies, a male voice pitched high as a girl's, and she couldn't even get her *cross* set. She was *furious*.

Natividad gripped the smooth wood of the cross in both hands, heaved it up and whirled it around with an effort she felt all through her back and stomach and shoulders – it was a lot heavier than she'd guessed – then she staggered and fell to one knee when a shotgun blast crashed next to her. But, once kneeling, she could brace the cross against the ground, haul it upright, embrace it with both arms to hold it steady. She called light into the silver-limned letters carved into the wood, and a net of light spilled down and around the arms of the cross. She expected all the time to feel claws tear into her back, powerful jaws clamp down on the back of her neck. There was another shotgun blast followed by a heavy, coughing roar then a huge dark shape loomed at her out of the snow, and she screamed...

Sheriff Pearson strode out of the blowing snow, leveled a shotgun at the black dog, and pulled the trigger twice in quick succession: pump, *boom*, pump, *boom*. The black dog staggered back a step, but his shadow writhed thickly as it carried away injuries that ought to have killed any natural creature, that would have killed even most black dogs. He didn't even seem to need to shift to human form and back again to shed his wounds, which seemed strange, but Natividad had no attention to spare for that. The light from her cross had tangled with the black dog's trailing shadow, *that* was what she was worried about, but she couldn't see anything she could do about it now. Lunging to her feet, she hauled the cross up as straight as possible, drew a pentagram where the crosspiece met the upright, and cried, "May the strength of God fill this cross! May this cross guard Lewis and all within against any who come with ill intent! And against the fell dark! *And against all manner of evil things!*"

She did not know whether she was shouting in Spanish or English, did not think the words in whatever language were exactly the ones her mother had taught her, but light followed her hands, running swiftly up and down the length of the cross. The light knotted where the blood spatters contaminated the wood, and everywhere it tangled up with the black dog's shadow, but it gathered strength despite that and exploded outward. Light, intertwined with blood and shadows, spilled out across the snow, reached left and right along the circle, and speared back along the cross that centered her mandala, rushing away toward the heart of the town. The power of the circle smashed out into the night as it closed, much greater than Natividad had expected; the force of it sent her staggering sideways and then she lost her balance and fell – away from the mandala, exactly the wrong way. Though she tried to scramble back toward safety, the black dog was too close and she ducked the other way even though she knew she shouldn't. But all her muscles spasmed with magic, and she fell again and then found she could not get back to her feet, couldn't even scramble away on her hands and knees, though she tried. The mandala was doing *something*, very strongly, but not the way she'd meant it to – even if she could get to it, it might not work to keep the black dog away, but she couldn't even *move*, she was helpless, and the black dog was going to kill her…

The black dog had taken several steps away from the mandala, but he had not fled from it. He was in human form now, laughing and cursing at the same time. The laughter and the curses sounded the same: aggressive and furious and savage, with nothing of humor, not even cruel humor. His human shape was tall, blunt-featured, angry. Natividad cowered down. She was sure he was going to kill her, but Sheriff Pearson stepped in front of her. His hands moved quickly to reload the shotgun.

Their enemy shifted again to his black dog shape. He showed no sign of any wounds, no fear of the sheriff's gun. He was enormous, the largest black dog Natividad had ever seen, with heavy shoulders and a thick neck and powerful jaws. His eyes were crimson, his breath black smoke that wreathed around his huge head; the snow melted away from his tracks. The cold air smelled of sulfur and blood.

Sheriff Pearson's movements were economical and quick – he had a shell in the chamber, he was lifting the gun – but even so it was perfectly clear to Natividad that the black dog would tear him apart before he could shoot again. She knew the moment the sheriff was out of the way, the black dog would tear *her* apart, too, but she still couldn't move.

Another black dog flung himself out of the blinding snow, trailing smoke and a hot gust of sulfurous air. He slammed into the first with such force that both were hurled backward and disappeared. A shattering roar tore through the blind snow-filled light. Natividad put her hands over her ears and tucked herself down as small as she could, like a little mouse trying to hide from a very big cat. But nothing lunged out of the snow to grab her, and after a moment she couldn't help but open her eyes and straighten cautiously, trying to see. She could still smell blood – she was sure she could still smell the blood, mixed with smoke and sulfur. But there was no sound, no movement except the blowing snow.

The sheriff stood over her, his gun ready but no enemy now to shoot at. He asked her, sharp and tense, "Can you get up?"

Natividad thought she *could* stand, maybe, now. She tried, cautiously, and found the power of her mandala had... not faded, exactly, but it had become less... less immediate. Less intense. Less something. If she couldn't get up, she could now at least crawl. The dubious protection of the mandala, whatever the contamination of the black dog's shadow had done to it, would almost certainly be a lot better than staying where she was.

The sheriff was not exactly illuminated by the light that radiated from the cross and the mandala, because that kind of light didn't exactly illuminate anything, but Natividad could see that raking claws had shredded his coat, that bruises were darkening on his face. But he seemed to be alright, mostly. He turned his head slowly back and forth, listening as he waited for her to do her part, to at least *try* to save herself. Nothing could be heard, now, but the wind.

Natividad staggered to her feet. She *could* get to her feet, now, barely, and looked for her mandala. She moved stiffly in that direction. Sheriff Pearson backed up beside her, watching not her, but everything else. The cross stood straight and firm, only a little way away. Natividad limped toward it. Neither her light, nor the black dog shadow tangled with it, were visible, now. Not exactly *visible* but she knew that both were still there.

Natividad didn't understand what she had made. Black dog magic and Pure magic shouldn't mix, though it was a little like blooding silver for a black dog. Well, not really. Had

Mamá ever said anything about contaminating Pure magic with black dog magic? She couldn't remember anything like that, but everything near the end had happened so fast and she had been so scared and her memories of those last days were all in bits and pieces. She wanted to study what she'd done; she wanted to figure it out; she wanted to be able to tell the townspeople what kind of circle she'd put around them. But she was sure that she wouldn't get the chance to figure out anything – any moment, that huge black dog would lunge out of the blind white snow surrounding them and kill first Sheriff Pearson and then her.

Deputy Denoux lay, crumpled and still, just near enough to be visible. The dark heap of his eviscerated body was already disappearing under the snow, which seemed a mercy, like throwing a blanket over the dead. All the blood, too, was already chilling and being covered over by the snow. She could see part of another leg that probably belonged to Belliveau. Natividad shivered, and then couldn't stop. They were all dead, those three deputies who had come to protect her: bad-tempered suspicious Belliveau and polite Denoux and young Harris. All three of them *had* protected her, with their lives. Would they feel like that was fair? *She* didn't. She put a hand out. The cross was only a step away, now, and she could feel the magic in it like a physical pressure against her skin: not exactly Pure, but she couldn't decide whether the difference felt bad or actually sort of OK. She knew it felt strange. It felt *powerful*, though.

The snow parted like a veil, revealing a black dog who loped toward them, fluid as a lion and a lot more dangerous. The black dog moved very fast, out of the blowing snow and

past the dead man. He straightened toward human form as
he moved forward, and he hardly seemed less massive in his
human form than as a black dog. It wasn't the same one as
before. Sheriff Pearson aimed his shotgun at the newcomer's
chest, but didn't fire, and at first Natividad didn't understand
why, but then she saw that the black dog had caught the
barrel. He twisted the gun out of the sheriff's grip, and closed
his other hand, nearly human now, around Pearson's throat.

It was Harrison Lanning. There was no sign of the other
black dog.

Harrison flung the shotgun aside, bore the sheriff straight
through the circle of the mandala right down to the ground
and pinned him flat, all in the same silent rush.

"It wasn't his fault!" Natividad cried. "It was mine!"

Harrison released Pearson, came to his feet, and swung
around to confront Natividad. He was fully in his human
form now, except for his fiery eyes. Behind him, Pearson
came up on one elbow, not hurt at all. To Natividad's relief,
he didn't get all the way up, and Harrison didn't whirl back
to strike him down to the ground. Natividad realized at last
– she was ashamed she hadn't understood it from the first
– that Harrison had thrown the sheriff to the ground not as
an attack nor even as the precursor for an attack, but as a
way to *prevent* an attack. Not the sheriff's, but his own. He
hadn't trusted Sheriff Pearson to know he needed to show
submission, hadn't trusted himself to tolerate any show of
defiance, so he'd knocked the sheriff down with enough
force to remind him to be prudent. That was actually clever.
Even kind, sort of. As kind as a black dog in a raging temper
was likely able to manage.

It was also a reminder Natividad should not need. Not
that Harrison would hit *her*, she was pretty sure, but she
crouched down in the snow anyway. Well, sort of collapsed,
really. It was very easy to just let her legs fold up. It might
be harder to get up again. She asked, "Was that Vonhausel?
Is he dead?" Her voice shook. She couldn't help that.

Harrison answered grimly, not shouting, "Of course it
was Vonhausel. Of course he's not dead. But if Grayson
hadn't sent me after you, *you* would be dead! We would
have lost you! Reckless, irresponsible child!" Turning his
head, he glared down at Pearson. "*You* brought her into
this danger, when Grayson explicitly forbade it!" Harrison's
black dog still showed in his eyes, a powerful echo behind
his human form.

Sheriff Pearson didn't try to stand up. And he remembered
not to look directly into Harrison's face, so that was alright.
He stayed propped up his elbow – his other arm *was* hurt,
Natividad was almost sure – and said, "I lost good men
protecting Natividad. Is the circle she drew for us worth it?
You crossed it."

Harrison Lanning glowered down at him. "Of course it
was worth it – to *you*. It's a good, strong circle. It's blazing
like a bonfire."

"It's supposed to shut out those who come with ill
intent," Natividad said. Her voice was not quite steady. She
wanted to explain that black dog magic had gotten tangled
up with her work, but didn't know how. Instead, she took
a deep breath and tried to calm her nerves. She said, "I told
it to shut out *evil things*. I didn't mean it to work against
Dimilioc wolves. But…"

"It's fine," snapped Harrison. "Anybody could feel its strength, but it's not directing that strength at me. Worth your men?" he added to Pearson, still glowering. "How not? Worth losing the only Pure girl we have? How could it be?" He transferred his glare to Natividad. "Reckless, self-indulgent, childish, disobedient–"

"Lewis needed help." Natividad was still trembling. "*Si una persona pide ayuda, hay que ayudarle* – if somebody asks you for help, of course you should help them! If Grayson had sent you with me in the first place, it wouldn't have been so dangerous…"

"I am here now," Harrison said harshly, "and so if anyone attacks Dimilioc now, there will be one less wolf there to fight. That *is* your fault."

He was still furious, but there was a lot less of the black dog in his voice now. Even his eyes were almost human again. When he held an impatient hand down to Natividad, she took it and let him lift her to her feet. She *could* stand up. For a shaky moment she had not been sure. "Are they dead? All those men?"

"Of course. How else? That *you* are not shows either violent luck or the direct favor of God, neither of which you deserve." He took her arm in a hard grip, though not hard enough to bruise, which under the circumstances showed a lot of restraint.

Natividad bowed her head, meek as a black dog puppy.

"I will consider your punishment as we drive back to Dimilioc." Harrison transferred his glare back to Sheriff Pearson, who looked down almost as meekly as Natividad, and, she was sure, with no more sincerity. "I will need a vehicle." He held out a broad hand. "Your keys."

Pearson tossed over his car keys without a murmur of protest.

"It's as well you have your circle to show for your stupidity," Harrison told the sheriff. If he was not mollified, at least he had not been further provoked. His tone, if not exactly gentle, was no longer so savage. But he added, "If you find it insufficient, don't call on Dimilioc. Dimilioc will not be interested in your troubles." He shoved Natividad back toward town.

Natividad walked meekly the way Harrison pushed her, but she also turned her head to meet the sheriff's eyes. He was gathering himself to his feet at last, moving as though it hurt, but he paused questioningly as she caught his gaze.

She winked. Harrison might have said, *"Don't call on Dimilioc,"* but in that wink, Natividad hoped she communicated a different message. *If that mandala doesn't work*, she meant to convey, *or if it's not enough, call on me.*

Pearson nodded back, and if the movement looked like it hurt, it nevertheless carried reassuring determination.

Natividad waited to speak again until they had found the car. The bulky, broad-shouldered Harrison looked exactly like the kind of man who ought to drive such a big vehicle. He had to put the seat back several notches and even then he had to slouch down so that he could keep an eye on the rearview mirror.

Natividad did not object to anything. She pulled herself slowly into the passenger seat, the effort showing her how stiff she was. As soon as Harrison started the car, she turned the heater all the way up. She hadn't realized *exactly* how tired and cold and frightened she had been until she was in this nice car with its wonderful roomy seats and excellent heater. Though she wished the car could also do something about the fear. She wished they were already back at Dimilioc, safe in the house. If that was safe. Well, it would be safer than this car...

"You're tired," Harrison said to her, his rough tone almost a growl on the words. Yet, he did not seem angry any longer. Not *very* angry. He looked at her closely, his attention probably caught by her slow movements. "But you are not hurt."

"I don't think so," Natividad said. Though she *was* very tired. She didn't want to make the black wolf angry, not again, not now when he seemed so much calmer. But she said tentatively, "My mandala... I should explain... Vonhausel..."

"You can explain to Grayson," Harrison growled. "But Vonhausel will not challenge any Dimilioc wolf again until he can bring overwhelming force to bear. So, not today nor tonight." Then he ruined the certainty of this statement by adding, "Or I think not."

Natividad did not want to think about what might happen if he was wrong. If overwhelming force came against them on the road, when she and Harrison were alone... She wished, suddenly and intensely, that Ezekiel was already back from Chicago. And Alejandro. She wanted to be safe in her room at Dimilioc, she and Miguel and Alejandro, all safe.

No, that wasn't what she wanted at all. What she *really* wanted was a cup of hot chocolate, very strong and dark, the way her mother had made it. She wanted a hot bath and a soft bed and some silly light romance to read... She wanted, fiercely and suddenly, to go *home*. Tears prickled at the backs of her eyes.

"Though it's true you will have a great deal of time to rest once we are home," Harrison added, in counterpoint to Natividad's sudden *melancolia*. "You're grounded."

"Grounded?" He'd said he would consider her punishment, but this was so unexpected that Natividad found herself shocked out of her homesickness and grief and the remnants of her fear, and actually struggling not to laugh. She hadn't known that Harrison had a sense of humor at all, and then he came out with something like that!

The black wolf gave her a look that was not exactly a scowl. Or if it was a scowl, it wasn't exactly bad temper behind it. He said, his tone still harsh but no longer angry, "Grayson cannot order his executioner to beat you. Ezekiel would not obey. Besides, you aren't a young black dog, to be beaten into submission. You're too thin to be refused supper. So. You are grounded. I believe girls your age consider this a significant punishment. You will stay in your room until I release you."

"I'm not a baby–"

"You are *very* young," Harrison growled, in a tone of finality.

Natividad looked at him uncertainly. "Grayson..."

Harrison turned his head to glower at her, heavy brows drawn down over dark eyes. "What? Will you go to my brother asking for a lighter punishment?"

This wasn't what Natividad had meant. She said, "No, alright," in her meekest tone.

For some time, Harrison drove in silence. He glanced at her now and then, sideways glances that she could not read. He tapped his fingers on the gear shift. He adjusted and readjusted the angle of the steering wheel. And at last he said, "Grayson told me about the pentagrams you put on the living room windows. For him, you did that."

Natividad, still mostly thinking about the strange mandala she had made, wondered why this was a problem. "Yes?"

The big black dog glowered out at the falling snow. He handled Sheriff Pearson's big vehicle with a casual skill that Natividad found didn't surprise her at all. But he evidently found talking a harder task. Eventually he said, "Grayson was married. His wife was a black dog woman. Of course they did not have children. Except one that was stillborn."

Natividad said nothing, but her stomach clenched with sympathy. It was even worse for two black dogs to have children than for a black dog woman to have a child by a human man. The children of two black dogs, inheriting the shadow from both parents, would inevitably be eaten by their shadows way before they could grow up – all the boys, and most of the girls. Sometimes those infants really were stillborn, but black dogs who strove for basic human decency might also say *stillborn* when they meant they had killed such a child at birth. She found that she wasn't at all surprised that Grayson Lanning had loved a fierce, angry, strong black dog woman, the sort of woman who could match his own ferocity and strength. But it also wouldn't have surprised her, either, if he had spared such a woman as much as he could by taking on himself the worst duty that could face a black dog.

"She was killed early in the war," Harrison said, and stopped.

"I'm sorry," Natividad whispered. She was. That was terrible.

Harrison gave her a quick sideways scowl. "Grayson was going to come after you himself. I said I would come." He stopped again.

Whatever he wanted to say was apparently hard for him to put into words. Natividad looked away from him, out her window, at the blowing snow and the naked trees, so that he might find it easier.

"You could hurt my brother badly," Harrison said abruptly. "Especially if you thought he could not be hurt. He wants you to think he's impervious. He wants everyone to think he's impervious to everything. He is not. Do you understand?"

"Yes," Natividad said softly.

"When he looks at you, he sees every Dimilioc woman who died in the war. His wife, his baby daughter, he sees them both in you. All his hope for Dimilioc's future. You are not to kill yourself by some stupidity, do you understand? Your death would hurt him. Or if you just do not care for Dimilioc, you could hurt him that way. Do you understand that?"

"Yes," Natividad repeated. She found herself liking Harrison Lanning much more than she had expected she ever would. She said earnestly, "I understand you. I do. I want Dimilioc to prosper. I really do. I want everyone of Dimilioc to do well, to be happy."

Harrison made a wordless sound, a sort of grunt. After a while he said curtly, "You're still grounded. No straying from your room. No visitors."

"Yes, but my brothers–"

"You will not need to speak to them. I will tell them so." But at Natividad's dismayed silence, Harrison relented enough to add, "Though your brother Alejandro may come to see you when he returns. For one minute."

Even one minute was enough to make sure he was alright – enough for him to assure himself that she was alright. Natividad said, "Thank you," in her very politest tone.

9

Alejandro stared into the freezing wind. He could see nothing useful in the blinding confusion of snow. He had no idea how Ezekiel had landed their plane in this weather and less how the *verdugo* could drive in it so casually. There were chains on the tires, he said. Alejandro wondered whether these were literal chains, and why they made it easier to drive. By improving the tires' grip on the packed snow? Could the rounded links of chains actually help that way? But if the links were sharp, would they not destroy the tires?

Despite the special tires, Ezekiel had to constantly correct for the car sliding. All the way between Newport and Brighton, they passed trucks fitted with shovels to push the snow to the side of the road and other trucks throwing out what Ezekiel said was salt. Alejandro had no idea why salt was supposed to be helpful. Certainly neither salt nor shovel really cleared the road. Maybe nothing would clear it until spring.

Alejandro supposed that driving in the snow was something Americans naturally learned. *Por otre parte,* there were not many other cars on the road, so maybe even those who lived here didn't like driving in this bad weather. He was glad he did not need to drive. If Ezekiel collapsed in exhaustion... but the *verdugo* provided proof against weariness or pain. He drove and moved exactly as though he had never been injured with Thaddeus's silver knife. Alejandro could smell the blood and knew the cut had opened again, but neither the injury nor the hours of travel seemed to affect Ezekiel in the least.

If Alejandro could smell the blood, though, so could Thaddeus. The black dog was chained in the back. The steel chains might not ordinarily hold a black dog, except he was still wearing those silver bands. Those bound him, and so the chains did, too. Ezekiel was confident enough that he had allowed the little boy, Con, to go back to his mother, where she sat next to her husband. DeAnn cradled him on her lap, her head bent over his. The boy, too afraid of Ezekiel to close his eyes in the plane, had tucked himself down against his mother and slept at last. Alejandro tried not to resent the boy's ability to find comfort in the arms of his Pure mother. A decent man would not resent such things... But it was hard. And harder, without Papá to remind him what he should feel and think and do. Alejandro tried to think only of the moment, of the immediate dangers they faced.

There were assuredly enough dangers, both outside the car and inside. Alejandro tried to stay constantly ready for Thaddeus to attempt some desperate last-minute defiance. He was tired and on edge himself, and so if there was violence, the hardest part might be to stop himself from going after DeAnn or little Con or both. Thaddeus probably guessed this. Maybe the fear of what might go wrong during a violent escape attempt was as good as another chain.

"Stop fretting," Ezekiel said, his voice light and mocking and absolutely impervious to any ordinary weakness. "Thaddeus knows perfectly well that even if he got himself and his family away, his woman couldn't possibly survive out there in that snow. Around here, anyone they asked for help *would* help them – and then call Dimilioc. Thad there couldn't stop them – a Pure wife isn't always an unmixed blessing."

Alejandro glanced at Thaddeus again, this time perceiving the knowledge of defeat that dragged the black dog down more heavily than the chains. So, Ezekiel was right. *Bueno.* Alejandro faced forward again and tried to relax.

They turned north from Brighton and reached Lewis at only a little past seven in the morning, exactly as Ezekiel had predicted. It should have been light by then, but the sun rose late in this frozen country, even if it had not been hidden behind a thick overcast.

Ezekiel grunted suddenly, lifting his head. Alejandro felt it a heartbeat later: a sharp astringent hum in the air, with a low undertone that buzzed in the back of the skull. Though one could not exactly hear it because it was not exactly sound. Nor feel it, as it was not *exactly* painful.

"Natividad's been busy," Ezekiel said, sounding surprised and pleased and worried and angry all at the same time. "What was Grayson thinking, bringing her out this far from Dimilioc? Asking her to draw a circle around a whole town. At her age! If Vonhausel…" He stopped short, shrugging, and glanced back at Thaddeus. "Keep an eye on him," he told Alejandro. "We may need to go around. That'd be a problem, in this weather."

Alejandro nodded, understanding. Natividad had never done a circle so big, but if Grayson had asked her to do it, of course she would try. And she would do it right; that wasn't a surprise at all. That was why he and Ezekiel could pass through it: Natividad's circle wouldn't be meant to keep either of them out. But Thaddeus might be exactly the kind of black dog it *was* meant to stop.

Thaddeus certainly felt the circle. His head was up, his lips drawn back in a grimace that was half a snarl. His wife put a hand on his arm and leaned her head against his shoulder, cradling her son with her other arm. Alejandro could see the tension run out of Thaddeus like anger, or strength. The boy stirred but did not wake.

"I think it will be alright," Alejandro said to Ezekiel. "DeAnn is protecting them."

"Just watch him," Ezekiel said shortly. "Watch them all." He eased the SUV forward.

Whatever Natividad had done, they felt the pressure of it all the way through Lewis. Then they drove out of it, with a sharp little "*pop!*" like going up too fast in a plane. Ezekiel only shook his head like a man shaking away a cobweb he had walked through, but Thaddeus shuddered all over and leaned his cheek against the top of his wife's head.

The road was rougher and narrower once they were through the town. Alejandro found that he could not reliably make out the edges of the road, could barely see the black trees that lined the way, could not begin to guess whether the darkness under those trees was thick with black dogs just waiting for their chance to run out, batter the SUV off the road, tip it over, haul them out to their deaths... His shadow pressed him, wanting to rise. Alejandro would not give way to it, but he wished they were already back at Dimilioc.

"Huh," said Ezekiel.

Alejandro glanced at the *verdugo*, waiting to see if he would explain his surprise.

"The road's clear."

It was not clear. There was a lot of snow on the road. But then Alejandro blinked, realizing what Ezekiel meant. He could see, now the *verdugo* had pointed it out, how the snow blew sideways off the road, piling up instead under the trees. Away from the road, the snow was much deeper, maybe chest high in places.

"Your sister is truly gifted," Ezekiel said. He sounded pleased about it. He sounded *possessive*. Alejandro set his jaw against showing a sudden blaze of angry resentment. Ezekiel cast him an amused glance and drove a little faster.

Ezekiel had not called ahead, but nevertheless the Dimilioc wolves were waiting, gathered in a tight-knit group on the front porch, just as they had been when Alejandro and Miguel and Natividad had arrived. Neither Miguel nor Natividad were among them. Alejandro wanted to see the twins, *para asegurarse de estaban bien*. But it was good they were not here, at this moment when violence burned in the air like fire.

Grayson Lanning stood at the front, autocratic and immovable. Harrison Lanning stood to his left side, aloof; Zachariah Korte to his right, disdainful and curious.

Benedict Mallory and Ethan Lanning leaned side by side against the snow-covered railing. A little to Alejandro's surprise, Keziah stood behind and to one side of the Master, hip cocked and arms crossed and black, black hair pouring like a waterfall to her hips, looking scornful and superior and elegant. Even Amira was there, though she had tucked herself half out of sight behind her sister.

The Dimilioc wolves may have gathered like that when Alejandro and the twins had come here, but that had not been the same. They had been afraid, but they had come into Dimilioc territory *deliberdamente*. They had had a plan, and followed it through the fear and the doubt, and it had worked – at least so far as to bring allies to their side against Vonhausel so they did not face him alone. So, they had been right to come.

It was different for Thaddeus, for his family. The boy was too young to understand what Dimilioc was, but not too young to feel the deadly strength of the black wolves. He clung to his mother, but he did not bury his face against her the way a human child might: he was angry as much as frightened. He might cling, but he was ready to push away, go into the *cambio de cuerpo,* fight. Even a little puppy like that one *would* fight.

DeAnn held her son tightly. If the child began to change, she would try to stop him. Alejandro could tell by the way she walked a little apart from Thaddeus that she thought there was nothing she could do to protect her husband. She thought Grayson Lanning was going to kill him. Thaddeus thought so, too. That was very obvious. It was almost painful to watch – it was so easy for Alejandro to imagine exactly how the big black dog felt. Alejandro wished, momentarily but strongly, that he had defied Ezekiel just so far as to tell Thaddeus the truth. *Papá* would have told him. But as soon as he thought so, Alejandro was not sure. Maybe Papá, too, would have deferred to the Dimilioc executioner. But probably not out of fear. *He* had not dared, and so now Thaddeus had no hope.

Ezekiel had taken off the steel chains, but not the silver bracelets that mattered so much more. Thaddeus's shadow had been pressed flat by the bright fire of that silver, but Alejandro could not imagine the black dog trying to fight now, even if he could get rid of the bracelets. The weight of all the powerful Dimilioc shadows filled the air, until it almost surprised Alejandro that the porch was not crushed under the load it had to bear, that the earth itself did not crack open in protest at the burden.

Thaddeus walked forward without lifting his gaze from the snow. A few feet from the steps that led up to the porch, he went down, not kneeling, but all the way down on his belly, his hands open, his face flat against the snow in absolute submission. Alejandro thought that Thaddeus might not realize that he appeared even bigger stretched out that way, his body dark against the white of the snow. He looked huge. Even bound with silver, his shadow radiated anger and power.

Grayson tilted his head, clearly pleased. Alejandro thought he was pleased by the black dog's obvious strength as well as his surrender, but he was not sure.

"Keep an eye on the woman," Ezekiel said to Alejandro. He strode past the prone black dog and leaped up to join the other Dimilioc wolves on the porch. He looked very young and slight beside the Lannings, but Harrison and even Grayson shifted aside for him as though he was much bigger than he really was, and Ezekiel accepted the space they yielded as his due. He gave no sign of weariness or injury, but the Dimilioc wolves turned their heads as they caught the scent of blood from the reopened cut. Ezekiel only said, pleasantly, before either of them could speak, "You didn't specifically ask me to bring the pup, but I thought you might like a look at him."

"That is an unexpected bonus," Grayson agreed, his deep, gritty voice growling through the winter quiet. "And his existence is instructive." He added to Thaddeus, "Up. Up, dog. Let us have a look at you."

Thaddeus pushed himself up to kneeling, the muscles in his arms and shoulders bunching. But he obviously intended no challenge. He kept his head down, glancing covertly up at Grayson the way a weaker black dog would look at a stronger... though one on one, Alejandro was not absolutely certain Grayson would actually prove stronger. But of course that did not matter.

"You'll kill me," Thaddeus said, speaking straight to Grayson, ignoring all the other Dimilioc wolves. His voice was as deep as the Master's, maybe deeper, rough with black dog anger. "That's alright. That doesn't matter. But don't kill my son. He's DeAnn's son. She's sensible – she's smart. Let the boy alone and she'll do what you want, anything you want. I swear she will."

He still didn't look at his wife, even when he said this. Alejandro did. He couldn't help it. Natividad hated it when

Alejandro spoke for her that way – she usually insisted on speaking for herself. But Thaddeus' wife didn't even change expression. She looked up, though; she looked into Grayson's face, met his eyes. But then, maybe because she still held her black dog son in her arms, she lowered her gaze again immediately.

"Tell me you'll let him live," Thaddeus said. He looked directly into Grayson's eyes just for an instant. "Just tell me that. Please. Before you kill me, tell me you'll let him alone–" He stopped, with an abruptness that suggested he didn't trust the steadiness of his voice.

Grayson studied him for a long moment. "Unusual, for a black dog to care so much."

Thaddeus' hands, set on his thighs, closed hard into fists. He said harshly, "What difference does it make to you? But if you want DeAnn for Dimilioc–"

Grayson held up a hand, and Thaddeus halted. The Master said calmly, "I've no intention of harming your son. A black dog's life is hardly secure, but he will come to no harm here from any Dimilioc wolf. Not while he is still a child." He paused and then asked, his deep voice making the question seem almost a threat, "Do you believe me?"

Thaddeus sat back on his heels. He stared at Grayson for a moment, then looked down again. He started to rub one big hand across his bald head, flinched from the silver band around his wrist and dropped his hand instead to rest again on his thigh. Clearly he did not know whether he believed Grayson or not – and did not know whether he should say that, or not.

"Well?" said the Dimilioc Master.

"I hope it's true," Thaddeus said. He glanced up. "I don't know why you'd lie. Maybe it's true. If you're lying, I hope you kill me before you do him."

"Take the silver off him," Grayson said to Ezekiel. "Let's take a look at him."

That clearly surprised Thaddeus, who nevertheless held out his hands one after the other so that the Dimilioc *verdugo* could remove the silver bands. He took a deep, shuddering breath when they were gone, some of the tension easing out of his back and shoulders. But then his muscles visibly tightened again as his shadow suddenly expanded, filling out the space around him, so dense it almost seemed it might take on physical form without him.

Alejandro half expected the huge black dog to explode into violence, but Thaddeus only took another breath, shut his eyes, and locked his shadow down tight with pure willpower. He did not otherwise move except to rub each wrist in turn, hard, as though trying to scrub away even the memory of the silver. His wrists showed marks, char-black against the dark brown of his skin, where the metal had burned him even through the leather backing.

DeAnn had given Grayson a sharp look when he'd ordered her husband freed from the silver. She said nothing, but she swung her black pup son down to stand on his feet beside her, though she kept hold of his hand. But the boy tugged, tugged again, black dog instinct driving him down. At last DeAnn let her son kneel, crouching so that she could keep an arm around his shoulders.

"Well?" Grayson said to Thaddeus.

The black dog flicked a glance up, then fixed his gaze

firmly on the ground. "You expect a fight? I won't fight."
He glanced up again, not quite as briefly. "You think I want
black dog violence here? Now?"

"He's had good control right through," Ezekiel said
casually to Grayson. "Once he got his shadow battened
down in the first place. Which was, however, a little difficult.
Alejandro was helpful there. It seems he's picked up your
special trick."

The Dimilioc Master turned his powerful stare on
Alejandro, who instantly dropped his gaze. It had not
occurred to him that Grayson Lanning might not welcome
a demonstration of that particular skill from any other black
dog. If that had occurred to him at the time... he had no idea
what else he might have done besides what he *had* done. He
knew he would have lost control of his shadow if he hadn't
managed to use it to force the boy's black dog down and
back. He did not dare say that. So he said nothing.

Before Grayson could respond to Ezekiel's comment,
however, the front door of the house opened and Natividad
stepped out onto the porch. All the Dimilioc wolves turned
toward her, a powerful reordering of their interest that
sent alarm of an entirely different kind down Alejandro's
spine. Only Ezekiel kept his attention tightly focused on
Thaddeus. The black dog knew it, staying very still under
the young *verdugo's* cool gaze.

Grayson, obviously displeased, began, "Natividad–"

"I'm sorry," she said quickly. "Really I am, I didn't mean
to disobey you, Grayson, only there's a phone call. It's
Sheriff Pearson, you know?"

Grayson's lip curled. "You may inform–"

"Yes, of course, only I think you should talk to him, I really do," Natividad said with earnest rapidity. "I'm so glad you're back," she said to Alejandro, and added to Ezekiel, "You're hurt, aren't you? I'm sorry." Alejandro gathered from her tone that there was some sort of trouble and that she was sorry for very practical reasons that the Dimilioc *verdugo* was injured. He saw Ezekiel catch this subtext too, and, a heartbeat later, Grayson, whose scowl deepened. The Master's hard gaze went to Ezekiel, judging the extent to which he might have been impaired by injury and hard traveling.

"I'm perfectly fine," Ezekiel assured him. He sounded fine: his voice was light and amused, edged with cutting scorn for anyone who might for even a moment think otherwise. He looked fine, too. It was hard for even Alejandro to guess how much the *verdugo* might be concealing, and *he* had seen the injury dealt and heard Ezekiel admit to being tired and in pain. As a tactic, yes, but he *had* admitted it.

Grayson grunted, said shortly, "Come with me, then. All of you, come with me." He stepped toward the door, pausing only to jerk his head toward Thaddeus and add to Zachariah, "He'll have to wait. You and Benedict may take him downstairs. All three of these can go in the main cage. Put Cass Pearson in one of the small cells."

Alejandro found it impossible to get a clear picture of whatever the trouble was from overhearing Grayson's conversation with the sheriff. In fact, Grayson's side of the conversation consisted mostly of wordless mutters of annoyance. Alejandro wanted to ask Natividad for details, but his sister had vanished. That was unlike her; usually she and Miguel would both be hovering at the edges of any excitement. But neither of the twins was in evidence.

Easing away from the crowd of Dimilioc wolves was simple enough. No one called after him as he backed away, tucked himself through a doorway, and ran up the stairs three at a time to find his brother and sister.

They were, of course, in Natividad's room, Natividad cross-legged on her bed and Miguel perched on the windowsill. That was fine. But they both looked up at Alejandro with guilty expressions. While unexpected, this was not actually a surprise. He glared at them both. "Well?"

"Well, I'm grounded, so you're not supposed to be here," Natividad said rapidly. "But–"

"Grounded!" He did not know whether to laugh or be angry. "What did you do?"

Natividad made an exasperated sound. *"Ahora no es el tiempo para armar un escándalo,* 'Jandro! If Grayson agreed with Harrison grounding me, he ought to have left somebody else to answer the phone. Now things are happening, so I can't still be grounded!"

Exasperating, stupid, foolish – she always thought she could get away with *anything*, that *no one* would ever really be angry with her. Alejandro said harshly, "You *cannot* defy–"

Miguel, holding up his hands, said quickly, "There's trouble in Lewis, 'Jandro, trouble with the black dogs, Vonhausel is attacking there and not here, they're attacking *right now*. Listen, listen now: yesterday Natividad laid out a big mandala around half the town. It should have stopped any stray black dog from attacking Lewis, but–"

"I should probably tell you…" Natividad began tentatively.

"But surprise!" said Miguel, too focused on Alejandro to pay attention to her. "The attack there isn't just some random black dog stray, right? The mandala's holding them for the moment, Pearson says, but from what we hear, the black dogs are really serious about killing *everybody*. Maybe for fun, maybe for practice, maybe to hurt Dimilioc, we don't know, but it's bad. And it's worse than it should be, because… Look, after that attack earlier, you'd think Vonhausel would have maybe twenty black dogs with him, right? Or not even so many if they got scared, which they should have been because we killed so many of them and they didn't kill even one of us. *Me entiendes?*"

Alejandro grudgingly tilted his head. "*Sí, sí, te entiendo.*"

"Well, Sheriff Pearson says they think there are at least forty black dogs outside Lewis right now. Forty!"

"Grayson was really angry with Pearson," Natividad put in. "And Harrison *said* don't call on Dimilioc. But forty black dogs, that's too many. Grayson *can't* just stay back and let them kill all those people, only I don't *know* how long my mandala will hold because, I tried to tell you, it came out a little strange."

"Doesn't matter how it came out," said Miguel. "Not during the full moon. Not if there are forty black dogs trying to take it apart – *and* Vonhausel."

Alejandro scowled. His brother was right. But he doubted Vonhausel really could have recruited so many black dogs. He said so, adding "*Especialmente cuendo su primero ataque pue un fracas.* Black dogs follow a leader who *wins*."

"Perhaps they still expect Vonhausel to win," Keziah suggested behind him. Alejandro didn't whirl around because he wouldn't let her see she had surprised him. But she had. He hadn't heard her approach at all, but she was poised, long and elegant and negligently scornful, in the doorway of Natividad's room. He was furious that she had come up so quietly and he had not heard her. She knew it, too. She smiled. "Or perhaps this enemy of yours has made a lot of little moon-called wolves," she said smoothly. "Those townspeople, perhaps they do not know the difference between those little crazy moon-wolves and black dogs."

"That's a really good suggestion," Miguel said warmly. "That could be exactly right, and if that's all Vonhausel's got, Lewis isn't in a lot of danger, which would be great."

Keziah glanced his way, her lip curling contemptuously. Alejandro didn't know whether he should laugh at his brother or snarl at Keziah, but before he could do either, Amira slid past her, met Natividad's eyes, looked away – a black dog looking away from a Pure girl, she *was* a nervous creature – but then crept forward when Natividad held out a hand in invitation. She ducked her head submissively, afraid of Alejandro. Keziah straightened and glared at him, not submissive at all. The light from the window caught in the crystals of her earrings, scattering into pinpoints of refracted light, brilliant against the density of her shadow. But she stayed exactly where she was, in the doorway, not moving to follow her sister.

Alejandro, pretending not to notice Keziah's aggressive stance, backed away from Natividad to let Amira come to her. Natividad gave him a warm smile, transferred the smile to Amira, and put her arm around the little girl's thin shoulders when Amira came the rest of the way in a rush and tucked herself against Natividad's side. Alejandro did not quite look at the child, in case Keziah saw his too-close attention as a threat to her sister. Keziah was not quite looking that way either, he saw – and no doubt for exactly the same reason.

Keziah said to Natividad, "All the time Amira asks, can she go visit the Pure girl? And I say no, she is not to have people visit her, she is being punished. But I think now you don't care about that."

"Well..." Natividad began.

Keziah glanced at Alejandro. She leaned against the doorframe, ostentatiously relaxed. "You said no one would hurt Amira. Because of your Pure sister. I thought, well, good, maybe it is even true. But now I think *I* will like your sister – because of mine."

Alejandro gave her a short nod. "I almost think *I* might like *you* – because of my sister."

Keziah smiled scornfully. "I will enjoy fighting you, Toland. Later. Now, of course, there are other black dogs to fight. It would be good if your enemy owns little moon-bound wolves and not so many true black dogs."

Miguel said rapidly, with that air of meek stubbornness that meant he wasn't going to back down to anybody, "I think we ought to plan for the worst case. If Vonhausel's really got a lot of black dogs, Grayson's going to have only two choices: either he's going to have to go fight Vonhausel and his black dogs there in Lewis or he's going to have to let them take Lewis apart and kill everybody there, and he can't do that because it'd be wrong, but even more so because if Vonhausel gets a clear, obvious victory, he'll get more dominant out there…" Miguel waved a hand, meaning out in the world, and continued rapidly, "and more powerful, which is obviously exactly what he has in mind, isn't that right?"

"A moderately plausible analysis," Keziah allowed. She was not quite laughing, but there was a savage humor in her eyes. "Obviously we cannot permit that."

"You will fight for Dimilioc, will you?" Alejandro asked her sharply. "My father taught me that it is right to protect human people against cur black dogs. What did yours teach you?"

Keziah grinned, a dangerous flash of white teeth with very little humor in it. "I should hardly have acquired a conscience from *my* father. Such a commodity was not in high demand in my family. So, now I make my *own* choices, Toland."

Alejandro smiled, showing his own teeth. "Then your father did teach you something important."

The Saudi girl lifted one shoulder a fraction in a minimal shrug. "Amira and I, we are not really Dimilioc. Not yet." She lifted a scornful eyebrow. "No more than you, *Toland*, which you know, if you are not a fool. Those of us who are foreign to Dimilioc must show that we will fight Dimilioc's enemies, and also that we will protect these human people who owe allegiance to Dimilioc. If we do not, then Dimilioc will shut us out in the cold wind."

"Exactly!" cried Miguel. "That's what I was going to say! All of us need to stick together, that's obvious! Listen, if Grayson leads you all out to fight Vonhausel and his lot, then you're going to need that new black dog, aren't you? Thaddeus Williams, I mean. Even one more black dog on your side could make a big difference. Territorial as you all are, that's something I don't think Grayson's going to realize. I mean, he'll certainly figure it out when you're actually in Lewis, fighting a million black dogs. But then it'll be too late! But you..." He glanced quickly from Alejandro to Keziah and back. "You see already that you're going to need Thaddeus, don't you?"

It would not have occurred to Alejandro to try to recruit Thaddeus Williams for a big fight the very day he'd been brought, by force, to Dimilioc. He glanced at Keziah, whose eyebrows had gone up in surprise or thought.

She said slowly, as though this was difficult to believe, "The human boy is right. That is perfectly true. I will fight for Dimilioc, but I did not come here to die. Certainly I do not wish to die for human townspeople I do not even know. If we go to fight in Lewis, it would be better to win."

Alejandro found himself smiling again, and did not know whether he was pleased because Keziah had admitted that Miguel was right, or because of her dry understatement. "He is very strong, that one," he conceded. "But will he fight for Dimilioc?"

Miguel jumped up and paced back and forth, thinking out loud. "Natividad, you need to work on Grayson. He'll listen to you even if he's angry, won't he? I mean, any male Dimilioc wolf will obviously listen to anything you say, isn't that right?"

"Wow, that's a reassuring idea," Natividad said drily. Amira was still tucked against her. Natividad was stroking her hair.

"It is true," Keziah said. "So, you would be a fool not to use that, Pure girl."

Miguel said very fast, before Natividad could answer, "You need to get Grayson to see that he shouldn't delay with Thaddeus, he has to make him that offer about joining Dimilioc, he has to do it right now. He's going to need *everyone*." He glanced uncertainly at Amira.

"My sister is strong," Keziah said, still amused.

"*She* isn't going to fight!" said Natividad, horrified. She put both arms around Amira as though cuddling a much younger child and glared at Keziah. Alejandro wanted to laugh, but he instantly moved forward, warning Keziah to keep back with a hard look. He said sharply to his sister, "Amira is not a tame little puppy, Natividad!"

Keziah had not moved. Now she laughed, with hard-edged aggressive humor. "This Pure Girl thinks Amira is just little. No, girl. You make her shadow settle low, so low you do not see it, but it is a good, strong shadow. Amira fights with me. Grayson knows that."

"If she can fight, we will need her," Alejandro said, though privately he wondered how much use a cowering little creature like Amira could possibly be during a real fight. But he said, "Natividad, think of me when I was twelve, thirteen – she is that old."

"She's not like you!" Natividad protested. "Look at her! She's a baby!"

Without looking up, Amira said all in one breath, muffled against Natividad's shoulder, "I can fight, I can fight better than anybody, I won't let anybody hurt Keziah – or you." She looked up at last, though she kept her arms around

Natividad. "I like you. I do. I don't want to kill you and you don't want to kill me. That's because you are Pure."

"That's right," Natividad said, looking a little stunned.

"I will fight," said Amira, fiercely. "I can fight."

"So," said Keziah, smiling proudly at her sister.

A sudden violent surge of jealousy surprised Alejandro. *He* had no little black dog brother or sister. He had fought against black dog *callejeros* beside Papá – it would be like that, fighting with a little brother, only different. He found himself struggling against a sudden desperate longing for his father, for the absolute certainty of his childhood, the certainty that nothing could defeat his father, that nothing could defeat the two of them together. That had been a false certainty. He longed for it now. He said harshly, not looking at Keziah or Amira, "We will need everyone. Ezekiel... you may not know, but he is acting. He's tired and hurt. All this smooth-killer thing, right now at least part of it is *una farsa*, a part. A role. I don't know how much."

"Ezekiel Korte is injured?" Keziah inquired, straightening.

"I'm *sure* it's nothing but a scratch," Natividad said in an extremely bland tone. "Isn't that right, 'Jandro?"

Alejandro glared at her. He wanted Papá, and instead he had *Ezekiel*. He snarled, "Oh, you are *worried* for him?"

Natividad glared back at him. "It's not like that!"

"Alright!" said Miguel, holding up his hands. "Whatever it's like or not like, don't we have other things to think about that are almost as important? Natividad, see Grayson, will you? That's important. OK?"

"*Sí, creo que sí*," Natividad agreed, though not happily.

"And, uh, Keziah," Miguel flushed when he said her

name, "can go with you, maybe, in case Grayson will listen better to a black dog, alright?" He said earnestly to Keziah, "And Grayson will really like seeing you with Natividad, don't you think?"

This was true, though Alejandro hadn't thought of it until his brother said so. *He* didn't like it, though. But Keziah didn't meet his warning stare. She was looking at the way Natividad sat with her arm still around Amira's shoulders. At the way Amira had tucked herself against Natividad's side. She said, "He will like that. And he will listen to me."

Alejandro thought of the way she had said *I will like your sister because of mine.* He said reluctantly, "Alright. Go, then."

There was a short pause. Then Miguel said, "Well, um, good, then. OK." He turned to Alejandro, "And while the girls are working on Grayson, you and me, we'll slip downstairs and explain what's going on to Thaddeus and make sure he gets which side his bread is buttered on, you know? Because Grayson's going to come across *como muy feroz,* isn't he, and Thaddeus is too strong to take that. Isn't that true? Everyone's been saying how strong he is. But it really *would* be best for him and his family to be Dimilioc, isn't that right? I mean, *por supuesto,* as long as we win."

"*Sí,*" Alejandro agreed, not very happily. "But you know, Ezekiel said very clearly I wasn't to talk to Thaddeus. *Don't muddy the waters,* he said. I guess it's clear what he meant. If Grayson finds out–"

"We'll be quick, we'll be careful, if Grayson finds out, we'll manage–"

"If Grayson finds out, if he's angry, this was *my* idea–"

Miguel made an impatient gesture of agreement. "Alright! I don't think it matters, but alright. But you know if Thaddeus doesn't get anything but threats and black dog posturing from Grayson, then he'll promise anything and mean nothing and turn on Dimilioc the first chance he gets – and if he's smart, either he'll find a chance or he'll make one. So, we have to make him *want* to be Dimilioc. Grayson will understand that, too," said Miguel. "Eventually." He jumped to his feet and stood looking at Alejandro expectantly.

"How do you talk me into these things?" muttered Alejandro. But he also got to his feet.

They took sandwiches downstairs. The sandwiches were Miguel's idea. It was a clever idea: obviously Thaddeus and DeAnn and the boy would have to eat something, and obviously this need wasn't important enough to bother any of the senior black wolves about, and the sandwiches would provide an excuse for going downstairs in case Grayson *did* catch them disobeying his order not to talk to the prisoners. When Miguel picked up the platter, Alejandro thought, *last chance to say no, this is* estúpido, *this is* peligroso, *we should talk to Grayson, not try to go behind his back*.

But Miguel had been right: black dogs were too territorial, too mistrustful of outsiders, too aggressive. Grayson wouldn't think of Thaddeus Williams as an asset to Dimilioc, the same as Alejandro hadn't thought of it, *por supuesto que no*. Not now, not yet. Not until Natividad or Keziah made him think of it. And then, yes, Miguel was right, Grayson would try to batter Thaddeus into

submission through sheer force of will and that wouldn't
work, not now, there wasn't *time*. They needed Thaddeus
himself to want to belong to Dimilioc to head off all those
conflicts of strength and rank and loyalty.

So, he only nodded and led the way out toward the stairs.

The things that had been brought down to the cage to
make Natividad more comfortable – the extra blankets,
the cord to hang them on, the chairs –were still there. The
sheets on the cot had even been changed, which Alejandro
wouldn't have noticed except the new sheets were rose-
pink. None of these small luxuries made the silver-wrapped
steel bars look any less a cage.

DeAnn was sitting on the cot, her legs drawn up. She
had one arm around her son's small shoulders. The boy was
leaning against her, his face pressed close, and for a moment
Alejandro heard Miguel pause behind him and knew that
his brother had been surprised by a surge of angry, jealous
grief for their own lost mother. Or at least grief: maybe the
anger and jealousy was a black dog reaction and Alejandro
only guessed at those emotions in his brother because he
felt them himself, because the boundaries between himself
and his black dog had become blurred, because he was no
longer absolutely sure he could draw out those boundaries,
not when it really mattered, not when he most needed to. He
touched his brother's shoulder, trying for a light, comforting
touch, trying not to show anything of what he felt himself.

The sounds of the opening door and descending footsteps
had brought Thaddeus to his feet. He stood between his
family and the cage's door, his broad shoulders squared
aggressively, the dim yellow light turning the skin of his

bald head and thick arms and big hands to a gold-tinged ebony. Even caged, Thaddeus looked enormous and *más peligroso* – dangerous. Alejandro wondered whether the black dog did that deliberately, and how, and whether it was something anybody could learn. Then he wondered if he should want to learn it. *Then* he wondered whether it was he who wished to learn that, or the black dog. He shut his eyes for a moment, shuddering, reminding himself fiercely that the present moment held enough danger, that he needed to focus and stay *in* the present and not borrow trouble. He wished, desperately, that Papá was here with them – or Mamá, that would be even better...

"Lunch," Miguel said cheerfully, holding up the plate. "Or breakfast, or both, I guess. You must all be starving." He stepped casually around Alejandro, oblivious to his brother's struggle against his shadow's influence, and set the plate down on the table outside the bars, where DeAnn could reach it.

Thaddeus, glaring at Alejandro, did not speak or move. DeAnn sighed, patted her son's hair, got to her feet, and reached through the silver-laced bars for sandwiches for herself and the boy. She put another one aside for her husband, if he decided to take it, said, "Thanks," to Miguel, and bit into her sandwich with enthusiasm.

"DeAnn..." Thaddeus began.

"Don't say anything yet," suggested Miguel. "Let me tell you something important first: Grayson didn't send for you to punish you for taking a Pure woman."

Thaddeus stared at Miguel – straight at him. Then he laughed, bitter and contemptuous. "Human, are you, kid? Come to tell *me* what it is?"

Miguel gazed back at the black dog with a bland, ingenuous expression. "Well…" he began.

"Miguel!" snapped Alejandro. He knew his tone was too harsh, but his awareness of Thaddeus' strength set him on edge, made him expect a fight despite the cage, made him expect blood and fire and remorseless battle – and here was Miguel, utterly disregarding everything he knew about black dogs. At least the fury and danger in the room made it much easier to focus tightly on this one single moment and not think about the past or the future…

"Oh, right," said Miguel, in a tone that implied he was only just resisting the urge to roll his eyes. "It's alright, 'Jandro, you can see he's got real good control." But he looked politely at the floor. He said to Thaddeus, "Yep, that's me, human as they come. But it's still true, what I said."

Thaddeus laughed, a sharp crack of sound. "Of course. He's the forgiving sort, is Grayson Lanning, we all know that! All sweetness and light and pink sugar unicorns! That's why he sent his damned executioner to bring me in, cause it's just fine with him…"

DeAnn laid a hand on his, like caramel over dark chocolate, and he stopped suddenly, turning his hand to grasp hers like a drowning man grabbing after hope of rescue. In Thaddeus' grip, his wife's strong hand and wrist looked almost delicate.

Thaddeus turned his head, touched his lips to his wife's hair, closed his eyes, and stayed like that for a long breath of time. Then he pressed her hand between both of his and turned to glare at Miguel once more. He demanded, "I know the Dimilioc executioner, that vicious young bastard, but who the fuck are you, boy? A couple of wetback kids like you, you're not Dimilioc, so what the fuck?"

Miguel wasn't offended, but Alejandro gave the other black dog a hard stare. After a moment, acknowledging his own difficult position, Thaddeus muttered, "Sorry. Sorry. I'm…" his voice trailed off. He lowered his gaze, a deliberate gesture of submission which must have been painful for him, since both he and Alejandro knew that he was the stronger.

Alejandro thought he might actually like the black dog. Or learn to like him. Alejandro's shadow hated and feared a rival, but Alejandro respected how hard Thaddeus was trying to protect his wife and son. The black man reminded him, suddenly and strongly, of Papá, which was both disturbing and comforting. He was sure Grayson had been right to want this black dog for Dimilioc, and now also sure that Miguel had been right to approach Thaddeus immediately. Thaddeus was going to be hard to recruit: mistrustful and angry and too strong to submit easily to anybody's authority.

Miguel didn't seem to be suffering from any doubts, though. He leaned casually against the silver-laced bars. "I know who you are, of course. I'm Miguel Toland. My brother is Alejandro Toland. Our father was Edward Toland. He went to Mexico, met my mother, hid the same as you, only for longer…"

"Mexico," repeated Thaddeus. He turned his dark face away, scowling. Thinking, no doubt, that if he'd taken his family to Mexico that the Dimilioc executioner would never have shown up on his doorstep. That was probably even true.

DeAnn leaned her head against his shoulder. "Lots of black dogs in Mexico. You told me that."

Thaddeus transferred his scowl to her. "I could've protected you from 'em. If this kid's dad could protect his wife, I could've protected you."

Alejandro made an impatient sound. "*No seas estúpido,*" he said. "*Cabeza dura* – worse than stupid; willfully obtuse. Our mother is dead: who do you think murdered her? How do you think our father died?"

Thaddeus swung around to stare at him.

Alejandro glared until the big black dog remembered his position and dropped his gaze. Then he added, "Before the war, Mexico was a good place to hide from Dimilioc. After the war, my father had enemies, but also there were too many black dogs for anyone to protect anyone. Lots of them weren't quiet, not them, too stupid and too vicious and not scared of anything with the vampires gone and Dimilioc broken, so after a while we also got a lot of soldiers down from Monterrey, wandering around the countryside shooting at shadows, almost as dangerous as the black dogs."

Thaddeus began a hot response, but his wife interrupted, her tone interested, almost friendly. "You two are brothers, of course? Your mother was Pure?" Her voice had gentled; she already knew the answers to both questions. She was sorry for their mother's death, pity that Alejandro would have bitterly resented if it had come from someone who wasn't Pure herself.

"We are," Alejandro agreed. "And my sister, she's Pure, like you. That's why we came here, when Mexico got too dangerous. To ask Dimilioc for a place, because Dimilioc protects the Pure." Well, it was mostly true. He deliberately looked back at Thaddeus. "Dimilioc needs wolves."

"Shit, kid," Thaddeus said, forgetting his effort to appear submissive. "No way anybody like you or me's going to be Dimilioc, Pure sister or no Pure sister. Or wife. They've got 'em a pure angel cake operation up here, kid, no place for anybody whose family wasn't kissing cousins with the *Mayflower* bunch–"

"Last year maybe that was true," Miguel said. He was still leaning against the silver-laced bars of the cage. Now he put his hands in his pockets, totally unafraid in a way that only a human, free of black dog instinct, could be. "But, hey, check it out! Just at this moment, Dimilioc does not care about your bloodlines. Grayson's even brought in a couple of Saudi black dogs, and that's no bloodline that's ever crossed one of Dimilioc's, you bet."

"Those girls," Thaddeus said slowly.

"You wondered about them, didn't you? They're Dimilioc now, and we're glad to have 'em on board, because there's going to be a big fight. Like, today. Looks like we've got these big bad stray dogs messing around Dimilioc territory, you know that? They want to tear down Dimilioc and grab any Pure women handy, and it looks like they're going to start by ripping into a town full of humans–"

"Shit, kid, stop before I cry big tears..." Thaddeus began... but then he halted. Not because his wife stopped him. He stopped himself, his aggressive air becoming edged with speculation.

"Yeah, that's right," said Miguel, watching him carefully. "Too bad, so sad! But not for you. For you, it's opportunity knocking good and loud. You get that, right? Stick around, join the fight, be loyal to Dimilioc – not just as a pretense but for real – and next year you'll be on the inside looking out instead of the other way 'round and your son will carry a real true Dimilioc bloodline because that's exactly what yours will be. If you want that. Which you should, if you're not willfully obtuse."

Thaddeus glared at him. "Lookin' for Pure women, you say, and here you've brought 'em one, haven't you?"

"Well, if Grayson lets you go, you could take her back to Chicago," Alejandro said, nodding toward DeAnn. "How long do you think it'll be before a big stray pack shows up, drawn to her like *mariposas* to flame? Only these moths hate the Pure fire that draws them."

There was a pause. Thaddeus drew breath to speak.

"Thad," his wife said, her voice low, "I'd do anything to protect Conway. But I don't want any man but you. You get that, right?"

Thaddeus stared at her, took a step, moved a hand to rest on her face. He touched his son's hair with his other hand. "It's not what I promised you…"

The sound of the door opening stopped him, brought him around again to face this new threat.

"It'll do fine," DeAnn said, still quietly but with a good deal more urgency.

Alejandro gripped on Miguel's shoulder, moved him firmly aside, stepped between his brother and the stairs and realized only then how similar his reaction had been to Thaddeus' protection of his wife. He found himself glancing over, meeting the big black dog's eyes, not in challenge, but in a moment of mutual understanding.

Grayson Lanning came down the stairs. Alejandro hadn't realized he could recognize the Dimilioc Master solely by the sound of his tread, but he could. Or maybe he had simply recognized the dense power of his shadow as it preceded the Master into the prison room.

He waited for Grayson to demand, *What are you doing down here?* But Grayson glanced at the plate of sandwiches – more crumbs than sandwiches now – and gave Alejandro a brief nod. Then he said to Thaddeus, "Interesting family you have here, Williams. A Pure wife. That's unusual, for a stray. You've had the *Beschwichtigend*, clearly. Did she do it for you? Did you ask her to?"

Thaddeus scowled. "A Pure woman can work the Calming magic on any black dog – it's not against your law…"

"No. But it's unusual for a stray black dog to voluntarily take the *Beschwichtigend*." Grayson paused, studying the big black dog. "You found a Pure woman and instead of killing her, you let her do the *Beschwichtigend* for you. Maybe that was just strategy: a precaution against drawing Dimilioc attention. Then you stayed with her, got her to marry you – *that* was not a way to keep clear of Dimilioc attention. *Then* you gave her a black dog son. A son you're willing to die to protect. Every step on that path more unusual than the one before."

Thaddeus had lowered his gaze, though his growled, "Well?" held very little sincere submission.

Grayson stared at him, his eyes fiery with temper. But his anger was not directed at Thaddeus, and obviously the black dog knew it because he did not even bow his head, much less drop to his knees.

"Dimilioc has enemies," Grayson stated.

"Shit, imagine that," said Thaddeus. "I bet they looked forward to the vampires and Dimilioc wiping each other out, like happened every place else. Must have disappointed 'em something fierce when they looked around after all the hellfire died down and Dimilioc was still there. Figured they might do something about that, did they?"

"You've got strength and control," said Grayson. "And a Pure wife. Only Dimilioc wolves are allowed to take Pure women."

"So, you're thinkin', if I was Dimilioc, there wouldn't be a problem with that," Thaddeus said. He was silent a moment. Then he said, "It's not what I expected."

"Well?" said Grayson.

"Well," said Thaddeus, "Considering the options... I'm in, alright. Hell, if you're offering, I'm in *all* the way. We'll see if you keep your end of the bargain after I fight your enemies." He didn't sound very trusting.

"*Our* enemies," DeAnn said, softly but firmly.

"Yeah. Our enemies." Thaddeus dropped to one knee and said much more formally, "Master."

"Good," said Grayson. "We expect to face roughly four times our numbers. This should present no insuperable difficulties, as our enemies are by no means a cohesive pack. We shall expect to demonstrate Dimilioc superiority. I shall expect *you* to assist in illustrating the principle, Thaddeus."

"Yeah," said the newest Dimilioc wolf, not impressed. "I'll demonstrate my own damned superiority, but you can call it Dimilioc if you want." Though his words were proud and even defiant, his tone was much more respectful... and he did not look Grayson in the face.

"That will do for the moment," agreed Grayson. He threw the key to Alejandro and added, "We're moving in five minutes. Eat something fast." Without turning toward him, he said peremptorily, "Miguel."

Miguel twitched, the first sign of nervous guilt he'd shown. But his face and manner revealed nothing but eager willingness to help as he straightened attentively. "Yes, sir?"

"Take DeAnn upstairs. If she can shoot, give her a rifle. When you see black dogs coming back across the snow toward the house... I don't imagine you'll have any difficulty telling who's won the battle."

"No, sir," Miguel agreed earnestly.

Grayson grunted, said, "Eat," to Alejandro, and walked away, back up the stairs. If he had any doubts about turning his back on Thaddeus Williams, they didn't show.

Thaddeus had already edged out through the cell's narrow doorway. He was tearing off big bites of a sandwich, gulping them down with more haste than manners. DeAnn had picked up the plate and looked at Miguel to show her where to go. She held her son's hand in hers, not exactly with the air of a protective mother, but more as though she was worried the child might attack Miguel if she let him go.

Once he'd thought of the possibility, Alejandro worried about this, too. He doubted the problem had occurred to Miguel, yet... He caught his brother's eye, then glanced at the boy.

Miguel followed his glance. "Right," he said to Alejandro,

and went on casually to DeAnn, "I'll introduce you to my sister first thing. You'll both like Natividad. Can you shoot?"

"I have a silver knife… somewhere."

"Guns are better," Miguel told her. "You never want a black dog to get up close enough to let you use a knife. But silver ammo is *tremendamente* expensive, so maybe we'll get some practice in with regular bullets, right?"

Thaddeus followed his wife and son with his eyes as Miguel led them away, still chatting about the possibility of a black dog attack as casually as though he was discussing a party he was planning to throw for friends.

10

By the road, it was a little more than ten miles from the Dimilioc house to Lewis, but it was only six if you cut straight across country – not as the crow flies, but as the black dog runs. Alejandro, running near the tail of the line, saw for the first time how deeply the snow had drifted in the black forest where no Pure magic blew it aside. He guessed it would now be well over Natividad's head. It might even be over his, if he took human form. Alejandro could hardly believe there could be so much snow in the world, far less that anyone – anyone human – would choose to live in a frozen country where it might bury them standing.

Snow never fell in the forests around Potosi, where Alejandro had hunted deer and boar with his father. And sometimes javalinas and the big mule deer in the dry country around Hualahuises. There were bears for sport. One did not touch cattle, but then cattle were boring anyway. Except the longhorns, which could be exciting. Even a grizzly or a puma respected the longhorned cattle. For a moment it almost seemed to Alejandro that he was at home, running with his father in the hot mountains around Hualahuises, hunting javalinas. Not the longhorned cattle. Never cattle. *Certainly* never men.

"We are not murderers," Papá said sternly out of memory. He was half-changed, but, though his voice was thick and his words slurred, *he* did not lose language. "*We* are not barbarians or animals or demons. You have Dimilioc blood in you, Alejandro, and we do not hunt men, no matter how our shadows press us. *We* remember who we are."

"We killed those men," Alejandro had protested. "Last month, when they came from Monterrey and said our people should pay the other tax."

"Those were *bandidos*," Papá had growled, amused even through the black dog anger. "The other tax! They're all *bandidos* in Monterrey! If they will not protect the villages, they should not take money and say they do! *That* was not a hunt. You said *our people*. It's right you should say so. *We* protect Potosi, from Monterrey *bandidos* as well as *callejeros*."

This was a very complicated thought for a black dog almost in the *cambio de cuerpo*. Alejandro could never have expressed a thought like that, not while his shadow pressed at him, wanting the hunt and blood. He could only almost understand it, and only around the edges of the black dog's blood lust. But Papá had been there to think those thoughts and remember who they were, so that Alejandro didn't have to, not when it was hard, not when it really mattered. Now, Alejandro could only barely even remember that moment, or make sense of it.

Papá was not here. Grayson... Maybe Grayson Lanning thought that way, even when he was fully changed.

Alejandro was sure the Dimilioc Master thought that way about Lewis, and about this frozen country.

Harsh as this country must be to human people, it was more welcoming to a black dog who did not suffer from the cold and who could run weightless across the surface of the snow. Though, weight or no, the heat of their bodies melted the snow where they stepped so that they left big, blurred tracks.

The tracks of the Dimilioc wolves were not alone on the surface of the snow. Stray black dogs had left deep trails melted into the snow around Dimilioc and leading to and from Lewis. Many trails. Vonhausel's brazen *desvergüenza* – effrontery – was outrageous. But it was also frightening. Alejandro had never imagined their father's enemy would pursue them so implacably, could hardly believe even now that any black dog would truly pit himself against Dimilioc.

The human part of Alejandro's awareness, settled in the back of his mind while he ran, also feared that maybe the black dog strays who ran in Vonhausel's pack might be too strong for the few Dimilioc wolves that followed Grayson Lanning. How many really strong *callejeros* had there been, before the vampire war? How many now longed to live and hunt free of Dimilioc's law, how many had been glad to follow a leader with the determination and cleverness to shove Dimilioc over the edge into the fell dark? All the strong black dogs in the Americas, maybe. And Dimilioc had only ten, counting Amira, whom Alejandro was not certain he *should* count. She was very small for a black dog, hardly larger than an ordinary wolf. And Thaddeus – black dogs loved treachery. He half expected the big black dog to turn on them during this battle, join Vonhausel. He was very glad that Thaddeus's wife and son were behind them, in the heart of Dimilioc territory. If there were no such hold on the newest Dimilioc wolf, Alejandro knew he would never be able to accept him at his back.

Thaddeus ran in his black wolf form, but he gripped his big silver knife – sheathed in black leather – in his powerful jaws. He would use that strange part-human shape of his to fight; he would use that knife of his against Dimilioc's enemies. The sheen of fresh black ichor clotting in Ezekiel's shaggy pelt was a reminder to them all of what that blade could do, though the *verdugo* ran with a smooth, effortless lope despite that injury. Ezekiel ran as though he could run all the way to Chicago and back without pause and still slaughter Vonhausel and all his black dogs by himself. This did not make Alejandro like the young *verdugo* any better.

Maybe thirty black dogs had joined together in Vonhausel's first attack on Dimilioc; Alejandro was sure at least a third of the attackers had been killed. But Vonhausel had found more somewhere, because the human warning had been right: many black dogs crouched along the edge of Natividad's mandala, and many more ran back and forth along its outside curve, pressing forward and then falling back. It was impossible to count them, there were too many in motion, but Alejandro thought there were at least forty in sight, maybe even closer to fifty.

A dismaying number. Dimilioc wolves were supposed to be the best, the very best, but how could Grayson expect to win against those odds? Alejandro's own black dog was strong and arrogant; it still thought they might win – but Alejandro himself doubted that every Dimilioc wolf could kill four or five or six black dogs. Yet Grayson did not seem dismayed – none of the older Dimilioc black wolves seemed dismayed. Could they truly be *tan seguros de sí mismos*, so confident?

The mandala glowed to Alejandro's black-dog sight: a pale, uneasy luminescence, like moonlight but not really. It had been damaged already, he saw: its light was threaded through with strands of darkness which must have come from the pressure Vonhausel's black dogs put against it. But it held. Its outer circle cut across streets and yards, right through houses and shops. How strange that would be, to have that circle curve its way through your kitchen or bath.

One of the crosses Natividad had used to anchor her mandala stood in sight, some distance away to the right of the black forest where the Dimilioc wolves crouched, hidden, to observe. The cross burned with the same pale light so that Alejandro, in his black dog shape, hated to look at it. He didn't even like looking anywhere in its general direction.

Some of the townspeople had foolishly not bothered to come into the circle of protection, or had not come in quickly enough. Human bodies lay sprawled here and there amid wide spatters of blood that were now freezing into crimson drops in the violent cold. One of the bodies, a young woman, lay in a huge pool of crystallized blood near the outside edge of the mandala. Her hands were stretched out toward it, the tips of her fingers only inches away from its protection: too far. She had been torn nearly in half by some terrible blow that had come down on her from behind.

No human townspeople were visible inside the mandala. They had retreated into their church, Alejandro assumed. A good stone church, Natividad had said. The sort of church made to withstand not only the intangible hatred emanating from the fell dark, but also the more physical threats of hellfire and the deadly influence of demon-souled vampires.

Vonhausel's black dogs pressed against the mandala with the intangible weight of their shadows, the smoke of their breath rising in dark wisps through the gusts of snow. There were at least twenty of them, larger and far more tightly controlled than those that ran back and forth. The others, the ones that ran along the curve of the mandala, waiting for it to fail, paused sometimes to cry aloud to the blank sky and blowing snow. Those would be weaker black dogs and the moon-bound shifters.

Keziah had been partly right, because though there were many black dogs, there were more of those little shifters. They were small compared to true black dogs, no larger than their human forms, but they were fast and savage. Their mad cries were filled with murder-lust. For the three nights and two days of the full moon, the shifters would run in black dog form. For Vonhausel's purpose, shifters – nearly mindless, burning with hatred and bloodlust, devoted to slaughter for the sheer love of slaughter and utterly heedless of their own survival – must be *even better* than true black dogs.

Against all those black dogs and those that had been moon-bound, ten Dimilioc wolves. Counting even little Amira. And counting Thaddeus. Alejandro swung his head around to stare at the newest wolf.

So did Grayson.

Thaddeus stared back just long enough to demonstrate his strength, then turned his head aside in deliberate submission. He straightened, the bones of his limbs lengthening, his powerful clawed paws becoming hands that could grip. He dropped his silver knife from between jet black fangs, caught it, threw the sheath aside, and stood in his half-man half-beast shape, his shadow gathered thickly about him, his eyes glowing with hellfire and bloodlust. If Thaddeus was afraid of the odds they faced, of what would happen to his family if Dimilioc lost here, Alejandro could see no sign of it. If he meant to betray Dimilioc and use that silver blade of his to finish what he had begun with Ezekiel... Alejandro could see no sign of that, either.

Grayson looked at each Dimilioc wolf in turn. They met his powerful gaze for one burning moment and then turned to stare out at the enemy. They would run out to attack; should they attack the moon-bound shifters first, because they would be easier prey; or the strongest of the black dogs, because they were the most dangerous? Either way, Alejandro saw no way they could enter such a battle with any hope of victory.

Grayson gave a low snarling croon to make them all look at him. Then he led the way, all of his wolves falling in behind him. But he did not lead them straight out to battle as Alejandro had expected, but rather in a path that curved back and around through the woods and came out at last from the precise east – from exactly behind Natividad's cross, Alejandro understood at last. From the direction that repelled the gaze and the attention of any black dog; the one direction in which Vonhausel's pack was blind.

Alejandro was ashamed he had not thought of that himself. But his black dog shadow had not wanted to look at or think about the cross anchoring this quarter of Natividad's mandala. Besides that, his shadow was fully absorbed in the lust for battle, in the longing for blood and death. It would have preferred to hunt among a crowd of weak humans, it would have liked prey better than strong adversaries – but if faced with real opponents, it was glad enough to fight. It did not press against Alejandro's control, it did not really want to turn against the Dimilioc wolves; it agreed that the time for that was past.

Alejandro's black dog also thought that maybe Thaddeus *would* betray them. It did not mind that, either; it thought the huge black dog would turn first against Ezekiel and then, if Alejandro was watchful, he could attack him from behind and tear out his spine and cast him into the fell dark, and thus be rid of a strong rival while putting Ezekiel and all Dimilioc in his debt. Alejandro looked forward to the moment Thaddeus turned – at least, his shadow looked forward to it. He pulled his own awareness apart from his black dog's enough to be able to find Grayson, watch the Dimilioc Master for the cue to attack.

Grayson gave that signal by the simple expedient of bounding out of the uncomfortable light of the cross and falling on the strongest of the nearby black dogs like a puma on a rat. He bowled the black dog over with his weight and the shock of the attack, ripping through his belly with scything black claws, tearing out his guts and shattering his spine in that same ferocious blow. The black dog died without returning even a single blow of his own. His body writhed and twisted back toward his human shape as his shadow, struggling furiously, pulled free and dispersed back into the fell dark. Grayson did not watch, but flung himself onto a second enemy.

Though no one had talked over the tactics they would use, Alejandro saw that Harrison first, and then Zachariah, and finally Ezekiel, raced past Grayson. Each in turn lunged to attack the next closest enemy black dog, and the one after that, and the one after that – Harrison took his opponent almost as much by surprise as Grayson had and tore him up almost as quickly; Zachariah's opponent, immediately on the defensive, also went down. Only Ezekiel's enemy had time to fully brace himself for the attack, but Alejandro saw that it didn't matter – the black dog might as well have been a puppy in his first *cambio de cuerpo*. Ezekiel feinted twice and then slid through the black dog's defenses with an attack that looked at first like another feint, but wasn't.

Then Alejandro lost track of Ezekiel's battle because he leaped into one of his own: Ethan had flung himself into a struggle with a black dog who overmatched him, so Alejandro lunged to take the black dog from behind, and then Thaddeus, though already battling an enemy of his own, crouched and spun and slashed his silver blade at their opponent, casually, in passing, opening a huge wound from his belly to halfway up his chest. The black dog screamed and scrambled backward, black ichor streaming from the slash, and then scarlet blood as the shock of the injury forced him into human form. But his human shape, though brawny for a human, was easy prey: before he could reclaim his shadow, Ethan tore his head off. The shadow writhed, crying voicelessly, then diffused like smoke in the cold air. Thaddeus dispatched his own opponent and freed that shadow as well before the first had altogether dispersed.

Alejandro, triumphant, wanted to laugh – he wanted to lift his head and howl challenge and threat across all this frozen country. His black dog, exultant and sly, smug in the confidence of its own strength, was happy now to fight alongside Ethan and thought it was clever to use Thaddeus's blooded knife against their enemies. When Ethan spun to face a new enemy, Alejandro separated from him only so that they could take the black dog from both sides and drive him onto Thaddeus's silver knife.

Another kill, and another, and then suddenly shifters crowded everywhere. Not one could be over two hundred pounds, most much less, but they were all mad with bloodlust, and there were so many of them. There were true black dogs among them, too, some of those heavier and stronger than either Ethan or Alejandro. Everything dissolved into a whirling confusion of slashing coal-black fangs and terrible claws, furnace heat beating through the air.

If not for Thaddeus and Ethan, Alejandro might not have survived that first wild struggle. Alejandro did not recognize this at once; he had little attention to spare for anything but battle and blood and death. But he and Ethan and Thaddeus found themselves continuing to fight as a team, foreign though that notion was to any normal black dog. Over and over, Ethan and Alejandro attacked to draw a black dog's attention, Thaddeus ripped him up with his silver blade, and then one of them finished the enemy without difficulty.

Several times Alejandro took serious wounds, or Ethan

did, or once an enemy black dog even tore claws across Thaddeus's back and smashed all his ribs on one side. But when any of the Dimilioc wolves was injured, he could fall out of his shadow, let his black dog carry away his wounds while his team protected him. Then he could call up his shadow again, shift through the *cambio de cuerpo*, and leap again for the throat of an enemy.

Alejandro was aware, dimly, at a remove, that Grayson and Harrison and Zachariah had formed a similar team. Even though he knew how formidable the three oldest Dimilioc wolves must be, even though he would never have expected to match them, he was furiously jealous that they were destroying enemies faster than *his* team. But Grayson could force black dogs into their human forms, Alejandro saw him do that again and again, and though he tried to do that himself, he couldn't now find the trick of it or else these enemies were too strong. His failure fed his jealousy, but that was alright; his rage only made him fight more ferociously.

Keziah and Amira also fought together, which did not surprise Alejandro, except that Benedict had somehow become a part of their team. Maybe Keziah was smart enough to realize that having a third black dog for her team might keep them all alive, and pragmatic enough to ally with the only Dimilioc wolf available to fill the role.

Whether Keziah had recruited Benedict on purpose or otherwise, her team was cutting through their gathered enemies almost as efficiently as Grayson's triumvirate. Keziah had been right about her little sister, for Amira, though so small, was blindingly fast – and, amazingly, fearless and savage in battle. She and Benedict drove one

enemy after another into Keziah's slashing claws, for
Keziah, not at all to Alejandro's surprise, was the killer for
her team. She was not so very much larger than her sister,
but just as fast, and she seemed to have a real instinct for the
killing blow. She cut down one enemy after another, tearing
them to ribbons, leaving them to twist, dying, back into
human shape. Keziah's deadliness made Alejandro's black
dog even more furious, though he was also savagely pleased
by Dimilioc's superiority.

Grayson had said that, about demonstrating Dimilioc's
superiority, but Alejandro had not understood. He
understood it now. No wonder Grayson had not been
worried about facing forty black dogs with only ten. He was
sure now that they would win, would crush their enemies,
would spill their blood out on the snow and howl after
their dispersing shadows – part of that was his black dog's
arrogant blood lust, but part of it was his own growing
confidence.

Of all the Dimilioc wolves, only Ezekiel fought alone, in
a deadly whirl of blood and ichor, with a clear space always
around him because the enemy black dogs tried to keep
away from him.

And Ezekiel did take them down. For the first time,
Alejandro really understood that the Dimilioc *verdugo*
had never for a moment been at risk from Thaddeus, silver
blade or no. He was as brutally strong as Thaddeus himself
and as fast as Keziah, and so profoundly in control of his
shadow that, as long as he was not killed outright, he could
let his black dog carry his injuries away and then instantly
bring it back – and somehow no blow he took ever seemed

to be a killing blow. Twice in ten seconds Alejandro saw one of Ezekiel's opponents lunge into a blow that should have torn him in half, but Ezekiel flicked into his much smaller human shape and ducked low to let the strike go over his head, then pulled himself instantly into his black dog form to strike his enemy from an unexpected direction. Both times, Ezekiel dealt so ferocious a blow that he left his enemy struggling and dying in human form, the freed shadow shredding away on the wind.

Ezekiel *had* claimed right from the beginning that he might kill all the black dogs in the world by himself. Watching him now, Alejandro almost believed he might.

All this Alejandro saw before the intensifying press of battle claimed his attention and he lost track of the other Dimilioc wolves.

He did not know how many black dogs and moon-bound shifters had been destroyed in the first clash – a great many, it seemed to him. And a great many more died after that first attack. Many of those were Vonhausel's true black dogs, which he would surely find impossible to replace.

The enemy should not have been taken so thoroughly by surprise. That occurred to Alejandro during a pause in the battle. He was contemptuous of Dimilioc's enemies – those enemies deserved nothing but contempt. If Vonhausel had not been so entirely focused on destroying Natividad's mandala that he forgot to watch for enemies; if he had realized someone might lead the Dimilioc wolves through the light of the anchoring cross; if the black dogs of his shadow pack had worked together against the Dimilioc wolves, especially Ezekiel – they might have won already instead of fighting and dying, each alone, right in the midst of their fellows.

But because of the mistakes their enemies had made, the Dimilioc wolves were going to destroy the shadow pack. Alejandro knew it, he felt it, he was swept along in a wild triumphant murderous fury that carried them all with it like a spring flood pouring down an arroyo...

Then Natividad's mandala cracked straight through. The magic infused in the mandala trembled and gave, and the mandala itself cracked, and the rest of the magic poured out of it into the air – gone, lost, and every house and shop that lay along its line burst into flames. The earth itself cracked open, burning, along the line where it had run.

Alejandro heard his own high, piercing shriek of terror, which slid down and down in pitch until it became a roar of rage before he understood that he was the one shrieking. Only the lifeblood of a Pure woman could have shattered Natividad's mandala so abruptly, and he knew, he *knew*, as soon as it broke, that Vonhausel had somehow gotten to Dimilioc and stolen Natividad out of its shelter and brought her here and poured her blood out in the snow so that it would run out across the mandala, *y prender fuego a la sangre*, he had called up his shadow and set her blood afire, and the mandala had broken because she was *dead*...

But then Grayson roared, and Alejandro whirled around and saw the body of a Pure woman, flung down and discarded at the foot of the burning cross, with the yellow-eyed silhouette of Vonhausel himself looming over it, blackly massive against the light and the snow, wreathed in smoke, fire glowing in his gaping jaws behind his coal-black fangs.

But Alejandro also saw, even in that first glimpse, that it was not after all *Natividad's* body that lay crumpled and broken at Vonhausel's feet. Vonhausel had brought some other Pure woman to this place; he must have found her and stolen her from her home and then kept her, who knew how long – kept her in reserve as a weapon and a tool. Now he threw back his head and howled, a long singing cry of hatred and triumph and fury, and his few remaining black dogs and moon-bound curs howled with him, swept up by the heavy moon-drawn tide of his killing rage.

Alejandro, furious at the death of that other Pure woman, was nevertheless so consumed by violent relief that she was not Natividad that he nearly forgot that Vonhausel was still there; that the battle was not ended; that the mandala was broken and all the town laid open to deadly enemies.

Then Ezekiel went past Alejandro in a silent, intent rush.

But Vonhausel did not stand to fight the Dimilioc *verdugo*. He whirled about and charged straight into the town, sweeping the remnants of his shadow pack along in his wake, racing along the path laid down by one of the crossbars of the burning mandala, heading for the center of town. What he meant to do there, Alejandro could not imagine; he had thought Vonhausel's attack on Lewis merely a tactic to forge all his wild undisciplined strays into a real pack and maybe to draw out the Dimilioc wolves to a battle where they might be destroyed, but if that was so, why did Vonhausel not rally his black dogs and fight? He thought that Vonhausel ran, not in flight but with some target in mind. His black dogs ran with and alongside him; his moon-bound shifters scattered to hunt through the town, testing the strength of any home where human prey sheltered.

Ezekiel pursued Vonhausel, never looking aside, utterly indifferent to the enemy black dogs who crowded him from either side. His very indifference frightened them, so they would not close with the *verdugo* – or maybe they had watched him fight, as Alejandro had, and that had understandably frightened them.

Then Grayson leaped away after Ezekiel, and Zachariah followed him, and belatedly Alejandro and Ethan and Thaddeus, and Keziah and her sister – Alejandro could not see Harrison or Benedict anywhere, but there was no time to look for them. His black dog shadow wanted to strike at any nearby enemy, wanted to fight, struggle, kill. But none of the other Dimilioc wolves turned aside to grapple with enemies. They all raced after Ezekiel, who pursued Vonhausel. No one turned either to the right or to the left; they went straight over fences and, almost as quickly, up and over houses – once Alejandro heard a human's terrified scream from one of the homes they passed, but Ethan ran at his left and Thaddeus at his right and he did not turn to look.

The church at the center of Lewis, the heart of Natividad's mandala, was burning. Like all Catholic churches, it had been made of stone expressly to withstand hellfire and then every stone had been blessed against demonic malice. Even so, it burned. The heat had broken out the windows; shards of colored glass glittered across the snow: red and purple, blue and gold, reflecting the hot light of the flames that roared through the open windows and crawled across the vaulted roof and charred the stones of the wall black.

The people who had been sheltering in the church were now huddling in the surrounding streets, staring up at the snow hissing into the flames. No one was trying to put out the fire, maybe because it was obviously too late or maybe because they knew that hellfire would irrevocably corrupt a church – or maybe because they knew the fire was not their biggest problem. They were turning toward the onrushing black dogs, but they moved so slowly – they looked like prey even to Alejandro, though he remembered even in the midst of bloodlust and battle fury that his own sister had made her mandala to shelter these people and would not want them torn down, torn apart, strewn across these streets *en fragmentos ensangrentado*... Fury poured through Alejandro like a substance with weight, with a presence of its own. His shadow thickened around him, dense and bloody, so that the whole world took on a crimson hue.

Vonhausel, black as pitch, surrounded by a miasma of smoke and fury, rushed toward the gathered humans. They scattered, but too slowly, like prey, like penned sheep. Vonhausel struck left and right among them – human screaming sounded so different from the dying screams of black dogs; their screams were sweeter and more satisfying. Their blood would also be sweet. For an instant, before he caught himself and remembered that he was Dimilioc and had a human brother, Alejandro wanted to turn on them himself.

Some of the humans, not such helpless sheep as the rest, were shooting, but either they did not hit Vonhausel or they were not using silver ammunition, or both. Vonhausel did not turn aside but raced straight toward the burning church; he had some aim in mind, but Alejandro could not tell what it was–

Ezekiel caught him before he reached the church.

The yellow-eyed black dog had no choice but to whirl around to meet Ezekiel's rush. The impact of their meeting seemed to shake the earth. They tore at each other, a blur of bulk and flashing claws and snapping jaws; the bitter scents of ash and black ichor filled the air; they were locked in a battle that had suddenly become not merely a fight but also a duel. Vonhausel's remaining black dogs crouched in a semicircle along one side of the street, all of them watching with avid, burning eyes.

The Dimilioc wolves matched them along the other side of the circle. Both Harrison and Benedict *were* missing, and though Alejandro would have said Dimilioc had been winning the battle, wasn't there a word for a victory so hard-won it destroyed the victor? But Alejandro could not remember that word either in English or Spanish.

The townspeople had mostly fled, which was the best thing they could do, though where they could go, with the church destroyed, Alejandro did not know; but he did not really care, either, and forgot them at once. Only a scattering remained, armed with their useless guns, but not shooting; they covered the retreat of the rest and maybe wanted to fight, but the man leading them kept them from shooting, wisely avoiding the attention of Vonhausel's black dogs. And even those were retreating slowly, which was also wise.

To Alejandro's amazement and fury, he saw that Vonhausel was matching Ezekiel. The black dog was heavy, strong, powerfully muscled and extraordinarily fast, even faster than Ezekiel – then Alejandro finally remembered that of course the Dimilioc *verdugo* had come into this battle already tired and injured. *Then* he saw that Vonhausel was not merely matching Ezekiel, but *over*matching him. Vonhausel took injuries fearlessly and they closed instantly – he somehow seemed to rid himself of wounds without needing to shift to his human form, which was impossible, but it was happening. Alejandro understood suddenly that Ezekiel might actually lose this fight, and with it the battle, and maybe the whole war...

Zachariah, too, saw Ezekiel's danger. Ignoring the conventions of the duel, with a cry that began as a bellowing roar and scaled up and up into piercing shriek of rage, he flung himself forward to attack Vonhausel.

The leader of the black dogs spun about as though to meet Zachariah's rush, but this was a feint, for he whipped right around and struck Ezekiel instead. And this time Ezekiel had mistaken his enemy, for he did not quite evade the blow. Vonhausel ripped claws right up through his belly and then on the backstroke tore out his throat, and Ezekiel, driven for once involuntarily into human form, collapsed to his hands and knees in a spray of ichor and blood. But though Ezekiel shifted so fast and so completely that he survived those terrible wounds, even he was not able to call his shadow back immediately, but was left helpless before his enemy.

Vonhausel did not pause to savor his enemy's defeat, but struck again in a blur of speed, meaning to finish Ezekiel immediately. But Zachariah crashed into him before he could touch the *verdugo*, and immediately the two were

locked in a tight blur. Thaddeus lunged to tear into that
battle, Ethan a beat behind him, and then all of Vonhausel's
black dogs surged forward, and the Dimilioc wolves rushed
to meet them, and Alejandro found himself fighting two
black dogs who were both larger and heavier than he was,
with a shifter harassing him from behind.

If his opponents had worked together, Alejandro might
have died then, but one got in the other's way and they
turned on each other, snarling, and then Grayson was beside
him, taking advantage of the black dogs' distraction to kill
them both with efficient speed before lunging past, with a
deep, guttural snarl of loathing, to hurl himself into a thick
knot of enemies.

Alejandro followed the Master, or tried to – Grayson had
disappeared into the melee. Alejandro could not find Ethan
or Thaddeus or any Dimilioc wolf – he glimpsed Keziah,
cutting a deadly swath through enemy black dogs, Amira
behind her, and leaped toward them...

The church collapsed, and for a moment all the fighting
ceased in the overpowering roar of falling stones and fiery
timbers. Then Vonhausel leaped up out of the battle, onto
the smoldering rubble. He howled, a long savage sound
of hatred and triumph, nothing at all like the howl of a
wolf. All around the burning ruins of the church, his black
dogs flung back their heads and answered, and, as though
in response to their cries, the burning earth cracked open
below the ruined church.

Grayson moved forward, crimson-eyed, heavy-
shouldered, his fury as dense and implacable as his shadow.
He did not answer Vonhausel's howl, but stalked him, head

low, smoke trickling from his jaws. Then Grayson gathered himself and bounded up onto the ruins of the church toward his enemy. His power spread out around him, forcing the shadows of lesser black dogs back and down.

Vonhausel snarled, a low sound that ached with fury and frustrated hatred. But he leaped from his high perch, skidding down the opposite side of the piled rubble. His black dogs scattered back and away from the Dimilioc Master, who stared around at them contemptuously.

Once he had ceded control of the ruined church, however, Vonhausel did not continue to flee. More black dogs – an impossible number – were even now sliding out of the flames of the church, flinging themselves up from the cracked and broken earth. Alejandro counted Vonhausel's *callejeros* twice and then again, and although he came up with different numbers each time, he was sure there were more than thirty. This seemed impossible, but when he counted a third time, he counted thirty-two enemy black dogs.

Against those numbers, even Grayson hesitated. Alejandro looked for, but still could not find, either Harrison or Benedict, and now he could not see Zachariah, either, or Amira. He could not believe Zachariah had been killed – he could not believe Dimilioc had lost both Zachariah and Harrison – but neither could he see them anywhere among the living, though he rose on his hind legs to search.

Ezekiel was up and back in his black dog shape, but clearly far from his best. He crouched near Thaddeus, with Keziah on his other side. Alejandro would never have guessed that either Thaddeus or Keziah would go out of their way to protect the Dimilioc *verdugo*, but so it seemed.

Ethan slid out of the fiery press of shadows to take a place on Thaddeus's other side, and Alejandro moved with some haste to join them – five Dimilioc black wolves together would still be a daunting target for Vonhausel's *callejeros*, however many of those might remain. And there was Amira after all, lamed, with slashes all down her flank and thigh, clearly unable to shift to human form or she would have let her shadow take away her injuries. But she was still on her feet, still moving.

Grayson, looming above them from his place, now uncontested, high on the burning rubble of the church, stared down at their enemies with a low singing snarl of loathing.

Vonhausel answered, and all around them dozens of his black dogs echoed that snarl. There seemed even more than before. Alejandro tried again to estimate their number and got an unreasonable answer; tried to count them in order and got a different answer, no more believable. There could not *be* more black dogs now than at the beginning of the fight – the numbers were impossible…

Somewhere near at hand, a deep-voiced motor rumbled to life, then another. And another. It took Alejandro a moment to place the sound, so unexpected: the deep roar of a bus engine. He thought first that the townspeople were fleeing, they had held a "Plan B" in mind all along. *Bueno*, good. He even wished, as far as it was in him to be concerned, that all those human people might make it out of Vonhausel's reach, get clear of all black dog wars – though this battle might end soon enough anyway, and then *Dios* protect anyone helpless on the road, away from shelter. But his shadow did not care about any of that. It wanted only to survive and to kill its enemies.

Alejandro agreed with those aims. He did not think any of the Dimilioc wolves were going to live through this battle, but if they could not survive, then he wanted to kill lots and lots of enemies. That, he thought they could do.

Along with all the rest, allies and enemies alike, he stared up at Grayson and waited for some signal to resume battle.

Then the first bus roared into the town square, *abarrotado* – crammed with people – with shotguns and rifles bristling out the windows. The second bus followed, one of those stupid yellow ones that advertised to any black dog, *Here are children, come and kill them*. But it was just as crowded as the first, with as many guns poking out its windows. After them came a car.

The first bus squealed to a halt beside the ruins of the church and everyone on one side began shooting. Shooting carefully, only at Vonhausel and his black dogs. It was immediately apparent that some of them had silver ammunition. The black dogs, snarling their rage, retreated from the open spaces of the town square, finding shelter behind the surrounding buildings. The shooting stopped... Alejandro guessed that the human people did not have very much silver ammunition, maybe not much ammunition of any kind. He suspected Vonhausel and his shadow pack would make that same guess very soon.

Grayson bounded down the rubble of the church amid a cascade of burning fragments of wood and shards of stone and glass, skidding to a halt a few feet from the bus. Amazingly, no one shot at him. The humans called back and forth to one another, but Alejandro had lost nearly all his capacity for human language and could not work out what they said.

A small man with fine features, a tight-set mouth, and eyes the hard clear gray of granite, leaned out the window of the car. He held a pistol in one hand, but he was not pointing the weapon at Grayson. He must have recognized the Dimilioc Master, because he said slowly and formally, in a loud voice, "We ask Dimilioc for shelter from the fell dark."

The words sorted themselves out only gradually for Alejandro, but Grayson must have worked out the meaning more quickly, or never lost his understanding of human speech, because rather than tearing the man apart for his temerity, he tipped his broad head down in something like a nod. The sound he made was savage, angry – but not hostile. It was a sound of agreement.

The human looked into the Master's face, ill-advisedly. So, the man was not so very experienced – he did not seem afraid, nor did he lower his gaze as he should have. He only went on, a good deal less formally but with considerable practicality, "Yours is the only road open. The road to Brighton's blocked, they've thrown trees down across it, but we hope the road to Dimilioc is clear."

Even speaking to the Master of Dimilioc in his black dog form, the man possessed a formidable composure. And despite his lack of proper submissive manners, he was obviously right. Because Alejandro had more or less understood the human's words, he was not surprised when Grayson turned his head to glare at his remaining wolves, then jerked his head at the buses.

The Dimilioc wolves did not ride *on* the buses, of course – not even on their roofs – except for Ezekiel, who lay stretched out on the flat-topped yellow bus and sank deadly claws right through the metal to brace himself on the curves. Alejandro did not want to think about the *verdugo*'s temper at being forced to show the world his weakness; he avoided even the briefest glance up at that bus.

The rest of the Dimilioc wolves, even Amira who was still injured, ran alongside the buses and car, keeping to the slow pace that was the best such cumbersome vehicles could manage. Vonhausel had apparently decided to let them go. He knew, of course, where they were going. Apparently he saw no need to risk his black dogs to stop them getting there. Anyway, he had made himself uncontested master in Lewis. If that had been his aim, he had succeeded.

If his aim had been, as Miguel had guessed, to give his shadow pack a victory, he had succeeded at that, too. If he had wished to defeat Dimilioc in battle and thus recover the pride his earlier defeat had cost him... he had also succeeded in that.

Dimilioc itself proved undisturbed. Alejandro had been haunted all during the run by the idea that Vonhausel's black dogs, not constrained to escort buses along the road, might make the shorter cross-country journey and be at the house long before the Dimilioc black wolves could return. However much silver ammunition Miguel might have made, however good his aim, or Natividad's, or Thaddeus's wife's, Alejandro was more than half convinced that the Dimilioc wolves would come back to find the house in

flames and their vulnerable brothers and sisters and wives
and children all dead. Or hostages, if Vonhausel was clever
enough to take hostages, and had the control necessary to
keep hostages alive. Alejandro thought the black dog was
certainly that clever, but could not guess whether he had
that kind of control.

But the house was fine. Whatever Vonhausel intended,
apparently it did not include tearing down the house that
was Dimilioc's heart. At least, not yet.

Natividad and DeAnn, and DeAnn's little boy ran out
to meet the vehicles, which made Alejandro nervous and
angry. What if someone from the buses shot at them? There
was no reason anybody should, but what if somebody did?
But Miguel had stayed above on the balcony with a rifle, so
they were not *so* careless.

Natividad ran to the car leading the first bus and put her
hands up to greet the man who swung quickly down from the
bus – the human leader who had spoken to Grayson and who
now said something to Natividad with similar familiarity.

Alejandro fought down a surge of black dog possessiveness
that made him want to rip the human's guts out. He should
be glad that Natividad knew the man, that she approved
him; he must be a decent man as well as a brave one. But
Alejandro resented him, almost hated him – or maybe his
shadow resented the man; it was harder even than usual to
tell where his black dog's thoughts and feelings left off and
his own began. Alejandro, suddenly weary beyond belief of
that confusion, struck out of his shadow, back toward the
clearer thought and cleaner emotions of his human self.

11

At first Natividad was so glad to see the Dimilioc wolves returning to the house, so happy to see Alejandro safe among them, that she did not think too much about the buses or what they meant. Then Miguel shook his head and said, "So, that's not good."

Natividad looked at her twin in surprise. "*Qué?*" Then she thought again about the buses and said in a smaller voice, "Oh."

"How many people do you guess they could cram onto those buses?"

Not very many, Natividad thought. She tried to count bus seats in her mind's eye, tried to guess how many people might be able to stand in the aisle. How many people could you cram onto a bus in an emergency? Fifty? More? She was pretty sure the answer wasn't *everybody in Lewis*.

Well, maybe the rest of the townspeople were OK, they just hadn't come on those buses, they were still sheltering in the church or someplace else in town. Except if that was right, why the buses at all? Had Grayson decided to bring a lot of humans to Dimilioc for some reason of his own?

But those buses looked really crowded… and the Dimilioc wolves escorting them looked *malísimo*. They looked to Natividad like they had been defeated. They looked like… well, like refugees. And… She counted twice, then again. "I think, only five Dimilioc wolves," she said, tentatively. Including 'Jandro, *gracias a Dios*.

"Seven, counting Thad, thank God," said DeAnn. "See your daddy?" she added to her son, pointing, and little Conway leaned forward, a breath away from shifting to his black dog form and leaping down off the balcony to run out and meet his father. DeAnn took a firmer hold on his belt, warning the boy, "Don't you dare!" Then the Pure woman glanced at Natividad and jabbed a finger to indicate the front of the little convoy. "Grayson's young bastard of an executioner's up on the roof of that last bus, see? And there's a black wolf behind the first bus, did you see that one? That makes it seven altogether."

Natividad hadn't spotted Ezekiel until DeAnn pointed him out, maybe because she just hadn't expected to see him riding up on the roof of a bus. She tried to think of any reason the Dimilioc executioner would be riding instead of running. The explanations that came to mind were all bad. She also tried to think of reasons why only seven out of ten Dimilioc wolves would be escorting those buses. Maybe Grayson had sent the others on some kind of errand. She couldn't see Zachariah or Harrison. It made sense for Grayson to send one or both of his strongest wolves and closest allies on some important errand. But the cold running through her bones was fear. She just did not believe any so-innocent explanation for the absence of black wolves who should have been there.

She said with stiff reluctance, "I think they lost. I think Vonhausel won. I guess… I guess that means he broke through my mandala." She paused, then added painfully, "It's my fault. I made them a flawed mandala and it didn't hold…"

Miguel shook his head, but he didn't disagree because how could either of them know what had happened? He didn't say anything. What was there to say?

DeAnn, leaning her hip on the balcony railing, swung the rifle Miguel had given her to a more comfortable position over her shoulder, gave her son a warning glare in case he took this for permission to slip off the balcony, and said, clinically, "Mandalas are good, strong protection. Stronger than plain circles, more resistant to demonic influence than helices. That's what my mama taught me. Your mama teach you the same?"

Natividad nodded. She felt numb. She felt sick.

"And you anchored your mandala with a church in the middle and a cross at each cardinal point, yeah? That right?" DeAnn stared out over the buses as though she might be able to see all the way through the winter forest to Lewis. "Your mama ever tell you how a vampire could take down a protective mandala?"

"*Sí*," said Natividad, but so softly she wasn't sure the other woman would hear. She hadn't thought of that possibility. She would almost rather… She *would* rather believe it was her flawed mandala that had been at fault. But she knew what DeAnn meant. She whispered, "Yes. Yes, she told me."

DeAnn nodded without looking at Natividad. "I guess a sister died out there today."

Natividad, her hands closed tightly on the balcony railing, did not answer. Below, the buses growled and slid as they changed gears and headed across the open ground toward the Dimilioc house.

"*No hay señas de los enemigos perros negros,*" Miguel said. But he did not seem very happy about this. He snapped the safety back on his rifle, frowning.

"I'm going down," Natividad said, and barely waited for her twin to nod agreement before ducking through the sliding door that led back into the house and heading for the stairs. Little Con jumped off the railing at last, and DeAnn swung around and ran for the stairs with a rough urgency that showed how much she wanted to get out of the house, get out there to meet those buses with her son.

Sheriff Pearson leaped down from the first bus just as DeAnn and Natividad came down the steps. Natividad headed for him, took his hands, and looked quickly into his face. The sheriff didn't seem to have been injured, but he had been badly hurt, she thought, in ways that did not show. She took a breath, dreading to ask, to know...

"I don't think anyone could have done better," he told her.

Natividad stared urgently at his face, trying to be sure he meant this. "You're sure? The mandala *did* help you, didn't it? I didn't make it... wrong?"

"Oh, yes," Pearson assured her wearily. "It held. Without it, we'd never have lasted long enough for Dimilioc to come."

Natividad nodded. It did help, a little, despite knowing a Pure woman had probably died, to know that at least the darkness she'd let tangle into her mandala hadn't hurt the town. That the mandala had held as long as any protective circle could. She asked, "The church?"

"Burned."

Natividad closed her eyes. "I'm sorry."

"Most everybody got out." The sheriff hesitated, then added, "Grayson didn't abandon us. I thought he would. That your doing?"

"No. I don't think so. A little, maybe."

"Ah." Sheriff Pearson glanced over his shoulder at the Dimilioc wolves. He was afraid of them, Natividad saw, but not nearly afraid enough. The shadows around the wolves were not merely dense but darker than they should have been. Deeper, like each shadow was really a crack in the world that led straight down to Hell. Natividad thought the sheriff did not see this. He said wearily, "Grayson's here, I know. I can't tell the rest of them..."

Natividad looked at the Dimilioc wolves, wincing from the absence of those she could not find. "Alejandro," she said, nodding toward her brother, who was straightening slowly back into his human shape. "*Gracias a Jesús, Maria y José,*" she muttered, not really meaning for Sheriff Pearson to hear her, though she could see he did. She didn't explain that she was not only glad to see her brother alive, but also to see him reach for his human form. The darkness of his shadow was really scary.

"Your brother, of course," said the sheriff.

"*Sí.* And there's Ethan, and that's Ezekiel, of course... That's Thaddeus Williams over there, and Amira and Keziah over on the other side of that bus. They're new wolves–"

"*New* wolves? New to Dimilioc?"

It was too complicated to explain. Natividad shrugged. Other townspeople were coming down from the bus, hesitating uncertainly in the snow. Lots of old people and women and kids. They hugged themselves against the cold, cast indecisive looks toward the house and frightened glances toward the Dimilioc wolves. Alejandro was all the way back to his human shape. His shadow must have carried away any injuries he'd taken: he stood with his shoulders slumped and moved with a dragging step when he walked to meet her, but there was no sign he'd been hurt. Only he looked really tired and angry and, she thought, maybe… maybe kind of heartsick.

The sheriff reached to touch her shoulder, then stopped, wary of the quick lift of Alejandro's head. But he asked, "Do you know what we should do, where we should go?" He hesitated. "My daughter?" But then he glanced over at Grayson, who was sitting on the high porch, staring out at the forest. The Master showed no signs of taking on human form. Pearson added reluctantly, "I should get these people inside, someplace… that is, maybe someplace…"

"Out of sight," said Natividad. "Yes."

Ezekiel, also still in black dog form, had disappeared into the house, trailed at a respectful distance by Ethan. Amira and Keziah had taken back their human shapes, but ignored the buses and the gathered townspeople as though they were all invisible. They walked slowly around the house, side by side but not touching one another, heading for a side door that would not risk any encounter with Ezekiel. Amira limped, but Keziah seemed almost untouched by the injuries or exhaustion of hard fighting – of course, no one important to her had died.

DeAnn had tucked herself against Thaddeus's left side, managing to look almost petite against her husband's bulk, not easy for a woman her size. Thaddeus had reclaimed his wholly human form. He'd swung his son up to perch on his shoulder, but he still held his silver blade. He held it casually, though, not as though he expected to use it again right away. His left arm was tight around his wife's waist, his head tilted down against hers as they, too, walked slowly back toward the house. Neither of them seemed at all concerned with the human townspeople or the Dimilioc wolves or anything.

Sheriff Pearson stared at this domestic little scene, distracted, his eyebrows rising in surprise. "*They're* Dimilioc?"

"Just very recently," explained Natividad, distracted. She reached out to take her brother's hands, and Alejandro took hers in a hard grip and sighed, like he might stand there just like that for a few hours before he found the energy to move.

The sheriff hesitated, looking at Alejandro, who ignored him. At last he asked, putting off any questions he might have had, "My people... It's cold... and all the babies... We should go in. But..."

"What, you want to know about rooms and baths and supper and how to keep anybody from eating the children?" Natividad asked. She'd thought she was joking, but then realized, almost before she got to the facetious comment about children, that she wasn't exactly sure. She glanced quickly at Alejandro, but he didn't seem to be listening. Whatever he was thinking about, she doubted it had anything to do with ordinary human concerns. She touched her brother's arm and he jerked back, then steadied and drew a breath. Some of the tight-wound tension slowly relaxed out of his muscles.

"Zachariah?" she asked reluctantly. She was afraid she had already guessed the answer. "Harrison? Benedict?"

"Lost," Alejandro told her wearily. "Gone into the fell dark."

He wasn't looking at her. He wasn't looking at Grayson, either, but Natividad knew his attention was tightly focused on the Dimilioc Master. She tried not to look at the Master, either, but her heart turned over in sharp sympathy for him. And, a little bit, in fear.

Both Zachariah and Harrison. And Benedict, too, which was bad, but *both* Zachariah and Harrison! And after losing his black dog wife last year! Natividad swallowed against a suddenly tight throat. She had to swallow again before she could tell Sheriff Pearson, "There's room, I guess, if you don't mind sharing. And there's lots and lots of food – not much fresh, we're out of eggs and stuff, but there's a huge pantry and a whole row of big chest freezers, I'll show you."

"Water?" asked the sheriff.

"There's plenty, I guess… "

"You're worried about a siege, of course," Miguel said to the sheriff, coming to join them. He had slung his rifle over his shoulder and nodded casually to the sheriff as though he'd expected all the time that the man might show up with a hundred townspeople in desperate need of shelter.

Natividad hadn't even known her twin had left the balcony, but he must have decided there was no need to stay on guard at the moment. "This is my other brother, Miguel," she explained, and wondered whether she should add, "*He always knows everything.*" She didn't know how it would sound. Lots of grown men resented a kid Miguel's age who knew anything, much less everything.

Miguel didn't seem worried about it, though. He said to Sheriff Pearson, "The house sits right on top of its own well, so that's fine, and there are three separate generators, so that's OK, and you should *see* the storage cellars. Well, you really should, I guess: I'll show you. This place is great for a siege, but I expect there won't be one. At least, not one that goes on and on until you start wondering when somebody really will start eating people."

Pearson tilted his head. "You think not?"

"Well, if we don't win soon, we'll lose soon," Miguel said matter-of-factly. "That's obvious." To Natividad he added, "The east wing is sort of separate from the rest of the house. I think that's where as many as possible of the human people should go. Maybe some of the older people can take rooms in the main wing with us, but not the kids – at least, not the little bratty kids who'll get on anybody's nerves." He didn't have to say, "*Dimilioc wolf nerves.*" He told the sheriff instead, "It's important for all your people to avoid the wolves, especially Ezekiel. Well, especially all of them. Actually, Thaddeus – the big black guy? He doesn't look it, but he's probably the safest, because he has a Pure wife. But even so – do all your people know how to behave around Dimilioc wolves?"

Alejandro made a soft, wordless *hsst!* of warning before Sheriff Pearson could answer, and everyone stopped.

Grayson had gotten to his feet. He was still in black dog form. His thick black pelt seemed to drift off into smoke around the edges, and blue-edged flames flickered here and there along his body as he shifted position. When he turned his head toward them, Natividad could have sworn that his crimson eyes contained the reflection of violent flames.

Everyone looked down – Alejandro first, then Miguel. Natividad had to kick Sheriff Pearson to get him to drop his gaze and for an instant was sure she'd been too slow.

But then the Dimilioc Master rose up, his body dwindling and straightening as he folded himself deliberately back into his human form. He must have let his shadow carry away his injuries earlier, but now he also dismissed the smoke and smoldering ichor and violent aura of battle that had clung to his black dog shape, emerging from the change as a civilized, self-possessed man. Even his clothing was ordinary: black slacks and a crisp white shirt that had never been stained by ash or blood or ichor.

But anger still clung to him like smoke, and informed his gaze when he raked a stare across them, across the empty buses and the confused crowd. Everyone felt it – the ordinary people fell back and looked away, and a couple of them made little frightened noises, which was not helpful. Grayson did not appear to hear them, though. He turned and stalked into the house, leaving behind charred spots on the wood of the porch and an echo of poised disaster that had not quite happened.

"You'll need to go after him," Miguel said to Natividad.

Natividad wasn't at all sure she wanted to do anything of the kind. "Um…"

"Not *now*," Alejandro said, shouldering forward with that aggression that infused every black dog's attitude and was especially strong right now. "Do you want to get her killed? Let him settle – let the anger fade a little…"

Miguel raised his eyebrows. "How long do you want to wait? He's lost Zachariah and Harrison. His anger's not going to fade. How can it? There's no time for him to deal with this by himself, isn't that obvious?"

Alejandro didn't move, but the look he gave Miguel was like a blow. He did not have Grayson's control: *he* still showed the rage and bloodlust of the recent battle in his face, and in the tension in his shoulders, and in the ash that streaked his hands and arms. The daylight that lay across his face was dimmed by his clinging shadow; the scent of burning followed him. He said, "*Deal* with this? With enemies that outnumber us by far more than they should, and with half the Dimilioc black wolves a step away from *callejeros*, and with a hundred human townspeople he never wanted to bring here, *and* with a wounded *verdugo*, and now with the loss of his closest allies? How is he supposed to *deal* with that?"

Miguel had looked aside, but this didn't mean he was conceding anything. He answered Alejandro's anger with his mildest, most stubborn tone. "I don't know. That's why Natividad needs to go to him. *You* shouldn't, I get that. You could tell me about the battle – about the enemies that outnumbered you more than they should, and about Thaddeus and Amira and Keziah, and just everything."

Alejandro glared at him.

"I need to know," Miguel said, even more softly. He added to the sheriff, still not looking directly at Alejandro, "You can tell us what you saw, too, while we get things organized for your people. Do you mind?"

"I need to see Cassie," said the sheriff. "My daughter. But after that... if you wish..."

"Better you wait for that," Miguel told him. "She's fine; I checked on her myself just a little while ago." He didn't say that no one who loved her should see her as she was now, but Natividad guessed this from his slightly too-brisk tone.

The sheriff didn't look convinced, but Natividad knew that her twin would get everybody to do things his way in the end. She thought Miguel was probably right about Sheriff Pearson staying away from his daughter and also about Grayson – about the problems he now faced as Master of Dimilioc, and about his need for her. And if there was anything at all she wanted less than to go find the Dimilioc Master right at this moment... well, maybe she could imagine a *few* things she wanted less, but only because she had a good imagination. She sighed.

Grayson had gone to the room with the fireplace and the view, the room where Natividad had drawn her pentagrams on the windows and called for peace. That might be kind of a compliment, because out of all the places in the house he could have gone for refuge, he had come to this room where she had drawn her pentagrams. *Por otra parte*, maybe he just didn't want to go back to the suite he had once shared with his wife... Natividad stood in the hall, studying the fine grain that ran through the wood of the closed door and trying to believe she really could draw confidence from Grayson's choice of retreats.

There was not so much comfort to be found in anything, right now. What Natividad *wanted* to do was turn around and walk away, go up the stairs to her own room, lock herself in and pretend she was still grounded. She really wanted to do that.

A grieving black dog ought to be left alone – but the Master of Dimilioc was too important to be left alone, because sometimes great grief and loss led a black dog into a terrible dark from which he never emerged. Somebody needed to make sure that didn't happen to Grayson. Natividad knew perfectly well that, of them all, she would least put herself at risk by going through that door.

Even so, it was hard to touch the doorknob. To turn it. Harder to swing the door open. Harder still to step through.

Natividad shut the door gently behind herself and leaned against it, her hands resting on the doorknob for a kind of covert reassurance – the smooth brass under her fingers a tactile reminder that she could run out again if she needed to. She knew she wouldn't retreat, but even so she didn't want to let go of the knob.

And yet, once she was in the room with the Dimilioc Master, she found to her own surprise that she was glad she had come. Grayson sat in his customary chair. He faced the window, but he was not looking out at the buses parked on the rutted snow or past them at the bleak winter forest. His elbows rested on the arms of his chair. His head was bowed. His forehead rested on his steepled hands. His eyes were closed. He did not seem to be aware of Natividad at all. He looked so alone... *was* so alone. She felt suddenly ashamed that she had not thought of coming here herself, that she had been ready to leave him so alone in the lowering dark of the evening.

Crossing the room quietly, Natividad sat down on the floor beside Grayson's chair. She didn't touch him or speak, didn't trace a pentagram on the window or the floor or even in the air. She didn't even look at him, though she was more intensely aware of him, of his physical presence, than she had ever been. His power might be leashed and hidden, but it was as obvious to her as the heat of a banked fire. She ought to be afraid of him, but now she found she wasn't. She grieved for him, for his solitude, for the wife he had lost last year, for the crippling of Dimilioc in the war and for the brother and friend he had lost today. She sat beside him, her arms wrapped around her knees, and waited.

After a while, Grayson said without looking up, "James was right. There is nothing left of Dimilioc. The thing we now call by that name is something else. If it survives at all, it will be nothing Dimilioc ever was."

Natividad let a respectful silence stretch out for a minute or so. Then, still not looking at Grayson, she said, "*Te ayudaría si pudiera.* I would help you if I could. I'm so sorry for your loss. I know it's presumptuous to say so because Zachariah was your friend and Harrison was your brother and who am I to say I miss them? But I do. I only knew them for such a short time, but I liked them both." She paused.

Grayson did not respond visibly. He didn't look at her. But hadn't there been a very slight catch in his breathing? She thought he was listening. She was less sure she was saying anything right. But how could she stop now? She said, "Black dogs aren't usually kind, but Zachariah was kind to me. I liked him. His shadow was so strong, but he controlled it so well you could hardly tell. He loved you, and he loved Dimilioc.

Anybody could see how hard he worked to support Dimilioc and you. He gave up his chance to be Master because of you, and self-sacrifice is so hard for black dogs."

No black dog would show weakness to another, or to an ordinary human, but Natividad was neither. Grayson made a wordless sound and pressed his hands hard across his eyes.

Carefully not looking at him, Natividad said gently, "And I admired Harrison. He was your brother. He was your *older* brother, and that's special. He always supported you and helped you. He didn't like what you were doing, bringing black dogs into Dimilioc, but he never said so in public, did he? But he argued with you in private, because he was never afraid of you. He loved you, and even when he thought you were wrong, he supported you because really he trusted you to be right. And trust is another thing that's hard for black dogs, isn't it?"

Grayson didn't move or make a sound.

"James was wrong," Natividad said. "Zachariah and Harrison, and Benedict, too – they fought for Dimilioc. They died so that Dimilioc would live. And it does. Grief and loss are part of life, but *you* are the heart of Dimilioc. Both Zachariah and Harrison would have agreed with that, wouldn't they? As long as you live, Dimilioc's future will be tied to its past, because its past is in you."

Grayson said harshly, "I am the Master of dust and ashes. How many indispensable wolves can Dimilioc lose and yet claim to have won this war?"

Natividad met his eyes. She felt old and sad and yet somehow strong. She felt, for the first time, that she was the Master's equal. They shared grief and mourning, but it was *she* who believed there would be, eventually, a spring to follow this bitter winter. She said gently, "Grayson, no one but you is indispensable. Dimilioc will live unless you yourself decide to let it die. You won't do that. You'll think of something. No one will have died in vain."

Grayson didn't answer.

Natividad leaned her cheek against his knee, as she had done for Alejandro when he'd been exhausted and *angustiado* with grief and anger after their parents' murder. At least then they had found their parents' bodies, at least they had been able to bury them in proper graves and pray for peace for their souls. This time, there were not even bodies. That was worse.

She turned her hands palm up and breathed quietly, long slow breaths, breathing in the rage and bitter grief that clung to Grayson, breathing out peace and acceptance of loss. She was afraid that Grayson would be angry if she sketched a pentagram in the air, if she called aloud for peace: he would not be ready to surrender the grief that is the just tribute the living pay to the dead. She understood that. So, she closed her eyes and made her wish silently to the dark behind her eyelids.

After a while, Grayson said, "Those people from Lewis…"

"Rooms, food, warnings to stay away from wolves, all taken care of."

"Ah." There was another silence, and then the Dimilioc Master began again, "Some of those people must be able to shoot…"

"Miguel is already figuring out which ones can hit what they aim at, and I'm sure Sheriff Pearson will help us figure out which of them can be trusted to aim at our enemies."

"Good," said Grayson, and was quiet once more. But now it was a quiet filled with thought as well as with grief. Natividad folded her hands in her lap and sat quietly next to his chair.

"I want Ezekiel," Grayson said abruptly. "He'll be asleep. You had better be the one to wake him."

Natividad, momentarily disoriented, blinked. "But... wasn't he hurt?"

"That won't matter," Grayson said, and though he didn't look at her, she could tell it was the Dimilioc Master speaking. "I want him here. Immediately." He put a bite to that last word.

Natividad stared at him for a second. She wanted to ask: *"Don't you care about Ezekiel at all?"* But that wasn't a question she *could* ask, and anyway she knew perfectly well that no one cared more about every Dimilioc wolf than the Master. She remembered, too late, that she shouldn't stare – but of course Grayson Lanning was *way* too powerful to worry about a girl's impudence.

Jumping to her feet, she gave the Master a slight bow to show she was obeying, backed up two steps, turned, and went to the door. She did not actually run. But she didn't stroll, either.

Natividad had not previously had any reason to find Ezekiel's rooms, which turned out to comprise a suite on the third floor of the main wing, above the front door. High enough, Natividad realized, to prevent any enemy from leaping to its window, but low enough that Ezekiel would be able to leap down to the balcony of the room below and from there to the open ground. If there was trouble, the kind of trouble where enemies came arrogantly to the front door, Ezekiel's sudden appearance among them must cause almost as much consternation as a vat of boiling oil.

When this thought occurred to her, Natividad concluded that life had definitely been much too exciting lately.

The problem was that she couldn't help but wonder, while studying Ezekiel's closed door, whether he might mistake anybody who woke him for one of those not-hypothetical-enough enemies.

The Dimilioc executioner *was* suffering from the lingering effects of silver injury, after all. Painful and slow to heal: exactly the sort of wound that would drive a black dog into a killing rage, and he would be embarrassed that he'd been cut, too. *Then* he had driven across Chicago, flown a plane halfway across *los Estados Unidos*, driven from Newport to Dimilioc, run eight miles across country, and then fought not only in the battle – he'd also personally fought Vonhausel. And lost.

That last was the worst. Natividad knew all about black dog vanity. And Ezekiel was a lot more arrogant than most other black dogs. He was going to be really pissed off about losing that fight – and it would be much worse because everybody had *seen* him lose, and watched afterwards when he'd been forced to ride on top of a bus because he couldn't run the distance back from Lewis to Dimilioc.

And now Grayson said he wanted to see Ezekiel. Immediately. Right. No wonder he'd sent *Natividad* to fetch his executioner. Probably Ezekiel would tear anybody else who disturbed him into little tiny pieces. Like confetti, only messier.

He wouldn't tear Natividad into bits, though. She was pretty sure.

On the other hand, if anybody else had turned up and volunteered to go wake Ezekiel up instead, Natividad's feelings wouldn't have been hurt at all.

Sighing, Natividad put her hand on the doorknob... took a breath... rolled her eyes at her own cowardice and finally, after an embarrassingly long pause, *turned* the knob.

The door wasn't locked. Right. Who would intrude on Dimilioc's famously vicious young executioner? Natividad pushed the door open and stepped into a big room with wall-to-wall dove-gray carpeting, low couches upholstered in black leather, and simple low tables of black-painted wood. No television, no stereo system, nothing like that. No bookshelves. A single thin bud vase stood on one of the tables, its transparent glass strangely contorted as though it had once been partially melted. There was no flower in the vase, though. She supposed this was because of the barren winter, and wondered what kind of flower Ezekiel put in the vase when flowers were available. A rose? An orchid? She couldn't guess. Maybe he always left the vase empty. That sort of seemed like him, actually.

That was all there was in the room, except for one surprising painting dominating the far wall. If Natividad had thought about it, which she hadn't, she would have guessed that Ezekiel might have chosen some horrible bloody scene of hunting or war, or else something disturbing by Dali. This painting – a real painting, she was sure, not a print –

was nothing like that. It was obviously Chinese or Japanese, because there were those kinds of letters across the top and a couple more at the bottom, maybe the artist's signature.

At first the painting seemed totally abstract, as though the artist had just splashed ink boldly across the lower third of a blank screen and called it good. Then shapes began to suggest themselves, first an angular tree – maybe a tree and a couple of shrubs? And maybe those triangular lines below the tree were a boat? Something little, like a rowboat. Maybe there was a person – two people? – in the boat. It was hard to be sure. Smooth pale-gray washes of ink below the tree implied water and mist. In the background, rising up through the height of the painting, tall skinny mountains were barely visible through the veils of mist. But most of the space had been left completely empty, the blank space used by the artist with as much deliberation as the grays and blacks of the ink.

It was a totally quiet, serene landscape, and it changed the whole character of the room. Without the painting, the room would have been stark and... What? Kind of soulless, maybe? Especially because there weren't any other personal touches anywhere: nothing cluttered the tables or had been tossed carelessly aside on either of the couches. But with the painting, the whole room took on a kind of serenity. It was sort of Zen, Natividad thought. Not that she had any idea what Zen was, except something Chinese. Or Japanese. Whatever. Anyway, she thought it meant something like peace, something like acceptance. Certainly nothing she would have expected from Ezekiel. Except now that she saw it, she sort of thought it fit him after all.

Two doors led out of this first room. Natividad walked across to the nearest and put a hand on its knob – it was unpainted metal, cold to the touch, and it, too, was gray. A dark gray, neither steel nor aluminum. Pewter, maybe. Did they make doorknobs out of pewter? She wondered whether the door would open into the bedroom or some kind of study or just a closet. In a way she hoped not to find Ezekiel too quickly because she was now much more curious about what else she might find in his suite, what other surprising things it might tell her about him. On the other hand, though she no longer really felt that she might be in actual danger, she was ashamed to be intruding into a privacy she was sure Ezekiel valued.

But the door turned out to open into the bedroom. The room was dim, not only because of the early-evening hour, but because, although there were windows in two of the walls, the curtains were all drawn. Natividad hesitated in the doorway, to let her eyes become accustomed to the muted lighting and also just to look for a minute.

After the first room, this one was not such a surprise. There was very little furniture, only the bed and a single table with a tall, angular lamp standing beside it. The table was very plain, like the ones in the other room, but painted in a pale color. Not white, though. A pale gray. A statue, maybe eighteen inches high, stood on the table. It was not exactly like a Buddha because the figure was standing and slim instead of seated and fat, but it sort of reminded Natividad of a Buddha anyway – although it held a spear in one hand, which didn't seem very Buddhist.

The bed was low, raised less than a foot off the floor, which was carpeted in the same dove-gray as the other room.

The bedcovers – sheets and blankets and bedspread alike – were all a dark charcoal gray. Ezekiel lay in abandoned exhaustion across the bed, on his back. His hands lay empty and open, one arm crooked back by his cheek and the other flung out straight. His head was thrown back, his throat exposed. He didn't stir. That he hadn't woken when Natividad entered the room told her even more clearly how desperately he needed sleep.

The top sheet – to Natividad's relief, more or less, now that other possibilities abruptly suggested themselves to her – lay across his legs and hips and came halfway up his stomach. His hair, damp from a bath, was a pale yellow: the exact color of *mantaquilla* – rich butter. His shoulders and neck were white against the dark sheets, except where the line of that nasty cut from Thaddeus's knife showed. Someone had stitched it up. The black stitches looked awful and ugly against his pale skin, but no other wounds marked him. Ezekiel might have sustained horrible injuries – of course he must have – but obviously nothing else dealt by a silver weapon. Nothing his black shadow had been unable to carry away.

Though Ezekiel might not show many wounds, the hollows of his face had deepened over the past couple of days. He looked thin and worn. It was easy, usually, to forget how young he was. But, asleep like this, his shadow hidden by the dimness of the room, his air of impatient disdain eased away by sleep, Ezekiel looked not only young, but also vulnerable, even helpless.

If she just strolled across the room and tapped him on the shoulder, though, Natividad suspected he would suddenly not look young or vulnerable or harmless at *all*. There was probably a better way to wake him up. A way that didn't involve getting too close.

Though, looking at Ezekiel like this, she didn't want to wake him up at all. Not just because he obviously needed sleep or because he might be angry when he woke, but also because then he would know that she had intruded on his privacy. Natividad might be safe to wake him – more or less safe – but she found she bitterly resented Grayson's order to do it.

Her embarrassment at her intrusion deepened as she hesitated, yet how could she just sneak away? Grayson would *look* at her and want to know why she hadn't got Ezekiel for him like he'd ordered, and what would she say? That she'd been too embarrassed to wake him up?

Natividad took a quick breath and switched the lights on, then clapped her hands and immediately dropped to sit cross-legged on the floor so she would look as harmless as possible.

He was across the room so fast that she barely saw him move, didn't have time to duck, barely had time to flinch. His eyes were a pale burning yellow with wicked pinpoint pupils, utterly inhuman. One long hand closed hard on her shoulder, pinning her back against the wall. Long black claws glittered on his other hand, foreshortened now into something that was almost a paw, ready to slash across her face or throat.

Natividad closed her eyes.

The blow didn't fall. She had *known* he wouldn't hit her, she'd known it from the first, but it still took a few seconds to make herself open her eyes again.

He knelt on one knee in front of her. His eyes, looking into hers with an intensity she could not read, was not sure she *wanted* to read, were again a completely human blue. Natividad had to force herself to look away from the concentrated ferocity of his stare. This was harder than she'd expected – harder than it should have been. Once she had lowered her eyes, she saw that though Ezekiel might not have let go of her, he had dropped his other hand to rest on the floor, and now that hand, too, was completely human again.

"Natividad," he said. His tone was light, cool, faintly mocking – utterly at odds with the violence of his response to her clap. Releasing her, he stood – an economical, fluid movement, but not nearly so fast as his initial lunge off the bed.

He was wearing shorts, Natividad was relieved to see. Well, more or less relieved. He didn't seem embarrassed to find her here in his bedroom. But then, he didn't seem angry, either. Or offended, or surprised, or even much interested. She didn't believe all this lack of response.

She said, trying to match his coolness, "I'm sorry to disturb you. But Grayson sent me to say he wants you. Immediately, he said. In the–"

"I know where he is," Ezekiel said. He didn't *exactly* snap the words. Turning, he walked unhurriedly across the room and, opening a door she had not noticed, reached in for a robe. The robe was medium gray, with here and there touches of odd off-tones: ash-gold and rose-gray and gray-lavender, the colors of the earliest dawn on a stormy day.

The robe looked Japanese to Natividad, but maybe that

impression had simply been created by the painting in the other room and the sculpture in this one. It ought to have looked too fancy for Ezekiel. Or maybe not too fancy exactly, but too... too something. But, anyway, whatever she meant, it didn't. It looked exactly right for him. It occurred to her for the first time that everything he wore always looked exactly right for him. She wondered if he chose clothing on purpose to have this effect or whether he would simply look good in anything, including, say, torn blue jeans and a faded plaid shirt.

"What time is it?" Ezekiel asked over his shoulder. He put on the robe and belted it. He still didn't seem embarrassed, but on the other hand he didn't turn and face her again until the robe was belted, either.

"Um," said Natividad, and looked at her watch. Her stupid pink kitten watch. It had never before occurred to her to be embarrassed about that watch, which Alejandro had bought her because they were running out of money and it was cheap and she needed a watch. She had even thought it was sort of cute. Now, one glimpse of Ezekiel's elegant robe and suddenly she was dying to own a nice watch, something tasteful.

She cleared her throat. "Almost... almost 5. In the afternoon. I think you've had about two hours of sleep. Maybe."

"Feels like it," muttered Ezekiel. He studied the contents of his closet for another moment. "Immediately, is it?"

From his tone, this was not exactly a question, but Natividad nodded. Then, because he wasn't watching her, she cleared her throat and said, "Yes."

Ezekiel turned his head, one eyebrow rising in mocking comment on her nervousness. He walked right into the closet, which must be a lot bigger than Natividad had guessed. His voice emerged, muffled, but now without that frightening edge to it. "I frightened you. I'm sorry. I wasn't properly awake. You don't need to be afraid of me." He came out of the closet again, now clothed in black jeans and a black T-shirt, the robe draped across his arm.

Natividad had never seen him in jeans and a T-shirt before. The casual clothing, it turned out, did in fact look just as exactly right on him as everything else. "You didn't frighten me," she told him, which was sort of the truth.

Ezekiel tilted a skeptical eyebrow at her and tossed the robe across the bed. Natividad suppressed an urge to ask him if she could borrow it. When he looked at her, she remembered only belatedly to drop her gaze.

"Natividad…" But then he stopped.

Her gaze was drawn upward by that pause, until she remembered again not to look at Ezekiel's face and made herself look aside. "Um?" She didn't hear him move, didn't know he was right in front of her until he put a finger under her chin and tipped her face up, gently. Startled, Natividad met his eyes. There was no anger in his face, none of the edgy temper that usually rode black dogs. There wasn't any of his usual mockery, either. She could see the weariness in the hollows of his face, in the shadows around his pale eyes, and knew it was a weariness of spirit as much of body.

"Look at me," he said softly. "Look at me, if you wish. I don't mind."

He *let* her see his weariness, his grief – it was a deliberate lowering of defenses. He could have hidden all his weakness from her if he'd tried. He was *allowing* her to see right through his hard-held privacy. This was frightening – or not exactly *frightening*. She felt somehow both vulnerable and oddly powerful at the same time. She said, a little breathlessly, "Grayson *did* say, not till my birthday…"

He did not lift his hand away from her face. "Of course. Of course he did."

"Ezekiel – you don't even want *me* anyway. You only want me because I'm Pure and almost the same age as you…" She stopped, startled and a little shocked because she hadn't meant to say *that*. Even though it was true.

"Is that what you think?" He began to lean forward – he was going to kiss her…

Then his eyes widened. His thin mouth twisted with a strange kind of bitter amusement that Natividad did not understand, and he said, softly but with some force, "Hellfire and damnation."

"Ezekiel…" Natividad said again, and again did not know what to say, but this time managed to say nothing at all. She had no idea what was going *on* with him.

He dropped his hand. Took a step back. Another. He looked away from her, looked back – ran a distracted hand through his pale hair, still disordered from sleep. He said, "I have to obey him."

"Well… yes?"

He glanced at her impatiently. "Not because of that! Because… look. Without… Without Zachariah and Harrison, he can't *force* me to do anything. He knows that, I know it. So I *have* to obey him. Damn!" He took a sharp breath and repeated, more softly, "Hellfire and damnation. I can't..." He stopped. She watched the mask of light, unconcerned mockery settle back across his face like he'd never shown her anything else. Then he took a smooth step sideways, opened the door, and stood back, inviting her, with a tip of his head, to go out before him.

"I'm sorry," Natividad offered, because she was, although it was hard to say for what, exactly. Just for everything. She could see what Ezekiel meant. She liked him better and better – she was beginning to feel *flattered* that he wanted her. Only then it occurred to her that when she'd accused him of only wanting her because she was Pure, he hadn't actually *denied* it. She took a quick breath and went past him quickly, not looking at him.

Grayson stood up, expressionless, when Ezekiel opened the door. Ezekiel walked into the room, faced him directly, dropped without hesitation to one knee, bowed his head, and said coolly, "Master. I beg your pardon for the delay."

Grayson nodded curtly, still grimly expressionless. He said to Natividad, "Everyone, here, in an hour. Your brother as well. Both your brothers."

Natividad nodded, startled and uneasy. But Grayson gave her a dismissive little jerk of the head, and she ducked and fled.

She also decided that if Grayson wanted everybody, all his black dogs, well, somebody else could tell them so. Ezekiel had definitely constituted her quota. She would find Alejandro, and *he* could wake up sleeping black dogs.

12

Natividad had thought her brother would be in his room, but he wasn't. She found him at last in a basement room she hadn't previously known existed. This basement had its own stairway hidden behind a forbidding door of iron-bound black wood, which suggested disquieting things about what might lie below. Natividad would never have tried it, only when she couldn't find Alejandro, she made a mirror in the entranceway of the house into a *trouvez*, a spell of finding. A hand mirror would have been easier to use – she could hardly carry the hallway mirror around with her – but once the glass shimmered with light, she caught the light in her hands, shut her eyes, turned in a circle, thought of Alejandro, and then walked briskly forward without paying any attention to her direction. When she found herself in front of the iron-bound door, she stood blinking at it, sure it would be locked. But its latch gave easily to her hand, revealing a dim, narrow stairway.

The stairway was angular and steep, with uneven treads. It led to a narrow, long, cold room with naked light bulbs dangling on thin chains, casting a harsh too-bright light across walls of unfinished granite and a whole row of cages like the one where they'd spent their first night in this house. All of the cages were much smaller than that one, and all but one were totally bare of furnishings. That one cage, nearest the door, contained a thin mattress and a single prisoner: a small, savage-eyed moon-bound shifter, who lifted her lip with silent loathing, fangs glinting dangerously.

Natividad resisted the urge to retreat back up the stairs. She said to Alejandro, who, beside Ethan Lanning at the far end of the room, was turning to her with surprise, "I guess that's Cass Pearson?"

"*Sí*," Alejandro said wearily, with a not-very-interested glance at the shifter. "I guess we could move her back to the big cage now. Unless Grayson wants it free for some reason."

"We've got more important things to worry about than any moon-bound cur, whoever's kid she is," snapped Ethan. He was almost as worn-looking as Alejandro, but far less welcoming; his eyebrows had drawn down in a disapproving expression when he saw Natividad. His father had just died, though, and Natividad knew exactly what that was like, the horrible days right afterward. She didn't want to think about it, but he had a right to be angry and upset with the world.

She also, however, made a mental note to remember to feed the little shifter, afraid that, if Ethan's attitude was characteristic, no one else would. She gave her a wary look. There was no sign, in Cassie's shadow form, of the fragile-seeming girl Natividad had glimpsed. She was crouching very still, but it was not the stillness of patience or resignation or surrender. Her fiery eyes gleamed malevolently. If anybody opened the cage door, Natividad bet Cassie wouldn't just sit there quietly. Miguel had been right: Sheriff Pearson definitely did not need to see his daughter right now. If her father reached between those cage bars – and he probably wouldn't be able to resist – she was pretty sure Cassie would rip his hand off.

Alejandro turned back to what he had been doing, which was, apparently, something to do with Miguel's guns.

Miguel's new rifles were neatly racked in one of the empty cells, his equipment for making ammunition arranged on a table in another cell. Two of the remaining cells were occupied by stacks of dusty boxes. Nothing she saw explained to Natividad why she hated the room, which she did. It wasn't just poor Cass Pearson. This was something else, a feeling, as though she could feel echoes of old despair and rage leaking from the walls and through the silver-laced bars of all the cells. She looked uneasily at the way the shadows of the rifles stretched, long and black and spidery, across the walls. She said, more or less involuntarily, "What an *awful* room."

Ethan grimaced and gave a speaking glance around the narrow room. "They say it wasn't so bad when it was Richard Lanning's private library, but Thos Korte decided Dimilioc needed more than one cell and turned this room into –" He opened a hand to indicate the cells "– his special prison. Ugly, yes, but the best place in the house to mess about with gunpowder. Who would care if we blew it up?"

Everything *anybody* said about the previous Dimilioc Master made Natividad more and more grateful that Thos

Korte had gone into the fell dark, and she found she liked Ethan better because he obviously felt the same way. "What does Grayson use this room for?" she asked.

Ethan shrugged. "Not much, I guess, until now. Mostly just storage for things no one wants, but no one wants to throw away."

Natividad took a rifle off its rack to see whether it was loaded. It was. Cass Pearson followed her movements with a steady, predatory stare. Natividad pretended not to notice, but the shifter's presence sure didn't help the ugly feel of the room.

"Can you shoot?" Ethan asked her.

"A little. Not like Miguel."

"Yeah." Ethan paused. "I had a human cousin who was pretty good... but Thos didn't like his black wolves to be too friendly with humans. She went to live in Lewis. She should have been safe there, but the war..."

Natividad wanted to say something to show she was sorry for Ethan's grief, only of course she couldn't. There was nothing to say, and anyway a black dog didn't like to have any kind of weakness noticed. In a minute, Ethan would begin to regret mentioning his cousin at all. She hefted the rifle. "I guess we should take some of these upstairs. Miguel should have one. And Sheriff Pearson and DeAnn, and maybe some of the others. Do you think?" she added, because black dogs always liked to feel they were making all the decisions.

Alejandro said, "Grayson can't have wanted them just to look at. We'll take at least a couple up."

The look Ethan shot Alejandro made it clear he didn't like any Toland upstart making decisions for Dimilioc.

Naturally Alejandro didn't notice. Or maybe he just pretended not to. Natividad said quickly, "And maybe some boxes of ordinary ammo. Can't practice with the silver."

"Your brother's set up a shooting range in the spare garage," Ethan said. "I'll show you." He gave her a tentative smile. She knew it was a peace offering. Maybe even the awkward beginnings of courtship. That was a scary idea in a whole different way.

The way Grayson had set it up, of course all the male Dimilioc wolves had to think about Natividad as a woman. It occurred to her now that this also made her think about herself that way, and she never had, really. Not even when she'd told Grayson she wasn't a child. She hated it. Well, they also had to think of her as a valuable commodity; *that's* what she hated. Ezekiel might court her, but he sure hadn't bothered to get to know her before he claimed her. To him, any Pure girl would do just fine. And now here was Ethan, *smiling* at her, one too many black wolves to deal with.

At least *Grayson* had been honest about what he thought of her.

It hadn't been like this for Mamá. The only black dog she'd ever met was Papá. What would Mamá say now?

She would say, "*Be nice to Ethan, Natividad, be nice to everybody, but don't be too nice, don't lead anybody on.*" She could almost hear Mamá say that. She bit her lip hard, hefted the rifle again and said to Ethan, casually, the way she might have spoken to one of her brothers, "You think a gun rack'll fit in with all the pink lace in my room?"

Ethan looked at her. For an instant, Natividad was sure he was going to smile – twice in two minutes, amazing and a little scary – but he didn't, so after a moment, she added, speaking now to her brother, "Grayson wants you all. In an hour, he said." She looked at her pink kitten watch. "Forty-five minutes, now. I figured I'd tell you and you could spread the word." She gave Alejandro a quick look. "Miguel too, he said."

Alejandro looked at Natividad in a silent question, like, *Dios mío, qué es eso?* He said, "A council of war."

"Not a council of anything," Ethan snapped, instantly on edge. "He'll tell us what he wants and we'll do it."

Black dog posturing: he and Alejandro hadn't sorted out their relative dominance yet and would be tense until they did. Natividad wished, briefly and fervently, that she was just dealing with ordinary humans. "Maybe he just wants to wish us all a nice night and pleasant dreams," she said in her most cheerful, encouraging tone.

Ethan, surprised, actually laughed, and Natividad, relieved, smiled back. Really, she still didn't exactly like him, but he wasn't so *totally* unpleasant once he got used to you.

Then Cassie Pearson snarled. It was the first sound she had made: a low singing sound of hatred. Natividad flinched and headed for the stairs without waiting for the others. But they were right behind her. Maybe the shifter's malevolence didn't bother them, but it really was an awful room. Natividad glanced over her shoulder and said, "Somebody should put her back in the other room."

This time, even Ethan nodded in agreement. "In the morning."

While Ethan went to tell the other black dogs about the meeting, Natividad and Alejandro found Miguel. He was hard to find, since he was over in the east wing of the house, explaining the subtleties of black dog manners to an interested group of townspeople, including Father McClanahan.

"Grayson wants to see you," Natividad told her twin, trying not to sound worried, and Alejandro demanded, "What did you do?"

"Nothing!" Miguel said defensively. "He probably just wants me there because I'm your brother."

Alejandro scowled. "I think you are not afraid enough of Grayson, Miguel – of any of the Dimilioc wolves. That's alright for Natividad, but for you it's different. You've put yourself forward too much. Of course he noticed you! Who knows what he noticed!"

"I'm safe," Miguel said reasonably. "I'm Natividad's brother." He stood with his hands at his sides and his gaze cast down, showing Alejandro a soft stubbornness that didn't give black dog anger anything to get hold of.

"We'll be alright," Natividad said, anxious. "Miguel's right." Which she wasn't sure of, actually, but she *was* sure they had better get moving if they didn't want to be late.

The meeting was in some ways an echo of the first time Natividad and her brothers had been brought before Grayson Lanning and the rest of the Dimilioc wolves, to hear what their fate would be. This time, though, the curtains had been drawn over the wide windows, shutting out the dark. That seemed sort of symbolic, though Natividad doubted anybody had meant it that way.

Grayson held court from his customary chair. His shadow, so dense that even to Natividad it almost seemed to have physical body and depth, lay beneath his chair like a hole in the firelight. The absence of the other two wolves of the Master's triumvirate was shocking. Zachariah Korte and Harrison Lanning should have been settled near Grayson, supporting the Master. Now only Ezekiel leaned against the back of the Master's chair. She was glad *he* was there, at least. Poor Grayson.

Ezekiel showed nothing of the exhaustion and grief that Natividad knew was dragging at him. He was not smiling, but his customary amused disdain showed in the tilt of his head and the crook of his thin mouth.

Keziah had curled herself into another of the heavy chairs, not too close to the Master. Despite her youth, she radiated dominance as well as unmistakable sexuality. Amira might almost have fitted into the same chair right along with her sister, but instead had tucked herself down on the floor beside Keziah's chair. Her arms were crossed over her small breasts as though for protection against the world, and she did not quite look at anyone. Natividad almost sort of liked Keziah, maybe, and she felt sorry for Amira, and she was glad they had both survived the battle – she really was. But the two Saudi girls seemed very poor substitutes for the lost Dimilioc wolves.

Thaddeus Williams had placed himself equidistant between Grayson and Keziah. Natividad was far less attuned to black dog posturing than Alejandro, but she guessed Thaddeus hadn't yet decided whether he was really inside Dimilioc or still outside. That would be a problem for Keziah, too. That was something else she had to do: work on pulling the new Dimilioc together. Mamá would have been good at it. Natividad sighed.

Despite the solidity of the chairs, the one Thaddeus occupied seemed barely large enough to support him. He did not exactly look comfortable, but he was leaning back, an elbow propped on one arm of the chair in a semblance of relaxation. DeAnn perched on the other arm of his chair, one hand moving in slow circles across his back. Natividad envied DeAnn's secure relationship with her husband.

Ethan, coming in right after Natividad and her brothers, flung himself into a chair that flanked Grayson's and sprawled there, trying, Natividad thought, for Ezekiel's easy disdain. He could not quite pull it off. Alejandro hesitated a beat longer than Ethan before also moving to a chair near Grayson. Natividad saw how he avoided looking at Keziah. The Saudi girl didn't look at him, either, but sort of gazed at the blank air, sexy and scornful.

Looking away from the black dog girl, Natividad found herself meeting Ezekiel's cool gaze and felt herself blush. She looked quickly away again.

The Master lifted a hand for their attention. Then, turning to Miguel, he asked abruptly, "Why did Vonhausel attack Edward Toland and his family after the war was ended, rather than coming directly after Dimilioc, which he should have considered his strongest enemy? If he hated your father so much, why did he wait twenty years before hunting him down? Once your father was dead, why did he trouble to follow his children – not merely to the next village, but across an entire continent?" He paused.

Miguel cleared his throat, but he didn't actually look surprised. Alejandro began to speak, but the Master pinned him with a long, slow stare and said, "Not you. I want

your young brother to answer me." Natividad wasn't sure
Alejandro would obey, but Ezekiel shifted his weight and
gave her brother a sharp, impatient glance, and Alejandro
lowered his gaze.

"Moon-bound shifters are easy enough to acquire,"
rumbled Grayson, "but where is Vonhausel finding his black
dogs? Why did he bring down the church? Why did he rush
to break your sister's mandala and then press forward into
Lewis rather than attacking us here?"

"I don't know, sir," Miguel said. Then he added, "But I
can guess."

The Master lifted his heavy eyebrows in ironic inquiry.

"Well," Miguel said rapidly, "You know, I wasn't there
for everything, but from what I've heard, Vonhausel really
does have too many black dogs. Like, about thirty when he
attacked this house, right? And you – we – killed about half
of those, but then there were about forty black dogs involved
in attacking Lewis, isn't that right? And you fought them
there, but even so there were lots left after Vonhausel broke
Natividad's mandala and brought down the church. Like,
still at least thirty. Which is impossible, from what everyone
says, but isn't that right?" He paused, looking at Grayson.

"Go on," the Master said quietly.

Miguel cleared his throat again. "Well, he's not...
He's... Look, this is only a guess. But I think he's cracking
open the gates of Hell. I mean, literally. I think you kill his
black dogs and send their shadows into the fell dark, but
Vonhausel catches them before they're gone. I think he's
found a way to put the shadows back again even after
their bodies are dead."

"No," said Keziah. Her beautiful, slightly *rasgados* – slanted – eyes had narrowed, giving her the look more of a fragile Oriental cat than a powerful black dog. She said, "Such a thing is not possible. One cannot bring back the dead! Once the body dies, it is dead. Once the shadow is gone into the fell dark, it is *gone*."

Miguel hesitated, thrown off balance by this challenge. Natividad wondered whom Keziah had killed that she needed to stay gone. But Grayson looked steadily at the girl for a long moment, until she suddenly lowered her fine lashes over her dark eyes and bowed her graceful neck. Her hair, straight and crisp and black as the long nights of this frozen country, fell forward to hide her face.

Grayson shifted his attention back to Miguel. "How would one do that? How would one gather up a departed shadow? Or put it back into the body from which it had departed?"

"I don't know, sir," Miguel answered. "But it wasn't just my *father* Vonhausel was afraid of. Vonhausel had allies – all that time, he did. I mean, blood kin. My father couldn't have protected us from them. It was my *mother* who hid us. *She* was the one Vonhausel most wanted to kill – her and Natividad. Mamá said Natividad is special. That she did something to give Natividad a special sympathy for the right kind of darkness. That Natividad should have a gift for making darkness cooperate with light–"

"What?" Natividad stared at her twin in surprise. She didn't know what he was talking about. She thought in just a moment she would be shocked and frightened and maybe even angry. Mamá had worked magic on her and not even said what she was doing? She had made up special kinds of magic to give her a *sympathy for darkness?* She had talked to *Miguel* about all those things and about Pure magic, and not to *her?*

Her twin turned to her, raising his chin, uncomfortable but stubborn. "It's true. I don't know… I don't know exactly what she meant. She said you have to be Pure to understand Pure magic. Only she couldn't talk to you about it. She said if you knew too much about the wrong things you'd be scared and – and being frightened would be bad for you. I'm sorry, *gemela*. That's what she said."

Natividad thought that maybe, in a little while, she would be able to understand that. At the moment, she just felt sort of hollow. She realized she was trembling, but couldn't stop. She whispered, "But what did she do to me?"

"I don't know," Miguel said. "Things she thought were important – things she thought would help us survive and defeat Vonhausel. But I'm not Pure and I don't know."

Neither did Natividad. She was supposed to know, but she didn't. She needed to *remember*, only she *couldn't*. She caught her breath against a shout or a scream or a sob and pressed a hand hard over her mouth.

DeAnn, frowning in sympathy, suddenly stood up and left her husband's side to stand behind Natividad, setting her strong hands on Natividad's shoulders. It wasn't the same as if Mamá had stood there like that, but Natividad leaned gratefully back against the other woman's support. She was trembling.

Her twin faced Grayson again. "Sir, I'm *guessing*, alright? But I think what Vonhausel *really* didn't want was an alliance between Dimilioc and anybody related to Mamá.

Or maybe taught by her. Or both. That's why he came after us – only he didn't know soon enough we'd gotten away, and Natividad's tangle-you-up spell probably got in his way when he followed us. It's a really good spell."

Grayson, gazing at Miguel, said absolutely nothing. It occurred to Natividad, with sudden force, that if they *hadn't* run north – if they *hadn't* come to Dimilioc – then Vonhausel wouldn't have come after them and everything would be different. Sheriff Pearson's daughter wouldn't have been bitten, the town wouldn't have been attacked – most of all, no more of the Dimilioc wolves would have been killed. Zachariah and Harrison would still be alive.

She could tell that Grayson was thinking about that, too.

Ezekiel said smoothly, "If Vonhausel had caught you outside of Dimilioc territory, you'd be dead. Then he'd have come here anyway, as we are indeed his strongest remaining enemy, and we'd have had no warning at all. And no daughter of your mother's would belong to Dimilioc." He raised an eyebrow at Natividad. "What can you do for us, Natividad Toland? What did your mother give you?"

Natividad only shook her head helplessly. Whatever Mamá had done, Natividad couldn't remember or hadn't understood... She'd been too slow a student, she hadn't figured things out fast enough, and now she didn't know anything and Mamá was gone, *dead*, and couldn't help her...

"You all saw Malvern Vonhausel fight me," Ezekiel said. He glanced coolly around the room. "He didn't need to shift from one form to another in order to dismiss his injuries. You all must have seen that. That is not something a black dog can do. That is a power possessed only by the true undead."

"I think Vonhausel destroyed the church in Lewis because he's worked out a new way to work dark magic, a way to kind of blend black dog magic with vampire magic," Miguel said, his tone careful. He kept his eyes on Ezekiel, probably, Natividad thought, because he was afraid to look at Grayson. He said, "I mean, vampires couldn't approach hallowed ground, and black dogs may not like to, but they can. So that's what I think Vonhausel might be doing – making, you know, weird zombie undead black dogs." He glanced at Grayson and stopped, swallowing.

"You suggest this only now," the Dimilioc Master said grimly. "Indeed, it seems you have a great deal to say, now. Sit down, Alejandro."

Alejandro was indeed on his feet. He turned his head aside and hunched his shoulders as against a blow, but, though he wouldn't look at Grayson, he didn't sit down again, either.

Without moving, the Dimilioc Master seemed to settle more deeply into his chair. Though she wasn't a black dog, Natividad could almost *see* his shadow gathering beneath him, pressing against the light, trying to rise. She caught DeAnn's hand and held it hard, laid her other hand flat against the wall and wished silently and fervently for *peace, peace, peace in this house*. DeAnn returned her grip, undoubtedly doing the same.

Miguel dropped to his knees, sensibly trying to calm everything down. He made urgent patting gestures toward Alejandro. "It's alright, it's alright!"

"It certainly is not *alright*," the Master said harshly. And, to Alejandro, *"Down."*

The Master hadn't let his shadow up, though he stared at Alejandro with a black dog's fire-ridden eyes. Ezekiel had straightened and now stood tensely by the Master's side. He was barely watching Alejandro: his attention was on the room and everyone in it. Natividad glanced quickly around, too, to see what he was watching.

Keziah was lounging in her chair, ostentatiously relaxed, but her gaze was intent. Amira had ducked back into her sister's shadow. Thaddeus had his big hands curled over the arms of his chair, ready to move. His lips were drawn back in a silent snarl. Natividad couldn't guess what he might do if there was a fight, except that his wife still stood with by her side, her arm around her shoulders, and Natividad knew that DeAnn would no more stand by and let Grayson hurt Miguel than she would herself. But Grayson wouldn't anyway, she was suddenly confident of that. No, the one at risk was *Alejandro.*

Alejandro took two steps out to the middle of the room, until he stood right beside Miguel. Then he set his hand on his brother's shoulder, took a hard breath, let it out, and sank down to one knee. He didn't bow his head, but he didn't look Grayson in the face, either. He said, "Master."

The tension in the room eased. Thaddeus leaned back in his chair, his shoulders relaxing and his expression smoothing out. Keziah raised an elegant eyebrow. Ezekiel's watchfulness didn't change at all. Grayson stared hard at Alejandro.

"Master," Alejandro said again, finally lowering his head submissively.

Grayson tipped his head back in satisfaction, the fire in his eyes ebbing. "Stay down," he growled at Alejandro, and glanced around the room. He looked back at Miguel last of all. "What else can this enemy of ours do? Now that he has pulled down that church, can he come against us here with new power?"

"I don't know," Miguel said. He hadn't gotten back to his feet. Natividad thought that was probably a good thing.

"*Will* he come against us here? Or against your sister, perhaps? One hardly believes he has yet achieved his aim here."

"I don't know," Miguel said again.

Grayson turned to Natividad. "Vonhausel's purposeful destruction of your mandala and the church that anchored it, even at considerable risk to himself; and the wide slaughter he attempted in Lewis: those acts are explicable if we stipulate that by this destruction he gains or enhances his ability to work demonic magic. Magic, in some measure, similar to vampiric magic, and thus threatened by the clean magic of the Pure. Even Vonhausel's determination to destroy Dimilioc is consistent with this hypothesis, for, as we have at last rid ourselves of vampires and the blood kin, he must guess that we would never permit a black dog to use any similar undead magic."

"Yes, sir," Natividad said shakily, since he seemed to expect a response.

"You know the things your mother taught you. Consider what you might do for us. You may wish," Grayson growled, "to discuss this with your brother."

"Yes, sir," Natividad whispered.

"You have a plan, I suppose," Keziah said, smoothly, to Grayson. "I trust it does not entirely depend on this little

Pure girl single-handedly defeating our enemies and saving us all."

The Master glowered, not at Keziah, but at Natividad. "Certainly if Malvern Vonhausel particularly wants you, he had better not get you." He looked deliberately around the room once more, compelling everyone's close attention. "However, I believe Vonhausel does suffer from one important disadvantage, which we may use. He cannot trust any of his followers. They are strays and curs, neither trained nor accustomed to any civilized standard. He cannot allow any of his black dogs to control his moon-bound shifters: any to whom he gave such power would immediately turn against him. He must either free the shifters to run as they will, or he must keep them gathered close about him and rule them himself. Ezekiel?"

Ezekiel gave a lazy smile. "He would sooner kill them himself than release them. To him, they are tools for his use, weapons to his hand – and weapons which might be turned against him if one or another of his followers were ambitious." The young executioner paused.

Natividad found herself trading a meaningful glance with Miguel. Her twin had cautiously gotten back to his feet but stayed beside Alejandro, who had not moved and did not look up. But they did not need their brother to explain to them that *all* of Vonhausel's stray black dogs must be ambitious to bring him down, either to rule in his place or just to get free of the constraints he imposed on them. That was what stray black dogs were like.

Grayson rumbled quietly, "Yet holding so many shifters under his constant rule must require a great deal of his attention. I believe we may safely assume that Vonhausel will find the remaining time of the full moon difficult. Yet this is also the only time he may use his full strength against us." He lifted heavy eyebrows at Miguel.

"Yes, sir," Miguel said meekly. "I guess that's probably true."

Ezekiel agreed, his tone light and unconcerned, "If he wants to keep the advantage of numbers, then he must come tomorrow. After that, the moon will wane and he'll lose half his cannon fodder."

"I guess you and the Master have worked all this out between you," Thaddeus said abruptly. "But I think maybe you should fortify this house. I guess you're right that the next thing he'll do, if he can't get us to a battlefield he chooses, is bring his pack here. We ought to arm a couple people who can shoot. We got all that silver ammo, be a shame not to use it." He glanced warily at Grayson. "Some of the townspeople must be able to distinguish between Dimilioc black wolves and the enemy. Maybe we could set up an ambush, you know?"

Grayson's eyebrow went up again. "An ambush."

"If we could draw Vonhausel's black dogs out of the forest into the cleared ground in front of the house, then people with decent guns and silver ammo could shoot them up. Catch the bastards in a decent killing field if we set it up right–"

"The humans could shoot them down like the dogs they are," Grayson said. "Then we could easily tear down the ones who survive. Indeed."

Thaddeus looked at him. "Yeah. You already thought of it, huh?"

"The Master and I have discussed it," Ezekiel said blandly. "Vonhausel isn't likely to know about the bullets our own silversmith has been making." He gave Miguel a cool nod, then Thaddeus. "An ambush such as you describe should be simple, direct, and difficult for Vonhausel to counter. Even if he knew about the silver and expects exactly such an ambush, what can he do but walk into it? He must attack, and he must do so during the period of the full moon. In carrying out such a plan, darkness would not be our ally. But if we expect an attack no earlier than dawn, we might reasonably expect an ambush to succeed. If he attacks before dawn, we shall have to hold him a little while. This should be possible."

"Well, but what if Vonhausel attacks Brighton? Or even Newport? At least, that's what I'd do," said Miguel. "It's an obvious tactic, isn't it? He'll have a huge numerical advantage over us no matter what, if he's been making zombie black dogs. If he makes enough of them, he won't need the shifters, will he? And that'll free him from the moon. He can attack one town after another and wait for you to come after him, and you'll have to, won't you? Because otherwise he'll get a new war, a war between black dogs and humans, and in a hurry, too, because now everybody knows black dogs exist. And the humans, they'll find out a whole lot more about black dogs *real* fast if they decide they need to, won't they? I mean, now the blood kin aren't messing with people's minds to stop them perceiving supernatural stuff, there's nothing to stop them coming after us just as hard as they went after the last of the vampires. That's obvious, right? It won't be Dimilioc that wins *that* war, will it?"

Ezekiel tilted his head, gazing curiously at Miguel. "And yet, he hasn't done anything of the sort."

"Well," said Miguel, as though this, too, was obvious, "I'm sure he still wants to kill Natividad, or at least take her away from Dimilioc, so there's that. He's probably resting in Lewis tonight, making zombies. But I don't think he'll come here tomorrow. I bet he'll take his black dogs and his *esclavos* and go hunting and wait for you to come after him, and he'll make sure the ground is of his choosing and not yours. He'll have the advantage, not you. He'll kill you all. Then he can come after Natividad at his leisure." The boy looked from one of them to the next, ending with the Master. "Don't you see? That's exactly what he'll do."

"I hardly think that likely," said Keziah, sounding faintly amused. "Of course a human boy will not understand. But no black dog ambitious to rule and to be free of the constraints of law would ever turn aside from the personal destruction of Dimilioc. Malvern Vonhausel will come here. I expect he would be here now, except he cannot drive his black dogs so hard. So, we see his control of his… minions… is not so complete, whether he finds or makes or compels them. He will come here, and here we shall destroy him at last, as," she finished with a definite edge of irony, "he so clearly deserves."

Miguel began to protest. Grayson lifted a hand, checking the boy. "Ezekiel?"

Ezekiel gave Miguel a thoughtful look. "Miguel's suggestion is interesting. But I believe Keziah is correct. I can't imagine Malvern Vonhausel will turn away from Dimilioc now, no matter how easy the hunting would be in a human town. He *needs* to be in on the kill himself. Any black dog would need that."

Miguel shook his head, shrugging in angry disgust, but he didn't argue. All of the black dogs agreed with Grayson, Natividad saw. All of them. It was a black dog thing, then, a bone-deep certainty that came from instinct and not from argument or logic or anything rational. Miguel was the most rational person she knew, so he wouldn't get that. But he could obviously see as well as she could that arguing was hopeless.

"We will all rest," Grayson ordered. "No one will leave the house without my explicit permission." He stood up, somehow looming almost as impressively as Thaddeus even though he was nothing like as big. He said, "We will be up no later than 5, if you please. I would like everyone to be ready for an attack at sunrise or a little before. That will be at approximately 7.30. You may all go. Not you," he added to Alejandro, who still knelt on the floor as Grayson had ordered him.

"Master…" Miguel began.

"No," Grayson said flatly. He looked deliberately from Miguel to Natividad and back again. "Before dawn tomorrow, I wish to hear from you regarding your possible contribution to the approaching battle. Go."

Natividad started to protest, not knowing what she should say, but Ezekiel gave her an ironic look and she stopped, confused but somehow also reassured.

Ezekiel left the Master's side. He took Miguel by the arm, gave Natividad a significant look, and herded them both out into the hallway. They were the last to leave. He shut the door behind them and leaned against it, his eyes on Natividad's face. She didn't look away. Meeting Ezekiel's gaze should have seemed dangerous, but didn't. His pale eyes were completely human. He was not smiling. Without that mocking smile, he looked younger and unwontedly serious. He said, "You and Miguel have things to talk about. Go talk about them. Don't worry about your brother. Grayson won't hurt him."

"You're sure?" Miguel asked sharply. "Because he mustn't punish Alejandro – it's my fault…"

"It certainly is. Yes, I'm sure. If Grayson was going to punish him, I'd be in there."

"Oh," said Miguel.

Oh, echoed Natividad, voicelessly.

She didn't know what she looked like, but Ezekiel put out a hand to touch hers, very gently. "It'll probably happen someday, if your brother doesn't learn to trust Grayson's restraint. But it won't happen tonight. Go to your suite. Your brother will join you shortly, I expect. I," he said, his tone once again edged and sardonic, "am going to bed. If anyone wakes me up, I will tear out his throat." He lifted an eyebrow at Natividad. "Unless it's you. *You're* quite safe to walk into my bedroom. Anytime."

Natividad blushed.

"Dawn tomorrow," Ezekiel said, still sardonic. He jerked his head at them: *go,* but despite what he had said about bed, he stayed by the door, guarding the Master's privacy and incidentally preventing Natividad or Miguel from trying to go back in.

Trusting Ezekiel – that he was right about Grayson, that he would even protect Alejandro if necessary – was surprisingly easy. Natividad touched Miguel's arm and headed for the stairs.

13

Alejandro knelt on the floor, head down, gaze fixed on the floor, waiting. He was intensely grateful the Master hadn't required Miguel to stay. He felt satisfied that he'd got the Master to focus on him instead of his brother. Yet was afraid of what Grayson would do, and ashamed to have earned the Master's displeasure. He had expected the satisfaction and the fear, but the shame took him by surprise. He had not realized until this moment that he cared whether Grayson approved or disapproved of him, not for practical reasons, but in itself.

He heard the door close, and knew he was alone with the Dimilioc Master. He knew when the Master came to stand over him, not because he looked up or because he heard him move, but just from the sense of the Master's dense shadow falling over him. He tucked himself down low, palms flat against the floor, forehead touching the rug.

"Your defense of your brother is admirable." Grayson's deep voice was surprisingly quiet, with only the faintest gravelly snarl of anger. "Your defiance of me, less so."

Alejandro pressed his face against the rug.

"Up," Grayson said.

Surprised, he rose to kneeling, cautiously lifting his gaze to look at the Master.

"Did you notice how Williams reacted to your defiance?"

Alejandro stared at him in surprise for a moment, then flinched away from the Master's hard stare and looked down. He said, glad to hear that his voice was steady, "No, sir."

"You have courage, but that is not rare. You have good control when you fight; you are able to think and cooperate with others. That is less common, and highly desirable. But when you are frightened, you focus too tightly. You must learn to watch everything that happens around you, even when you are frightened."

This was exactly the sort of reprimand Papá might have delivered when disappointed in his son. That tone, utterly unexpected, intensified Alejandro's sense of shame. He lowered his head.

Grayson said, "Williams was pleased to see you defend your brother. He thinks now he might like you better than he expected. He thought I would punish you harshly – he still thinks I may do that. He will judge his safety here, and his son's, by what I do with you. Then he will either be easier in his mind or more fearful. You have put me in a position where I cannot punish you as you deserve without frightening Williams, which I do not wish to do."

Though he did not look up, Alejandro nodded to show he understood.

"Now, Keziah. Whether or not she approves of your defying me for your brother's sake, she will think I am weak if I do not punish you. She, like you, is of an age where she wishes to press the limits of my authority, and she is naturally very dominant. You have put me in a position where, if I do not punish you as you deserve, Keziah will think that I will also tolerate *her* defiance. Which I do not wish to do."

This was all immediately obvious, once the Master pointed it out. Alejandro nodded again.

"I suspect Keziah has never been accorded respect by any male black dog. I will give her the opportunity to earn mine. That may suffice. If it does not, I may eventually be required to kill her. I am not pleased that you have contributed to this difficult situation." Grayson paused.

"I understand," Alejandro whispered.

"You're a fool – and unnecessarily. Do you think I would punish a human boy as though he were a defiant black pup?"

Alejandro swallowed. He shook his head.

"You had better learn to trust my restraint," said Grayson. It was a warning, and an order. "Do you understand?"

"I understand, Master."

Reaching down, Grayson closed a powerful hand around the back of Alejandro's neck – a threat, but a gentle one. He shook him, still gently. "You could be an asset to Dimilioc. Learn to think of that." Releasing him, he ordered curtly, "Go."

Alejandro crept backward on his hands and knees, got cautiously to his feet, and, not looking up, made his escape into the deserted hallway. He was shaking – he was very grateful to have a chance to collect himself without an audience.

"*You had better learn to trust my restraint… You could be an asset to Dimilioc.*" It had never occurred to Alejandro that he might actually *trust* any black dog except Papá. Nor had he ever really thought of making himself into an asset for Dimilioc. From the first, they had all thought only of Dimilioc being an asset for *them*. Only... Grayson had been right. Right both times. "*Pendejo*," he muttered out loud, meaning himself. He *was* an idiot.

Nothing about that difficult interview just past had gone the way he'd expected. Alejandro did not know what he felt, now. Except anger. But he was almost sure he was not angry with Grayson Lanning. No. He was angry with himself, because Papá had told him plainly, "*If you ever meet them, Dimilioc wolves may think you are a callejero. You must remember who you are and show them otherwise.*" He knew he had probably not yet shown Grayson otherwise, yet.

Alejandro hated it when he was angry with Miguel, and hated it worse on those rare occasions when Miguel was angry with him. He didn't care about the disagreement. He just hated the way any argument made him want to hit his brother, *force* him to submit.

He didn't do it. He never did. He wouldn't. But he hated that he wanted to. He was proud that Miguel didn't know he wanted to. At least, he was almost sure his brother didn't know.

Miguel certainly showed no fear of Alejandro. At the moment, he did not even show any caution. He was angry, not with irrational black dog fury, but with the colder anger of a frustrated human. He was still arguing. An angry black dog could not argue like that: thought and language became too difficult when black dog temper rose.

"He doesn't *understand*," Miguel said furiously, pacing

fast across the length of Natividad's room and back again. His quick movements made Alejandro's shadow want to lunge after him. Instead, Alejandro stayed exactly where he was, leaning his hip against the windowsill, his arms crossed over his chest, and Miguel kept pacing. The boy turned fast, glaring at Natividad but ending with an especially dark glower for his brother. "He doesn't understand that Vonhausel isn't an ordinary black dog. *You* don't understand. *None* of you black dogs understands Vonhausel, and it's going to get us all killed!"

Alejandro nodded – not in agreement, but in acknowledgement of his brother's anger.

Miguel glared at him. "You think I'm wrong!"

"*Sí*," Alejandro agreed. "*Estás seguro que estas correcto?*"

The glare intensified. Miguel snapped, "Yes, I'm sure! And if everyone else thinks I'm wrong, maybe it is because you're all black dogs and don't know how to think!" He whirled to his twin and demanded, "*Y tú y qué piensas?*"

Natividad held up both hands palm out, shaking her head. "Oh, no, no. *I* don't think *anything*. Don't look at me!"

Miguel whirled on Alejandro again. "*Think* on everything Vonhausel's done so far and tell me he's a normal black dog!"

"He's strong and clever and he may be using undead magic," Alejandro conceded. "But he's still a black dog. That's what he *is*. Grayson's right, Ezekiel's right, Keziah's right, and for once you're wrong."

Miguel shook his head. "Let's entertain the idea, just for a moment, that you've got it backwards. That I'm right and all you black dogs are wrong. What would that *mean*?"

Alejandro snarled soundlessly. He was too tired and angry to argue. *He* was not human. When he tried to frame his brother's question to himself as though it made sense, he couldn't do it. "It doesn't matter," he said, trying not to sound as frustrated as he felt. "It doesn't *matter* that we have no way to protect human towns from Vonhausel! Because you're wrong. He will come *here*, and then we'll kill him. We'll use silver, and then it won't matter whether he's using undead magic or what he's been doing with the shadows of dead black dogs, because he'll be *dead*."

Miguel gazed at Alejandro. He was not used to being so unable to sway his brother, and he looked like the recognition that he'd lost this argument might be choking in his throat. He said at last, his shoulders rounding with defeat, "*Puede que tengas razón*. I hope you are right. I think Vonhausel *wants* a war of all against all, I think he truly believes he can use his new kind of magic to win it, I think if we let him attack Brighton or wherever, we may have no hope of stopping him at all. But I hope I am wrong and you are right about everything."

Despite his anger, Alejandro did not like to see his brother like that, so defeated. He said as gently as he could, "*Lo siento*. But if Vonhausel does what you say... *entonces estamos fregados*. We can't guard every village and town in Vermont."

From the doorway, Keziah said in a very dry tone, "I think we have seen quite clearly that we can't guard *any* town in Vermont. This enemy of yours has too many black dogs and we don't have enough."

Alejandro snarled at her, furious because once again he had not heard her approach. He moved sharply toward her, his shadow rising fast – it was so tempting to let it up all the way, to let himself fall into the *cambio de cuerpo*. He could not fight Grayson Lanning, he didn't even *want* to, but he could fight this arrogant too-beautiful Saudi girl, he could force her to recognize that he was stronger, he could make her respect his strength and dominance...

Keziah did not want to fight. She turned her head aside submissively, and Alejandro, found his shadow subsiding almost willingly. He snarled, "Well?"

The girl watched him warily through the lashes of her lowered eyes. "If your human brother is right, then Vonhausel will begin a war with all the many ordinary human people. Then either he or they will destroy Dimilioc. What if he is right? If I knew it was like that, I would go to your enemy and join him, except what if he uses that undead magic of his on me, on Amira? I could not stop him if he wished to do that. I would take Amira and run, except what place will be safe if Dimilioc falls?" She turned to Natividad, "So, I came to ask, what is this about your mother's special magic? Have you found a way to counter your enemy?"

"I've thought and thought about it," Natividad said earnestly. "But I don't *know* what Mamá thought I could do, I don't know what she could do that was special, Miguel doesn't know either. We *don't know*." She bit her lip. "I *want* to help. But I don't know *how*."

Miguel said, his tone flatly certain, "But we have to go after Vonhausel tonight anyway." He took a step toward

Keziah, hoping for the support his brother hadn't given him. "You know Vonhausel won't expect an attack tonight." He turned back toward Alejandro. "We can't wait. *No podemos esperar más tiempo.* Not past tomorrow. After that, you're right, *nos fregamos,* it's too late."

Saying nothing, Alejandro looked away, at the window, which the gathering darkness had turned into a mirror. It showed him his own reflection, and his brother's. He thought he looked older than he had a week ago. Harder. More temper-ridden. But he also thought that, maybe just because of the contrast, Miguel looked somehow younger. More vulnerable. More like the child he'd been so few years ago. It was not an observation his brother would have wanted anybody to make. And anyway, it was just an illusion created by the glass.

But nevertheless, when Miguel stepped toward him, Alejandro found himself nearly overwhelmed by memories of his brother as a child, as a boy. He wanted to protect him, to guard him from harm. It was a kinder feeling than the black dog urge to force Miguel's submission, but not, he thought, something his brother would welcome.

Miguel said urgently, "If Vonhausel's planning to make a lot of undead zombie black dogs and start a war with ordinary humans, then we *have* to figure a way to stop him doing that, and we *have* to do it right away–"

"If, if!" snapped Alejandro. "We do not know what he is doing tonight, we do not know what he will do tomorrow!"

Miguel stared at him as though he would think, *milagrosamente,* of some way to crush Vonhausel and his shadow pack like so many poisonous *bichos*. This seemed an especially outrageous confidence because *Alejandro* was not the one who usually thought of dramatic things to do or try or say. He said reluctantly, "I will go out. I will go to Lewis and watch. Where's that phone of yours? Does it have minutes left? I can call and tell the Master if Vonhausel comes toward us here or if he goes away to hunt somewhere else."

"Yes," Miguel said instantly. "Yes, please, that's so much better than nothing."

Natividad protested, "Wait, wait! Grayson *said*–"

"That doesn't *matter!*" snapped Miguel.

Alejandro held up his hands, quieting them both. "I will go out, I say–"

"I will go," said Keziah. She met his eyes, smiling faintly. "I can come and go so quietly no one will ever know I slipped away or back unless I choose to say I have. Can you say the same? They will not see me, there in that town; they will not catch my scent. Nor will anyone in this house. I will come and go as though I am nothing but a true shadow."

Now, she did not look aside or down, and Alejandro understood suddenly what he should have realized at once: that she had never meant anything of the submission she had shown him. That had all been a show, a lie. How strictly she must be able to control her shadow, to lie like that! Doubtless she had learned that as a child in her father's house. Doubtless that was also where she had learned to come and go so silently – because she had certainly shown him that she could do *that*. He wanted to hit her, force a real submission – but he also wanted to laugh. He said, "It's true Grayson forbade it."

Keziah shrugged. "Grayson Lanning will not know unless I have reason to use this phone you will give me, and if I call, he will have other things to think of. Besides, he did not punish you for your defiance. Why should he punish me?"

Alejandro did laugh at that. He did not want this girl close to Natividad or Miguel. She was still too beautiful and dangerous and much too sexy. But even if he knew he should avoid her, he almost thought he *did* like her. He said, "If it comes to that, I will support you."

"Well, that relieves my mind," Keziah said drily. She caught the phone Miguel tossed her and turned to go, but added over her shoulder, to Natividad, much more seriously, "*You* must guard Amira for me, if there is trouble and I am not here."

"I will," Natividad promised her instantly. "We all will."

"*That* relieves my mind," Keziah said, and strolled out, hips swaying, slanting a glance back over her shoulder, deliberately seductive.

"I hope she finds out you're right," Miguel said awkwardly once she was gone, half an apology.

Alejandro hoped so, too, but he also longed to go after Keziah, leap out into the frozen night, run under the black sky. He would not give way to his shadow, but he could manage only a curt nod and a swift retreat to his own room. He did not like leaving Miguel to think he was angry, but he was, still. If he stayed, he would show it. He was too tired; he needed a respite from innocent human gestures that grated along black dog nerves, that continually pricked him toward violence. He shut the door of his own room behind him and he stood for some time, his hands resting on the cold metal of the deadbolt and his head bowed against the painted wood, lacking the energy and will to even turn and cross the room and throw himself down on his bed.

A sense of peace gradually crept over him as he stood there, though. At last he recognized Natividad's influence: she had been here, had stood where he was standing, had drawn her pentagrams on his door, on his windows.

The knowledge of his sister's care was almost as warming as the subtle whisper of *tranquilidad* that emanated from her work, and eventually he did turn and cross the room. He barely remembered dropping down full length on top of the bedcovers, and after that, nothing.

He woke to a hard grip on his arm and Miguel's voice, sharp and urgent, calling his name. If he hadn't recognized his brother's voice even before he was awake, he would certainly have taken Miguel's head right off with a slashing blow – as it was, he only just managed to turn his first, violent reaction into a snarl of, "*Suéltame*! *Estupido*!" and a back-handed slap that only rocked his brother back on his heels rather than cutting him to pieces.

"*Lo siento*! *Lo siento*!" Miguel belatedly crouched down low to help Alejandro recapture his control. His breath was coming fast with shock – no, with terror.

"*Que quieres*?" Alejandro demanded. "There is an attack, there is battle? Vonhausel has come?" His brother's fear and urgency swept over him like a fire kindling in the dark and he rolled to his feet, dimly glad he had not had the energy to undress before collapsing across the bed. How long had he been asleep? Not long enough, not nearly long enough... The glowing red numerals on the clock told him it was 12.05, the hinge of night where the dark swung around at last and headed back toward day.

He shook his head hard, fighting to flatten his shadow down out of his way so he could think clearly. Lingering exhaustion made it difficult, but one urgent thought occurred to him, far later than it should have, and he asked sharply, "Natividad?" Abruptly certain that whatever the trouble was, his sister was the heart of it, he did not wait for Miguel to answer before striding across the room and through the connecting door to Natividad's room.

It was empty. There was no sign Natividad had ever lain down in that bed. The room was filled with a sense of emptiness and abandonment – was that only in Alejandro's head?

"She's gone," Miguel said, very quiet-voiced. He was hesitating, with vastly uncharacteristic diffidence, at the door Alejandro had left open behind him. "I woke up and I knew something was wrong and I came in here to see and she was gone. *Es mí culpa– es mí culpa...*"

Brutally, Alejandro did not disagree with this judgment. He demanded only, "What do you know? What do you guess?"

Miguel took a quick, hard breath, gripping his hands together. Whatever he saw in Alejandro's face must have frightened him, for he also dropped down to kneel on the floor at the edge of Natividad's pink rug. He said, "She believed everything I said about Vonhausel and she went to find him. I'm sure that's what happened. She made something. Look at her table..."

The little dressing table had been cleared of all the little perfume bottles. The only thing that now occupied its lace-covered surface was their mother's old wooden flute and a single silver bullet taken from one of the rifles they had brought upstairs.

"I heard her playing earlier," Miguel whispered. He looked wretchedly into Alejandro's face. "I thought... I didn't think..."

"No," Alejandro said furiously, and saw, with both guilt and savage satisfaction, that this single word hit his brother like a blow. He picked up the little flute and stood for a moment, holding it in his hand, trying to think.

Miguel, visibly gathering his nerve, said, "She made something, a weapon, I guess. I don't know what someone Pure would make – maybe not exactly a weapon. But I think she thought she had to do something special. It's my fault, I know it's my fault. She made *something*, and then she slipped out. I think I heard her door close. I was dreaming and I heard a door close in my dream and the sound scared me and woke me up and I came to see if she was OK and she was gone..."

"How long ago?"

"I don't know, I just woke up, but I don't know how long ago she left. It can't have been long..."

That guess was based on hope rather than any kind of knowledge, Alejandro thought, but even so the guess was probably accurate. He looked at the window. The glass, opaque and glowing with moonlight, revealed nothing. But she would not be visible from this window anyway. He said out loud, "She could not have gone on foot. If she's gone out of the house, she must have taken a car." Natividad was not a good driver, and there was the snow – but then, hers was the magic that had kept the road more or less clear. If she thought she needed to drive back to Lewis, she wouldn't let fear of the dark or the snowy roads stop her.

Miguel's eyes widened. "Pearson's car. That's the one she'd take."

"I'll find out," Alejandro said grimly. "If she took that car, I'll follow it."

"She took it," said Miguel.

Alejandro was sure his brother was right.

The window was not locked, but it was frozen shut. Alejandro cracked the frame forcing it open, but at least the glass did not shatter. He could scent the icy night wind through the gap. He wanted to leap out into the dark, surrender to the *cambio de cuerpo*, and stretch out in a long lope across the snow. But he paused, gathered his will and what he could of his wide-scattered human thoughts, and turned instead back to Miguel.

He could not make his tone gentle, but he said, "Who would guess what she would do? Have we ever guessed from one moment to the next what she will do? This isn't your fault. *No me habría enfedado tanto si…*" He realized he had shifted into Spanish, could almost hear Natividad's scolding command: "*Speak Gringo!*" He shook his head and said carefully, in English, "I would not be so angry if my shadow did not press me so hard. I will find her. This cold air holds scent well. I will find her. *Arreglaré las cosas* – I mean, I will make this right."

"*Lo prometes?*" said Miguel: *do you promise?* Like the child he so seldom seemed.

"*Lo prometo*," said Alejandro. He gripped his brother's shoulder, shook him gently. "Now, you. Maybe she has not gotten far. She is not a good driver, and the road is bad, and she does not know it well. I will go through the forest and try to catch her before she reaches the town. But if I do not return with her in half an hour, forty minutes, then you must go to Grayson – hush! You must." He shook his brother again, not so gently. "Yes, I know he will be angry, but you must tell him anyway."

He was surprised, dimly, that he cared about Dimilioc enough himself to make this demand of his brother; more surprised that he trusted Grayson not to harm Miguel no matter how furious the Master was at what had happened. He did not think about this, it was too hard to think anyway, but he said harshly, "If Natividad gets to Vonhausel and she does some clever thing and destroys him, that is well. But if he takes her, she will either be dead or she will be a weapon in his hand. If I do not bring her back, you must warn Grayson so he will know. *Comprendes?*"

Miguel nodded, but so unwillingly that Alejandro shook him again, not quite so gently. "*Harás lo que yo te diga*," he demanded. "*Prometeme que obedecerás!*"

"*Sí*," Miguel said in a low voice, and Alejandro let him go and at last pushed the window wide, taking a deep breath of the winter-scented air.

"*Ten cuidado!*" Miguel called after him, hopelessly. But Alejandro did not turn. He had already leaped out into the night; he had at last let his shadow rise; he fell into the *cambio de cuerpo* and already, with the change barely on him, had almost forgotten his human form. He did not look back.

The forest was empty of everything but dark and cold and the moonlight that shivered through the naked branches. In better times, probably Dimilioc wolves had run out on many full-moon nights such as this – to hunt the deer or merely to run until dawn, dreaming of fire, the snow melting from the faint tracks they left behind them.

On this night, the forest was empty. He saw nothing, felt nothing running in the forest save for himself.

He did not really think in words, in language. He thought about his sister, about her scent, which was faint but mingled with the distinctive scent of Pearson's car. He thought about the music of their mother's little wooden flute, which Natividad had insisted on bringing away with them after the destruction of the village. He had not, at the time, asked, "*Why that?*" Now he wished he had been more curious.

At first Alejandro followed the road, but then, once he was sure he had truly found his sister's trail, he went through the forest, straight as a flung spear toward Lewis.

For some reason, when he tried to picture her there in his mind's eye, he saw instead fleeting glimpses of the ruined church in the center of the town, of its cracked stones and splintered beams, and of Vonhausel poised atop those ruins, in black dog shape, his head tilted back, singing a terrible song to a moon that was tangled and gripped in the angular grasp of leafless branches. It was like the song of a wolf, only it was not merely wild; it contained a terrible darkness that was born of rage and hatred. It was not merely sound, for it cracked stone and burned bone and brought everything that lived to ruin; it made the simple darkness of the night into the fell dark that burned at its heart with black-edged fire.

It had no words, that song, but nevertheless Alejandro thought he understood it. It was the kind of song that if you heard it once, you would hear it forever in your dreams. He was not sure whether it echoed only in his mind or also through the frozen air around them.

Then, as he approached Lewis, he was sure.

14

The black dogs that surrounded Natividad on the road were nothing like the Dimilioc black wolves. Natividad couldn't exactly explain the difference. Vonhausel's black dogs looked just like the Dimilioc wolves. Powerful muscles moved under their coal-black shaggy pelts, burning eyes smoldered yellow or orange or crimson above their long black-fanged jaws, smoke trickled from their mouths when they turned their broad heads to laugh their terrible, silent black-dog laughter at her... Alejandro looked like that when he changed, Papá had looked like that, Ezekiel or Grayson or any Dimilioc wolf looked like that. Only they hadn't, they didn't, they never did.

She was afraid of these black dogs in a way that she had not feared Ezekiel, not even the first time she had seen him, when none of them had been sure whether the Dimilioc executioner would kill them right there in the snow. She had *known* Ezekiel wouldn't do that, even though at the time she had not realized that she knew it. She had been frightened, but she had not really been *afraid*, and she had not known that.

This was different. *Now* she was afraid. *These* black dogs wanted to kill her. They really did. They *wanted* to kill her, but they only ran beside the car instead. That was horrible, because it wasn't the magic on the car that stopped them – they could run her off the road and break her windshield with stones and wait for her to come out or freeze. They didn't do that because they were *escorting* her.

Vonhausel had captured a Pure woman, but he had killed her – used her up – breaking Natividad's mandala. Of course he would want another Pure woman. *That* was why his black dogs were escorting her rather than trying to run her off the road. If Miguel was right, Vonhausel would especially want *her*. She expected that, she even counted on it, but she had not exactly realized how it would feel, to be surrounded by black dogs who hated her, to be heading toward a worse black dog who wanted not just to kill her but to use her for something awful.

This was not like any fear she had ever felt before. It made her feel small and stupid, like a rabbit trapped against a garden wall by a dog. She wished Ezekiel was with her now, lifting a disdainful eyebrow at the rabble of black dogs surrounding her. Or Grayson, solid and immobile as a mountain, sheathed in granite, with fire at its heart. She did not know which of them she longed for more. She would be so much less afraid if either of them were here with her.

But of course if either of them had been here with her, he would have died. That was why she hadn't been able to tell Grayson her idea: he wouldn't have let her do it, and he couldn't have helped anyway. Not all the Dimilioc black wolves together could help her do this. Not even Ezekiel could fight so many black dogs, not even Grayson could make so many run away through the sheer force of his will. It was just stupid to think about how much safer she would have felt with either of them standing behind her. It was *not useful at all* to think about how frightened she felt now. How alone.

She had been afraid when she and her brothers had found Papá and Mamá – she shied away from that memory, but others crowded in at her, inescapable: the torn bodies left in the streets, the trees and flowers burned, everything burned and destroyed. But the black dogs who had done that, they had been gone. She had been afraid, but she had not even known that because her grief had been so much stronger. The grief then had weighed on her like she'd swallowed all the stones in the world.

And all the death had been her fault, at least partly her fault, because if she had been braver and stronger and had not run away to hide, maybe she would have been able to learn the things Mamá had tried to teach her. Then maybe together she and Mamá might have protected the village. Instead, Mamá's magic had broken... Though she wanted now to remember exactly what Mamá had done and what had happened, though she had been trying all night to remember, she could not. She thought she would be crushed from the inside by the jagged weight of grief and memory.

She longed to go back, to go *home*, but that home was gone. Her home now was this frozen territory, filled with the ancient authority that Dimilioc was trying to hold and Vonhausel was trying to steal.

Her hands, where she gripped the high steering wheel,

were cold. It had stopped snowing at last, but this only helped a little. She was not used to driving. Her shoulders ached from holding the wheel too tightly, and her neck from craning forward to see.

It was about ten miles from Dimilioc to Lewis. She remembered that. Sheriff Pearson's car was much better than the one they had bought with their little store of money, and the wish she had put on the road still held, and so actually it was not that hard to drive. Except for the black dogs, from which she kept trying to flinch, so that again and again she had to stop herself twitching the steering wheel one way or the other. There was no sense in flinching. She knew things would only get worse. More dangerous. Scarier. Knowing this didn't help. Knowing that everything would be *over* if she did everything right and if Vonhausel did everything she expected, *that* helped.

She tried not to let herself think about Vonhausel doing something unexpected instead. She definitely didn't want to think about what his black dogs might do to her even if she did absolutely everything right. She tried not to think about that. She wouldn't. She didn't.

Except sometimes she couldn't stop her mind from going to Alejandro, to Miguel, about what her brothers would think and feel when they knew what she'd done, where she'd gone. Alejandro would be so angry, so afraid for her. It would be even worse for Miguel. He would blame himself, he would think it was his fault. She hadn't even left a note to tell him it wasn't, that this wasn't something a black dog or an ordinary human could do. Only someone who was Pure. She should have left a note.

She should have left one for Grayson, too. He had tried so hard to protect her. She should have left a note explaining that really the Pure weren't supposed to be protected. That really they were supposed to protect other people. Mamá had taught her that. Mamá's whole *life* had taught her that, and then at the end Natividad hadn't done anything but hide. *This* time would be different.

But she hadn't left any notes for anybody. Now she tried not to think about her brothers at all. Those thoughts were bad ones. They made her feel weak and young and stupid and afraid.

And thinking about Ezekiel was somehow almost worse. She knew he would take her death even harder, if she died. But really he hardly knew her. She told herself so, and tried to believe it. Any Pure girl would suit him, he would find another one to court, he could flatter any Pure girl and make her feel special. It was stupid that knowing that made her want to cry.

She saw the first opening of the road in front of her, a high blackness that spread out above the denser blackness of the trees. She had come to the cleared land that surrounded Lewis. The lower blockier darkness that stood against the sky: that must be the edge of town. The black dogs came up on either side of her, keeping pace with her car. She slowed a little, and a little more, letting them think that she was afraid to arrive where they meant her to go. She did not let herself think, not ever, not for a second, that this was true.

There should have been lights before her, showing where the houses stood and the roads lay. But there were no lights. Not ordinary lights. Only blacker shapes looming closer out of the black night, and a disturbing dull red glow behind the layers of blackness, like coals just before they guttered and dimmed and burned out. That glow did not combat the dark, but somehow made it seem darker than ever. It made the night seem dense, like a black dog's shadow.

She took her foot off the gas pedal as she passed the first of the empty buildings, allowing the car to coast forward under no power, only its own inertia. The car rolled past the scorched line where she had drawn her mandala. That narrow crack in the earth lay like the mark of a whip across the road. On either side, the snow was trampled and melted to show winter-barren earth that had been torn up in the fighting and then frozen again, jagged and hard as iron.

The red glow was not exactly brighter here, but it was more distinct. The air smelled of ash and burning even through the car's closed windows; of charred wood and smoke and a deeper, grittier scent, like burned earth and stone. Two of the black dogs ran in front of her car, turning their heads to stare at her, snapping at the air to frighten her. Or maybe that was a kind of black dog laughter. They wanted her to turn and drive into the center of Lewis. She had to remind herself very firmly that she wanted that, too. Now that she was here, this seemed so unbelievable that she half wondered whether she had just dreamed her plan to come here. Maybe she had dreamed this whole unspeakable drive. Maybe she was dreaming now.

But she knew she was not dreaming. She steered cautiously because it was dark and the streets here were filled with chunks of things: broken bricks and shattered stones and pieces of timber; the town's sole octagonal stop sign that glowed red as blood in her headlights, uprooted like a young tree so that she had to drive across it... Natividad turned carefully around one last corner and found the ruined church before her, dozens of black dogs gathered at the base of the rubble. She took her foot off the gas again, coasting gently to a halt. Nearly all the waiting black dogs turned their broad heads to stare at her. Their lips curled back from shining jet-black fangs in snarls that were also laughter; their eyes flared with all the colors of fire. Some of them were true black dogs, she saw; but some were the smaller moon-bound shifters and others were different again: too quiet and still and just, well, different. She studied those black dogs uneasily, wondering if they could be the kind Miguel had guessed might exist: dead black dogs, possessed now only by their shadows. She stared at the closest of the too-quiet creatures. Was it just her imagination that it seemed to lack something undefinable that any black dog, even a stray lost to bloodlust, ought to possess? An essential humanity, a memory of having been human? She wasn't sure, but looking at that black dog made her uneasy. She looked away from it, trying to find Malvern Vonhausel instead. He had to be here somewhere, surely.

Fragments of the church walls pierced through the tumbled wreckage. The rubble had burned. It still smoldered. That smoldering, of course, was the source of the red glow she had seen from the edge of Lewis. Smoke and powdery ash and glinting sparks still drifted in the air. Even from within the car, the bitter smoke coated the back of her throat.

The huge stones and cracked bells and broken cross from the church's highest steeple, thrown down before her, blocked the road completely. But maybe it was just as well the way ahead was blocked, because beyond that obstruction the road itself was cracked. Not just cracked: that was too simple and small a word for the gaping fissure that ran right across the road and away out of sight to either side. It looked wide enough to drive even Sheriff Pearson's car right into it. It looked deep enough to lead straight down to Hell. The bloody light from the smoldering ruins of the church seemed to run across the ground and down into that fissure, pooling in it like light, or like blood. Maybe it really did go down to Hell.

Natividad released her fierce grip on the wheel for the first time since she had begun this drive, and turned the key in the ignition. The sudden hush as the engine fell silent made her twitch with nervous startlement, and she reached out at last to lay her hand on the *aparato para parar las sombras* she had brought with her.

It was a new kind of *aparato*, not one Mamá had ever exactly taught her. She had thought and thought about all the magic Mamá *had* taught her. The Dimilioc wolves had taken her in and she had drawn all this danger right to them, and they had protected her anyway and wanted to go on protecting her even now. And she had known it was time to stop hiding and being protected and go out to face Vonhausel herself.

So, then she had thought of this, and she believed it would work. But now that she was here, where was Vonhausel?

He wanted her, Miguel said – her especially. Mamá had told Miguel she had a gift for making darkness cooperate with light, which Natividad didn't understand at all, but what Mamá had told Natividad herself was that she had a gift for making things. If that gift was enough, if she had made this *aparato* right, if it did what she had made it to do, then the thing she had made would destroy Vonhausel and then everything would be alright after all.

She had made her new *aparato* from Alejandro's silver knife and from moonlight and from her *maraña*, the tangle of light and magic that was meant to confuse the eye and mind. She had made that over into a *teleraña*, an orderly web, because confusion was no longer her goal. Now she wanted to catch and bind.

She had made this new kind of *aparato* with music from Mamá's little flute and with the clarity of her intention. That clarity was hard to remember, now that she was here in the dark. But the *aparato* was strong. It was cold to the touch, a biting clean cold that seemed to push back against the slow-beating heat from the burned church.

The base of the *aparato* was Alejandro's knife. To her the heart of it still looked like a knife. Sort of. If you glanced at it only carelessly, or if you were thinking about sharp-edged weapons. To her, it seemed to be surrounded by a kind of shimmering haze, like mist gathered together into something long and narrow and not exactly solid. That was one thing she'd used the *teleraña* to do: catch the eye. To a black dog who longed to tear down his enemies, to spill their blood across the dead earth and burn their bodies to ash and their shadows to a memory of darkness... to that black dog, the *aparato* should look exactly like the sort of weapon that would give you everything you wanted. She hoped it would look like that to Malvern Vonhausel. She couldn't see it that way herself and had no way of knowing for sure if she'd made it right. Except, of course, by trying it out.

She picked it up, cradling it against her stomach. But the *aparato* was too cold to hold like that for long, and she put it back on the car seat next to her, though she left the tips of her fingers resting on its hilt. Or the part that had been its hilt. It numbed her hand, but kind of in a good way.

The black dogs that had escorted her all turned their heads, looking toward the north, toward the ruined church, their hackles rising, the unholy light of their eyes dimming. They no longer looked like they were laughing at Natividad – they seemed to have forgotten her. They all lowered their heads and crouched down like nervous dogs, slinking back and away, clearing a path from her car to the burning rubble.

Natividad knew exactly what that meant. Of course it meant that Vonhausel was coming. She took a deep breath and moved her hand to open the car door. Or she tried to. She couldn't actually make herself move. This must be what people meant when they said they were paralyzed with terror. How strange, and not very nice. She felt as though she was an observer outside her own body, outside the car, outside all the action; like she was watching some other girl stare, frozen with fear, out through the car's windshield into the dark. It was as if she herself was distant and not really even very interested.

Then Malvern Vonhausel strode down the tumbled wreckage of the church, and that sense of dislocation trembled. He was in his human form. Somehow that seemed much worse than if he'd been in his black dog form. Not scarier, exactly, but worse.

He was taller than she had expected, though maybe that was because he was still above her, walking leisurely down a charred timber and then stepping lightly to one great broken chunk of granite and then another. He moved with the weightless confidence of a black dog, never missing his footing or dislodging any rubble.

He had a broad strong-featured face with wide-set cheekbones and a thick-lipped mouth, crooked now in amused contempt. He didn't look like he would ever smile except when he was hurting something. He didn't look young; his hair was black, untouched by gray. His eyes were also black, but not a clean black: to Natividad's sight they seemed filled with the heavy black smoke of a great burning. Those black eyes caught her gaze and held it, at once fiery and contemptuous and compelling, like a black dog's eyes but not exactly, though she couldn't tell where the difference lay. Again, the sense of remoteness and distance she clung to trembled. She closed her eyes for a moment, until the fear became once more a remote thing, something that belonged to somebody else, something not really hers. It was sort of like the blank distance that grief put between a person and the world and she was grateful for it.

Black dogs followed Vonhausel, one to either side. These did not slink low in fear of him like the others, but strode cat-footed and confident down from the ruins of the church. Once she could manage to force her gaze away from Vonhausel to look at them, she found they held her attention in a way she didn't at first understand.

Then she did understand it, and that was much worse. Horror shattered the remote detachment she had clung to and the present came crashing down on her all at once, like an avalanche of broken timbers and shattered stones.

The taller of the black dogs, walking at heel on Vonhausel's left, was Zachariah Korte. The other, on Vonhausel's right, broad and massive-shouldered and moving with a heavy stride that somehow was not at all lumbering or clumsy, was Harrison Lanning. Even in their black dog forms, she knew them. Only she had no idea *how*, because they weren't really the people she'd known, not *really*, not anymore.

Even when Alejandro's shadow rose all the way and he was entirely in his black dog shape, there was something still there that was *him*. All black dogs were like that: a low-burning memory of who they were stayed with them through the change. She had wondered if those strange, quiet black dogs might be different, might lack that kind of memory.

But she knew beyond doubt that all memory of who they had been was gone from these. The black dogs that had been Zachariah and Harrison... the human parts of them were gone. Because she had known them, she could see that what walked toward her now was only their shadows, given physical form but wholly lacking any trace of the human identity that had once shaped and restrained them. For the first time she really understood what it meant, to recall a shadow from the fell dark and put it into the corpse of the man who had once held it. It was horrible. Worse than what a vampire did to somebody... No, it was *exactly* what a vampire did. Or what vampires had done, and thank God the vampires were gone, but now there were these... these shadow-possessed dead things, just as bad.

Zachariah was dead. Harrison was *dead*. These shadow-possessed undead things were *not* anybody she had ever known. She knew that. But she couldn't help but look again and again for traces of the men beneath. And find nothing, because there was nothing there to find. It was horrible.

Vonhausel stepped away from the wreckage of the church and stood at last on the road amid chunks of shattered pavement. He was staring straight at her and smiling.

Natividad's *aparato* burned in her hand, but it was a cold clean burning that had nothing at all in common with black dog fire. The pain that struck into her palms and up her arms was a clean pain, an antidote to black dog burning. It cleared her mind and drove back the dark that pressed so close around her; it brought back that sense of distance and separation. She clung to it harder despite the pain, and found the courage to meet Vonhausel's gaze.

Malvern Vonhausel came closer to her, halting only when he was only a few feet away. Natividad was glad, distantly, that the dead black dogs that had been Zachariah and Harrison stopped at the base of the rubble and did not come forward with him. Vonhausel alone was bad enough. He was still smiling, that terrible contemptuous smile that had so much of his shadow in it and so little of anything human. But now Natividad found that she loathed him more than she feared him. She'd come here to destroy him – or to get him to destroy himself. Now she *wanted* to do that, especially now that she'd seen the undead things he'd made. Anyway, she was here, so she had to go forward. She had to. She would.

She moved a hand – in a way, it seemed again like she only watched some other girl move her hand, someplace far away where nothing mattered. So, she wasn't afraid. Not really afraid. The girl who was afraid, that wasn't exactly her. That was why she could move her hand and open the car door and slide off the seat and down to the broken pavement of the road. The dark and the winter air rushed in at her, but it wasn't really *her* who trembled with the cold.

She gripped the *aparato* tightly in both hands and stepped around the car, holding it in front of her, like a weapon or a shield. Or an offering. It glimmered in the dark. She felt the fire that hid behind and within the shadows of the black dogs rise up in answer, almost visible but not quite, at least not to her. The earth seemed to shudder under her feet. Though maybe that was just part of the ruined church settling. But it didn't feel that way. To her, it felt like the earth might crack open at any moment until the chasm that lay not ten feet away finally gaped wide enough to swallow the whole world.

Vonhausel was still smiling. If he thought the earth might crack wide open, the idea didn't bother him. He stared at her. Somewhere close by a black dog snarled, a long low vicious sound. Everything Natividad looked at seemed both far distant and incredibly vivid. The world seemed to dip and sway. All around her, the air seemed to waver like a curtain, ready to rip in half and reveal the *real* truth behind the looming shadows of buildings and broken church and shattered pavement.

"Well, well," Vonhausel said. His voice was smooth, relaxed, even pleased in a horribly vicious way. He spoke with a faint accent that didn't sound American. It might have been German, but maybe not. He said, "How very unexpected. Can this possibly be Concepción's daughter? Running from Dimilioc straight to me. Rather like leaping from a burning building directly into the flames below." He looked her up and down, amused and contemptuous.

"Stay away!" Natividad said breathlessly. "Stay away from me!" She jabbed her *aparato para parar las sombras* at him with a short, stiff little movement.

Vonhausel tilted his head, casting a quizzical glance at her *aparato*. "What have you brought me?" He lifted his gaze suddenly, caught her eyes as though doing so was a kind of attack.

Natividad felt that it was. She flinched and tucked herself against the side of the car. It took no effort to look like she was too frightened to answer.

"Do you think that will protect you?" Vonhausel asked her. "You little Pure bitches, you do amuse me. You always think so highly of yourselves. You *are* Concepción's child, of course." He paused, then, when Natividad said nothing, went on, "But your magic is weak, isn't it? Or you were too stupid to learn what your mother might have taught you. What a disappointment to her you must have been. Though in the end even she died as easily as any other human. Though I admit that particular indulgence might have been rather short-sighted. I think you will be rather more useful to me than your mother." He paused, studying her.

Natividad still did not answer. Despite his scorn, Vonhausel had not reached out to take the *aparato* away from her. She had expected him to grab it first thing. She had *made* it to attract him, to attract any really strong black dog. Maybe he was right about her after all – maybe she *was* stupid. She couldn't have made it right. He didn't even care about the *aparato* at all, he'd barely even *noticed* it, she had put herself in his hands for nothing – she *hadn't* learned what her mother had needed to teach her–

"What *is* that?" he asked her, so suddenly that she jumped and bit her tongue. When she didn't answer at once, he asked again, an impatient edge hardening his smooth voice, "Well, what? Speak, girl!"

"It's… It's a shield," Natividad whispered. This had seemed much more believable when she'd just *imagined* herself answering some question like that, before she'd left her safe pink room at the Dimilioc house. She could read both anger and contempt in Vonhausel's eyes, in the set of his mouth, but was that because he realized she was lying or just because he was a black dog? She said, not having to *try* to make her voice falter and fade, "My… My mother showed me. It's for vampires really, only it's the strongest thing I know how to make and I thought it would work…" She let her voice trail off into helpless silence.

There was still no clear sign that Vonhausel suspected that she was lying. Only there wasn't any sign that he wanted the thing she'd made, either. He wasn't even looking at it. He was studying her. She ducked her head to avoid meeting his unnatural gaze.

"Stupid little girl," he said to her. "Grayson Lanning didn't know what he had in his hand, when he gathered you up. Did all his black dogs trail after you like dogs after a bitch in season? I'm sure they did. That's all they thought of you. Is that why you ran from them, pretty little bitch?"

Natividad shuddered, wondering desperately if she could

possibly be fast enough to get back into the car and slam the door before he touched her. Probably not. He was so close. But she was poised to try it anyway.

Only then he said in a soft, absent tone, "And such a pretty little shield you've made. So delicate. Not very effective. But I wonder whether I might find some use for it?" He paused and then added, even more softly, speaking now more to himself than to her, "I wonder whether that little thing of yours really is nothing but a shield? Is that what your mother told you it was? It doesn't look like a shield to me."

His gaze had been caught at last by the *aparato*. It had grown brighter, she realized, and vaguer, and even colder to the touch. It numbed her hands. She caught her breath in a little gasp, and dropped it. She hadn't meant to actually let it go and snatched after it again at once. But dropping it turned out to be the perfect tactic, because Vonhausel moved with black dog speed and precision to seize the thing before it could hit the ground.

It turned in his hand so fast that Natividad didn't really see it turn, only knew that it had moved: it wrapped around Vonhausel's hand and flung itself up his arm. The misty glow surrounding it flared into sharp-edged brilliance and flicked out like a blown-out match. But the thing itself was not gone. She knew it was still there, really, though she couldn't actually see it, exactly. *Vonhausel* certainly knew it was there. He was trying to shake it loose, tear it off, cast it away. But he obviously couldn't.

A short, sweet phrase of flute music danced in the air, the individual notes like sparks from a new-caught fire. The music trembled just beyond hearing, but Natividad could hear it if she sort of listened sideways. And the black dogs must have heard it, too, or at least perceived it somehow, because they had all frozen into immobility, even the soulless dead creatures that Vonhausel had made out of Zachariah's and Harrison's bodies. Vonhausel was screaming now, a horrible sound that scaled up and up until, like the music, it was something Natividad could only hear in her mind.

Her *aparato* twisted up Vonhausel's arm and then across his whole body. It had become a silvery net of not-exactly-visible light. To Natividad, it seemed as fine and delicate and ephemeral as frost on a window. It had closed around… not Vonhausel's body, she saw now, but his shadow. It clung to his shadow and tore it free of his body. The screaming she couldn't exactly hear was the screaming of the shadow. It *was* a weapon she had made, after all, and it flared bright silver against the thick darkness of the shadow until both the weapon and the shadow went out together with a sudden *snap* that wasn't exactly audible.

Natividad stared at the husk of Vonhausel's body as it trembled and swayed and at last collapsed. He didn't fall all at once, though, but slowly, so that at first she wasn't sure he was falling at all and then she almost thought he might put out his arms after all and catch himself. But he didn't. He was dead, he was gone; he'd gone into the fell dark after his shadow and his body sprawled lifeless and limp across the cracked pavement.

The soft thud his body made as it hit the ground seemed strangely anticlimactic, as though he should have fallen with a tremendous crash, as though the whole world should have been shaken by his fall. But there was nothing like that. Dead, stripped of his shadow and of his life, Vonhausel looked just like anybody. This seemed very strange and unexpectedly disturbing. The way his body sprawled bonelessly at Natividad's feet made her stomach turn suddenly over. She couldn't believe he was dead. She couldn't believe *she* had killed him. She'd come here to do exactly this, but now that it was done, even though she knew she ought to be glad, even though she *was* glad, she was appalled, too. She had never killed anything before, except sometimes a chicken. This was… not the same at all.

But then her attention was jerked away from the thing she'd done because the air began to vibrate with a disturbing new sound, a sound like the howling of wolves set to music, only turned dark and bitter. This sound wasn't just in her head: it was deep and loud and getting deeper and louder all the time. It shook dust and ash into the air. The pavement and rubble surrounding the gaping crack across the road began to break up and crumble into the chasm. The fire-edged darkness within that chasm seemed to creep out into the night. Natividad shuddered and crept back along the side of the car.

At her movement, all the black dogs, who had been staring fixedly at Vonhausel's body, turned and looked at her. She froze. She thought it was fading, it *was* fading. She knew the black dogs would do something as soon as it had stopped. Some of them, the weaker ones, would just run, put distance between themselves and all the magic and power that had been loosed here. But a lot of them would probably fight. That was what black dogs did if no one stronger controlled them: they fought for dominance and for the pleasure of killing, and then they went out and hunted helpless prey because they loved slaughter better even than fighting with one another. Without Vonhausel, there was no one strong enough to hold so many black dogs.

Or... maybe there might be, sort of. Natividad turned her head the tiny degree necessary to look at the dead shadow-ridden black dogs that had been Zachariah and Harrison. They, too, were staring at Vonhausel's body. She'd hoped they would collapse when their master died, but of course they hadn't. That would have made everything too easy. What *they* would do now, she could not begin to guess. Would they want to butcher the ordinary black dogs, or would they want to rule them and use them as Vonhausel had, or would they want something else entirely?

There were more undead black dogs scattered here and there among the ordinary ones, too. Natividad recognized them, now that she knew what to look for. They were more completely still than any living black dog could be. They were more... more something. Or less something. More foreign, maybe, and less human.

It finally occurred to Natividad that she should actually get back in the car, that she could even try to drive away. Probably the black dogs wouldn't let her go, but she ought to *try*. She slid a covert glance sideways, toward the open door of the car. So near. She took a small step that way, trying to slide along unobtrusively.

Every moon-bound shifter and black dog in the whole crowd swung its heavy head around to stare at her, even the dead ones. Natividad stopped as though physically pinned in place by the weight of all those fiery eyes. Heat pounded around her until she half expected to see flames flickering out of the pavement, melting the shattered blacktop to molten tar. When she drew a breath, the air tasted of smoke and bitter ash. It choked her. She stifled a cough, afraid that if she made a sound they would all be on her at once.

She had not really expected to survive the night, but she realized now that she had never really believed, not even for a second, that she would actually *die*. Not until she had seen Vonhausel and the undead black dogs that followed him. And *really* not until now, when the brutal attention of dozens of black dogs came down on her like the weight of the darkness given substance and heft. *Now* she believed it. These black dogs were going to tear her apart before they turned on each other. She stood helpless and horrified before them, not so much afraid, now – although she was afraid – but stricken at the thought of Miguel, of Alejandro, of how her brothers would feel when they knew...

A blur of black through the darkness, hot and furious, and Alejandro hurtled straight over the top of Sheriff Pearson's huge car and came down in front of Natividad with a controlled lightness that seemed impossible for a creature his size. Every black dog in the crowd surrounding her gave way, wary and astonished, maybe expecting all the Dimilioc wolves to come over the car in his wake. Natividad thought they might – she hoped they would – but they didn't. Alejandro had come alone.

15

Natividad was sure her brother was going to die. He crouched in front of her, snarling around at all the gathered black dogs with furious loathing. He would fight, but how could he win? Vonhausel's black dogs would tear him apart and then – much easier – they would tear her apart, too.

Would the Dimilioc wolves come here, later, find the marks of the fight and guess what had happened? Would Miguel ever know? It would be worst of all if he didn't know, if he had to guess and wonder and imagine – if he wasn't even sure whether she and Alejandro were dead or not, *that* would be the *worst* – but Keziah was supposed to be out here somewhere. She would be watching. She could tell everyone what had happened. It was almost a relief to remember that.

Several of Vonhausel's black dogs edged forward, their eyes burning with fire and the savage joy of killing. The shadow-wolf that had been Harrison stalked toward her as well, and that was even worse, because there was nothing recognizable in those dead eyes. She felt she was being stared at by death itself, only it was really something worse than death, because death was just death but this thing was really evil.

Alejandro swiveled around to face first one and then another of their enemies, trying not to leave Natividad exposed. She looked with longing at the open car door only steps away, but was afraid to move.

Alejandro had crouched low, readying himself to lunge for the nearest of the enemy black dogs. He was still snarling, a vicious thread of sound that was strangely high-pitched and almost inaudible... In fact, it was not a snarl at all, nor any sound a black dog might produce. Nor was it actually coming from Alejandro. This was a new sound, one which had started as a thin, bodiless whine, and was now rapidly turning into a bright hum scattered with piercing phrases of music. This was not the same music that had wrapped Vonhausel up in fog, though. This was something else, something related but not the same... Natividad looked from side to side, searching for its source. The hum was darkening, thickening, swallowing up the musical phrases until those were wholly subsumed, like the sparks of a fire extinguished by too great a darkness. All the black dogs had drawn back, which was good, but Natividad could not feel relief at this apparent reprieve. She felt it wasn't a reprieve at all.

The dark hum coalesced above Vonhausel's body, like a swarm of insubstantial black bees made out of shadows and smoke, scattered with crimson glints like reflected fire and silver flickers like flashes of moonlit silver. This strange cloud settled on the body, and sank in, and disappeared. The hum ceased. The silence that followed was deeply shocking, though Natividad could not have explained why. Alejandro shifted to put his bulk between her and the body, and she put an arm across his shoulders both to brace herself and to hold him back.

Vonhausel took a breath and closed his eyes. The silver net of her *aparato* reappeared, seeming almost to rise out of his body – it was really rising out of his shadow, Natividad realized. It clung to him for another moment, then slid aside as he took another breath. He opened his eyes again, and then moved to get up. He made it to one knee first and stayed there, head down, panting, as her *aparato* condensed rapidly back into a misty object of light and silver – dimmer than it had been, and smaller, and mottled here and there by indistinct blotches like bruises. It had been corrupted by its fall into the fell dark, that was obvious, but it hadn't been destroyed. Natividad wondered if she dared run out and get it back – it might still be useful; her mandala had still been useful, and that had been corrupted, too – but then Vonhausel shook his head and got to his feet, and the opportunity was lost.

Vonhausel stood for a long moment, breathing slowly and deeply, his head down. Though he ought to have looked terribly vulnerable, somehow he did not. If Alejandro tried to attack him, Natividad knew she would try her best to stop him. She was terrified of what might happen if her brother attacked Vonhausel, and she didn't even know why.

Then Vonhausel took one more deep breath, lifted his head, and looked at Natividad. Right at her. And his eyes were exactly the same as they'd been before he'd died – before she'd killed him. *Exactly* the same. She saw now that the smoky appearance of Vonhausel's eyes was because he was dead, he was *dead*, she hadn't killed him at all because he'd been dead long before she'd ever come here with her special weapon. What was strange was that this realization was kind of a relief even though it also terrified her: she *hadn't* killed him, *she* hadn't killed anybody. She was glad of that almost as much as she was sorry for it, and the confusion of feeling that resulted made her shudder. She closed her hand tightly on the shaggy pelt of Alejandro's neck and told herself she shivered only because of the cold.

Vonhausel smiled, a tight smile that suggested she had hurt him somehow even though she hadn't killed him. Killed him more. She thought she could see, now that she looked for it, that his skin had the kind of waxy appearance that she'd seen in dead people. But he wasn't like those awful dead things he'd made out of Zachariah and Harrison. Nothing was left, as far as she could tell, of the people they'd been: they were pure shadow now. But Vonhausel... His shadow might have come back out of the fell dark to reclaim his body, but *his* soul had come with it. She was sure this was true.

"Stupid little girl," Vonhausel said to her. He ignored Alejandro contemptuously, speaking only to Natividad. He shifted a foot as though to kick at her *aparato*, but then did not touch it after all. Maybe he was nervous about touching it, though as far as she could see he had no reason to be. She wished she had it back in her hands, but she didn't know what in the world she could do with it anyway.

Vonhausel smiled at her. "Stupid little Pure bitch. Nothing can kill me. If you'd been paying attention, you might have realized that before using some ridiculous Pure weapon made of light and good intentions. Don't you know what they say about good intentions?"

Natividad did. Given... Given everything, that saying seemed entirely too applicable. She said nothing.

Vonhausel looked slowly around at the crowd of black dogs. The dead ones stood stolidly and looked back at him without fear, but the ordinary black dogs cowered low and turned their heads aside and tucked their tails... They were terrified of him, which Natividad hadn't exactly understood before. Now she did. She was sure they were afraid he would kill them and then bring their shadows back to possess their bodies. No wonder he could control them so much better than he should have been able to.

Turning back to Natividad, Vonhausel said, "Now, I believe..."

Alejandro shifted away from her a step and straightened away from his black dog form, his body seeming partly to shrink and partly to dissolve into smoke as he slid into the change. It was not as smooth as he usually managed. He was afraid, that was why, Natividad thought. Fear made a black dog angry, and anger made the black-dog-to-human change harder. And the full moon made it harder, too. But at last Alejandro dragged his human body back out of the darkness and the smoke and stood there in human form, facing Vonhausel, still between him and Natividad. He said, his voice low and husky with the change, "I'll join you. I want that."

Natividad stared at him in astonishment. Then she blinked, trying to get control of her face, though she couldn't decide whether it was better for Vonhausel to know she was surprised or to believe she'd seen that coming.

Alejandro didn't look at her. All his attention was on Vonhausel. He jerked his head northward, toward Dimilioc. "They can't win. Anybody can see it. *Esos dearriba estan locos, completamente locos* – they're all crazy up there. You're going to win and they're going to lose. Only I figure they can lose hard or easy. I'll tell you all about the house, where everybody sleeps, where you're likely to find Grayson Lanning, where you'll find Ezekiel Korte. He's been recently injured – a silver injury, not fully healed: I can tell you exactly what that injury is."

"Ah, treason, sweet as blood in the mouth," said Vonhausel. He was frowning, but he was also listening. "Is that what you want?"

Alejandro angled his head to show the undead black dog his throat. "Maybe you've meant to go in, kill them all, or maybe you've meant to leave them there, because what difference does it make, now, they're nothing, you can ignore them and hunt someplace else. But I can make it easy for you to destroy them all. The blood of your enemies is the sweetest blood." He glanced over toward the unnaturally still black dogs that had been Zachariah and Harrison. "You can do that to all of them. I'll do everything I can to help you–"

"In the hope I won't do it to you, pup?" Vonhausel was beginning to sound amused again.

Alejandro reached back without seeming to look, catching Natividad's arm and pulling her forward, steadying her with a hand under her elbow, though he still didn't look at her. "To keep her safe," he said to Vonhausel.

The black dog leader smiled slowly. "Your sister, is it? Are you another of Concepción's get? Or is this *your* pretty little bitch? Black dogs should stay with their own kind. Humans are only prey, and the Pure are only human."

"She's my sister. The Dimilioc wolves, they want to make her a *puta*. It's a whitebread operation up there: they say they value the Pure, but they don't mean Mexican girls, you know? Lanning promises – they're worth that!" He spat on the pavement, then went on with savage passion, "No one will ever be part of Dimilioc unless their ancestors came right off the *Mayflower*, and that's the truth. And now it's obvious Dimilioc is going to lose anyway. The Lanning Master…" He spat again. "*Aquél pedazo de basura!* He doesn't have a clue."

"And so you came here to me." Vonhausel seemed to find this, too, amusing.

"You're clever, everyone says, and it's obvious, anyway. I want to be on the winning side – and I want my sister safe."

Vonhausel laughed. His laugh somehow managed to be even more horrible than his smile, which Natividad wouldn't have thought possible until she heard it. She tried not to look at him. She focused on her brother instead. He sounded so sincere. Was it possible he could make Vonhausel actually *believe* all that nonsense?

"You offer me Dimilioc for your sister's safety," said Vonhausel to Alejandro. It wasn't a question, but a statement, and there was something nasty about the way he said it. Then it got worse, because he went on, "But I don't care about Dimilioc. Grayson Lanning is nothing. His executioner is less than nothing. The long history of Dimilioc, that I value, but…" and he leaned forward, holding out a hand, which he closed slowly into a fist, "I will begin a new history."

"But…" said Alejandro, but then stopped. Natividad knew that this response was not what he had expected and so he floundered, trying to think of a new tactic. She put her hand over his where he held her arm, trying to be supportive, but subtle.

Vonhausel straightened, relaxing. He opened his hand again in a wave that encompassed the dead black dogs that had been Zachariah and Harrison. "I have what I need from Dimilioc: Concepción's brat, and those. Look at them! *They* will serve to tear out Dimilioc's throat. They can't die – and there are so few true Dimilioc wolves left. Harrison Lanning will hunt his brother, and Zachariah Korte his nephew. It's a pity I can't send Benedict Mallory against his brother, but this will do. It will do." He paused, contemplating this vision with a small smile.

Natividad contemplated it, too. The idea made her want to vomit. She slid a covert glance up at her brother. His grip on her arm tightened until it bruised. She was pretty sure he was as horrified as she, but nothing showed in his expression.

"But if Dimilioc… If you… If they…" Alejandro began, but stopped in confusion.

Natividad said for her brother, "But if you don't move against Dimilioc yourself, if you just send your… your zombie black dogs against them, what will *you* be doing?" She was proud that this question came out in an almost steady voice. But she couldn't keep from flinching when Vonhausel turned his attention to her.

The master of the shadow pack moved his shoulders in a small shrug, glancing around at the broken pavement and up at the ruined church smoldering behind him. "This has been my proving ground. Do you know, I believe there's *no* black dog shadow that's truly beyond reach, if I have the right tools to hand?" He glanced significantly at Natividad. "I hadn't expected that, but it is so. It opens up so many possibilities."

He didn't elaborate, but Alejandro looked down at Natividad. She met his eyes, sure they'd both made the same guess about what Vonhausel meant. If he'd discovered a way to do more than just catch the shadows of fresh-killed black dogs, if he could recall the shadows of the long dead, then everybody had been wrong about a possible war between black dogs and humans. If Vonhausel couldn't be killed, if his black dogs couldn't be killed after he brought them back as shadow revenants... maybe he might actually *win* that war. Or at least, and this was what was important, Vonhausel might really *think* he could. If he thought that, he wouldn't hesitate to start it. Could that be possible?

It wasn't. Surely it wasn't. Natividad stared at Alejandro, hoping for some sign he didn't believe it. But her brother's expression was so carefully blank that to Natividad he looked... not only disturbed, but sick and afraid. Alejandro never looked like that, even when he *was* sick and afraid.

"*You'll* be useful to me," Vonhausel said to Natividad. "A gift from your mother to me, from beyond the grave. Pure magic to braid into shadow magic: she *owes* me that for the trouble she caused me. She escaped me, unfortunately, but here you are, in my hand after all! I'm so pleased she taught you how to weave light with shadows before she died."

Natividad stared at him. He thought she'd made her *aparato* deliberately to weave together with his shadow? He thought... What *did* he think? Had *Mamá* ever let black dog shadows contaminate *her* work? At the last, had she done something... What *had* she done? Natividad had tried so hard not to remember, and now she couldn't, except for brutal flashes of memory: pine trees burning, a towering circle of flames all around her. Oak leaves floating through the air, burning. Screaming, screaming in the dark... Someone had been screaming... Mamá had done something, Papá had fought, but there were too many, he could not reach Mamá, and Mamá had done *something*... But braiding light with shadows? Natividad couldn't *remember*...

Vonhausel added to Alejandro, "You'll be useful as well, to be sure. Though not in the same way." He sent a long, measuring look around at his gathered black dogs. All of the living ones crouched down a little lower when their master's glance fell on them. The undead ones simply stared back with fiery, unreadable eyes. When he lifted a hand, half a dozen of his black dogs began to edge forward.

Alejandro, snarling with incredulous fury, melted into the change, and only then did Natividad understand that Vonhausel meant to kill him right now, right this moment: Vonhausel meant to kill him and then call his shadow back and put it back in the body. He was going to *kill* Alejandro, but he wasn't going to *leave* him dead. She darted forward and sideways and snatched up her *aparato* from where it had lain, disregarded, since Vonhausel's return from the fell dark.

No one stopped her, maybe because they were distracted by Alejandro or maybe just because they didn't care what she did. She might not remember everything the way she should, but she was Mamá's daughter, and she bent and drew a pentagram right in the ash with the tip of the *aparato*. It felt strange in her hands; she thought she could feel each of the mottled dark patches that had altered it, patches of rough warmth scattered across its cold smoothness. But she poured its remaining power into her pentagram anyway because the moonlight and starlight were so weak, here where the fires of the fell dark were so close to the ordinary world.

The pentagram came alight as she drew it. Natividad could feel the power in it before she even sent the light pressing outward against the surrounding darkness. The power felt strange, as the power of her mandala had felt strange: not weaker, but different. Its light was strange, too, dabbed and mottled with patches of shadow.

She almost thought she *did* remember Mamá making a pentagram sort of like this, or, well, not a *pentagram*. A spiral or a helix, something to draw the eyes of enemies inward. Mamá would have made a spiral to keep Vonhausel's attention focused on her and Papá, away from her children. But what else... What else might Mamá have meant her spiral to collect? Black dog shadows? Natividad almost thought Mamá had done something... *Papá* had helped her. Right at the last. When fighting wasn't enough, when a black dog couldn't do anything, Papá had done something else, or he'd tried to. Mamá had done something, something with Pure magic and *Papá's* shadow... Fire, fire in the dark, and the earth cracking open, and then blood, so much blood...

Alejandro crowded close to Natividad's pentagram, jostling her, putting the mottled light at his back. He snarled his defiance at them all, and Natividad lost the memory she had almost captured, and was glad. She felt sick with dread and grief.

Vonhausel shook his head, like a chiding adult faced with annoying children. *He* didn't seem afraid of the moonlight or the pentagram or the *aparato* Natividad had made or anything. He didn't even bother to slide into his black dog form, but walked forward in his human shape. The dull crimson glow from the smoldering fires and the broken earth surrounded him, clung to him, filled his eyes, and dripped from his fingers when he reached out toward Natividad. She cringed. She couldn't help it. Vonhausel was going to reach right through her pentagram, she knew it: nothing she'd done would even begin to slow him down. Alejandro was crouched, preparing to lunge at him, and he would kill her brother and then he'd do whatever he wanted to her. He'd said she would be *useful* to him...

Then a long, resonant howl that was almost a roar echoed and re-echoed through the night, and all of Vonhausel's black dogs lifted their heads, listening. Natividad, listening also, couldn't believe what she was sure she heard. But the howl echoed again, undeniable, until she had to believe it. Grayson Lanning and all the Dimilioc wolves had come after all.

16

Alejandro was astonished by the arrival of the Dimilioc wolves. He didn't understand it, but he didn't wait for the Dimilioc wolves to close with the black dogs of the shadow pack, either. He hurled himself straight at Vonhausel, who in his arrogance was still in his vulnerable human form. But Vonhausel only gave way before his first raking blow, and though Alejandro's claws ripped right across his belly, his shadow roiled around him and his wounds closed immediately. Vonhausel did not have to use the *cambio de cuerpo* to get his shadow to carry away his injuries; his shadow could just take them away as they were dealt. Alejandro had never fought anything that could not be wounded. It was like fighting a vampire, only worse. Even the strongest of the vampires and their blood kin had been vulnerable to a black dog's determined attack.

Nor was Vonhausel going to stop at merely showing off his control over his shadow: he was now allowing himself to slide into the *cambio* after all. His change was almost as swift and effortless as Ezekiel's, and from the vicious ferocity of his smile as he changed, he intended to enjoy the blood and death of the Dimilioc wolves, and then enjoy putting their shadows back in their dead bodies. That terrible smile lingered longest, because Vonhausel's head and face changed last. It was utterly grotesque, that human head and face, changing but still recognizable, on the brutal black dog body. He lunged forward even before he was all the way changed, his jaw lengthening into a muzzle as he leaped, jet-black fangs glinting in the ruddy light of the low-smoldering fires. Alejandro leaped away.

Shots cracked out, one-two-three and then two more in quick succession, and Vonhausel staggered, fell, rolled, and was up on his feet again at once, and rushing now at Natividad. Alejandro lunged, crashed into him, bore him to the ground with weight and speed. He slashed, trying to tear out Vonhausel's throat – surely that would at least slow him down – but his fangs only raked his enemy's shoulder, and Vonhausel was both stronger and faster. His jaws closed on Alejandro's foreleg, crushing as well as tearing, and his claws ripped across Alejandro's side and flank. Now Alejandro only wanted to get away, get clear – his shadow, furious, wanted to press the attack but did not dare. Under the pressure of that conflict, all Alejandro's rage and fear was transmuted to a furious desire for murder and destruction. Alejandro fought to break away from Vonhausel, but he also had to fight his own shadow, and knew all the time that he was losing both battles.

Then Keziah dropped from above as though she had simply appeared out of air and darkness. She pounced like a great cat on Vonhausel, ripping with fangs and claws at his neck and face and shoulders. He whirled, trying to shake her loose, but she had her claws set fast and did not lose her grip. She had leaped down from the remnants of the church; Alejandro understood that after the first instant. He could not imagine how she had got around all the enemy black dogs and up onto the jumbled timbers and stones, but he was desperately glad for her appearance. He had forgotten that she would be here, hidden; that she must have come here before Natividad had even arrived; that she could call Dimilioc with the phone he himself had given her. Though he was still astonished Grayson had brought his wolves against Vonhausel.

Natividad, ducking low, darted from the relative safety of her pentagram to throw her arms around his neck. Straightening into human form, half blind and nearly wordless from the *cambio*, he put his arm around his sister's shoulders and let her guide him, as quickly as he could move, back toward the pentagram. His arm ached even after the change, so he knew the bone had been badly broken; no guessing how long the limb would be weak. His side hurt, too, where Vonhausel's claws had torn at him.

Once safe – safer – in Natividad's pentagram, it was possible to understand a little more of the ongoing battle. Like any black dog, Alejandro loved to fight and kill – but not in a battle like this one, against creatures that weren't exactly black dogs and couldn't be killed. All the Dimilioc wolves were battling such creatures.

Grayson Lanning fought the dead corpse of his brother, but could neither injure him nor force down the shadow possessing the corpse. But he held his own, and at least he faced no other immediate enemies. This was not the case for Ezekiel, fighting the shadow-creature who had been Zachariah. The *verdugo* was hard pressed by several other black dogs also, including another of the undead creatures who could not be wounded.

Ezekiel flickered back and forth between human and black dog forms with his usual fluidity. If facing his dead uncle horrified him, the horror didn't translate to any loss of speed or deadliness: as Alejandro watched, the *verdugo* ducked his head and chopped sideways, catching and crushing his opponent's foot in his powerful jaws and nearly wrenching off the whole limb with a powerful shake of his head. Not even the shadow-possessed Zachariah could ignore so serious an injury, withdrawing step by lame step. But there were more of Vonhausel's black dogs to prevent Ezekiel from pressing his advantage against Zachariah or attacking Vonhausel.

Ethan hurtled out of the dark to slash left and right at Ezekiel's living enemies, then fell back to defend the *verdugo's* left flank from a shadow-possessed black dog who had not, thankfully, ever been a Dimilioc wolf. But even with that support Ezekiel could press forward only slowly toward his target – clearly he was trying to reach Vonhausel and just as clearly, embattled as he was, he was not going to be able to close with the master of the shadow pack unless Vonhausel allowed it. Which he was not going to.

Vonhausel had thrown Keziah from his back and stalked her, now; Keziah evaded his attack by retreating toward Ezekiel, then whirled to face black dogs pressing the *verdugo* from the right – at least those seemed to be ordinary black dogs who could be killed. Alejandro hadn't seen Amira anywhere near when Keziah had struck at Vonhausel, but the little female black dog was with Keziah now, and no enemy seemed able to get through their defense. For the first time, it seemed possible that Ezekiel might reach Vonhausel – but Vonhausel was not staying to meet him, but racing away, back up onto the tumbled wreckage of the church.

Thaddeus Williams, half changed, his silver blade in one clawed hand, huge even among the crowd of ordinarily massive black dogs, had meanwhile been fighting half a dozen enemies, not quite on his own: the Dimilioc wolves had brought Cass Pearson along with them. The slim little shifter seemed no match for the much bigger black dogs, but she was wickedly quick and savage, and entirely fearless – Alejandro saw her slice her claws across the throat of an enemy black dog twice her size, then spin to snap at the face of another. She leaped away from her enemy's return strike and darted forward to slash at the rear legs of one of Thaddeus's opponents, trying to hamstring him. *That* injury would certainly challenge a black dog's healing ability, but her attack was even more effective than Alejandro had expected, because when the black dog whirled to face her, Thaddeus lunged forward, ripped his knife across the black dog's throat, tore his head off and threw it like a missile, thirty feet or more, to smash into one of the shadow black dogs fighting Ezekiel. Alejandro was certain – almost certain – that actual beheading was something that not even Vonhausel could repair.

And all the time, the *crack-crack-crack* of rifle fire went on: how Grayson had got humans here from the Dimilioc house so fast was a mystery, but however he had managed it, the gunmen were firing all the time. Dimilioc might almost have brought twice the number of black wolves to this battle – Alejandro couldn't believe how *enorme* a difference the gunmen made. One after another of Vonhausel's black dogs went down howling, the silver bullets leaving smoking tracks through their bodies.

If all the enemies had been ordinary black dogs, that would have surely been enough to shift the battle in Dimilioc's favor. But the silver didn't work as it should have on Vonhausel's dead-shadow black dogs. Alejandro saw one bullet after another strike Zachariah, strike Harrison, strike another of the shadow-possessed black dogs. But the undead black dogs did not fall. They might stumble or hesitate. But then they pressed forward again. Black dogs couldn't do that; vampires could not have done that. But these creatures could.

Alejandro wished that the Dimilioc Master or the executioner would do what Thaddeus had done: tear off their enemies' heads, or at least limbs – inflict damage which would actually *count*. But the press of fighting was too intense and they couldn't. It amazed Alejandro that the Dimilioc wolves continued to fight, that they had come here at all – that they did not retreat. They must have recognized now that they would all die here. Unless they could kill Vonhausel before they were all overwhelmed and dragged down. And Vonhausel was staying far away from any enemy who might kill him.

"I'll go," Alejandro said, barely aware he'd spoken aloud. "I'll help Ethan, help them all get Ezekiel clear. If the rest of us can just get him clear of those black dogs and let him reach Vonhausel–"

"No!" Natividad said sharply. She was up on her toes, her eyes brilliant with shock and terror. She was staring at Vonhausel, who had bent to do something to one of his freshly killed black dogs. It shook its head and rolled to its feet. So fast. Vonhausel had caught a shadow to possess that dead black dog so *fast*. Alejandro started to leave the pentagram, heading toward the wild tangle of combat surrounding Ezekiel.

Natividad gripped Alejandro's arm hard. Alejandro hesitated. He was losing language; he couldn't frame an argument in either English or Spanish. But he *had* to go; obviously Dimilioc needed all its black wolves for this battle. He shook himself free of his sister's grip, calling his shadow up, inviting the *cambio*. The lingering weakness of his recently broken limb was not good, but if Ezekiel could still fight, so could he–

"No!" Natividad said again. She caught Alejandro's arm again, this time with both her hands. "Alejandro, no, you'll just get killed and it won't make any difference anyway!"

Her words went past Alejandro like wind in the leaves. He heard her and knew she was upset, but he would have had to stop and think hard to make sense of what she had said. And there was no time for that. He could see another of the undead black dogs closing on Ezekiel, and now another undead black dog had joined Harrison, and what if *Grayson* was killed? It didn't bear thinking on, and yet it could happen, and Alejandro just stood here like an ordinary helpless human...

Vonhausel himself, in black dog form, was standing over the body of yet another of his own black dogs. He merely beckoned to it, and that dead black dog got to its feet, looking around with burning eyes that contained no trace of humanity. It shook itself and headed for Ezekiel. Worse, toward the periphery of the battle, Alejandro could see black dogs heading out into the night – going, he was sure, to stalk the men with the guns. If Dimilioc lost the supporting fire of the gunmen, the battle would be over, the slaughter of the remaining Dimilioc wolves merely a formality.

There was nothing he could do that could change what was going to happen. But he would fight anyway. He stepped toward the edge of her pentagram, hauling Natividad with him, his bones broadening, his arms contorting into the powerful forelimbs of the black dog.

"It's not Vonhausel who matters," Natividad cried in his ear. "Alejandro! It's not *Vonhausel* who matters, it's his *magic*. Stop, will you, and listen to me! *Stop!*"

The desperation in her voice dragged Alejandro to a halt despite himself. He tilted his head, staring at his sister in impatient anger. The meaning of her words gradually came clear to him – or at least the meaning of each word in turn. She was speaking in Spanish, which helped a little. But what she actually meant, he did not know.

Releasing him, Natividad waved her *aparato* under his nose. There were traces of his silver knife in the thing – the knife itself might have been useful, but Alejandro had no idea what Natividad meant to do with this indistinct tool that seemed more a dense glowing mist than a knife. Though a glowing mist mottled with blurred patches of darkness, which seemed very strange for a work of Pure magic.

"I've figured it out! I *remember!* I think I do! I think I've figured it out!" his sister shouted at him, still in Spanish. "Did you hear what Vonhausel said? Look what he did to this! *Look* at it! It's light and shadow both! Like my mandala, do you see? And Mamá said that, about making darkness cooperate with light! I remember what she did, I remember her *doing* it, I didn't understand, but now I do! I can *use* this, I think I can, I think I see how. It was Papá who helped her, at least he tried to, only he couldn't reach her, but I know what she tried to do, I think I know, I'm sure I do! 'Jandro, listen! You have to help me! *Trust* me!"

Alejandro stared at her. He longed for fighting and blood and death... but Natividad seemed so sure. He had tried so hard to keep her safe, but she had not come to this place tonight to be *safe*. He could not protect her, but she was not looking for protection. Natividad wasn't asking for *rescue*, but for help. For help *doing* something.

And Alejandro found that he did trust her. He wanted to help her do whatever she had thought of to do, but he had no idea how he could. The kind of magic she did was for the Pure, not for black dogs.

"I need your shadow!" Natividad cried, half command and half plea. "I need your shadow, 'Jandro! I don't think... I think it won't... I'm pretty sure I can... If I can't – but I have to have it. *Please*, 'Jandro!"

Alejandro had no idea what his sister was trying to say. Except that she wanted to do something with or to his black dog shadow. This seemed impossible. But she sounded very urgent. He crouched down and stared at her, waiting. But then for a long moment, it seemed she would do nothing after all. She was afraid – afraid of him, he thought at first; then he realized that she was afraid of what she meant to do, afraid of hurting him, maybe afraid that what she needed to do might even kill him. Fury and terror and a strange wild grief tangled inside of him, but though the anger was only anger, he did not understand the grief.

Then he did. It was grief for Natividad, who might kill him by what she did and then feel the horror of that for the rest of her life; and it was also grief for Dimilioc, which would surely be destroyed in a very few minutes if the magic she worked didn't succeed. He wanted to tell her – he wanted to say – he did not know what; his mouth was a black dog's savage muzzle, incapable of framing human words, and anyway he no longer possessed any clear command of language. But he turned his head aside, offering Natividad his throat.

She caught a sobbing breath, laid one hand on his massive heavy-jawed face, and stabbed him at the base of the throat with the *aparato* she had made, with the part of it that had been a knife. Alejandro was only just able to turn his instinctive leap away into an abortive twitch, and reduce his equally instinctive snap to a ferocious snarl. Natividad utterly ignored her own danger. She twisted the *aparato* and jerked it back out.

She had stabbed Alejandro at the base of his thick black-dog neck, which should have been a very dangerous wound because the knife was silver, only of course it was the knife she had blooded for him. But the *aparato* was not exactly a knife anymore, not really like a knife at all, and the injury it dealt was not exactly a normal injury. Neither blood nor ichor flowed where it had stabbed into him. The injury hurt; it burned, only not exactly, because the burn was cold instead of hot.

When Natividad jerked out the *aparato*, it felt to Alejandro as though all the blood and fire in him was torn out with it. Cold struck inward through his body, threaded through all his veins, froze him from the inside out. Alejandro felt his bones turn to ice. He groaned, folding to the ground – he was in his human shape again, though he had not even realized he was changing. He was wearing jeans and a T-shirt, but neither protected him from the horrifying cold. He could not speak. He could not move.

But he saw his sister leap to her feet, silver mist and black shadows trailing like water from her fingers. He knew she had somehow taken his shadow. She was doing something with it, braiding her light and his shadow together into a thick rope that sparkled and flashed and dripped with darkness, whirling this over her head and casting it up and out, like a *vaquero* with a lariat, so that it twisted as it rose and then settled as a huge loop, broadening as it fell, broadening far more than seemed reasonable, so that by the time it fell, it encompassed half the town and the whole surging pack of embattled black dogs.

Then she knelt down by Alejandro, her hand warm on his cheek. She was weeping, he realized. She thought maybe she had killed him, and he wanted to tell her he was alright, but though the words were there on his tongue, he could not make his numb mouth make the sounds. But he was shaking with cold, so she must have realized he still lived. She put one slim arm around him, helping him sit. So then they sat together, shaking with cold and fear, and watching to see what exactly would happen.

Natividad's magic did not seem, in that first moment, to touch the true black dogs. But all across the battleground, the moon-bound shifters were suddenly forced into human shape. Alejandro saw it with Cass Pearson first: the little shifter was fighting with Keziah and Amira, the trio supported by Thaddeus on one side and Ethan on the other. Cassie held her place in the trio with silent, vicious intensity, the tight teamwork keeping her alive when so many other shifters had been killed. But when her corrupted shadow was torn out of her by the shadowed circle Natividad had flung around them all, she staggered abruptly into human form and stood, fragile and dazed and helpless, in the midst of the battling black dogs.

With a kindness that Alejandro would never have expected, and with startling aplomb, as though shifters that suddenly turned human during the full moon were perfectly ordinary, Keziah caught the girl's arm and flung her out of the way, against the shelter of a broken wall. Many of the other shifters were immediately killed by the black dogs who surrounded them. Only the black dogs were then distracted by the collapse of one shadow-possessed undead black dog, and then another. And another.

The shifters were just an accident. Something about the magic that corrupted their shadows must be like the horror Vonhausel had made of dead black dogs, because really those undead black dogs had been Natividad's target all along. Alejandro understood this at last, and then was ashamed it had taken him so long to grasp it. She had woven her *aparato* with his shadow and made both together into a *literal* tool for catching shadows. The shadows of the living black dogs must be too much a part of them to be torn away, but somehow Natividad's *aparato* was ripping the shadows away from Vonhausel's dead black dogs. The Zachariah-creature collapsed almost last, a heartbeat before it might have finally torn Ezekiel in half, and Ezekiel, at that moment in human form, stared down at his uncle's body without expression. Everything had paused, all the combatants hesitating in wary disbelief as they tried to understand what had happened and what it meant.

Vonhausel himself, in human form, turned in a circle, staring around in outraged dismay. Alejandro saw the exact moment when he realized who had done this to him. He turned to stare across the broken ruins of the town at Natividad, who straightened her shoulders and returned his stare. Alejandro was briefly afraid Vonhausel would rush across the field of battle and attack her.

But Vonhausel did not come. He could not. He, like all the black dogs in which he had invested shadows, was actually dead. Alejandro saw him realize this, too, and what it meant. He flung back his head and stretched out his hands to the dark, to the crimson fires that still smoldered through the town and in the depths of the shattered earth. He might have done something, worked some corrupted magic, if he had had time. But he did not have time. He lost his shadow last of all the dead black dogs. But he lost it. Alejandro almost thought he could see the shadow tear itself free and disappear, or dissolve into the darkness – or maybe fall into the glowing chasm that gaped at Vonhausel's feet; he could not exactly tell. It almost seemed to somehow do all of those things at once. Vonhausel's body, left untenanted, collapsed slowly. There was no question about what happened to it. It fell into the break in the street and disappeared without a sound. The ruddy glow from the fires below flared up, dully crimson, and then went out, leaving only darkness.

Or not quite only darkness. In the east, beyond the ruined church, the first pale glimmer of the dawn shone across the winter sky, magically transmuting the smoke and ash of burning to silver and pearl.

Once they lost the unkillable shadow-possessed black dogs, and especially once they no longer had Malvern Vonhausel to drive and rule them, the remaining black dogs were after all nothing but strays. Alejandro was surprised, despite everything, to see how utterly overmatched they were by the Dimilioc wolves.

All of Vonhausel's black dogs now gave back, and back again, searching from side to side for a way to flee. But the circle Natividad had flung around them, of moonlight and silver and magic and Alejandro's black dog shadow, closed off all lines of retreat.

Alejandro sat on a half-burned timber, his arm around his sister's shoulders, and watched as the black dogs of Vonhausel's shadow pack forgot their advantage of numbers. As before, if they had supported one another, if they had fought together, then they might still have been able to defeat the Dimilioc wolves, especially as it seemed that the gunmen could not shoot through the shadowed circle. But fighting together clearly didn't occur to them at all. Alejandro watched, fascinated and disturbed, as the uncontrolled violence and treacherous nature of the black dogs drove them instead to turn on one another. Though he had been a black dog all his life, he could not at this moment exactly remember the way black dog instincts *felt*. He was uneasily conscious of the *locura,* the madness, to which those instincts now drove Vonhausel's strays.

Furious and panicked, one black dog would turn and fight to clear a way past his neighbors, even though there was no point to his efforts because no line of retreat existed. Even so, he would snap left and right, until a black dog stronger and more brutal than he drove him back – and then half the time this small fight would spark a savage melee that spread right through half the remaining black dogs.

Ezekiel drove all this violence. He deliberately threatened the remaining strays, one and then another, touching off small, vicious conflicts within each group. They were too afraid of him to face him, even all of them together, and so Ezekiel shaped the violence and more or less directed it, prodding the black dogs to defeat themselves. To be fair, Ezekiel did look very dangerous, even now. He showed no sign of weakness save for a very slight catch in his gait when he turned to the left. Even so, Alejandro would have been ashamed to let anyone manipulate him that way. He would have been ashamed of that when he was a child. But only a few of these black dog strays resisted the *verdugo's* threats, staying quiet and still and well away from their fellows, refusing to meet any threat or return any insult, only waiting to see what chance might come to escape. Alejandro did not expect they would find such a chance, but at least they showed decent control.

It was very strange to watch all this and feel only weariness. He was not possessed by burning rage, nor furious contempt, nor a hot desire for blood and violence. He felt empty. Peaceful. This must be the part of himself that was real, that was *him*. The part that was still here when the black dog shadow was gone. He had fought all his life to get a space narrow as a knife-blade between himself and his shadow, to understand what *he* was. All his life, he had wished to know what it would be like to be ordinary, to be human.

Now his shadow was gone, and he *was* human and ordinary, and he found he *hated* the cold and empty peace that had replaced his shadow. There was nothing in it to fight against, and without that struggle, he couldn't catch his balance. He kept reaching after the anger he *ought* to feel, and there was *nothing there*. He felt as though some power had reached into his mind and heart and soul and pithed him like a hollow reed. It felt like the winter wind could blow right through him. Anger was hot. He had never in his life really felt the cold. Now he felt as though he might never be warm again.

Alejandro slid a glance at his sister. She leaned against his side. Her head rested against his shoulder. He wondered what it would be like when she let go of her shadowed circle, released her light and magic. Would his shadow force itself back into his mind and heart and soul, or would it disappear into the fell dark after all the other freed shadows? And if it was lost into the dark, what would that do to him? He thought most likely if that happened he would either cease to be a black dog or die, and he wasn't sure which of those possibilities seemed worse.

Grayson came back toward the center of the shadowed circle, toward Natividad. He did not even glance at Ezekiel. But his *verdugo* nevertheless left off fomenting violence among the thinned ranks of the enemy and came to join him. Behind him, the remaining black dogs gradually settled. Even now there were at least a dozen left, but they seemed very few after the outnumbered hopelessness of the battle.

Thaddeus, now fully in his black dog form, had been resting quietly beside the unconscious Cass Pearson, but turned his head to watch the Master. Ethan limped slowly after Grayson, too lame to conceal his injury. Keziah, who had been lying on the rubble of the church, glanced at Amira, who was clearly hurt but unable, at the moment, to drive back her shadow and force it to carry away her injuries. Then Keziah abruptly got to her feet and slid down toward her little sister. Jagged fragments of stone and brick and splinters of broken timbers showered around her, then she allowed Amira to lean on her as they came down to join the others.

Grayson came to Natividad, shifting out of his black dog form so that when he reached her he was once again in his fully human shape. The Master showed no trace of injury, though he had not entirely shed the black aura of violence or the scents of smoke and burning. He gazed at Alejandro for a long, thoughtful moment. Alejandro, shivering with cold like any ordinary human, stared back at him for a beat before he remembered to look down. It felt very strange to have to *remember* to look away. He had never really understood how ordinary humans could be so dangerously slow to respond to black dog threats. It was strange and unpleasant, like a kind of blindness.

Grayson removed his jacket and handed it to Alejandro without comment. Surprised – he had not expected the Master to realize that he was cold, far less to care – Alejandro took the jacket and shrugged it on. The jacket, or maybe the unexpected kindness, made the cold a little more bearable. Maybe in time – in a lot of time – he could learn to tolerate the cold emptiness inside too, even if he never got his shadow back. He shuddered, and could not tell whether it was from the cold outside or the cold within.

"This is not precisely what I expected, when Keziah told me what Vonhausel had done with our dead," Grayson said to Natividad. "Nor when she told me what you had done to Vonhausel, nor when she warned me your magic had failed. I see that last warning was mistaken." He paused, then asked, "You can release this magic you have made here? You can undo it?"

The Master's heavy voice had a dark-edged resonance to it that seemed more than weariness or anger. Alejandro involuntarily glanced up at him again. Was this how ordinary humans heard black dogs all the time? Maybe not, maybe it was something else, something about this night or the shadowed circle or about Grayson himself: if this was how black dogs sounded to humans, how could a black dog ever pass unnoticed among them?

"Yes," Natividad answered. Her voice was small and weary and did not echo with any surprising resonance. She didn't avoid looking the Master in the face; it obviously didn't occur to her that she ought to. "Yes. I think so. I'm pretty sure. Whenever you like."

Grayson nodded. There was a world of weariness in that

nod, but no visible anger. Turning, the Master crossed his arms over his chest and stared around at the black dogs enclosed in Natividad's circle. Now, at last, with so few enemies remaining and all of those defeated and afraid, Grayson could use the weight of his powerful shadow to roll all of theirs at once under and down. He did that. Alejandro didn't – couldn't – feel it. Not now. But he knew what the Master had done because all around the circle, Vonhausel's black dogs shuddered and cried out, their bodies contorting and twisting as they were forced back into human shape.

Most of the Dimilioc wolves shifted as well, but smoothly: Grayson wasn't forcing any of his own wolves into the *cambio de cuerpo,* only helping those who wanted to change. Even Ezekiel shifted, which from him was probably an expression of disdain for all their remaining enemies. He was looking at Natividad, his expression odd. After a moment, he said, "Brave little kitten, aren't you? Don't you know daring single-handed assassinations are my job?"

Natividad blinked at him, wordless. But after a moment, she smiled.

Only Keziah did not change. She leaped up to stretch out, contemptuously relaxed, along a broad timber above Grayson's head – as disdainful, and nearly as dangerous, as Ezekiel. Thaddeus pulled himself gradually into human form, seeming nearly as big as a man as he was as a black dog. He lifted Cass Pearson in his arms with no sign of effort and came to lay her down near Natividad's feet. In her proper shape, the girl was fine boned and fragile, with corn-silk hair. Alejandro stared at her. Her exquisite delicacy was an entirely different order of beauty from Keziah's burning splendor. The human girl was unconscious, but her breathing looked steady. Alejandro couldn't tell about her shadow. Maybe she would be alright.

All but one of Vonhausel's black dogs threw themselves to their knees or all the way down to their bellies, pressing their faces against the broken pavement. The man who stayed on his feet had been the quietest black dog, one with good control even after Vonhausel's death and the turn of the battle. He had accepted the forced change without resistance. Now he was a tall man with slender hands, a high-boned face, and close-cropped dark hair outlining his skull. He stood very still for a long moment, then walked slowly toward Grayson.

No. Not toward Grayson. Toward Natividad. She pulled herself away from Alejandro and stared at the stranger, not exactly alarmed, but wary. But then she glanced up at Grayson, then at Ezekiel, and relaxed again.

The black dog dropped to one knee a few feet from them, but he spoke to Natividad rather than the Master. "Good job killing that bastard. That's one good thing to come out of all this." His tone was light and almost conversational. He even ignored Ezekiel, who had stepped around behind him. He spoke quietly, his vowels soft and round in an accent Alejandro did not recognize. He paused, then shrugged. "I just wanted to say that."

"It wasn't just me–" said Natividad.

The black dog shrugged again. "Near enough."

"Étienne Lumondiere," said Grayson.

The black dog turned to Grayson. He did not seem surprised to be addressed by name. Lumondiere... Alejandro had thought all the Lumondiere black wolves gone into the fell dark, but this one obviously had lived through the war. Only to come, somehow, into Vonhausel's grip, until Natividad had freed him. Now the Frenchman lowered his gaze and waited to hear what the Dimilioc Master would say.

"You are far out of your usual territory," Grayson observed.

"Yes," said the black dog, in a calm, amused tone which Alejandro couldn't help but admire. "Yes, and little enough profit I've had from my travels. If I were, by some remarkable chance, able to go home, I think I would never again leave." He bowed his head low, fixing his gaze on the broken pavement at Grayson's feet.

"You did not come here intending to join Malvern Vonhausel?"

The black dog shrugged. "I came to America to try to find the scattered remnants of my House – several Lumondiere wolves came here during the war. I cannot say what became of the others, but I..." He opened his hands. "As you see. Joining Vonhausel was... Actually, that was a surprise to me."

Grayson's expression didn't change, yet he somehow looked faintly amused. He looked at Ezekiel, lifting one eyebrow in query.

Ezekiel glanced at Natividad, a look Alejandro couldn't interpret. Then he shrugged. "Spare them all, if you like. It doesn't make any difference to me. I can always kill them later."

"Let go of your magic," Grayson told Natividad. "Let it go, and we will all go home."

"Oh, yes, please!" Natividad said longingly. But then she looked anxiously at Alejandro, reaching to pat his arm. "I can... I have to... But you – I never wanted to take away your shadow, 'Jandro, and then put it *back*. That's awful. I'm sorry..."

Alejandro touched her cheek. "It's alright. Either way. *Verdaderamente*."

She gazed into his face for another moment. Then at last she tried to smile, closed her eyes and did something to the shadowed circle that surrounded them all. It dissolved into the air, silver moonlight and black shadow and little flickers of crimson fire. Alejandro threw his head back as the darkness came across his sight; fire-edged shadows smothered him, he could not breathe, he was falling, he would die... His sister's hand gripped his, one point of reference in the dark. Another hand, painfully strong, closed on his shoulder... The darkness shifted around him and snapped into focus with a shock that was almost but not quite physical. He drew a breath filled with familiar heat and anger, and recognized himself at last, his *self* defined by the constant need to draw the border between himself and his shadow, and more clearly than ever by his shadow's absence.

Grayson looked at him closely. Then, frowning, he let him go and stepped back, his expression closed and neutral. "Good," he said to Natividad, and walked away.

"Alejandro..." Natividad said tentatively, not quite a question.

"Yes," said Alejandro. He got to his feet, and lifted his sister to hers with easy, familiar strength.

17

Natividad didn't know which surprised her more: that Grayson should think for one minute about sparing the rest of Vonhausel's black dogs or that Ezekiel shouldn't care one way or the other. She had time to think about it during the long ride back to the Dimilioc house, though, and she decided that really neither reaction should have surprised her. Grayson had already made it very clear that he wanted to recruit a lot more black dogs, and probably Ezekiel thought she wouldn't like watching him slaughter them. Or maybe he was just too tired to care. Anyway, he was totally right: he really could kill them all later. Probably he would kill some of them. They couldn't all be from a civilized House like Étienne Lumondiere.

Of the rest, she suspected that Thaddeus approved of Grayson's decision, but Keziah definitely did not. She had said so straight out, which, Natividad had decided, was one thing Grayson actually liked about the Saudi girl – that she would argue with him. She said that guarding prisoners was stupid, they were all tired; what was the point of slaughtering their enemies at Dimilioc where they would have to actually dig graves, or else build a huge bonfire and either way it was too much trouble; they should kill them all now and throw the bodies into the chasm Vonhausel had opened in the earth, that was a fitting end for the strays he'd ruled. But Grayson didn't change his mind, and at last Keziah shrugged angrily and said why should she care, as long as *she* didn't have to bury the corpses later, but if any of the black dogs gave *her* a moment's trouble on the way back to Dimilioc, she'd just kill him right then and throw his body into the snow and it could wait for spring to rot.

That was certainly clear enough, and maybe it was why Grayson gave Keziah and not Ezekiel charge of the prisoners on the way back. They were all bound in silver, and if it burned them, no one much cared. They wouldn't have to wear it long, at least. They rode in a bus, but not the one Natividad and everybody else occupied. The townspeople Grayson had brought to the battle mostly did not come back to Dimilioc at all, now that it was so much safer in town, but Sheriff Pearson rode back with them, to be near his daughter. Cassie had changed again, which was too bad. The shadows of the undead black dogs were all the way gone, Natividad was sure of that, but the shifter's corrupted shadow had come back up to its living body when Natividad had let go of her magic. Thaddeus sat next to Cassie, one broad hand gripping the back of her neck, preventing her from attacking her father or anyone else. But she seemed less vicious now, perhaps because she had fought enough to satiate even her shadow, or perhaps because of the brief respite from it that Natividad's magic had given her.

Natividad sat between her twin and Alejandro. She was

still shivering with reaction to everything. It was hard to believe that they were really safe and that this time no black dogs would run out of the forest to attack them. The bright sun and cloudless sky helped with that. So did Miguel. Her twin didn't ask her any questions or try to say anything comforting. He told her instead about the way it felt to cling to a black dog as it raced through the forest, the rushing dark and cold wind, the bunch and spring of muscles under him, so much more fluid and strange than the feel of riding a saddled pony. The bulk and heat of the black dog and the way he'd clung so tight to Thaddeus's shaggy pelt that his fingers had cramped.

That was what Natividad wanted: harmless chatter that didn't grate along nerves still raw from... from everything. She could see the flow of Miguel's talk working on Alejandro, too, so that he could slowly relax. The sharp whiplash changes he'd undergone, from black dog to nearly human and then back again, had obviously confused and upset him.

And she almost thought... She wasn't sure, but she almost thought maybe a tiny bit of her Pure magic might have been tangled and caught in his shadow. That would confuse any black dog. She didn't say anything about it. She wasn't sure, anyway. What she had done to him must be hard enough for a black dog to cope with all by itself, and anyway, she really wasn't sure. At last he managed to smile. Not a very good smile, but something to start with. So, she felt better after that.

She had been so glad her use of his shadow hadn't killed Alejandro that she hadn't worried about what *other* effects her magic might have caused until now, when she finally saw the hidden confusion in his eyes. *Now* she worried, but now it was too late, and anyway she had no idea what she might have done differently. At least now everyone was safe. Alejandro could rest and recover. He *was* safe. She was sure that even a trace of Pure magic left behind in his shadow wouldn't actually hurt him. Almost sure.

So, he was fine. *Everyone* was fine. So, that was reason to be really glad. And she was. Mostly. She never thought about killing Vonhausel. Killing him twice, seeing him fall – she didn't think about it. Though refusing to think about things... She kind of realized now how that had stopped her remembering what Mamá had taught her there at the... at the end. About black dog shadows and Pure magic. She wasn't sure now how much of that she sort of remembered and how much she had figured out on her own.

Once they were finally back at Dimilioc – she seemed always to be coming back to Dimilioc, usually after something awful had happened – once the black dog strays were safely locked up in that awful prison room of old Thos Korte's and everyone else cleaned up and been fed breakfast, lots of good things happened. Cass Pearson, released at last from the moon's grip as the new day dawned, woke up in her proper human body, so she could go back to her father for a little while. She would have to begin learning how to control her shadow, so Natividad supposed she would be around Dimilioc a lot for the next few weeks.

And Lewis might have suffered a lot of damage, but now all the black dogs were gone, the townspeople could go back and start fixing everything. Father McClanahan hugged Natividad before he climbed on the bus to leave and promised her they'd even rebuild the church, reconsecrating every stone as it was laid back in place. So, that was alright.

And, yes, a lot of people had died, but not as many as they'd all thought because it turned out a lot of people had managed to hide in basements and things, and now the final battle of the war really was over. They all hoped it was the final battle, anyway. They thought it was. Sheriff Pearson said they had special equipment to dig graves even in the frozen ground. The people of Lewis could lay their dead properly to rest and then go home and know it was *over*.

So, really, lots of good things. Natividad sat on her pink bed, hugging a frilly pillow and staring out her window at the cloudless sky. She was horribly tired. She sort of wanted to talk to Ezekiel, she sort of wanted to know if he really thought she'd been brave, or just stupid. Maybe if he thought she was brave, maybe that meant he really might like her as a person and not just as a girl who happened to be Pure. Unless he thought she was stupid.

Of course, he would be asleep. He'd said she could wake him up. Obviously that would be stupid and pointless.

She ought to pull the curtains shut and burrow right down into this bed and pull the pink coverlet over her head and sleep for about thirty hours. She wanted to. Miguel was safe in his room and Alejandro was safe in his, they were probably already asleep, and everything was fine. Only, although Natividad was desperately tired, she knew she couldn't sleep.

And if the aftermath of the battle was so bad for her… she wondered about Grayson. He'd lost so much. More than anybody else. Everything, nearly. And she'd so nearly pulled him into a battle where he'd have lost everything else. He hadn't said a word about it. She knew he wouldn't. Of course, everything had turned out alright, but that was mostly luck.

She knew exactly where he would be now. He would be alone. More alone than anybody else in the house. She remembered – it seemed like a long time ago – thinking that about Ezekiel when she'd first seen him, but really it was true of Grayson. Who would both want to intrude on the Master's privacy and dare to? Well, Ezekiel, maybe. But exhausted black dogs, even friends, didn't usually dare seek each other out, lest their control slip. And Ezekiel and Grayson were allies, but they weren't exactly friends.

Natividad jumped out of her pink frilly bed before she could change her mind, and went to find something clean to wear.

She found Grayson, not exactly to her surprise, in the big room with the fireplace. Alone, so she had been right about that. She had only known him... had it really been less than a week? That was... That was really unbelievable.

Grayson didn't glance around at Natividad. He was sitting in one of the big chairs, his hands resting on his thighs. He was staring into the fire. To Natividad, he didn't look as though he was exactly worried. Or troubled – exactly. But he had lit a fire in the big fireplace; he, who could not be cold. He had lit it for comfort, then. Natividad hoped it comforted him. She doubted it could.

She walked across the room and, as she had the other time, sat down silently on the floor by his feet. She leaned her cheek against his knee, hoping to give him a measure of peace. Maybe she succeeded, because after a moment, he let his breath out in a long sigh and rested one of his broad hands on her hair.

She had not realized until that moment that she had stopped being even a little bit afraid of Grayson. That was kind of a surprise. She wondered when it had happened. Then she stopped thinking about it and just settled herself into the quiet stillness that was part of being Pure – so much a part that even all the violence and death of the past days hadn't broken it.

That was how Ezekiel found them, when he opened the door and stepped into the room.

At first Natividad didn't realize how it might look to him. Even after the warning stillness, brilliant with tension and danger, made her lift her head and turn to look at him, even when she saw Ezekiel's eyes change from winter blue to pale flame-gold, she didn't understand immediately. Then she figured it out, but she still didn't understand just how bad a problem they had. Of course she knew that Ezekiel had been pressed far past any normal black dog's breaking point, but he wasn't a normal black dog and she hadn't realized that he, too, had a breaking point or that he might actually have reached it. Grayson, of course, knew both those things far better than she. That was why he was on his feet and tossing her away to safety, already halfway into his own change, when Ezekiel hurtled across the room and smashed into him.

Ezekiel had shifted so fast that he was already fully in his black dog shape when he hit Grayson. Even though Grayson was the more massive when fully shifted, when Ezekiel actually slammed into Grayson, he was much bigger than the half-changed Master – and he already had jet-black fangs and terrible claws, the better to rip out Grayson's throat or slash his spine into pieces. Which he was definitely trying to do, both, and he would have, too, except that Grayson shoved his half-human arm into Ezekiel's jaws as he went down, and then twisted and threw the other black dog half across the room with a powerful kick delivered with legs that were almost entirely the heavily muscled limbs of a black dog. Blood and black ichor sprayed across the carpet – both of them were injured – but Ezekiel twisted in midair, flickering from black dog to human and back again before he landed, shedding his injuries and launching himself once more at Grayson before the still-wounded Master had even regained his feet.

Natividad finally got enough of her breath back to scream, which was useless and stupid, except she distracted Ezekiel just enough that Grayson was able, barely, to meet his charge. So she screamed again, just in case it might actually help, but it didn't seem to: Ezekiel and Grayson crashed together and ripped at each other. Ezekiel was going to kill Grayson. Natividad knew there couldn't be any other outcome. The grief of it tore her apart – not only grief for Grayson, but for Dimilioc, which would never hold without the Master; and for Ezekiel, who would surely never recover from the knowledge of what he'd done.

Everything was so fast. She wasn't a black dog, she couldn't follow every move, but there was a brutal exchange of blows and afterward Grayson was down, with horrible gashes all across his chest and side, and Ezekiel was rearing above him. In the next instant he would plunge down with all his immense strength and weight and his terrible black claws would tear Grayson in half. Natividad knew he was going to do it and she screamed again, weeping as well, and this time her cry had a word in it, and the word she cried out was Grayson's name.

Alejandro slammed the door open and plunged into the room, with Thaddeus behind him – then they both froze in horror. But the embattled black wolves seemed somehow fallen into a vibrating stillness as well, which Natividad didn't understand: Ezekiel hadn't completed his kill after all, and didn't, and *still* didn't, and that first instant stretched into a full second, and then Grayson was up and using his superior size and weight to hurl Ezekiel off balance, and then their positions were somehow reversed because Ezekiel was the one down, and Grayson was the one with his powerful jaws closed around his opponent's throat. And Ezekiel *was* fighting then, but it was too late, Grayson had him, he was going to kill him – he was going to *kill* him, and he couldn't, he mustn't. Natividad was horrified at the idea that Ezekiel might die, but even worse, if Grayson killed Ezekiel, Natividad was sure he'd never recover. She screamed his name again, this time in a totally different kind of horror, and Grayson turned his burning eyes toward her. There was nothing human in those eyes, but he didn't close his terrible jaws.

And then Alejandro flung his shadow forward and across both Grayson and Ezekiel. Natividad felt it as a smothering darkness that wasn't exactly visible and a bodiless pressure that wasn't anything like weight but somehow forced both the Master and Ezekiel back into human form. It wasn't smooth this time, especially not for Ezekiel. The change was slow and shuddering for Grayson, but for Ezekiel it happened in a series of painful, twisting jolts and convulsions that was horrible to watch.

Grayson got to his feet, slowly, once they were both back in human form. He moved as though it hurt him and as though he didn't care who knew it. Ezekiel did not get up at all. He stayed down, braced on one elbow, his head low. The carpet where he lay was spattered now, like everything else in the room, with black ichor and red blood. He didn't look at Grayson. He didn't look at any of them.

"Cage," Grayson said, rasping, his voice not at all human. "Now." He turned a dangerous stare on Alejandro and Thaddeus. They both immediately dropped their eyes. He said harshly, "Once he is secure, leave him be. Is that clear? No black dog is to approach him." Then he looked away from them, his temper locked down so tight it almost hurt Natividad to watch him. "You," he said to her. "Come with me." He stalked away, not moving exactly like a normal human even now, and went through a door across the room.

Natividad threw her brother an urgent look, hardly knowing what she meant to convey, and ran after Grayson.

Grayson wanted calm. He wanted her to draw pentagrams on all the windows in his suite, especially his bedroom. Natividad had been curious about what Grayson's suite might tell her about him ever since she'd seen Ezekiel's. This was not the way she had meant to break into the Master's privacy, when she was distracted and anxious and stumbling with exhaustion and he was clinging to his control by a thread so tight she was afraid even to breathe too loudly. She was afraid for him, afraid that grief and anger might still lead him to fall into the terrible dark that always waited for black dogs. But, even so, she couldn't help but be interested.

The bedroom wasn't much like Ezekiel's. The suite wasn't. Where Ezekiel's rooms were Zen, Grayson's were very English. Or what Natividad thought of as English. All polished walnut and antique brass; tables with carved legs and chairs with ornate backs – all probably antique, not that she would know. In the bedroom, a rocking chair with an intricate border of fancy inlay around its worn cushions faced another of those big fireplaces, this one with a hearth of black granite. The bed, with an old-gold coverlet, had an intricately carved headboard and bedposts.

The heaviness of the furnishings and the richness of the colors might have made the suite seem close or oppressive, but the rooms were so big, with high vaulting ceilings, that they seemed instead luxurious and sort of… gracious, Natividad decided, was the word. She had not pictured rooms like these for the Dimilioc Master, but as soon as she saw them she knew they fit him. She wondered whether his wife had furnished these rooms, chosen the colors… They had probably been happy here.

And now his wife was gone, leaving the wrong kind of silence and emptiness. Natividad knew too much about that herself, but Grayson had lost so much more. She was happy to draw the signs for a different kind of silence. For peace. There were already signs on the windows: Stars of David, and, older, fainter traces of pentagrams like hers. And, even older than that, so old even Natividad could barely see them, mandalas – circles with crosses in them, but not a evenly quartered circle such as she was used to, but offset crosses more like the Christian symbol. But all the signs were alike, really. She could tell that when she brushed her hand across them. All of them were meant to bring peace. To quiet the stricken heart.

Natividad didn't mention the older signs. She drew her pentagrams one after another, fitting them in among the others, and set them alight with wishes for peace and acceptance, with the memory of sorrow and a wish for heart's ease. Drawing them brought *her* a measure of peace, at last; too much so, so that she was stumbling and yawning when she finished drawing her last pentagram on a bedroom window.

"Go to bed," Grayson told her when she was finished. His tone was curt, but no longer inhuman. No longer dangerous. Though he did not thank her, he touched her shoulder very lightly when she went past him. Natividad lifted her hand to rest on his for a moment, and looked briefly into his face before she remembered she shouldn't. But when he didn't seem offended, she didn't bother to lower her gaze.

To her, Grayson looked worn, tired. But she could not see anger in his face. "You go to bed, too," she said to him, and waited for his nod – curt, like his tone, but still not angry – before she left. She did not remember, later, finding her way back to her own room or climbing into her pink bed or falling asleep.

18

Natividad was not surprised that Grayson wanted her with him in the morning, when he went down to confront Ezekiel. Of course he wanted her there, for lots of reasons, which was fine because she wanted to be there anyway. She felt quite fiercely that she wouldn't have *allowed* Grayson to go down those stairs without her. But she didn't have to worry about it anyway, because there was a note waiting for her when she woke up.

It was late, after 8. That wasn't surprising, but even so she didn't take time for breakfast. She wasn't hungry anyway. She didn't exactly feel sick, but she was nervous enough that she didn't want anything to eat. But the note, signed with a strong angular "*G L*", said "*I will require your presence downstairs. Come find me when you are ready,*" in big blocky letters. So, that seemed to mean she had time to splash water on her face and dress carefully in her best and most grown-up blouse, one without any girlish lace or frills, and a plain brown skirt. She had time to put her hair up and find her pink crystal earrings. She looked at herself carefully in the mirror as she put the earrings in. The girl who looked back at her looked so much like Mamá... but her eyes were darker now, Natividad thought. Or maybe that was her memory of shadows and darkness.

She found Grayson not in the room with the fireplace, but in his own suite, in his study, seated in a big chair behind an ornate walnut desk. He was working, a pad of paper open on the desk and a thick pen of bone or ivory in his hand, but he put the pen down when she knocked gently on the doorframe. He looked tired, but not with the previous night's desperate on-the-edge exhaustion. He looked almost entirely human. His shadow, pooled beneath his chair, was very dense but also very quiet.

He shoved the pad away, looked her up and down without expression, nodded, and got to his feet. "You are well?"

"Yes, of course," Natividad assured him. "Um... you?"

Grayson gave her a scant nod.

"And, um... Ezekiel?"

"That, we shall have to determine."

Natividad nodded. "Only I meant, that is, you won't..."

"We shall have to determine," Grayson repeated tersely. He indicated with a gesture that she should proceed him back out to the public areas of the house.

Natividad took an obedient step backward, but she also said, "But..."

"Last night we all discovered the limits of our control. This morning we shall discover whether we have redrawn those limits. Your presence may be an asset – or, for Ezekiel, perhaps otherwise. We shall determine that." Grayson paused. Then he said, as gently as his deep voice could manage, "But nothing of this is your fault, Natividad. Nor anything of what will happen now."

Natividad knew that wasn't true. The Pure helped black dogs stay civilized, they helped black dogs keep the peace. If she couldn't do that, which was the most basic and important responsibility of the Pure... She *would* do it, though. She didn't say so. But she knew she couldn't bear it if Grayson let Ezekiel out of the cage and there was another fight. She was more and more nervous. She wanted to run down the stairs, see for herself how Ezekiel was this morning... but Grayson offered her his arm, so she had to take it and match his measured steps.

To her surprise, Alejandro was already downstairs. Grayson had said, "*No black dog is to approach him,*" but Alejandro had anyway. A tray of bacon and sweet pastries on the table by the cage provided an excuse. Kind of a thin one. She knew very well the real reason her brother had come down those stairs was that he, too, had thought maybe there might be another fight when Grayson opened the cage door. He lowered his gaze and backed away as Grayson led her down, trying hard to look unobtrusive and obedient and like he wasn't really there and certainly hadn't disobeyed Grayson's order, but he didn't make any move to leave. Grayson gave him a long, steady look, but to Natividad's relief said nothing.

Ezekiel looked... alright. He looked like he had been awake for a while. He was seated in the cage's one chair, one elbow propped on its plastic arm, his legs stretched out and his feet resting on the cot, which had been made with a care for precise corners and a wrinkle-free blanket. He managed to look not merely rested, but cool, neat, and assured. Natividad didn't believe that pose for a minute.

After one quick glance at Natividad, Ezekiel paid attention only to Grayson. And Grayson, after that one glowering stare at Alejandro, looked only at Ezekiel. The Master showed no expression, but Natividad felt the hard tension of his arm under her hand. He did not speak.

Ezekiel's mouth twisted with bitter amusement. After a moment that stretched out uncomfortably, he rose, took one step forward toward the bars, and dropped to one knee. He turned his head to offer Grayson his throat. "Master."

"Well?" said Grayson, his voice hard.

"I forgot myself," said Ezekiel, which was something that, Natividad knew, he meant literally: he had forgotten his human self and his shadow had broken his control. He went on, speaking slowly, "I thought I could endure anything." He glanced up at Natividad. "I forgot that you're too young and that spring has not yet come."

Natividad had no idea what she should say, or if she should say anything. Her throat ached. It was all hard and too much of it was her fault.

"It wasn't your fault," Ezekiel said to her, quietly, without a trace of mockery in his cool voice. He looked Grayson in the face, then bowed his head. "All the fault was mine. I know that. I pretended so hard that I have no limits, I didn't realize I had gone beyond them. I beg your pardon."

There was a little silence. Then Grayson said, a little less harshly, "You turned away from your kill. I am not mistaken in this."

Ezekiel glanced at Natividad once more, fleetingly. Then he again lowered his head. "That's so. So did you. I admit that surprised me." His mouth twisted again. "Not the only time recently I've been surprised."

Grayson didn't answer.

Ezekiel said, "You have warned me once or twice that arrogance is my besetting sin. I don't argue it. I beg your pardon, Master."

"Dimilioc needs your strength and your skill."

Ezekiel bent his head a degree lower, acknowledging this.

"But that isn't why I held back from the kill," Grayson added. His heavy, deliberate voice added emphasis to the words. He stopped, regarding Ezekiel in silence.

But at this Ezekiel finally brought his head up to meet the Master's eyes. They stared at one another for a long moment, their gazes locked. It wasn't a dispute, though. It wasn't defiance. It wasn't a black dog sort of look at all.

Eventually, Ezekiel bowed his head again and said, his voice low, "Alright."

Grayson did not nod or smile. If he had won anything by Ezekiel's concession, Natividad did not know what it was. If that had been a concession. She sort of thought there hadn't actually been a contest.

The Master asked, his heavy voice inexpressive, "Shall I open the cage?"

Ezekiel answered, still quietly, "I swear I will not challenge you." He looked up suddenly, not at Grayson but at Natividad. "In April... In April, if you choose Grayson... I will not challenge him."

Natividad's eyes widened. She glanced from Ezekiel to the Master and back again. "But I..." she said, and then stopped. "I'm not..." she began again, and stopped once more. She took a step toward the cage and stood for that moment alone between the two Dimilioc wolves.

"I can't promise as much for anyone else," Ezekiel warned her.

"I... You..." Natividad took a deep breath. Then, rallying, she cocked her hip forward provocatively, set a hand there, tipped her head challengingly to one side, and said, "It's true Grayson's got that super-sexy older guy thing going, but if I choose somebody else, you know, I'll get you to promise to leave him alone before I announce it." When Ezekiel began to answer, she held up a hand and asked warningly, "You think I can't do it? You want to double dare me?"

After a stunned moment, Ezekiel actually laughed. Grayson, too, looked about as amused as he ever got. He held out the cage key to Natividad, who took it with a feeling of deep relief that made her want to laugh out loud. She wasn't even sure exactly why she should feel so relieved and suddenly so happy, only she did, and she knew she was right. Everything was going to be alright after all. Everything was *fine*. She opened the door with a confident little flourish, as though inviting Ezekiel out into a kingdom that she herself owned and ruled.

Ezekiel rose to his feet. He did not immediately move toward the door, however, but looked deliberately to Grayson for permission. Just as deliberately, the Master lifted a hand in summons: *come*. And Ezekiel stepped forward, out of the cage, to reclaim his place at Grayson's side.

Alejandro, aware he had missed a good deal of the subtext between Grayson Lanning and Ezekiel Korte, found himself relieved and confused in almost equal measure as he watched his sister go up the stairs with Ezekiel. The young *verdugo* offered her his arm, and she laid her hand there and walked beside him up the stairs, just as she had come down with Grayson. She did not even look at Grayson for permission. Nor did she look at Alejandro. She didn't look back at all.

But when Alejandro would have gone after them, Grayson stopped him. All along, after that first hard stare, the Dimilioc Master had not seemed to pay the least attention to Alejandro. But now he stopped him with just a glance, waiting while the other two disappeared up the stairs. Alejandro tried not to show his nervousness. He dropped his gaze and backed away from the steps, moving automatically, but not without realizing he had moved and why.

It felt strange to notice the working of black dog instincts, but the thing that Natividad had done, borrowing his shadow like that, that had left him with a new and not entirely comfortable awareness of the impulses and emotions that moved his black dog shadow. Nothing he did yet felt entirely normal.

Though the feeling of *separación* was less now than it had been, he thought he would never again risk losing track of the boundary between himself and his black dog shadow. He even suspected he might have learned the secret behind Ezekiel's extraordinarily control: the new clarity of that boundary made him understand, in a way he never had before, that it was *his* choice where to draw that line. His choice whether to hold fast to human self-control or allow black dog violence. Not his shadow's.

That had always been true. But he knew it much better now.

"Come," Grayson ordered him then, once Ezekiel and Natividad had had time to get out of the way. He led the way up the stairs, down the hall, and out into a winter day glittering and sharp with light and frost. The Master did not stop on the porch, but strode down the steps and out across the broad open area. The tracks of buses and vans and many human feet marred the smooth white expanse of snow, but almost all of the signs of the earlier battle were hidden. There was no wind. The forest, lying bright in the sun before them, was very quiet. At last, just before they reached the trees, Grayson stopped and turned his back to the forest, staring back the way they had come, toward the house.

Alejandro turned with Grayson and followed his gaze, wondering why the Dimilioc Master had brought him out here. He tried not to think that maybe he already knew. He tried not to think that maybe…

"You came to Dimilioc a week ago," Grayson said abruptly. He turned his head to stare at Alejandro. "How many times have you lied to me in this week? Whose decision was it to approach Dimilioc? You told me it was yours, but that's not true, is it? Was it your sister's idea, or your brother's?"

Taken utterly by surprise, Alejandro said nothing at all.

"You will not answer? Well, then, tell me this: why were you downstairs just now, when my order was that Ezekiel was to be let alone, that no black dog should approach him?" The Master added, with heavy sarcasm, "Perhaps you believe my orders do not include you? You have certainly appeared to believe that you have special dispensation to defy me. How many times have you disobeyed me in this week?"

Alejandro still said nothing. He had no idea what to say. He dropped to one knee instead, turning his head to expose his throat. He had known he risked punishment for disobedience. He had believed Grayson had brought him away from the house to punish him. But he thought now this might be worse. He was now almost sure that the Dimilioc Master meant to send him away. The Master wanted Natividad and probably didn't care about Miguel, but a young black dog who wouldn't take orders? A black pup who argued and lied and defied him and would not obey; who went out windows and pulled all of Dimilioc after him into ill-considered danger?

Now Malvern Vonhausel was dead, and Grayson had all those other black dogs, at least any of them he decided to keep, and also the ones James Mallory was supposed to bring when the roads opened... maybe the Dimilioc Master thought he could dispense with one disobedient black dog pup. Alejandro shut his eyes, breathing slowly, trying not to show his dismay. He knew he should be grateful that Grayson couldn't actually kill him without offending Natividad. She and Miguel would be safe, that was the important thing. But Alejandro's heart sank at the thought that the Master might send him away – he would be alone, just another solitary stray black dog, maybe for the rest of his life. He did not know what to say to make Grayson change his mind.

"You are loyal to your sister," Grayson rumbled. "And to your brother. That does you credit. But Dimilioc itself is nothing to you. *Can* you broaden that loyalty of yours to encompass Dimilioc entire? I wonder about that."

Alejandro opened his mouth, but closed it again without speaking. He had realized as Grayson had spoken that the Master was wrong; that Dimilioc *was* important to him, that he wanted it to belong to him as a home, that he wanted to belong to it in turn. But he did not know how to say any of this. He did not even know when the change had happened, or exactly why. It was Natividad who immediately cared what happened to anybody and everybody she met, and it was Miguel who cared about Dimilioc as an institution, as a concept. But he... Grayson had been right about him: *he* had not cared about Dimilioc at all.

When he had told Miguel he had to warn Grayson about Natividad being gone, he should have realized then that this had changed. When he had found himself utterly dismayed to think first that Ezekiel might kill Grayson, and then the reverse: he should have realized it then. But he had not known it until now, and now it was too late. He did not have his brother's quick tongue or his sister's charm, and he was sure that Grayson would not believe any protest he made.

Grayson's voice dropped into an even lower tone. "Keziah cares about herself and her sister, no one else. Andrew and Russell Meade will care about their sisters and possibly about each other. Thaddeus is less limited. He cares about his family, but also he wishes to be a man his wife will respect and love. He, I believe, will be a great asset to Dimilioc. You..." He turned his heavy gaze on Alejandro and fell silent.

"I care about Dimilioc." Even to himself, Alejandro sounded defensive.

"Do you?" Grayson studied him. "Perhaps you do. Or perhaps you might, in time. Your Pure sister may offer you both a good example and an incentive. That seems possible to me. Dimilioc's previous Master... Thos Korte was strong, but he cared for nothing but strength. In his mind, Dimilioc owned resources. Those included its black wolves, which, as with all his resources, he put to hard use. He was not a good Master for Dimilioc. But he was *strong*."

Alejandro glanced at the Master, confused by the change of topic and doubtful of the implication he thought he'd heard. Just as quickly, he looked away. He tried to imagine anyone thinking Grayson weak, and failed completely. Ezekiel might outfight the Master. But Ezekiel was not *stronger*. He tried to think how to say this, realized he did not dare say anything of the kind, and was silent.

"I think you will develop considerable strength," Grayson said, with no great emphasis. He was no longer looking at Alejandro, but again at the house. "And you have the gift of forcing down the shadows of other black dogs. That gift, too, will become more powerful with age."

Worse and worse. Grayson saw him, then, not merely as a disobedient black pup, but also as a potential rival...

"It's a necessary gift for any Dimilioc Master," said Grayson. Turning his head, he thoughtfully looked Alejandro up and down.

Alejandro stared at him, incredulous.

The Master's mouth crooked with a slow humor that was edged with savagery, yet not unkind. "You have proper

Dimilioc blood from your father, which is symbolically important; and Pure blood from your mother, which strengthens your control over your shadow. You hold your temper when you fight, which is crucial. You have a human brother, so you value ordinary people; you have a Pure sister, so you cherish the Pure – and if Ezekiel wins Natividad, your tactical position within Dimilioc will be strong. Especially since you will find Ezekiel does not want the Mastery himself." He paused.

Alejandro said nothing. He could think of nothing to say.

"So," said Grayson. "You will accustom yourself to the notion. It will not be soon. But in time. *If* you learn to care about Dimilioc. It is your commitment I doubt, not your strength."

Alejandro could hardly imagine being strong enough to take mastery of the Dimilioc black wolves. He said, hardly aware he was speaking aloud, "Thaddeus – and Keziah..."

"You must make Thaddeus into your ally. The strength of your allies can be as important as your own strength. Keziah may be more difficult, I admit." The Master added after a moment, "If your sister accepts Ezekiel, you will be well-placed to succeed me."

This had not occurred to Alejandro, but it was obviously true. He drew a breath, but then closed his mouth without speaking. Another breath. He said at last, "I thought you... I thought I..." but stopped again, trying to reorder all his thoughts.

"It will not be soon," Grayson repeated. "Nor at all, if you remain indifferent to Dimilioc. I will not permit any black dog locked into a narrow self-centeredness to take the succession. I will kill you before I permit that." He looked away, at the house. He seemed in that moment... not exactly old. But worn. The humor had left him. He said quietly, "Alejandro... Dimilioc must never again have a Master who views his black wolves merely as resources to be used. It must not have a Master who cares for nothing but strength. You cherish your family. *That* is the drive that sets true determination beneath your control. If you would take Dimilioc, then Dimilioc must become your home and your family."

"Yes," said Alejandro, understanding him completely. That was not a warning, or not *only* a warning; it was also an invitation, and a promise. He said, finding the words at last, "It is. It will be. That's what I want it to be. Not just for me. For us all."

He knew he meant it. He had not realized that was true until that moment. But the words stood bright and clear in the brilliant morning light, and he knew he had never in his life been so certain of anything.

Acknowledgments

Thanks are due to the entire Strange Chemistry team, and as always to my agent, Caitlin Blasdell, without whose insight every one of my books would be the poorer. But for this one, I also owe a great debt to Sarah Prineas, whose advice was instrumental in turning *Black Dog* from an adult to a young adult story; and most especially to Abril Warner and Concepción Beyer, whose help with colloquial Spanish was invaluable. It really is true that any remaining mistakes are entirely my fault.

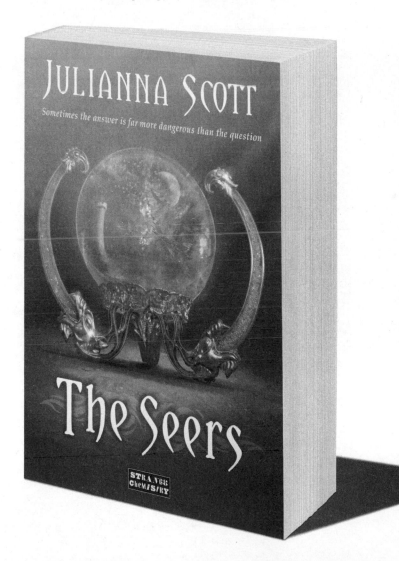

EXPERIMENTING WITH YOUR IMAGINATION

A tale of phantom wings, a clockwork hand, and the delicate unfurling of new love.

LAURA LAM

SHADOWPLAY

"Pantomime took me into a detailed and exotic world, peopled by characters that I'd love to be friends with . . . and some I'd never want to cross paths with."
Robin Hobb, author of the Farseer Trilogy

STRANGE CHEMISTRY